Listen to

GOLDENBORN LEGACY: REBIRTH
ORIGINAL SOUNDTRACK

A cinematic soundtrack created to accompany book 1 of the *Goldenborn Legacy* series. Each composition reflects the early stirrings of Olivia's journey—through reflection, loss, and a fragile awakening as the first whispers of prophecy begin to take root. Best experienced with headphones, full volume, and a heart open to the unknown.

Scan to listen to the official score.

I0630025

bitly

*The above code links to the **official original score** created for The Goldenborn Legacy—a cinematic soundtrack composed to reflect the emotional arc of the story.*

A separate chapter-by-chapter reading playlist, featuring curated songs that mirror specific moments in the book, can be found in the back.

a
miki starr
novel

Olivia

REBIRTH
of the Anointed

BOOK I

A REIGNSTORM PUBLISHING
ST. PAUL MINNESOTA

PUBLISHED BY REIGNSTORM PUBLISHING

St. Paul, Minnesota

Copyright © 2010 by S Michelle Johnson

Edited and re-released 2024

ISBN: 0-9721246-6-7

Printed in the United States of America

Book design by Em Jay for #BEINGCREATIVE design depot

www.mikistarr.com/books

Thank you **GOD** for giving us dreams
and opportunities to realize them.
Thank you for your children who encourage us
to bring those dreams into reality.

Thank you Shay Glorius L. Martin & Michele Adams
– Children of GOD

I LOVE YOU
Dawn Rooker,
Mildred Johnson, Berta Richard,
Delores Adams, and Ernestine Johnson.
– Women of GOD

My heart swells for the HSRA class of 2009 – 2010
– Gifts from GOD

REBIRTH

Definition: A renewed existence, activity, or growth; renaissance or revival.

"Power tends to corrupt, and absolute power corrupts absolutely. Great men are almost always bad men."

- John Emerich Edward Dalberg Acton

ZEPHYRNOX THETA
SYSTEM
"Shadow Realm"

Eastern Sun

AMIRONTE

MARIEUX

STARR OF TAYLE

Western Sun

NTOZAINT

DOROLARD

Velox Continuum

MILTAVER

CTIOBER

ARETHOXX

Marieux Glossary of Terms

Amen Deus – (org. Amironte) to praise God.

Ami – a derogatory term for Amirites, used as a term of endearment amongst Amirites.

Black Berries – seeds of the Black Atelus flower used as a potent narcotic.

Caniron – (cani) ground from imported canitheron herbs.

Codila – derogatory term for a gay female who behaves like a man.

Com Device – Walkie Talkie

Concealor – term for a woman who uses special clay or mud and/or film and other tactics to hide her looks.

Crack – areas beneath porches and in corners where residents hang out.

Dashii – Marieux currency Marineal – an animal very similar to a lemur.

Day – can refer to a span of time from Western sunrise to Eastern sunset or one's birthday.

Facilities – SRA jail.

Galê/Golê – term of respect for an elder.

Ganti – derogatory term for a gay male.

Gelish – Ancient language of the plant Marieux.

Giji Boy/Girl – a young boy/girl who spends money to be used strictly for sex.

Hold – tunnel

Legatus – (Lega.) Title for high ranking officer.

Lil'eail – (org. Marieux) term of endearment.

Mangalee – a citrus fruit.

Marineal – an animal very similar to a lemur.

Mariuchan – a derogatory term for Marinites used only by Amirites.

Mateles – veggie similar to a tomato.

Meli – (org. Amironte) term of endearment.

Mira – term of endearment for a great grandmother.

Musha – term of endearment for grandmother.

Obi Red – drug made from red obi berries altered to be much more potent than the berry picked from the bush. The powder version is smoked or snorted. A liquid version is shot into the neck (only hard core addicts use liquid obi red).

Pendi – fish that swim in Apigara River (also Lamilen).

Poppy Beer – a light, fruit flavored alcoholic beverage preferred by women.

Port – strong illegal liquor made with caramel, red obi berries, and other ingredients by Amirontians.

Seer – an individual chosen to bear spiritual responsibility for a deity's anointed.

Shunti – derogatory term for any female.

SOTA – Sisters of the Allegiance. Sisters may rank as:

Elite – Gifted to Board Officers by Henry Kelsard.

Level 2 – Resides on SOTA Compound A and B and are available to SRA soldiers only for a tax which is 100% paid into SRA.

Level 1 – Resides in downtown SOTA building and available to anyone for a tax, of which a percentage is paid into SRA.

SRA – Shadow Realm Allegiance; regulates conditions on planet.

Tms – tanometers; a degree of measurement.

The Board – Twelve top SRA leaders responsible for creating laws and keeping order.

Turk – man who pays for sex.

Volat – a small flying insect.

"For in the depth of despair, the divine flame of Deus is ever-present, a beacon to those who hold steadfast to their belief. Fear not the darkness, for it is but a veil, and beyond it lies the dawn of hope, like a rebirthing, shining eternal for those who do not falter."

Book of Luminaries, Chapter 14, Verses 4-5

A Child is Born

Prologue

WHERE I AM FROM IT IS SAID THAT LITTLE GIRLS ARE BORN into their fate.

Some are born to be wives of the farmer, help toil the land and birth the many boys that will carry forth the family name. Some are born to teach the children in the ways of our people and keep our beautiful history alive. Other girls are born to be healers of our people, practicing the ancient medicinal secrets that have been passed down for generations.

The lesser fortunate girls ... the most beautiful of us all are born to please the men that control us. They are born into captivity of the oppressor and spend their lives hiding who they are and attempting with all that is in them to change their fate.

My birth marked a different purpose.

I was born to be the Anointed Daughter of the Marinites.

†

THE STORY WAS TOLD TO ME SO MANY TIMES THAT I AM no longer certain whether or not it was actually relayed to me at all, or if I recall it from a past life experience. It was my great-grandmother, Elizabeth Alpha Ylai, daughter of the clan Aleyk and who later married Franklin Kalaath, who shared her memories. This was not so much done for the sake of passing along history or assuring that I was aware from which I came, but rather as a warning for me to heed, a means of keeping me safe and free of the clutches of the men who have oppressed our people for more than two decades.

It began with Diana, my mother and Elizabeth's granddaughter, saved from the womb of Elizabeth's own dying child. Diana, a wild, untamable beauty whose own fate was sealed the very moment a boy from a nearby village acknowledged her resplendence, encouraging her to flaunt it in disobedience. My *mira tried her very best to conceal Diana's looks, an allure perfectly suited for the desires of the soldiers of the Shadow Realm Allegiance.

Diana certainly would have known very well the dangers associated with her looks. Exceeding the ideal features and traits of what was considered to be most attractive, it was guaranteed that were she ever seen by an SRA soldier she would most assuredly be recruited. Her skin was the rich dark color of the kakali bean that hangs from the large panati trees that can be found on all edges of our quaint planet Marieux. Her hair, thick and long, was dark and shone beneath the sun, the soft feel of the silky strands brushed low across her narrow back.

She was taller than she should have been, taller than what is traditional of my race and built much sturdier than the average Marinite woman. Every feature was designed and placed ideally. Were she drawn by the most talented artist in the sector she could not have been more perfect. I wish I would have had the opportunity to see her that way.

Diana was not an anomaly but certainly a rarity amongst the Marinite's; the blessed dark skin with rich red hues that our people are known for coupled with the sturdier physique generally reserved for the descendents of the neighboring planet Amironte. She was exactly what the SRA looked to recruit. She had hardly seen her fourteenth day when she was spotted and taken.

Mira never shared with me whose bed Diana wound up in. I suppose it was of little importance if she was even aware. What was most significant about the tale as she told it was that Diana had been fixed for the prevention of pregnancy, as all girls recruited into Sisters of the Allegiance (SOTA) are. A year into her captivity, she discovered she was with child.

She successfully concealed her condition before taking the risk of disappearing into the night. I imagine that it was the best chance she had for our survival. Though her skin tone and long, beautiful hair was standard for the SOTA, her beauty far out-matched any other recruits and she was immediately sought after. She managed to remain in hiding just shy of two months when she caught wind that SRA had picked up on her scent. It would be a matter of time before she would be discovered hiding in the abandoned shanty in the thicket that bordered the village of Kalaath.

Diana went into birthing prematurely, possibly from the stress of it all, and made her way to her grandmother Elizabeth who served as her midwife just as she had done for her own daughter fifteen years earlier. While word spread through the village that soldiers were en route, Mira worked diligently to bring me into this world.

It was a long, laborious birthing. Maybe it was because I knew what the hell I was being born into or, more specifically, what hell I was being born into. Maybe it was simply as a result of the trepidation that was placed upon both women as their lives and mine literally hung in the balance. But finally, I was born. And to the horror of both women, this child that they had fought so hard to retrieve and protect was born with golden skin of a variety that no one had ever before seen, a skin that practically glowed and eyes bright and gleaming and the color of an imperial topaz.

Now, more fearful than ever, Diana convinced Mira to take me immediately and go into hiding. All knew of the prophecy of the chosen one ... the Anointed Daughter of the Marinites, and they knew with certainty that if the soldiers (or anyone for that matter) saw this child, all would immediately be put to death as a means of ceasing the bloodline once and for all as they believed they had done years earlier with the murder of Carolyn Kalaath.

Mira escaped with this child ... with me. I have been told that before we departed, Diana kissed my forehead softly and blessed me with the gift that only a birth mother could give ... should give. The gift of the first of my four names – Olivia.

†

Marinite culture requires that children are bestowed four distinct names. The first is ritually decided by the birth mother alone. For the past hundred years or so mothers preferred to give their newborns the beautiful exotic names originated by the humans on the planet Earth, rather than historical Marinite names. My name, Olivia, means olive tree, a symbol of peace and prosperity.

The second is given the child by her *musha or her mira, whichever is most fit for the task. The second name is the most important of them all for it speaks directly into the child's life and destiny (or so legend has it). The third name is a collective decision and rooted in Marinite culture and the clan of which the child belongs determines the last.

My full title as completed by my mira became Olivia Vala Eso Kalaath, Vala being the *Gelish word for chosen.

Although Mira acknowledged the belief that I may very well have been *the one*, even naming me according to this belief, she did everything in her power to prevent me from accepting any parts of this prophecy. Instead of raising me as a warrior, she raised me to be a *concealor.

We survived in a small hut built on the edge of the Apigara River. There we fed on fish from its mouth, milk from the kakali bean, and obi berries that grew in great abundance in the brush surrounding (the green berries, not the red).

As I grew, Mira taught me how to place the dark film into my eyes to hide their true color and to apply the perfect coat of the special mud dug from the banks of the Apigara to mask the glow of my skin. Done properly, anyone who encountered me would believe that I was born the correct color of the Marinite.

Her training with me proved successful, possibly because it was my nature to be reserved, or maybe because I was being raised in seclusion from other Marinite children.

Whatever the reason, I learned very early to work the land for my survival. I learned to be aware of my surroundings. I grew strong. Some would say mannish even, but it mattered not as these lessons were crucial for my survival. In spite or as a result of her efforts, I became a warrior in my own right.

When I was four, Mira negotiated with the nearest village elder for a small plot on their land which was not too far from the Apigara. There we were able to add a variety of vegetables to our meal and I could stretch my legs that were growing at an accelerated rate requiring more freedom for me to roam.

In those days, I never wondered what happened to my mother; my mira was enough. Life on the small plot of land in the minute village of Ashtwor was everything to me. But there was a sadness that cloaked Mira. Though she laughed kindly when she taught me to pull the stalks and shuck the corn, though she smiled brightly as I played, perfectly content with the piece of rope that had been given to me by the barren Sarai Ashtwor, whose husband owned our land, and although she beamed with pride when I picked up on my academic lessons quickly and with little effort, when she lay in bed at night, I would often hear her weep. I would go to her, stroke her soft hair with my small hands, and she would fall asleep in my tiny arms.

†

DIFFICULTY SURROUNDED MIRA'S LIFE DURING THE DAYS

following the Shadow Wars. That was when the sovereign leader of the planet Amironte, Claude Ustek, used his *gift of the poison tipped tongue* to sway our leader, Vincent Ittas, into the signing of a treaty that he summarily violated. In his quest to join forces with Katashi Kedt, ruler of Arethoxx, the largest planet in our system Zephyrnox Theta, the rogue Ustek took control of our planet, thrusting my people into captivity and inhabiting it with his fellow Amirontians.

Ustek controlled both his planet and ours for years, until his greed ultimately led him to a fate that he had previously bestowed upon the Marinite leader Ittas. Kedt slaughtered Ustek and all of his leaders, dumping their bodies into the Velox Continuum and sent our planet Marieux, without a leader, into chaos and complete civil unrest. Many lives were lost during this dark period, including Mira's first-born child, a son, Thomas Kalaath.

Pre-shadow Wars, Marieux had been a peaceful and upstanding planet where the concept of violence was foreign. Now the streets ran with blood. The climate was perfect for the rise of a new leader and it was the Marinite, Henry Kelsard (with the guidance of a rogue Amirontian named Taaman Dupec), who stepped up to the challenge. And so began the reign of The SRA and further destruction of my mira's life, a woman who had already lost her husband in a failed attempt to rescue their daughter Carolyn, a child with the skin of the Anointed and eyes of a see-er, and an original Sister of the Allegiance. Her pregnant daughter was murdered when Kelsard sent soldiers after her, fearing that she, or the child that she carried, would be the one to bring forth the destruction of The Allegiance and return Marieux to its original inhabitants.

All of the pain and loss Mira experienced took a toll on her, and the morning following my thirteenth day I awoke to find that my mira was deceased.

†

CRYING IS NEVER AN OPTION. I HAVE NO TIME FOR TEARS. To show emotion is to reveal weakness and being in the world – in *this* world, alone – to show weakness can be disastrous. Mira was my family, she was my world. She was all that I had and all that I had ever known and I buried her with honor in the tradition of the Marinite, and secured a promise from Pete Ashtwor to return her to her home village of Aleyk so that her soul may rest in peace, with dignity.

Sarai and Pete insisted that I live with them. *Galê Sarai had always wanted a child and now there was a refugee orphan to fill that void. I loved them both dearly for what they had done for us, what they had done for Mira and me, but I would not stay. I left their home under the cloak of darkness and made my way to The City in search of Diana ... in search of my mother. I believed that she was alive and I knew that if she were, I would find her there.

Finding Diana was suddenly everything to me. If she were alive, she would be all that I had left of my family. Finding Diana would give me a part of my mira back. I did not know that finding Diana would help me to find my own self and the fate that I was destined to realize.

One
Jayde

Where I am from, to be different is dangerous. If you are male, being different can get you beaten, or worse – jailed. If you are a female, being different can get you enslaved. And if you are lucky, being different can get you killed.

I was thirteen when I fled from the land of Pete and Sarai Ashtwor in the night. They were wonderful, upstanding citizens who maintained their strong Marinite morals and ethics despite the horrors that they had lived through and I will always remember their kindness and to include them in my prayers. Mira always spoke of life before the Shadow Wars and how much the Ashtwor village represented those values. They were a sign of pride to the native race of Marieux.

I am certain that Golê Pete searched for me when they awoke to find my bed empty and cold. I am sure he would have scoured the banks of the Apigara, seeking out my young body, washed ashore, my life taken by my own hands in the height of my grief. I am positive they mourned the loss of me and what they deemed as a failure to the memory of the Aleyk daughter, Elizabeth, when they could not find me.

I feel guilt for that still.

I wanted to leave behind a note. I wanted to leave some message behind for Galê Sarai to find and know that I was alive and that I would be just fine, but I was too afraid that something in my writing would betray me. I could not afford to be found. I could not return to them for they could not provide what I needed most which was that missing part of my mira.

Furthermore, I could not take the chance of their finding out my secret. I could not put their lives at risk. They were old and had been through so much in life already. They deserved the opportunity to die an honorable death ... to die in peace.

Nearly four years had passed since I made the journey from the tiny far away village into the centre of town, the area known simply as The City. Mira said that pre-war, The City was a grand place to visit and, for the younger generation, to live. She told tales of the days when Thomas and Carolyn were small, how she and my great-grandfather would enter The City every weekend to trade at the markets, purchase wares from the shops, and oft times catch a film or a play.

Mira had actually lived in The City herself for a couple years when she was much younger. She had attended the University School and been taught by the great Zanti teachers who had transplanted from the faraway planet Ntozaint to share their vast knowledge. That is where she met and married the Kalaath son,

Franklin, defying the laws of Aleyk that required that her parents arrange her marriage, as was custom.

Mira was the original rebel, living up to the second name Alpha that was bestowed upon her by her own mira.

The City was no longer a place for scholars and friendly proprietors. During wartime, the University School that the fortunate bunch who wanted a little bit more out of life willingly entered, suddenly became a place where all whose hearts pumped Marinite blood were remanded whether they had ever wanted to be there or not.

Its once bright walls were now gray and dull and held the souls of many – too many – fallen Marinite men, women, and children. The hallowed halls that once bred greatness, post the death of Ustek and rise of Kelsard and Dupec, became nothing more than our own personal Velox Continuum where bodies went in but rarely ever came out.

It was a frightful thing to be near the former University School at nighttime. It is said that a thousand souls come alive and tug at the heels of Marinite and Amirontians alike that are held there as prisoners of the SRA. The shrill screams that arise at all hours pierces the souls of all that hear.

The cinema was no more. Throughout my lifetime it has been nothing more than a dumping ground for illegals, abandoned children, girls and boys that had not yet reached their sixteenth day. Run by an awful Amirontian woman from an unknown clan by the name of Tagali, it is rumored that she was brought especially for the purpose of caring for the fosters, hand selected by Dupec himself, from a village on their home planet.

A ghoulish woman of at least 6' and 300 lbs who is known to use children as her own indentured servants, forcing deeds upon them that range from preparing her evening dish of the Amirontian delicacy of boiled carrupe, a bitter tasting fish imported fresh daily from Amironte and purchased by the elite, to satisfying her own twisted sexual desires.

At age sixteen the illegals become legitimate and are released and allowed to find ways to fend for themselves. Few survive the ordeal and a high majority of the ones that do are those that were taken only a year or two prior to their sixteenth day. It is not uncommon for a newly released foster to find themselves quickly thrust into the *Facilities shortly after their release for thievery, or if female, raped, beaten, or even killed for being caught taking money out of the pocket of SOTA and SRA by stealing their customers. But how else is one to survive under such depraved circumstances?

†

AT AGE THIRTEEN BEING IN THE CITY WAS DANGEROUS. SRA soldiers blanketed the area serving many vile purposes. Some to collect dues from the level 1 SOTA that resided in buildings that Kelsard provided. Some to collect the outrageous taxes imposed on those that continued to do business there. Some watched for thieves that they would beat mercilessly if they opted not to turn them in. Others kept their eyes peeled for minor citizens, just like me – underage girls that had no family – that they could rape and pass around before handing over for further humiliation and degradation under the watchful eye of Galê Tagali.

That would not be my fate. I kept my eyes low and wore the garments of a male. I stalked the shadows of the soldiers and avoided being seen. I followed what my instincts commanded, never once betraying or second-guessing an order. Some might say it was as though an anointing covered me and had they seen me without the mask of the contents of the large jar filled at the banks of the Apigara that I carried at all times in my satchel, they would truly believe that.

I did not.

I was smart, raised well by my mira who trained me in the stealthy ways of the Marinite, the art of following in the shadow of the pendi as they swam near the shallow banks of the Apigara ... following patiently and spearing an entire family without them ever sensing they were in danger. Their deaths were as peaceful as if they had fallen asleep and never awakened.

This skill was the key to my survival then just as it is today.

†

"WHERE DID YOU GET THAT?" JAYDE ASKED FAINTLY AS we walked together toward Mole's, one of many underground gathering spots for people in my age group that operated just out of range of SRA's radar. Mole's was the perfect place for Jayde and me, our favorite hangout. The owner, an Amirite who was simply called Mole, welcomed everyone, black, brown, and other, Marinite, Amirite, Citoberian. I had even once met a young rebel Zanti there. All he cared about was red, the color of the *dashii's that were handed over to him to gain entrance.

"I bought it," I answered simply and without the reserve that had been clear in Jayde's tone.

"Bought it with what?"

"With dashii's, what else?" I responded, looking her directly in the eyes.

An awkward grunt escaped her and she stopped abruptly, grabbing me by my arm and almost making me drop the fresh pendi and rutarb sandwich that I had purchased just before we met up on the predominately Amirontian side of town.

"Hey," I cried out, switching my delicacy to my other hand and snatching my arm back.

"Where did you get the dashii's?" Jayde asked, her eyes darting back and forth as though she feared that she may somehow be overheard by the invisible presence of SRA that constantly loomed.

I smiled devilishly, my eyes already darkened by my contacts, I was sure darkened further with my mischief.

"Olivia, where did you get the dashii's?" she asked again, sternly.

"Relax, my Amirite sister," I responded, continuing forward toward Mole's. "It is legit."

"Since when?"

"Oh, do you think that little of me?"

"Um, yes."

I rolled my eyes, not the least bit offended by the unvoiced accusation and verbalized insult.

"Jayde, *meli," I began, stopping before her and cutting her short as she had done me. "I did a job for Wally."

"Wally."

"Yes, Wally."

"Let me ask you a question, Liv. Since when does Wally pay enough for you to pay Diana your cut, go to Mole's, and have enough left over for a pendi and rutarb sandwich from Kel's Deli?"

I turned and continued forward. "He does not. Diana paid my cut this month." I took another bite, savoring the flavor of the moist fish mixed with the tangy orange sauce and for a moment – just a moment – flashed back to Ashtwor and my days with Mira. I shook off the overwhelming sadness attempting to cover me and wrapped the rest of my sandwich and tucked it away inside my jacket.

"Diana paid your cut," Jayde asked more than stated.

"Yes. It is her early gift to me."

"Your cousin, Diana Kalaath. Since when does she do that? Since when can she afford to?"

My stride slowed and my jaw clenched. "What are you trying to say, Jayde?"

"Nothing. I am only saying that it is not like her, is all. I mean, if she somehow had extra money would she not spend it on *obi red?"

I folded my lips in and nodded my understanding of the accusation before sucking my teeth and turning away.

Jayde called after me. "Where are you going? Olivia, why are you leaving?"

I could hear the sound the tall heels of her shoes made on the pavement as she ran after me. She grabbed my arm gently. I stopped.

"Olivia, why are you upset? It is just so unlikely. You have to understand my doubt."

"I am not a liar."

"Meli, I know you are not."

"I may be a lot of things ... a lot of things but I am not a liar."

"I know. I know, I am sorry. Please, forgive me. My concern is less about you and more about – never mind. It is unimportant."

Jayde was looking down at me, her brown eyes boring into mine, pleading for a stay of execution.

I looked away. I could not stay angry with her for very long. She was my friend. Besides Diana, she was all I had on Marieux.

"I forgive you, Jayde. Of course I forgive you. I just ... I am just going to go home."

"Oh come on, Liv. You know I look forward to this all week. This is the reason that I even survive the week, to get to the day that I get to party at Mole's."

"No one is stopping you from going."

"You said you forgive me."

"And I do. I am just no longer in the mood."

"Liv, please. You cannot send me in there alone. Aissa's off at Moxi with Raz and hoping to hook up with that bartender Lakew ... Lakin, whatever his name is. And I cannot take Tabi following up under me all night."

"Faraji should be there if he did not go to Moxi with Aissa and Raz."

"*All night*," she stressed, ignoring my suggestion about her other roommate's potential presence. "Please, Liv … please. I will buy you your next pendi sandwich myself, the next time I get paid."

I fought the smile emerging. Jayde pleaded and pouted, forcing a laugh out of me. "Can I get it with *mateles on it? You know Kel started charging extra for mateles?"

"You can get mateles."

"And a kakali milkshake? You know they make the best kakali milkshakes on the planet."

"Okay, now you are pushing it," Jayde answered in her beautifully husky voice, grabbing my wrist and pulling me after her.

†

I HAD GOTTEN UPSET WITH JAYDE FOR THE ACCUSATION because I was insulted by the implication that I was a liar. I had been quite self-righteous and made my best friend feel bad for having suggested such a thing.

But I am a liar.

I have been lying to Jayde since the very day she led me to my mother.

Jayde filled in the blanks where my own instincts left off. Moving in the shadows, living on streets beneath stoops and just out of view from doorsteps, was the perfect entry into the world of small time thievery. A talent that could see me locked away in the west wing of the Facilities and, at that age, could have easily had me under the control of that witch, Galê Tagali.

That is where Jayde found me, at the most dangerous point in my young life. Behind an old rundown building where I watched turks* and sisters enter horny and anxious and exit separated and satisfied, obi red dealers selling their lethal product on the steps above where stray *marineals and diseased rats attempted to steal what I had already stolen for my own survival, that is where a young Amirontian girl, brown skinned and nearly 6' tall, discovered me, dirty and hungry.

She offered her assistance to me because she thought I was one of her people. I was tall when I stood upright, not close in comparison to her but exceeding the height expectation of a Marinite my age.

She was floored when I asked that she lead me in the direction of the location of a Marinite named Diana Kalaath. "Why in the world would a young Amirontian with clearly no ties to SOTA want to find a whore, not to mention a Marinite whore, like Diana Kalaath?"

I had not known what I would find when I located her. A beautiful home and a four-door transport car imported from Ntozaint? A beautiful woman, a husband, two new siblings and a pet? Not likely. She had been a SOTA escapee when she gave birth to me; I only truly hoped to find her alive.

Though I had not ever seen her in life, she was still my mother and my initial reaction was to defend her honor. But she had been reduced to a level 1 SOTA whore. She had no honor.

I recalled the teachings of Mira, the gift of the Marinite that she passed on to me. Be calm. Be patient. Be in control.

I spoke in the small voice of a new teen but with all the passion of a seasoned adult. "I am not Amirite. I am full blood Marinite and I have just lost the only family I have ever known. I am only thirteen, I am an illegal and I am desperate to find the only known relative I have, a distant cousin my mira once mentioned. A cousin from Kalaath. If you will not help me, I will find her myself. I have come too far to give up."

I had not understood why I had given her so much information about my plight, but as I have already stated I had always followed my instincts and never once second-guessed. She was an Amirite and, though I could not care less about such things, clearly it mattered to her. It would have been nothing for her to flag down the nearest SRA soldier and have me turned over to Galê Tagali.

But more than a proud Amirontian, she was a victim of the injustice of the society in which she and I both lived. She was barely legal herself, but a year beyond the danger zone.

She did not turn me in. Instead she introduced herself to me as Jayde Nestyton.

I introduced myself as Olivia Aleyk.

I am a liar.

†

MOLE'S WAS FULL AS IT WAS EVERY ENDWEEK, FILLED TO THE brim with Amirites and Marinites. A couple Citoberians laughed over shots at a table in the back that they shared with a few

Amirontian girls and boys and a tiny pale-skinned, red-haired girl who was likely a Dorolard transplant. Since the Shadow Wars, my planet had become a regular nesting spot for transplants that were either outcast or bored with their own planets.

The DJ, a popular Citoberian female on the underground circuit who simply referred to herself as Silhouette, mixed dance beats with heavy bass lines through the most powerful speakers Mole could afford to acquire from Ntozaint. Half-dressed waitresses who stood no less than 5'10" without the additional 4" that their heels provided, worked the crowd. Sturdy bodies of Amirontian women, replete with full breasts and round rears and thighs that could crack walnuts, offered watered down drinks at hiked up prices and commanded a tip greater than the last girl to pass by.

Jayde's face lit with joy as she danced through a crowd smiling and stealing air kisses from the many patrons that recognized her. I followed along barely noticed, the way I liked it.

"Jayde! Jayde," a voice called over the music.

It was the voice of Jayde's roommate Tabia. If I had heard the shrill cry, certainly Jayde had, yet she kept moving forward. She was going to make Tabi work. Tabi would not speak to me, not until she had to. She did not care for me. Not so much because of my Marinite blood but mainly because of my relationship with Jayde. She envied me for that though she was not likely to ever admit as much.

I turned, catching Tabi's eye and shrugged my shoulders, unwilling to plead her case and attempt to stall Jayde. That is until I spotted Faraji. His crown displayed his Amirontian ancestry, bald on all sides except down the centre.

"Hey, Liv," Faraji called, smiling and showing perfectly even teeth.

I tugged Jayde's top and nudged her toward the table while informing her that roomie #1's presence would take some of the pressure off her and share some of Tabi's attention.

Jayde grunted, leaning toward my ear as she and I walked toward the saved table. "I so wish Raz would take this little *shunti off my hands sometimes. I swear I do not think she understands that I do not like girls like her. She should count herself fortunate that she is the only *ami in the house that is dependable for rent."

I laughed heartily, a chortle made stronger at the sight of Tabi looking on nervously between Jayde and me, her expression betraying her thoughts.

"Hi, Jayde, I did not think you would make it," Tabi said uncomfortably.

Jayde only nodded and offered a brief wave.

"Tabi. Can you not speak?" I said to her.

"Hello, Olivia," she answered reluctantly.

"I thought maybe you two changed your mind and decided to stay home with poppy beer and girl talk." Faraji laughed as he stood to give Jayde and me a welcome hug.

"And we would do this without the biggest girl of all?" Jayde jokingly responded.

I nodded at the attractive Citoberian who sat at the table beside Faraji watching closely every move he made and phalangering the material of his top. My mind flashed to Razi and the pleasure it would give me to see the look on his face if he ever found out about Faraji's secret obsession for pretty Citoberian males.

Faraji caught the eye of the tallest waitress, waving three phalanges.

I felt Jayde's hand press discreetly into my spine firmly as she, at the last moment, swapped positions, forcing Tabi and me to share personal space in the booth. It bothered me none, but I felt Tabi's entire energy shift.

The waitress returned with three small glasses filled with a potent dark liquor manufactured secretly by Amirites at some heavily protected location not very far from where we sat.

Faraji stood, passing one shot to Jayde and the other to me. On cue we stood for the chant.

"May your life be long and full, may your days be never dull, if you battle with soldiers may you aim to kill, and when between the sheets may it be surreal," we cried out in unison, toasting our glasses and sending the feeling of flames shooting over our tongues and down our throats to warm our bellies before landing with a thud in our seats, laughing along the way.

Faraji leaned to his right, planting his full lips against the mouth of the smooth faced Citoberian boy. The kiss was extended and wet and filled with much more lust than passion.

When he was done, he wiped the moisture from the boy's mouth before addressing us. "Girls, this is Madan. Madan, these are the girls. Girls, thank Madan for the drinks."

"Not if I have to follow your lead," Jayde stated with laughter in her voice.

"Oh no, save the dirty work for me," he said, kissing Madan again.

I chuckled. "Thank you, Madan, for helping to kick off my endweek binger."

Jayde saluted her thanks. "Oh Raj, if Raz could only see you now."

"Not funny, J," Faraji said apprehensively.

"I will never tell," she said in a singsong voice.

"Better not." He turned his attention away from Jayde. "Why the scowl, Tabi? Mad because you cannot spend the night sniffing Jayde's forearm."

"Screw you, Raj, you silly *ganti."

Faraji hissed. Jayde and I folded into one another in laughter. I could feel Tabi's eyes boring into my side. She wanted me gone, but she could never make me disappear.

†

IT WAS JAYDE THAT LED ME TO DIANA. TWO BUILDINGS over from where I had hid for the first twenty-four hours after my arrival in The City. Though the sight was not what I had expected, still I was not terribly surprised.

She was emaciated and doped up on obi red. Her right eye moved a hint slower than her left one. Her hair was dirty. She did not match the pleasant visuals that Mira had left with me but when I looked deep into her eyes, I knew the stories were once true.

I told her that I was her cousin, separated from Aleyk in my youth and raised alone by my mira Elizabeth Alpha Ylai Aleyk and watched as, for the first time since Jayde left me in her presence, life entered her eyes. When I gave her my name her knees buckled.

"Olivia," she had whispered with relief while wrapping her arms tightly around me, pulling me into her body. Her tears soaked the jacket that I wore where her head rested on my shoulder. My tears filled up my throat and I fought hard to swallow them, but not before one or two escaped.

I came to live with her in the small two and a half-room flat that she rented from Kelsard in the downtown SOTA building. She could not afford to have me there, but she did not complain. I did not eat much better in Diana's home than I had behind it. From that moment on thievery became my chosen profession.

Mira would have been terribly disappointed.

I saw Jayde often but only by chance. She resided on the outer edges of The City's downtown in a heavily Amirontian populated area, but she frequently visited the SOTA building that she had discovered me loitering behind, checking on the well-being of her own cousin, another demoted Sister (in her case for age and weight gain that conveniently seemed impossible to lose).

We acknowledged one another out of courtesy ... in passing. But soon our discreet head nods led to casual conversation. She came to be concerned about me and my health and well-being, as it seemed to her that I was disappearing before her very eyes. This did little to help improve the opinion of the woman that she thought was my cousin.

She offered her home as a legal, viable option for me to have food and a quick rest without being subjected to the sighs from Diana and grunts from whatever turk that happened to be contributing to the paying of our household expenses that hour. The only condition she imposed was that I pretend to be Amirite. She lived with four other Amirontians who were none too fond of the Marinite race, for how they saw it, we were prone to demonize them all for the sins of others and for them that injustice was greater than any sin Kelsard and (particularly) Dupec could commit.

It was just that simple. I would be fed and rested and the only cost imposed upon me was to take advantage of my inability to properly darken my skin and the several inches I towered above a typical Marinite woman.

I told her thank you, but I would rather continue to starve. To deny who I was would be to deny everything that Mira represented. I would die before I further shamed my mira.

I did continue to starve. I ate the meager rations that Diana remembered to purchase. I ate from the proceeds of what I could acquire on my own. I continued to roam amongst the shadows half dead and waiting for Mira to extend her hand to me and take me home to be with her and our ancestors until Jayde's latent motherly instincts kicked in and her concern for me far outweighed the importance of maintaining an allegiance to a prejudice.

From then on she became my big sister. She fed me, protected me and stood by me despite the opposition she faced from all, but most pointedly Razi Las, pro-Amirite – which for him is equivalent to anti-Marinite.

In time I came to win the respect of Faraji and Aissa (twin sister of Razi) and they dubbed me their friend. Tabi saw me only as an inconvenience, someone who stood between her and whatever disturbed affections she held for Jayde. Despite the great efforts of Tabia and Razi to convince Jayde to rid herself of me, *a dirty little *Mariuchan girl who dresses and behaves so much like a boy that she is probably a nasty *codila who is just waiting to pounce the first chance she gets,* Jayde stood by me and I will forever love her for it.

†

WE STOOD TOGETHER IN A CLUSTER NOT TOO FAR FROM the 5 cement steps that led from the secret *hold to the thicket in the abandoned yard, which led to the heavy metal gate that separated our world from our reality, passing around a *caniron stick supplied by Faraji's date for the evening.

Faraji inhaled deeply the smoke the little purple leaves created as they burned in the treated film that they were wrapped in. Tabi waited impatiently for Faraji to pass the cani her way. She stood as close to Jayde as possible, breathing in her scent and getting her high from that as she waited.

Faraji finally finished his turn and passed the drug my way. I declined as I always did.

"Loser," Tabi commented as she anxiously put the stick to her lips.

"Just remember that OR addicts were first caniron addicts."

She responded with the age-old display of the center phalanx.

It was the end of the night and Mole's was shutting down, its remaining patrons sneaking off into various directions, careful to keep a watchful eye for the soldiers. They would not be very diligent at this hour; they never were which is why most of the underground spots in every sector closed down at this time. Many of the soldiers were likely asleep at their posts, between the legs of a Sister, or locked in their own cani or OR haze.

Faraji inhaled the stick that had, like magic, materialized between his tips once again. He looked on lovingly at the remains as he held the purple haze in between his jaws while Madan fondled him unabashedly.

"It has been great, guys," Faraji announced diverting his attention to the horny young fair skinned Citoberian *giji boy that was commanding his attention. He handed the remainder of the stick to Jayde. "Liv, see you around. Jayde, Tabi, I will see you two in the morning ... or afternoon ... or the next day..."

Faraji's voice, low and laden from the effects of the cani, trailed off as he led Madan away flirting and clearly excited for what was to come.

"What shall I say to Razi of your whereabouts should he ask?" Jayde questioned playfully as the couple ascended the steps.

Faraji responded, "Tell him to try it. He just might like it."

We laughed. Razi had no idea about Faraji's secret weakness and, best case, would consider him a traitor and complete embarrassment to the Amirontian race if he ever did. Worse, he would probably kill him.

Jayde took the cani stick to her lips and adjusted her skirt. "We should go, too. In another hour it will be too dangerous to venture about this side of town. Olivia, why not stay over? You know I am always so nervous about you creeping through downtown this time of night. You know SRA is always heavy near anything SOTA."

"We go through this every endweek. Razi would have a fit if he woke to breakfast with a *dirty Mariuchan* at the table."

"Screw that arrogant, ami," she said, mashing the end of the cani stick with the tip of the exotic shoe she wore.

"Yes, pleasant though it may be for some, that arrogant ami pays a fifth of your rent and keeps you from having to live in the heart of downtown with me and D. I am going home, that is all to it. No time for Razi's drama or Tabi's either for that matter once she is sober."

Tabi showed me the tip of her tongue. I, in turn, showed her my friendly phalanx.

"Ugh, you are so stubborn. Whatever, let us go."

We walked together quietly, immediately sobered by the constant threat present. At the edge of downtown, Jayde offered her brief goodbye as she and Tabia made their way east and I took to the shadows. The presence of SRA was evident where I lived as it always was. I had never been caught sneaking back onto the block in the four years that I had resided there and I would not now.

I entered the building from the side entrance and traveled the five flights to the home I made with Diana. I used my key though it was unnecessary, as she had forgotten to lock it behind Ja'ali Dupec, an SRA ranking officer and her regular, yet again.

I stepped lightly but even doped up she was a light sleeper.

"Olivia, is that you?" she asked in a terribly groggy tone.

"Yes, Diana, it is me. Go back to sleep."

She made an odd noise that sounded faintly as though she were trying to tell me something as she drifted back into slumber. She laid across the foot of the bed, nude and sweaty, her dark hair matted to her head. She was not hot, the sweat beads were not caused by heat but rather as a reaction to the obi red I was sure she had snorted.

I took her firmly beneath the pits of her arms and pulled her higher upon the worn down bed. The moonlight streaming through the smeared window reflected off the long, jagged scar that extended from above her rib cage and across to her lower back. I touched the raised skin gently, following its trail from top to bottom, wondering who had inflicted the gruesome wound and why.

I grabbed the tattered blanket and tucked her in tight, noticing for the first time that her teeth were chattering. She mumbled some incoherent words to which I respectfully agreed.

My legs were heavy as I crossed the room toward the small section of the flat hidden behind a pale yellow curtain, the area we called my bedroom. I fell onto the old mattress that took up nearly the entire space, staring at the ceiling.

I eased the green wool hat from my hair that was turning curly again from the sweat I worked up at Mole's. I measured its length with my phalanges. It had already grown nearly two inches since the last time I cut it. I would have to cut it again in the morning ... *yawn* ... maybe color the roots... Yes, in case my hat were removed at an inopportune time.

My heavy eyelids closed and I drifted away to the place I waited all day to get to. I drifted away to meet Mira for lunch of fried pendi with rutarb sauce on a bed of lettuce with matele's on the side, enjoyed near the Apigara not far from Ashtwor ... same as I had done in a past life ... same as I did in all of my dreams.

Heart of The City

Two

At the conclusion of the shadow wars, when Katashi Kedt, sovereign ruler of the planet Arethoxx, leader of a clan in rule for over four hundred years and certainly not known for diplomacy, overthrew the Amironte leader Ustek and all that ruled beside him, a young Marinite named Henry Kelsard was making a name for himself and creating a following during captivity and the subsequent uprising.

It is commonly known that he had always had ambitions of political power, but tradition on the planets that make up the sector of the galaxy called Zephyrnox Theta dictates that the ruling clan retains power as long as there is a first-born son to carry forth the family's name. In this way, a family can retain power indefinitely.

Unfortunately for Henry, he could never expect any

opportunity to be in any position of power in the ranks of the reign, for he was the eighth-born son of a poor farmer from a limited lineage with no education.

But with the murder of Ittas and extinction of his bloodline, the subsequent murder of Ustek, and a race war on the streets and in the valley's of Marieux, Henry finally had the playing field leveled. It is said he did much to fight *for* the people during and post captivity, which gave him the appearance of a savior. But it was Taaman Dupec, a handsome young Amirite with political ambitions of his own, that took the most notice to his potential.

Marinites were fighting to regain control of their home. It was theirs and with Ustek forever gone they saw no reason that Amirontians should not jump into their shuttles and return to their own home planet. Amirites who had now lived here for many years and made Marieux *their* home, felt they had a claim staked in this place and had as much right to be here as the natives. Both could agree that the bloodshed had to stop; the season was ripe for new leadership. The citizens, native and transplants alike, craved guidance. It matters not what planet one is from or race they are, at some point everyone simply desires to be led.

In the beginning, the newly formed Soldier's Alliance was a godsend from the perspective of the citizens on both sides. They policed the streets, created laws, and ultimately reinstated a decent economy. But there was a saying taught to the former students of Zanti professors, a saying that originated on the planet Earth and made its way via space and time, a saying that was passed down from one Marinite generation to the next – power corrupts and absolute power corrupts absolutely.

While Henry Kelsard and Taaman Dupec were taking charge of the streets of Marieux, there was no one in charge of them. Something that can only be described as greed consumed both men inspiring them to create even more unreasonable laws and institute excessive punishments for the smallest infractions.

In the midst of this recognition of ultimate power, their goals changed, their name changed, and Sisters of the Allegiance was born.

†

FROM THOSE EARLY, COMPLETELY CHAOTIC DAYS OF SRA reign, the pair found a perfect way to use SOTA to satisfy multiple purposes. Ranking officers were given access to nearly any Sister of his choosing, within his race (with the exception of Level 1's where race is irrelevant). All others, whether SRA or not, could have their time with a Sister for a price. But only level 1 Sisters were allowed to retain a share of the profits earned as they had to pay their own way in life, despite having no choice in how they earned a living. Elite's and level 2's were 100% provided for.

Understanding that the day would come when Kelsard would retire the Sister and immediately evict her from her residence in the downtown SOTA building, many downgraded Level 1's began to follow the Marinite practice of sacrificing 10% off the top of their profits. A figure normally reserved in sacrifice to Deus but would instead be used as their retirement fund. The likelihood of returning to their home village or meeting a successful man who would care for them after having lived such a degrading existence was slim to none. When the day came, they would have a little something to help them get on their feet. The personal retirement fund was essential to a former Sister's survival.

Diana had nothing.

From our first meeting she was fragile with sunken jaws and shallow eyes. Much of her dashii's were spent on the purchase of cani and obi red. But somehow through it all she could still be quite lovely. She had something special and men, from the hard-hearted Sector Leader, Ja'ali Dupec, to the husbands of the many upstanding Marinite women who lay with her most nights, seemed to have a weakness for Diana.

There were months when she would attempt to become sober, kicking her OR habit once and for all. During those times signs of what I assumed to be her former self shone through. She ate more and picked up enough weight to put a rosy glow into her dark cheeks. She would wash her long, luscious hair with a mangalee-based shampoo, twisting it into the intricate and elegant Valian bun, and adorn it with a bright yellow flower.

On those mornings, during those months, she would apply a bright red lip paste and pierce the holes in her ears with a beautiful and valuable pair of jewels made from the shell of a conchi, a rare crustacean found only on the deep south end near Ittas Lake (named in honor of the former ruling family).

But as the years pressed forward, somewhere along the line, she simply gave up.

†

"THERE IS NOTHING IN HERE TO EAT. DIANA. DIANA!"

She sat on the edge of the bed, seemingly in a daze. An old, pale yellow brassiere concealed small, pendulous breasts. She wore a pretty green skirt that had seen better days. It was one that I had used my *special skills* to acquire for her a year earlier. She was rolling a stocking on her leg. She had been attending to that one leg for a good five minutes.

I walked to where she sat and gently touched her shoulder. "Diana."

She looked up at me. Looked at me like this was the first time she had noticed that I was in the flat.

"Olivia."

"Yes, it is me. Are you okay?"

She eyed me oddly ... longer. "What? Of course I am okay," She stuttered. And like that, she was back.

"Where were you?" I asked, scratching my scalp and walking back to the tiny kitchenette to scour the cabinets in case I had missed something.

"What are you talking about? I am right here."

"I was speaking to you."

"Well, what did you say?"

"Food, D. There is none," I answered with exasperation, allowing a cabinet door to swing closed with a thud.

She frowned. "Please, do not call me D. I am your ... I mean, I know you very well cannot ... just do not be that casual with me."

"Apologies," I mumbled.

"Can you not buy food this time?"

I stood at the mouth of the kitchen, watching her dress in her corporate wear, dumbfounded and speechless. She paid me no mind. Instead she finally made progress with the other stocking. She stood and walked to her dresser, sifting through her meager belongings (most acquired by me) seeking out a top to wear.

She was too tall for a Marinite woman, exceeding the expectation by a good 4". I had already grown beyond that by at least 2. Evolution was changing much of what was expected to be reality. My eye was drawn to the red ink embedded into the pigment in her shoulder, barely noticeable for her skin was so richly dark. It was the ancient Marinite symbol for PEACE.

"You said that you would buy food."

"I said no such thing."

"You did so. You told me you had extra. That you would pay the full house bill for the month and buy food."

"Wait, what?" She turned to face me, halting the process of pulling the thin, white top over her body. "You have your share, right?"

"What? No. You said—"

"I said no such thing."

"Yesterday—"

"Voshon will be coming to collect first thing tomorrow. You had better have that money or we are in trouble."

"I spent the money."

"Why would you do that?"

"Because you insisted you would pay it. You insisted, Diana."

She flipped her hair, heavy and weighted from oils and dirt, from inside her shirt and walked to the mirror.

"Then you better find some way to get it back."

She leaned forward and began smearing lip paste across her pouty mouth. I could not be bitter, it was my own fault, I should have known better. I should not have trusted her. She was my everything, all that was left of my mira. In this city filled with corruption, she was how I survived. She was my heartbeat and I wanted to trust, but I knew better.

She walked toward me smiling, as though she had not just betrayed my desired confidence in her. She stopped in front of me, her eyes just below my own. Her dirty nails created a path through my curly locks. Gold shone through at the roots and I knew my skin color must be uneven.

"You better dye this pretty soon. You should probably cut it, too. I can do it later if you wish."

She was my heart in this horrible city.

I nodded. "I am going to dye it today ... after the floor is cleared out. Maybe ... maybe I will cut it myself if you are going to be, you know, busy."

Her eyes dropped to the scuffed floor and the light that had flickered there moments earlier, extinguished.

"Yes, that is probably best."

She stepped away and walked to the door. She called to me without pausing or looking back. "Be careful, Olivia. You are all I have left in this world."

She closed the door firmly behind her before I had a chance to respond.

"Right back at you."

†

THE DAY WOULD COME WHEN VOSHON, THE ODD LITTLE MAN from a system to the north of Zephyrnox Theta, would make the rounds to collect the tax and he would walk though our door with the typically dreaded announcement, "Congratulations. You are being retired. Your services are no longer needed." It would be said in a tone befitting of the news, said in the annoyingly nasal and monotone voice that was unmistakenly his.

Though every level 1 Sister dreamed of the day that Kelsard allowed them to retire, they dreaded its arrival. With the emotionless announcement came the instruction to be out within 48 hours.

Many Sisters were left with no place to go. Some roomed with others that they had come to be close with but because spaces were small that did not usually last for very long. If Bea had a bed available, the Sister would take advantage of her 3-month policy.

Bea Yalei was a former SOTA recruit who was demoted and ultimately retired for excessive weight gain. Legend around the building has it that she gained the weight purposely as a means to break free from the clutches of SOTA and Kelsard. Though she garnered a great deal of respect for her ability to maintain control over herself and her life in a controlled society, few had the stomach for the task. Bea Yalei diligently saved her earnings and soon formed a privately funded home for Formers in the underground circuit.

A lucky few returned to their village. The others, those that hid their money away, were able to begin again. That was the afterlife that I wanted for my mother, Diana. I followed in the footsteps of the wiser of the Sisters, but since there were two of us I took it a step further. I put 12% off the top of every dashii that came my way.

Whether I earned it doing errands for the Marinite Wally or acquired it from my former side hustle of relieving the Amirite proprietor Tiakalu out of his dashii's, 12% always went into the envelope I kept hidden away deep inside my old, pre-used mattress.

The day would come when Kelsard would retire Diana and we would not have to grovel at the feet of aging whores or pay for a temporary bed beside a former one. I was hoping to use the dashii's to purchase one of the many vacant shanty houses in villages around town. We would live there and make a home. We would find one near the banks of the Apigara and we would grow our own veggies that we would sell at market, and fish for pendi in the river. We would plant our very own Mangalee tree and drink the nectar from the ripened fruit.

We would lie in the sun, her dark skin getting darker and mine concealed, sucking on the sweet juices of green obi berries.

†

I MET WALLY DURING MY EARLY DAYS IN THE CITY. A huge flirt with a sizeable frame who grew on Jayde and became an associate; she connected me with him to do odd jobs that would keep me from stealing and potentially being locked in the Facilities. I tried to remain on the straight and narrow for not only my sake but also Diana's and Jayde's. At the news that Diana was going back on our arrangement I went directly to Wally. I found him at his little shop and begged and pleaded for something ... anything that would earn me the money that I would need to pay the balance of the tax before Voshon arrived the next morning.

He had nothing for me but promised if any opportunity arose he would seek me out. I did not have time to wait for opportunity to knock. I had to create my own opportunity.

I stood next to the side door of Kel's Diner at nightfall. It was the one on the Marinite side of The City, the one where he did his most rip-offs. Kelikee Tiakalu was one of few wealthy Amirontian businessmen, who owned three such diners throughout The City, amongst other ventures. He had sold his soul and it served him well.

Much of what was served in each diner varied by location. If it was on the Amirontian side of The City, boiled carrupe platters with couscous and topped with mantele's was the number one sale. Where I was, the most famous dish was the fried pendi sandwich on a roll with rutarb sauce. He charged extra for mantele's. He charged us extra for everything. A green obi kakali nut shake cost us Marinites twice what it cost at the Amirontian location.

He had been robbing us blind for years. And I had been doing the same to him.

Fortunately, I spotted the camera before it spotted me. Tiakalu had wisened up it seemed and purchased one of the pricey new surveillance cameras manufactured on the industrial planet Ntozaint and sold locally. I would have to be even more cautious.

I knew the layout of the shop and I knew the rotation of the clerks and soldiers. This was the one uncoordinated time of day. I had twelve minutes to get in, get the seventy dashii's I had come for (fifty for the house bill and twenty for myself. If I were going to do it anyway, I may as well profit). I had not accounted for advanced security but I would not allow such a thing to count me out.

I stayed close to the building, blending in, and becoming one with the structure. I was unsure if he had ordered one of the alarms that some shop owners were investing in. If he had, I did not know that I would be able to get around it.

I reached over to test the handle. I took a deep breath. If a sound cried out I would have to move quickly to avoid the ray of the Harbinger, a weapon that the soldiers carried and used to immobilize (and sometimes slaughter) the innocent and guilty alike.

My hand gripped the handle. I pulled slightly and the door opened – no alarm. Opening the door wide enough for me to fit inside would cause it to pass the eye of the observing technology and if someone were monitoring from the inside, alert them to a problem. I determined my best option would be to shift the fixture slightly away from the door so that I could get inside.

A nearby dumpster acted as my stepladder. I carefully, but swiftly, climbed on top. I balanced myself and tipped to the edge, reaching for the device. My phalanges brushed against it but I could not grasp it unless I stepped closer. If I stepped out further I would run the risk of losing my balance and falling to the ground below. If I got down and pushed the dumpster closer, the loud noise it would make scraping across the ground was bound to command attention.

I tipped further out onto the edge delicately. Beads of sweat that had spontaneously popped onto my forehead trickled down between my eyes and passed by my nose. I closed my eyes tight and extended my arm as far as it would go, managing a loose grip onto the camera. I held my breath and moved it slowly, carefully. If anyone were indeed watching, hopefully they would not notice.

When I felt I had gone far enough, I paused and waited. According to my mental clock I had, maybe, seven minutes before the safe would be guarded, nine before the soldiers would return.

I jumped down, landing softly and ducked beneath the device and to the other side of the door. I turned the handle and eased inside the back of the diner. I could hear voices not far away. My adrenaline intensified. I kept low and out of sight and quickly made my way to the unlocked safe. It was between shifts and the clerks, despite all the years I had been shorting their delivery, had a terrible habit of leaving the safe open while the transition was made. My actions had led to the termination of numerous clerks who were blamed for the shortfall that their carelessness caused.

I reached inside the safe and quickly counted out the seventy dashii's I had come for but at the last moment decided on an extra five for good measure.

"Did you lock the safe?" a voice asked. The voice, deep and sultry sounded closer than it should have been.

"I forgot."

"You forgot."

"What is the big deal, no one is here but us."

"The big deal is that it is Tiakalu's procedure, that is reason enough."

"To hell with that greedy, ami. Had I the nerve, I would rob him myself."

The voices were moving closer. Quickly, I pushed the door closed. I looked to the exit. I wanted badly to make a break for it but I could not without passing the workers and if they spotted me, they were certain to flag down a soldier. The consequences for stealing from a man like Tiakalu, a man that was in bed with the devil, would be severe.

My heart pounded but I steadied myself. I remained calm and clearheaded. I moved backward, centimeters away from the large metal counter, the centerpiece of the room. The footsteps approached to my left so I dashed to the right.

"Just keep talking like that," the bass-filled voiced warned. Curiosity consumed me. If I were going down I wanted to see who would take me there before he saw me. I peered around the corner, careful not to take a breath. I could see the owner of the voice from where I sat in hiding but unless he turned and leaned forward, he would not see me. I was fairly certain he was Marinite. His barren, kakali nut colored scalp gave way to his heritage. He bent down and entered the combination on the safe and my shoulders relaxed. To my relief he had not first checked the contents.

As the men disagreed, I took inventory of my surroundings. There were two entrances to the kitchen from the interior of the store. The one the workers had come through and the other directly across from where I crouched. The dilemma I faced was that the shop would be locked during the transition.

The voice spoke again. "Just stay back here and get to work. I will finish up in the front and get ready to open the store again."

I had to move. No time to contemplate what could happen; I darted across to the doorway, keeping low, unsure of what other obstacle awaited me on the other side. Footsteps moved in the direction of the front of the store as I arrived at the edge of the counter. I glanced to the door. There was no way out without being seen. The one thing I had going for me was that there were no customers, or worse, soldiers present to witness my emergence.

I crept from the side of the counter to the front. I had no choice; if I wanted any hope of escaping I would have to take my chances. I stood upright, coming face to face with the owner of the voice. He jumped, startled by my presence.

"What are you doing here?" he asked. "How did you get in here?"

"Through the door," I answered calmly as though what I said were absolutely true.

"What door?"

"That door. What other door is there?"

"That door is locked."

"No, it is not." I stepped slightly to my left hoping to obscure his view. "How else would I get in?"

He paused, looking from me to the door. "What were you doing down there?"

I chuckled nervously. "Tying my shoe."

His facial expression said he was not completely convinced. "So ... what do you want?"

"I wanted a kakali nut shake."

The question mark remained as he began to service me. "Certainly. What flavor?"

I glanced out the glass of the door in time to see two soldiers approaching. I cursed inside. If they pulled the door and proved it was indeed locked there would be no way for me to explain my presence.

"Hey, what flavor?"

"Never mind." I turned quickly and walked toward the door.

"Hold on. Hey, hold on for a second," he called after me. I continued forward, walking faster. I could hear him moving from behind the counter. My eyes stayed on the approaching soldiers.

"I changed my mind. I can get it cheaper across town."

He stopped. I faced him as I turned the lock quick and discreet while pushing the door moments before one of the soldiers reached out to open it.

"Thanks, anyhow," I said before disappearing into the shadow of night.

†

"WHAT TOOK YOU SO LONG?" JAYDE ASKED. NOT WAITING for a response, she leaned in and pulled me into a tight embrace. "Happy 17th, you old *shunti!"

I half-smiled. "Thanks."

Jayde stepped back and looked into my eyes carefully. "Okay, what is going on?"

"What do you mean?"

"We have not just met, Liv. It is a big day. You do not seem very excited about it."

I bit down on my lip, contemplating my response before I spoke. "Is it, Jayde? Really. What is so big about it? I am officially old enough to be tossed into the Facilities. Maybe it is a big day on Amironte or even in some villages around Marieux but what of the rest of us? Those of us who have to live in this God-forsaken city? Whose mothers have been taken by men with no conscience and forced into a life of servitude?"

"Whose mother?"

"Mothers, sisters, cousins. There is no future for us. The Starr of Tayle does not even shine on us here in The City, nevermind ever dreaming of seeing what life looks like to the west of it. And yet I am expected to celebrate the start of another seventeen days of pure hell."

Jayde took my hands in hers and pulled me close. "What happened?"

An outsider had noticed me. I was but one carefully executed fib away from being captured and found out by SRA. Someone had seen me, knew what my face looked like aside from the substitute mud powder mixture used to conceal it. And when it was discovered that seventy-five dashii's had gone missing, I would likely be number one on the radar.

I opened my mouth to speak but closed it when my eyes locked on Aissa approaching in the distance, preparing to share in the joy of this most anticipated day. How could I rejoice? If I were lucky I would be allowed to live to experience another seventeen of dodging SRA, caring for a drug addicted mother who I called cousin, and going out of my way to hide the most dangerous characteristics I had the misfortune of being born with.

Happy day to me.

"I ... I have to go. Thanks, Jayde. Thanks for being here for me. Diana did not remember."

"Olivia, no. It is your seventeenth. We have been looking forward to this day."

I paused. Jayde did not fully understand – would not because I could never be 100% honest with her. Aissa approached, waving and smiling and ready to celebrate what, for me, was not worth the energy.

I leaned forward, taking Jayde into my arms. I spoke softly into her ear. "Apologies. I cannot do this. I cannot celebrate this."

I turned away quickly, leaving Jayde behind to explain to an even more confused Aissa what she did not fully understand herself.

†

THE AIR WAS THICK WITH MUST AND SWEAT, BREATH AND conjoined flesh and Diana's moans and the groans of a stranger bounced off the paper-thin walls. The space was dark and I crept silent and unnoticed across to my room, stumbling over some discarded garments along the way.

She had not told me happy day. The past three she had remembered and found a way to make good on. Her only present this year was nearly having me tossed in the Facilities as a result of a reneged gift ... and she did not even know it.

Three

High Stakes

I SHIFTED ON THE TATTERED MATTRESS IN DESPERATE search of comfort. A loose spring that had broken through the material jabbed my leg, forcing my mind from the cloud and sweet relief of slumber. I twisted my body away from the sharp metal and tried to find my way back into the calm of my dream state I was only allowed a few hours of at night.

Breathless mumbles between a hired lover and her temporary owner began to rise and become coherent as they fell upon my previously deaf ears. I gauged the time of day. It was nearing the rise of the western sun; it was unusual for Diana to have company at this time of morning. She wanted him to leave, he wanted one more round but what he did not want was to pay for it. I would not become involved. It came with the territory and I learned my lesson long ago. Control your emotions.

I growled and slowly sat upright. I stretched my limbs as far as they would go and scratched the back of my scalp. I reached for my green hat but it had fallen to the floor. My eyes wandered to the stained window and fell upon the early sign of the orange cast glow that signified the start of yet another tumultuous day. Voshon would make his way to our door in less than a few hours looking to collect.

The disagreement became louder. The negotiations began.

I reached beside me and grabbed my jacket, pulling it across my lap. I stuck my hand inside the interior pocket and pulled forth the dashii's I had nearly lost my freedom for, all because Diana reneged on her word. I had promised Jayde I would not resort to thievery again but Diana had not left me a choice.

I separated the dashii's, setting fifty aside for the tax after the 12% for Diana's and my retirement. I pressed my hand against the dirty wall, pushing the bed partway to the other side of the barrier that separated me from Diana, and eased onto the dusty floor on the other side. There was a small opening that I had cut into the mattress, enough that my hand would just fit. I reached inside, the fibers tickling the back of my hand. I felt around seeking out the edge of the piece of folded papyrus that contained the dashii's.

My heart paused. I found the edge and pulled it forward knowing that once again my world would come crumbling at my feet.

"No, no, no, no, no." My voice was low and hoarse.

I grabbed the edge of my jacket, sliding it toward me. I reached inside and pulled forth the blade I kept hidden there in the seam for protection. I scrambled back to stretch the opening further so that I may better feel around inside.

"No, dammit. No!"

I stood and rushed from my personal area, from the place that was to be my bedroom, waving the empty piece of papyrus. I had been saving 12% of everything I ever earned or otherwise acquired without fail. Three years as a matter of fact and now, in one day, it was gone.

"Where is it?" I said suppressing the urge to scream, caring not for what the man on top of Diana may say or think, caring not for what those in the neighboring rooms may overhear. "Where the hell is it?"

"Do you mind?" the man snarled.

"Get off of her. Your business here is concluded," I spoke with relative calm.

"Olivia, not now. Please," Diana begged. I cared not what she had to say.

"Now."

The man waved an arm back at me, not missing the rhythm in what he was doing. "Beat it you stupid little shunti."

I moved forward instantly, not first thinking of my actions. That same instinct that had kept me safe all these years was now placing me dead center in confrontation and I was not fighting it. He was Marinite. There was just enough light cast across the room for me to see his clean head and dark skin. My hand was on the back of his neck and my mouth to his ear before I had even realized that I had moved.

I did not bat an eye. I spoke clear and firm. "Do you not have a wife and children you should be spending your dashii's on?"

"Little girl ... let me *cough* go," he struggled with his response, reaching back and trying his best to pry my phalanges from his neck.

"Olivia," Diana whispered, fear in her voice. "Please. Stop this. You will cause a scene."

I ignored her. "Do I not know you? Have I not seen you around here before? Your wife, the beautiful Marinite who teaches the little children right under the nose of SRA, and this is how you repay her sacrifice?"

"How do you–? Who are you?"

"Please, stop this." Tears were stuck inside Diana's throat.

"I know all, I see all. I am only going to tell you this once more, sir – get off of her. I would like to have a private word with my *cousin* if you do not mind." I stepped back, allowing the man room to rise.

His hand moved to the back of his neck, massaging out the kinks I had just twisted in it. I could smell the fear rising from him but knew that he was not yet prepared to admit his own cowardice in front of a young female and the property that he had paid for the extra time to own.

"I ... I paid her. I am getting my dashii's worth or you will have a soldier at your door before the rise of the eastern sun."

"Ah, perfect. A threat." I stepped forward and relished in the sight of him curling into himself.

Pre-Shadow Wars, the Marinite people had very little concept of violence and aggression. We are, by nature, quiet and peaceful beings. During years in captivity some Marinite's learned that it was necessary for one to do all they could to defend themselves and the ones they loved, yet our peaceful nature persisted.

With the creation of the SRA, the vast majority of soldiers that Kelsard placed in position have been the descendants of Amironte, while Marinites tend to take on more administrative roles. Besides the obvious advantage of being larger than my people, Amirontians are natural born fighters with warrior instincts.

Mira was very much against the Amirontian practice of resolving disputes through violent tactics and because I had not given much thought to it one way or another, I could not help but be equally as surprised as Diana and her client when my hand wrapped firmly around his neck and lifted him with force, pulling him away from her body.

"Consider this the climax of the evening. If you leave now, I will not bother crushing your larynx. How I would love to be a *volat on the wall when you try to explain such a thing to that pretty little teacher of yours."

I released him, allowing him to fall heavily to the floor beside the bed. Left him trembling and questioning how a little girl who he had never before noticed could have such strength. I was wondering exactly the same. He leaned forward, squinting his eyes and trying to get a better look at me in the darkness but it was of little use. My eyes went to Diana's. She moved back on the bed as far as she could manage, pulling her sheet tight to her chin as though it would provide protection should I decide to turn my wrath upon her.

I turned again toward the adulterous man. "By the way, I would not bother any of the soldiers with what has happened here if I were you. Not if you value your family. I am rather certain that underground teacher that you are married to thinks you are pulling an overnighter at Kelsard's plant. I would hate for her to discover your dirty little secret almost as much as I would hate for SRA to discover hers. And just so there is no misunderstanding, should a soldier show up at this door, so shall a soldier show up at yours."

He paused, a look of pure horror flashed across his face. I could only guess that he was imagining the awful things that would be done to his wife should the soldiers find out about what she had been doing, as he dashed half-nude out the door.

"What has gotten into you?" Diana whispered. "What are you?"

"Why do you not tell me?"

There was a moment of silence as she asked and mentally answered her own questions ... questions I knew that she would not answer for me.

"I apologize, Olivia." Her voice was small and frail when she changed the subject. "I so apologize."

"Why, Diana? Why would you take it? I do not understand ... how did you even know I had it?"

"Because unlike me, you are responsible. You would not see me retired with no place to go. You are a good ... a good relative."

"And your way of thanking me was to take all the dashii's I had saved."

Water poured from her eyes. Her head dropped low. "You do not understand. I just needed ... I just – you know I am not worth much anymore."

"You would be if you would stop killing your body with obi red."

"It is not killing me, Olivia. It is what is keeping me alive ... it is what is keeping me from killing myself."

"Is that what you did with it? Is that what you spent my dashii's on?"

"I need to be numb, Olivia. You do not understand. Praise Deus, you may never understand."

"You did not use it all. Impossible. Where is it?"

"They took me away from my musha. The soldiers came and just ripped me away. I was only a child, but fourteen days. They gave me to him. I could have loved him like he ... loved..."

I paused and looked to her in the darkness with only the glow of impending daylight shining across her face, illuminating her tears. "Wait, who? Diana, for goodness sakes who? Do you know who my father is?"

She stared in the distance, reflecting upon a time which she would never share with me. She had information that could answer so much. She wiped the wetness that hung from her nose with the back of her hand. "I have not a clue."

I swallowed hard the aggravation that was building from her lies. "Where is it? Just tell me, where is what remains?"

She did not speak. She did not have to. Her shifting eyes led me to my answer. I walked to the dresser and jerked open the top drawer. Sifting through her garments I found what was left. I sighed, relieved as I counted the remaining dashii's laying there crumpled beside three OR vial's. Two were empty, the third partially filled.

I took what remained of the dashii's, what she had planned to spend on her next obi red fix. I took the dashii's that were to help start our new life. If I could have saved enough and steal just a bit of luck, maybe we could even escape the oppression of this planet altogether.

Maybe. Maybe even without this setback it was impossible but all I had to keep me sane were my dreams. Without those the things Diana did to me just may have caused me to crumble.

A pounding on the door jarred me. I reached to adjust my green hat but realized I was not wearing it. I stepped back into the shadows as the door flung open. The black uniform with the tan chest patch identified the man before us as a soldier. He was tall, Amirontian, with angry eyes that could be read even in such dim light. Those dark eyes immediately latched onto mine.

I steadied my breathing. I wondered if the turk had told of what happened though I did not believe he had. I was not afraid for myself but for Diana.

She began to plead immediately. "Apologies, *Legatus. I am very apologetic. My cousin and I just had a bit of a disagreement. It will not happen again."

His eyes were now absorbing the fear in Diana's. He twirled an unlit cani stick around with his tongue. "Keep it down in here before the three of us have one *big* disagreement. Understand?"

"Yes, Lega. Many apologies." She bowed her head to his

authority.

His eyes returned to my own and I hoped that the shadow cast would conceal the look of defiance which I was certain was upon my face. "We understand."

He grunted before turning to exit. We were silent, stilled. The soldier's loins had led him back to from whence he came lest there could have very well been a great deal of trouble.

My words were much softer when I spoke this time. "I am leaving with you the house note for Voshon. It will be in your best interest not to spend it on more obi red." I walked to the door that the soldier had only moments ago walked out of. "By the way, *my* day was yesterday."

I heard the gasp and attempt at an explanation. "Apologies, Olivia. I did not mean—"

I closed the door behind me before she could finish her sentence.

†

As a small child while living near the banks of the Apigara it seemed the world was all mine. Though I had no friends, I found great joy in playing alone and with the fuzzy marineal that lived in the woods near the river. I named her Ibidia (e-bye-dee-ah), a traditional Marinite name from historic times, before names originating from the planet Earth became trendy.

The Apigara runs along the outer northwestern edge of the planet for 45,000 tms. where both the bright western sun and smaller eastern sun shine together generating clear, blue skies and causing the water below to sparkle like a bed of jewels. I gravitated toward its glisten daily, oft times sneaking away from beneath Mira's nose to take a dip. She would suppress laughter as she feigned chastising me for my disobedience.

Fortunately the mixture my mira used on my skin and hair was so dependable that I could swim side-by-side with the pendi and lamilen that resided there and never fear hints of my true identity sneaking through.

During that time in my life I ran for as long as Mira would allow me, crashing onto the softness of the green ground below whenever I grew tired. Feeding Ibidia the dicami nuts that grew on the trees as the Western sun disappeared from the sky at the close of day.

Long gone from the village, life in The City did not afford us very many opportunities for fun and certainly not freedom. Besides time shared with friends hiding beneath stairwells and concealing giggles in alleyways and the endweek frolics at underground meeting places like Mole's and Moxi, the greatest joy my friends and I found was a little cove hidden away near the much smaller River Lux.

A quarter of the size of what I felt prompted to call upon comparison, the Queen Apigara, and not quite as appealing. It was surrounded mostly by granite with the occasional obi patch peaking through. But the water sparkled almost just as hypnotically.

Somehow the location managed to miss Kelsard's planet-wide radar and to get to it was no easy task. It required a great deal of courage and willingness to chance hitchhiking across the northeastern part of the planet followed by a tedious and potentially disastrous hike through 30 tms. of thicket to the cove on the other side.

†

"Ah. I did not think I would ever be able to look upon this place again. It has been so very long," Jayde said as she eased down, sitting carefully on a rock at the edge of the river, dipping her bare feet into its warm waters.

I stood beside her with my face tilted high, embracing the feel of the eastern sun upon it. Because this side of Marieux did not see quite as much of the western sun as near the Apigara, it was not as bright as I had been accustomed to in childhood, but it was a relief from the dimness of the orange sky that we lived beneath in The City. The cast was a permanent creation caused by a lack of direct light from either sun and the gasses emitted from Kelsard's many factories mixing in our atmosphere.

The sound of two sets of footsteps crushing brush caught my attention but I did not turn.

"It is so beautiful out here." Aissa's voice fell onto my ears as I continued to bask in the glow of a natural light. "It is much warmer here than in The City, Liv. Why not take off that awful jacket you are forever glued to?"

I smirked. "No thanks."

Faraji approached, sitting down beside Jayde who was now splashing the water with her toes.

"Tell me something, Liv."

"No."

"Why do you refuse to part with that monstrosity of a garment?"

"Simple. Because it is mine."

Aissa said, "And that miserable hat."

"Mine as well."

"One day," Faraji began, leaning forward to dash his hands across the water, "someday, I am going to hide those ugly things from you."

I turned to face him, a smile on my face. "And that is the day that I will kill you."

He halted his movements and glanced at Jayde whose eyes remained closed, a grin fixed to her mouth. He looked to the water. "If I did not know any better I would swear you meant that."

I raised an eyebrow before looking away and taking a seat.

Aissa danced along the rocks. "One day you are going to have to share your little secret with us, whatever it may be." She glanced back at me while continuing to dance.

"Who says I have a secret?"

"Jayde," Faraji spoke up. "What is it? What is Liv's secret?"

"If I knew do you think I would tell you? Have I ever shared your secrets?" she replied, opening one eye to peer at him then shutting it immediately.

"Touché."

I sat with my knees to my chest and hands in my pockets,

gazing upon the River Lux, imagining that it was indeed the Apigara and Mira would soon be calling me back to the shanty for dinner.

Jayde spoke suddenly. "I would like to know what happened to you on your day."

And like that, my visions were instantly disintegrated and I was thrust back into the cove on Lux ... my mira once again dead and forever gone.

"Nothing happened."

"That tone tells me otherwise."

"And now you are my mother."

"I have been the only real mother you have known for near four years."

"Diana does not have to *be* a mother, she is a cousin."

"She is your guardian."

Faraji interrupted. "Do you two wish privacy while you figure out exactly who is Liv's mother?"

Jayde and I gave opposing answers in unison. Her answer, yes. Mine, no.

Faraji stood. "Aissa, meli, if I am not mistaken I believe there is a healthy patch of obi berries down the way."

"Raj, I think you may be correct. Shall we?" Aissa agreed.

"We shall."

The two stood and, arm in arm, walked carefully along the rocks to where the green obi berries grew.

Jayde and I were still ... silent. She, apparently awaiting an answer that I was hesitant to provide. She pulled her feet from the Lux and turned to face me.

"Olivia, please talk to me."

I chewed my lip for a moment, and then sighed. "'Tis a difficult life we lead here on this planet. Is it too farfetched to believe that one would not wish to celebrate?"

"I know it is hard. I live it, daily, just as you do. I see it firsthand every day that I show up in that god-forsaken SRA factory to process their paperwork. Smiling in their faces and pretending to be one of them just so I can get by. Even more reason why the little things ... escaping to the cove, Mole's at endweek, and the most coveted, celebration of one's day means so much. Especially when so few get to see as many days as they are meant to."

My eyes and Jayde's locked. She claimed to want honesty but it would only disappoint her.

"It seems that Diana forgot about her promise to pay the full tax."

"Oh no." Jayde sighed first then gasped. "Olivia, you did not."

"I had already spent it, you know that."

"But Olivia, you promised."

"I knew you could not handle this," I said rising to my feet and walking to the mouth of the cove.

"That is not it."

"How else was I to get it? It was due the next morning."

She looked away. "What about Wally?"

"He had nothing for me." I paused and looked down to my phalanges. "But that is not the worst. I was nearly caught. A clerk saw my face."

Jayde turned quickly to me. "Oh my, Liv. How did you escape?" she asked sounding more intrigued than angry.

"I am not really certain. Somehow convinced him that I had walked through the front door that he had forgotten to lock. Only, it actually *was* locked. "

I looked up in time to see her eyebrows rise. "And you are sure you are not at least part Amirontian?"

I turned toward the sound of Faraji and Aissa walking our way in the distance.

"There was a great patch back there," Aissa called. "We brought you guys some. They are really juicy, too."

Jayde stood and dusted the gravel powder from her clothes. She walked toward me, taking a seat beside me and wrapping her arm around my shoulder.

"You must find work, Olivia."

"I cannot do as you do, Jayde. I cannot work administratively for a man whom I despise."

"'Tis better to survive than live off pride."

My eyes moved to hers. "'Tis better to be true to oneself in spite of the cost."

We looked at one another in silence until Faraji leaned in, redirecting our focus.

"My, how intense it is over here. Have an obi berry; it will help you live longer."

I laughed. "Please, do not threaten me."

†

THROUGHOUT THE YEARS RESIDENTS OF MARIEUX, NATIVES and transplants, have discovered many ways to find themselves in discord with the long arm of SRA law. Some laws were broken with full knowledge and intent. Others were broken by the good-intentioned who had found themselves without options.

Nearly just as many others who found themselves in trouble with SRA did so completely unbeknownst of their offense until it was too late. This was the primary way in which new laws were discovered.

Kelsard had the dreadful habit of enacting laws that were to be immediately enforced without prior warning to the people whom were affected. There was solid reasoning behind this crude practice. It kept everyone on their toes, both citizens and enforcers. And by keeping a looming cloud of panic in the air, residents were kept in line. It increased pay offs and maintained the constant state of paranoia that Kelsard preferred his citizens to live in. If the people were intimidated, who would dare have the courage to stand up against him and his ranks?

SRA representatives were certainly not exempt from this psychological game whether they realized it or not. It kept them from becoming too lax ... too cozy with residents. It assured that they stayed connected with what was going on at SRA headquarters for if they failed to do the duties required and uphold the laws instituted by Henry Kelsard, they were subject to the same consequences as all else who committed an infraction against the regime.

Each and every citizen of the planet Marieux, whether resident of The City or a farmer in a village or in the valleys, were subject to the consequences of any and all rule change without prior notice or fair warning.

†

JAYDE, AISSA, AND I STOOD IN THE FADING LIGHT BENEATH the stairwell in back of their building making small talk, the pair passing the remainder of a lit caniron stick back and forth. It was one that Raj's little giji boyfriend Madan left behind before their earlier departure. The cool nighttime air made the wearing of the green colored jacket I took so much hassle for, that much more welcome and appreciated.

Alarmed, we quieted and slipped deeper into the shadows at the hurried sound of what we believed to be a soldier's footsteps coming our way. The sound of footprints crushing gravel became much closer.

"Jayde. Jayde, are you back here?" the voice cried out in a desperate whisper.

Jayde stepped forward and peered out. "Raj, is that you? What happened?"

"Please tell me Liv is still here," he said as he stepped deeper beneath the stairwell.

"I am here," I spoke up. "What is going on?"

He was breathless and even in the shadows we could see that he was drenched in sweat. Jayde placed a hand on his shoulder.

"Raj. Raj, meli, take a deep breath."

More footsteps and voices grabbed our attention. Faraji swore, and then cautioned us by putting a phalanx to his lips and guided us deeper into darkness. Jayde snatched the cani stick from Aissa and squeezed the tip firmly, extinguishing its flame. Fortunately for us, smoke from caniron leaves is odorless.

I looked toward the slats in the stairwell in the direction the voices were coming from. Two soldiers stopped short, glancing in both directions. One asked whether the other thought they should check all *cracks and we froze. His partner expressed his sentiment that they should do so but once the streets were secure.

We held our breath and focused on becoming invisible until the soldiers footsteps disappeared into the direction they had originated. We exhaled collectively once we were sure the two soldiers were indeed gone and none had taken their place.

"Raj," Aissa whispered, "what in the world is going on out there?"

"New SRA law. This one is not good for Liv." His gaze landed on me.

I stepped closer. "What is it?"

"Kelsard just enforced a law stating any citizen found in a sector other than one established for their own descendants after the setting of the eastern sun is subject to prosecution." He made a pained face.

"You cannot be serious," I responded.

"Wait Liv, Raj's expression tells me there is more. What is it?" Jayde asked.

"It is Madan. We were coming from ... you know, and a soldier stopped us, asked of our ancestry. I said Amirontian, Madan said Citober. The soldier took him, just like that. Said he was breaking protocol by being in an Amirontian sector after eastern sunset and he was subject to be prosecuted to the highest extent the law allows."

Jayde said, "Which with Kelsard and Dupec is however far they are in the mood to go."

"Since when is this law?" Aissa asked foolishly.

"Since now."

Jayde crept closer to where the light shone. "We have to get Olivia inside."

"Jayde, no." I whispered. "I am not going to put anyone else at risk. I will take my chances getting to SOTA no different than I always have."

"No," she said with force. "No. This *is* different, much different. This is not up for debate."

I did not find that I feared much but in that moment I feared Jayde. I swallowed hard my disagreement and nodded. She slowly looked away as though if she turned too quickly I may just make a run for it.

Jayde bent at the waist and removed her shoes. She crept closer. "There are soldiers at the mouth, I can hear them. We can rest assured that it will not be much longer before they begin a search of all cracks. If Kelsard has a new law, they all have something to gain and some ranks to vie for."

She turned her face to us. We were ready to be instructed.

We had all dodged SRA together enough times to know that if we wanted to survive we would need to be in sync.

"We are ready," Aissa whispered.

Jayde nodded. She glanced again into the alley and listened carefully. When the time was right, she, without looking, pointed to Faraji who took her post as she darted out into the alley and up the steps to ready the door. We stilled ourselves and waited, Faraji looking on and listening, with Aissa and I ready to move. We watched as his hand slowly rose. When he pointed, Aissa grabbed my wrist and she and I exited the darkness and crept up the steps. Faraji followed closely behind.

Aissa, Raj, and I rushed to the flat while Jayde stayed behind listening and making certain that we had not been seen.

†

TABIA RUSHED TO THE DOOR AS WE ENTERED. "RAJ, what is going on down there? Sounds like chaos."

Aissa held firmly to my wrist. We said nothing and neither did Faraji, not until Jayde was safe inside. We could hear commotion from the street below. Jayde signaled for us to hold our positions while she walked over to peer out the window and see what was happening.

After apparently seeing more than enough, she stepped away and pressed her back against the wall and faced us. "This is unbelievable. Why? Of all the despicable laws this monster has enacted, why something that would bring harm to his own people?"

"What is happening?" Tabi asked frantically.

"SRA is taking citizens caught on the wrong side of town after sunset into custody."

"What does that mean?"

Jayde walked heavily in our direction, tossing her heels into the corner. "All that matters, Tabi, is that it does not concern you. You are Amirite in an Amirontian neighborhood. You are fine."

"But Liv–"

"Is not."

Tabi collapsed onto a chair and glanced at me looking every bit of distraught. I found her reaction confounding. Aissa looked down and realizing she was still holding me in a vice, released my wrist. Faraji began to pace.

"They are going to hurt him, I know they are. Amirontian soldiers, they hate giji boys. They will probably kill him. I lied. I had to ... I had to lie and pretend not to know what he was. Said I was giving him directions."

Jayde grabbed my arm forcefully and pulled me aside while Faraji continued to vent his guilt and Aissa attempted to salve it through sound reasoning. Jayde opened her mouth to speak and said words that floored me more than the sudden change in SRA law. She asked that I re-adjust my color in an to attempt to pass for Amirontian.

I stumbled over the response I attempted to lie my way through. "H-how can I possibly–"

"You are a Concealor. I am no fool. For the past three years you have tended to be an awful lot darker than the year I met you."

I stood speechless, feeling a strong urge to explain but uncertain what to say. "Jayde—"

She raised her palm to stop me. "I do not need an explanation, I do not care. You have your reasons and that is enough for me. I need you to try and be Amirontian tonight ... just in case."

There was a standoff between her and me. I walked away. She had asked me to do the one thing that I could not, the one thing I ironically have done every day of my life. Deny who I am ... be what I am not.

She said my name again. I looked back in time to see the intense fear and pleading in her eyes. Faraji, as though sensing what Jayde wished for me to do, put an end to all hope of my trying to be another.

"Soldiers are requiring proof of ancestry."

I was jarred back to the conversation on the other side of the room. "W-what? How so? How might one *prove* ancestry?"

Jayde swore under her breath and walked back toward the window. "All Amirontians have a distinguishing mark someplace on their person identifying them as full blood. It is genetic. Mine is on the back of my thigh."

"Razi's and mine are on our lower back," Aissa shared. Tabi told us that hers was on her left foot. Faraji, lifting his shirt, showed his stomach. My eyes grew as I took in the darkened patch of skin resembling the shape of a crescent.

Faraji informed me, "If you claim Amironte yet cannot show

one of these you will be taken into custody."

The room hushed. Jayde stood near the window with her hand covering her mouth and wet eyes. If I stayed the night, it was possible that I could escape and make the journey home safely after the rising of the western sun. If only the soldiers did not begin door-to-door checks, we could manage.

The sound of the door opening caused us all to hold our breath in fear. We all turned in time to come face to snarling face with the one obstacle standing in my way.

"She has to go. I am not breaking the law for her." Razi had barely entered the home and had yet to make eye contact with anyone but me before making his announcement.

"Raz, please," Jayde pleaded, "now is not the time for this."

"The laws have changed, Jayde. It is just that simple."

"It is never simple."

"As we speak the soldiers are cleaning the streets, checking cracks. I will not be surprised should they begin to do a door-to-door sweep. I will not harbor a Marinite, even if she is your friend." He spit the word out as though it alone were contaminated.

"She is not just a Marinite. She is Olivia. She is family." I could hear the pain filling Jayde's throat and I knew she was aware that Razi could hear it too. She fought hard against her weakening emotions for, by nature, Amirontians held contempt for the weak and she would not stand any chance against Razi if she expressed fragility. For as strong as Jayde truly was it was always very clear that the ultimate authority in the home belonged solely to Razi Las.

Razi stepped closer to Jayde. Her back straightened and her head tilted so that their eyes deadlocked, but her intimidation could be felt by all.

There was a tone of pleasure in Razi's voice when he addressed her. "She is a Marinite and is no longer welcome here after dark. I am going to change my garments. I am giving you fair warning, Jayde. If she is not gone when I return, I will report her."

There was a fight in Jayde that could not be brought to the surface. With limited options she had no choice but to back down. Razi walked past her toward his space, eyeing me with satisfaction. I felt Jayde's eyes come to me. Maybe hoping I would stand up in my own defense. But I would not beg.

I looked defiantly at Razi as I pulled my hat further onto my head. I turned away and walked to the door.

"Olivia," Jayde called to me. I glanced back. "Please, be safe."

I opened the door and headed into the shadows.

Four
Blackberries

FOR FOUR YEARS I HAD LIVED WITHIN THE LIMITS OF THE City. The journey from Ashtwor was long, dangerous, and impossible for an inexperienced child of my age to make on her own safely but somehow, I managed.

I had a talent, a gift. I would not attribute such a thing to the true color of my skin but, rather believed it had everything to do with the heritage passed down through genetics beginning with Mira.

For four years I lived in the shadows, coming out now and again to socialize with my Amirontian brethren, the ones I discovered the cove with and took shots with at endweek at Mole's and now ... now some egomaniacal dictator on a power trip was determined to tear us apart.

For four full years I followed the crumbs that the darkness left behind and I had never been caught – until now.

†

"UH, UH, UH. NOT SO FAST."

Razi had sent me out to fend for myself in the midst of a warzone. I was alone in the trenches with no team on standby to implement an emergency strategy to set me free. I had survived through a great many law enforcements and knew just what it meant. Soldiers were constantly trying to claw their way from the bottom barrel "beat cop" to a rank and a room of their own, fully equipped with a private Elite SOTA at Kelsard's compound. Every capture represented a unique opportunity.

The night was crawling with soldiers shaking down innocent citizens who were unable to prove an ancestral tie to Amironte. Some, like me, were visiting with friends. Others were simply on their way home. Worse than not being an Amirontian was being the significant other of one. Intergalactic relationships were a practice that was highly frowned upon. Plenty were raising shirts, taking off shoes, lifting skirts, whatever was necessary to find the distinctive little mark that identified one as full blood.

I ducked beneath stairwells and in every crack and hold along the way. I had memorized them all. The trouble was the many soldiers spread about the area doing the exact same as I was.

I had not seen the soldier approaching though I had sensed a presence and turned quickly to blend with the shadows in the hold that I had began to emerge from. It was by chance that I had been spotted. One soldier was clearing the stairwell nearest but it was the ground soldier who looked over in time to see me in my attempt to vanish and caught me by the wrist.

I had an urge; one unlike I had ever had before. No sooner did his hand grasp me did I reverse the maneuver and take his wrist firmly into my grip. I turned my face to his and took note of the surprise in his eyes. He tugged, tried to break free but the more he fought the tighter my grip locked.

I realized that I had him if I wanted. I offered him a quick celebratory, albeit surprised, smirk just to make sure he was aware that I knew this.

"All clear." The cry went out from the bottom of the stairwell. "What is your call, Soldier?"

My eyes were on the soldier that had attempted to capture me and his eyes were on mine. He was afraid ... afraid of something. Maybe afraid of me. I could hear his partner approaching.

"Hey, Pystran, what is your call?"

The soldier, Pystran, fearfully looked from me to the direction his partner was coming from. He fixed his mouth to respond but froze and looked back to me. I loosened my hold but held my smile as I allowed the soldier to carefully take my wrist into his grasp once more.

"What are you, citizen?" he asked quietly.

I straightened my spine and tilted my head higher. I did not blink as I looked at him. "Full blood Marinite."

He eyed me a moment longer before the blood flow to his manhood regenerated and he regained the courage that came with the patch that he wore.

He cleared his throat. "One," he replied through a cracked voice.

I knew then and there that I could have taken him down. I knew that, but I also recognized that I likely would not have escaped. There was no back exit from the hold I was in, the heavy door was locked and the second soldier would have realized there was a problem and sought me out, and a dead or maimed soldier would have only complicated things. By turning myself in I actually stood a better chance of getting away.

The soldier, once again filled to the brim with testosterone, aggressively pulled me into the light and in view of his partner who looked a little too pleased to see me. He sucked his teeth and shook his head as he leisurely approached. He offered praise to his partner for the capture.

"Awful tall for a Mariuchan shunti, is she not?" he stated more than asked. My captor laughed uncomfortably. "What are you doing on this side of town so late at night, Mariuchan?"

I chuckled sarcastically. He was awful short and hairless for an Amirite.

"Something funny?" he asked.

"Yes, a bit. But you would not get it."

"Try me." His hand moved to the weapon attached to his waist. A not so subtle threat.

I looked from the weapon to the eagerness in his eyes. "Nothing is funny."

"I did not think so. Take her to the wagon. I will deal with her later."

The soldier, Pystran, placed a firm hand around the back of my neck, pushing me forward down the alleyway. I glanced around. I had nearly made it. Home had been within my reach and now I was being forced to a wagon to sit with other unjustly detained Marinites and Citoberians and await persecution.

"You are attractive beneath that filthy garment, are you not?" he spoke into my ear as he guided me along. "Yes, I believe you are, that is why you wear all of that. You tried to make me look like a fool in front of my partner. Do you not think you owe me for my trouble? Yes, yes, I think so. Now, how do you think you and I can make this right?"

He stopped short. I glanced up; I could see the wagon in the distance. My body was jerked backward, the momentum sending me crashing into the wall with a great force. A sharp pain shot from the base of my skull and crept steadily to the front causing a heavy throbbing.

Pystran leaned forward, his face so close I could smell the stench of carrupe on his breath. I remained stoic as he used one of his phalanges to graze the material of my hat. I hoped that he would not touch me and hoped he would at once. If he did, I likely would have died on this night for I would have certainly killed him where he stood.

"What do we have here, soldier?" Pystran and I both turned at the authorative sound of the voice. "We are on strict orders from Dupec himself and yet, somehow you believe that you have time right now for a little Mariuchan fun. Interesting."

Pystran stepped back and at attention. "No, sir."

"So tell me, what is it that you think that you are doing with our prisoner?"

"Taking her to the wagon ... sir."

"Well, carry on, soldier."

The light shining behind the Legatus cast a shadow, which obscured his face. I could not make him out but there was something familiar about his presence. Pystran wound his hand tightly around my arm and jerked me forward. My eyes remained curiously fixed to the face of the Lega, the ranking officer, hoping to get a glimpse of who was in charge. Pystran, feeling a need to impress, pushed my head straight, forcing me to look ahead.

"Hold on." The Lega stepped closer and looked carefully into my face. He gently tilted mine to meet his. "Do I know you?"

I knew him all right, or at least knew exactly who he was. "Lega Dupec," I addressed respectfully. A junior ranking officer. Brother of Taaman Dupec and regular lover of Diana.

"Let her go," he spoke the order which my captor reluctantly obeyed. "You are Diana's cousin, are you not?"

"I am."

He laughed heartily. "What are you doing on this side of town?"

"I have friends of Amirontian ancestry."

He raised an eyebrow. "She speaks ... she has friends. *Very* interesting. Your cousin takes care of me, has for many years. She is umm ... good at her work."

"So I hear."

Ja'ali Dupec laughed. "Humor. I appreciate that." He stood still, eyeing me curiously, offering a discomforting smile. "Release her."

My captor's eyes widened. "What? I mean, sir?"

"I said release her."

"But sir, we have been ordered–"

Dupec quickly approached the soldier and placed a large hand around his neck. "First you were to take it upon yourself to take a break from your ordered duties to pleasure yourself and now you wish to advise me on my job, soldier?"

"N-no, sir." Pystran struggled to catch his breath.

Ja'ali Dupec turned to face me. "You are still here? Tell Diana what I have done on this night so she will thank me properly."

I cringed. "Of course." I turned toward the shadows.

"Little one," he called to me. "I know that you will not forget this generosity either."

I swallowed hard and vanished, more cautious than ever before, into the night.

†

I RECALLED A PARTICULAR NIGHT AS A SMALL CHILD LIVING in a neat little shanty with my mira. I paid special attention to my small body after she had given me my weekly scrubbing. It was the day of the week that she cleared away all of my concealant so that she could apply a fresh coat. Back then I was fascinated with the golden tone that shone through from beneath the darkness of the mud that latched into my skin, altering my pigmentation while becoming a living, breathing organism. And though I understood my flesh to be a curse, the contrast still amazed me.

My tiny phalanges traced the visible areas of the flesh on my exposed belly. It was then that I first noticed a spot there that would not wipe clean with the wet cloth that Mira was scrubbing me with. It was a small patch of darkness shaped similarly to a crescent that had the tail hastily erased.

I poked at it and attempted to scratch it away. I pointed it out to Mira near hysterics, asked her why it would not come off. She grabbed my wrists in her small hands and stilled me. Told me that it was fine, it was a part of me and, no, it would not come off. She referred to it as a stain, said it sometimes happened at birth. This partial crescent ... this stain, it made me unique (as if I needed one more way to be different).

And now many years later, I stood alone in the bathroom in the middle of day before a foggy mirror that was barely capable of displaying a reflection, wiping clean the area around the stained flesh beneath the dim overhead light. I scrubbed aggressively until the partial crescent shown through.

I traced the outline of the shape. I wondered what it could mean, if anything at all. I recalled Faraji's stain. He had said the mark proved his identity as Amirite, full blood. Jayde, Aissa, and Tabia boasted of having the same. But how could I, a Marinite, have nearly the same mark?

A heavy pounding on the door jarred me and I instinctively pulled my top down to my waist. I exhaled my nervous tension.

"What?" I cried out.

The muffled female voice of a resident Sister came to me from the other side complaining of the time that I was spending in the community bathroom. She likely needed to prepare for a pending date or freshen from one just past. My eyes rolled to the back of my head. I instructed her to wait a moment to which she mumbled some incoherent and profane insult.

I took the jar of concealant with the revised recipe and scooped a small amount out and rubbed it over the area of my stomach until it blended with the rest. I fanned with my hand to help it dry faster. Once I was comfortable with the result, I pulled my shirt back to my waist and screwed the top back on the jar and shoved it inside my bag. I opened the door and came face to chin with a particularly large Amirontian Sister.

"It is about time," she complained as she forcefully pushed past me. "Such a weird one."

I brushed it off and made the trek down the hall back to the flat shared with Diana in slow motion, heavy in thoughts related to the events of the night before. There were answers to questions that were beginning to plague me that only Diana could supply.

She appeared nervous and frenzied when I stepped inside. She was oblivious to my presence. I crept across the room in contemplation while she awkwardly sifted through the small black bag filled with the various colors of clays and paints she used to decorate herself with.

I softly spoke her name. She stopped and turned to face me with glassy eyes, high in an OR daze though, for the moment, still functional. She responded as she returned her attention to what she had been doing.

I did not know exactly how to poise the question and so I

went the route of blurting it out. "Have you any idea who my father is?"

"What?" she responded in a thick, phlegm-filled voice. "Why would you want to know now? After all this time?"

I paused. Most children coming up on my planet were fully aware who both of their parents were. Knowledge of ancestry was not privileged information but a right. For some reason I had never thought much about it. It had not ever really mattered to me – until last night.

"Is it possible ... could it be possible that my father is Amirite?" My eyes moved to the back of her head. She stopped what she was doing, slowly turning to face me. Our eyes locked. The blood drained from her dark face.

She looked away. "It is impossible."

"How are you so certain, Diana? You are SOTA. You have shared your bed with many over the years. Could you have possibly known the ancestry of every one?"

"Do not insult me."

"It is not meant to be an insult."

"Do you see this mark?" One dainty phalanx guided my eye to the red mark of the Marinite sign of peace embedded into the pigmentation on her shoulder. "This labels me Marinite."

"I do not understand. There has been no discrimination in this room since I have shared it with you."

"Certainly not. At this level, who cares what I am? I am only an object to be used when convenient, when a greater option is not viable. I was not always a leech on the soles of man, holding on for a hot meal and tax payment. I was once respected as an Elite where my ancestry was treasured and reserved for those soldiers and officials whose blood ran the same color as my own."

"I have the mark of the Amirite."

"What mark?" she asked disinterestedly as she lifted a brush to stroke her hair.

"The crescent."

My eyes followed as the heavy brush slipped from her grasp and landed powerfully against the hard floor. She stared at my reflection in her mirror. In her expression was truth. She scrambled to retrieve the brush.

"What does that mean?" she asked unconvincingly.

"It means you know something," I said as I stepped nearer.

"I know nothing," she answered with great force, her voice rising ... her gaze piercing.

I snatched the brush from her hand, slamming it onto the dresser.

"That is a lie! You know who he is, do you not? You know who my father is." I hissed the words, keeping them from reaching the prying ears of anyone who may be nearby listening for good gossip to share. I leaned closer. She had answers to the questions beginning to burn within yet she was refusing me a birthright. In that sense she was true SRA. "What are you keeping from me?"

She rose from her chair. "You believe you are so special that if I had this information which you seek I should share it with you? What makes you more important than me? I have survived thirty-two days on this planet without knowledge of who was responsible for my birthing and I troubled no one."

"Exactly who would you trouble?"

Reflexively, Diana's palm landed forcefully against my cheek. I deserved the hit. My question was callous and insensitive but I was angry and she was being selfish. It was because she was stripped of her dignity and rights that she owed it to me to grant mine as best she could.

Neither flinched. Neither offered an apology and though deep down we were both sorry for our actions, neither would admit to it. In that way we were truly mother and daughter. She returned her attention to preparing herself for her pending date. I turned away and walked to the mouth of the kitchenette, my fist tapping against the wall.

"In case you have not realized, this conversation is complete. You may want to find yourself something to do. I have received word that Lega Dupec is en route and shall be here soon."

That caught my attention. "I wish you had told me sooner." I turned immediately, walking to my space and retrieved my jacket. I would not wait around for a confrontation with him, a man who had not noticed I even existed for the past four years. I could have stood to keep it that way forever.

"What difference does it make? It has not mattered before, why should it now?"

"It matters."

I threw my arms inside my jacket and walked back across the room, stopping to lift my bag from the floor just in time to see the door push open. Again, I was face to face with Ja'ali Dupec.

His smile was wide and sinister. "Ah, look who is here. Nice to see you again Diana's cousin."

I glanced at Diana, catching the odd look she aimed at me. "I think I will give you two some privacy," I said attempting to pass but was halted when he took my forearm into his hand and eased me back.

"This is your home as well as hers. You do not need to leave on my account."

"How generous you are, Legatus."

His eyes were affixed to me but his words were directed to Diana. "I am sure your child cousin told you how well I cared for her last night."

My eyes shot to Diana's. Murder mixed with confusion was present in hers.

I spoke up quickly, clearing the air before turning my face back to Dupec's. "Yes, I did ... tell her how gracious you were for saving me from the bête noire of the Facilities. Now I really must leave. I am sure my cousin has plans of thanking you properly for your ... kindness."

He did not move immediately, but rather took the time to allow his eyes to scan the length of me while offering a smile that revealed a hint of the vulgarity of his thoughts. "Certainly," he said, finally stepping aside, allowing just enough space for me to squeeze by.

†

I WAS THE DAUGHTER OF A LEVEL 1 SOTA WHORE, A CHILD of debauchery and yet I had never myself been with a man.

Jayde and Faraji took great pleasure in teasing me for it. I was missing out on life according to them. And in an environment so restrictive with such little joy as it was, this was the one thing that I could do to have pleasure without risking the wrath of SRA.

"What I do not understand is how you can *not* enjoy a man." Jayde would say, assuring me that the act itself did not make me like them ... did not make me like Diana. Intellectually I was aware of that. But Mira had enjoyed the last thirty-three years of life raising her granddaughter and subsequently her great granddaughter without a need for that sort of intimacy. And with four years observing such an intimacy that led Diana to drug herself more frequently and with greater effort, proved to me that I was better off without it.

That I had not nurtured many relationships since journeying to The City helped to maintain a distance between my loins and that of the male species. I had never been exposed to a situation where temptation could rear its ugly head. I did not plan to ever give myself over, never marry, and certainly Diana could not count on me to make her respectable by having children of my own and making a musha of her. Ja'ali Dupec would not change that.

†

THE DAY WAS THE BRIGHTEST IT HAD BEEN IN A GREAT WHILE. Ironic that it was the gloomiest just the same. Tension was etched into the faces of all that wandered the streets. Sisters were on their best behavior with soldiers. Unusual faces sprinkled about, citizens who were hesitant to take leave of their own area of residency to visit friends on taboo sides of town for fear of not returning in time or worse, being detained by corrupt soldiers looking for an opportunity to take someone, anyone, in for any reason.

Across the lane, two soldiers were harassing a citizen for likely no plausible reason. I jogged down the flight of steps and took to the walk. Soldiers were posted about, never too far from wherever my eye landed. I turned in time to see a large Amirontian soldier forcefully pushing a smaller citizen into his transport car. I involuntarily caressed the place on my body where the crescent was located.

I could not take my eyes off the action of the Amirontian soldier as I walked. My mind was elsewhere, my focus off. Not a good thing during the early days of enforcement. My eyes wandered, venturing into the distance as I passed by Sisters thirsty for attention and the financial support of distracted soldiers.

My arm contacted forcefully with a passing citizen. "Excuse me," I mumbled while continuing forward.

"Hey. Hey!"

I turned my head toward the deep voice calling after me. My heart leapt into my throat. I swore as I turned away, pretending to be oblivious and stepped quicker. The set of footsteps on the pavement behind me came closer, moved faster. I was trapped, looking for a way out. The owner was soon beside me trying to get a look into my face as I fought to keep from being recognized by the man that I recognized as the clerk from Kel's.

"Slow down. Why are you moving so fast?" The silky, bass-filled voice nearly buckled my knees.

"I am in a hurry," I mumbled, preparing to cross the lane but quickly changing my mind at the sight of two soldiers who were just itching for action.

"My apologies. May I just speak to you for one moment? I will not keep you long, I promise."

I had been spotted on the street by someone I had stolen from. This was not a good thing and there was little to be done about it. Soldiers were at every turn. I stopped, about-faced and came eye-to-eye with the head clerk, preparing myself for what was to come.

His hands rose defensively. "I do not wish to trouble you. I only recognized you and wanted to meet you formally."

I remained suspicious. "Hi. Okay, we have met."

"You are a feisty one. I am Charleston–"

"How can I help you, Charleston?"

He paused, displayed a defeated smirk and scratched his temple. "I ... I just ... I see you around here often. I wanted to speak for some time. I thought now was as good a time as any. But I apologize for the bother."

Charleston turned away. I stood confused. He had recognized me from the area but not as the culprit who had lifted seventy dashii's which he undoubtedly took the blame for.

"Hey, Charleston," I called. He turned to face me. "Nice meeting you."

He smiled and waved before continuing on his way. Warmth washed over me. I shook the odd feeling away and cleared my thoughts. There had been too many close calls in such a short period of time. I would have to be much more aware lest suffer the consequences.

†

I RECOGNIZED THE FACE OF THE MAN EXITING THE FLAT AS I approached. It was not difficult. He was an odd looking man of uncertain ancestry. Height of an Amirite, skin of a Marinite, and a crown difficult to decipher. He was always around, popping in and out of shadows on a mission to turn Sisters into addicts. His job was made easier by their jobs. Sisters were always looking for a mental escape, some more than others. It was the latter ratio that made his business so successful.

It was not illegal for pushers to sell caniron. The soldiers benefited from its affects as well. However harsher drugs were heavily restricted for they had the ability to turn a Sister's (and even a soldier's) allegiance from the cause and to the pusher himself.

Though there were many who slithered among the cesspool of the underground, this one leaving Diana's company was particularly alarming for he was known to push more than the average obi red fix. He appeared satisfied as he passed me by hardly noticing my presence. A knot formed in my stomach and I moved faster.

The air was thick and an unfamiliar odor clung to it. The room was dark, save for a single candle that emitted a pitiful glow. Words, incoherent ramblings, came to me and I felt around for the string connected to the bulb overhead.

The sight of Diana horrified me. She sat on the edge of the

bed, topless and barefoot. She was drenched. I did not know if it was from sweat or if she had been doused with water.

I rushed to her side and called her name repeatedly but it was as though she were not there. It was Diana's body ... her voice speaking random strings of nonsensical verbiage but her mind was not present. Her eyes were red and glazed and face stained with tears.

"Diana. Diana, what did you take? Can you hear me?"

I had not cried in many years but I felt as though I could now.

It was not an OR daze, could not have possibly been. I had never seen such a reaction in anyone that I had witnessed take the drug. Her skin was extremely warm to the touch. I wondered whether I should bother another Sister and ask for help. They had experienced much more than I where poison was concerned. There was one Sister in particular she seemed to be close with. She resided only two flights up.

I did not need this info to be spread around; she had enough to contend with. I did not want it to get back to Ja'ali Dupec. I did not know how he would react if he found out. I turned to rise ... and that is when I saw it. On the small table beside the candle sat a syringe, dark on the inside from the black fluid that had been there.

I lifted it from the table, praying that it was not what it appeared to be. Slowly I put it to my nose, smelled the pungent odor emitted. I dropped it and turned back to Diana. I grabbed her clammy forearms in my hands and forced her to face me.

"Diana, wake up. Snap out of it, please." I groaned and shook my head in frustration. "Diana, what is in that? Did you shoot blackberries? Please, tell me that is not blackberries."

Her glazed over eyes came to mine. She gurgled out words but all I could understand was my name. I cursed and pulled her arms forward and began to check for an entry point but found nothing. I sat astonished ... frustrated. She was wearing a skirt, short and purple. She had it for quite some time.

My hands went to her outer thighs. I touched the flesh, moving my hands until I felt it, the small raised patch of skin. She had shot the drug into a vein in her thigh.

Blackberries was a very potent narcotic, the worst known on the planet and Diana had discovered it. I allowed the heaviness in my heart to spill forward as I walked to the kitchen to warm a cup of kakali nut milk to try and bring her down.

Five
Decisions

THE PERIOD OF ENFORCEMENT IS BY FAR THE MOST dangerous of times for any citizen of Marieux. Kelsard and Dupec randomly instituted a new rule for no better reason than they could do so, and would have word transmitted to all soldiers on foot and in transport car within the hour of its inception.

Day one of enforcement totaled the greatest amount of captures for any law simply because citizens were unaware of the new laws existence. The typical period of any enforcement spanned approximately 2.5 – 3 weeks before the diligence in upholding it began to wane and the soldiers inevitably returned to their usual ways and habits.

While the law itself remained on the books and punishment for the infraction would be enforced like any other, the rigorous seek and destroy missions and heightened presence of SRA began to diminish.

Offenders were dealt with in a number of ways from a "simple" warning (nearly always accompanied by a severe beating which one may or may not survive), to being placed in holding to await a final decision by the Magistrate. Marked criminals (former convicts whose wrists were embedded with the SRA icon signifying their criminal past) and those spirited citizens who did not go into custody easily, or those recognized by the Magistrate as repeat offenders (though never convicted of a crime), were nearly 100% of the time remanded to the custody of Chrekal, the small, angry Marinite warden of the Facilities.

Despite the dangers and consequences, citizens looked forward to the end of enforcement, when all would return to normal. Though the laws remained and the risk was high, with cracks and holds no longer routinely investigated, citizens were certain to return to the behaviors that had brought them their greatest joys in the first place.

I was no different.

†

I STOOD AS ONE WITH THE SHADOWS IN THE CRACK BENEATH the stairwell that led to Jayde's building, leaning my back against the stone wall and bouncing a tiny ball that I had found. Probably one that a child lost track of while being shooed home in haste. I had been there for nearly an hour but I was nothing if not patient.

The click of a pair of heels reverberated throughout the back alleyway. I pushed myself from the wall and stepped forward quietly. As the sound grew nearer I shrank into the shadow closest to the mouth of the crack and melted into the wall. I could hear words of greeting being spoken, likely out of a respected fear of a soldier passing by. I waited until the owner of the heels was in plain view and identifiable before emerging.

"Hello, Jayde," I said, all smiles.

She faced me, standing momentarily frozen in place in her black SRA approved uniform. Her face lit with excitement and she scurried to join me.

She took my hand in hers, the other touched my head ... my cheek. "Amen Deus, you are safe. Not that I ever doubted your abilities but needless to say I have been most concerned. Clearly I have been no freer to roam than you have. How is Diana? Have you seen *my* cousin? Is she surviving this okay?"

"She is fine. They are both fine."

"Thank goodness. Faraji convinced me that I should not worry. Said that there is something special about you ... something that protects you and he was certain you had made it and well, I was too but you know, it was pretty bad out here for awhile." She stopped speaking and smiled. She opened her arms wide and pulled me into an embrace. "I am glad that you are safe. Come on up. Aissa and Tabi should be there. We are not expecting Razi until his usual time."

I followed her up to the flat she shared with her Amirontian brethren. I nearly felt at home the moment I crossed the threshold. The fragrant scent of the Pelarulata, a flower native to Amironte but grown in the mini garden Jayde created on her windowsills, captivated my senses. The home was clean and bright with a relaxing breeze ever present. Were it not for Razi's disdain for me and Diana's need, I could have very easily been persuaded to call this place home.

Aissa did not contain the excitement she felt. Tabia did not display the same outward expression of joy as the other two women but the faint hint of a smile that could not be withheld betrayed her true feelings. Surprising.

The little family of Jayde, Razi, Aissa, Faraji, and Tabia had established long before I ever arrived beneath The City's orange skies. A group of outcasts come together to help one another survive in their quest to avoid capture by SRA and an acquaintance with Galê Tagali.

Jayde could never bring herself to confess why she had left her village on the far east side of the planet, not even to me. I did not push as I had a secret of my own that she would never know the full extent of. Razi had been forced out, no doubt for some sort of unsavory behavior. His twin Aissa stood by him as an act of loyalty.

After one too many drinks at Mole's, Faraji confided to having fled his village in the southeast to avoid repercussions he would most assuredly have to suffer after being caught in the family's shanty with a young boy from a neighboring village. Tabia was orphaned when her father was remanded to the Facilities for failure to pay overdue taxes. Her mother, devastated, hung herself in response.

Were it not for my heritage, or rather Razi's intolerance, we could make for quite the band of misfits.

†

I SAT IN JAYDE'S CUSHIONY CHAIR, SIPPING ON A COLD glass of juice from sweet carraplums, an Amirontian beverage. I wanted to confide in Jayde about Diana's newly acquired addiction but I was not sure that I could speak of it.

"Sometimes I really hate it here," Jayde said. She was stretched across the sofa, upside down, her head hanging over and bare feet crossed at the ankles, toes pointing in the air. "I think about leaving ... going to Amironte."

"How would you even get there?" Aissa asked. She sat on the floor with her back against a wall.

"I know people. I guess you can say it is the benefit of working for SRA. It would be dangerous ... I would be taking a great risk to do so but it is not impossible. People do it, Marinites and Amirites alike. They leave. Just get up and leave."

I looked at her over the rim of my glass. "I would really miss you if you left."

"I would never actually go. I am not strong enough ... not brave enough. No, I only think about it. Besides, I know nothing of Amironte. My people came here during the war, one of the first families to do so. I do not know that things are any better there anyhow. I have never heard many good things about it to begin with."

Tabia walked across the room and took a seat at the opposite end of the sofa. "Most who escape tend to return ... if they are able."

We were rendered speechless for a moment. The thought

of possibly escaping this planet had us all fantasizing. I had not known Jayde was even pondering escaping to Amironte. But I could not blame her for considering it. If there was any glimmer of hope of a place better than this, she certainly deserved the opportunity. I did not want her to leave and honestly hoped that she would never consider following through but if she ever felt the need to try, I knew that I would not attempt to stop her.

"Amironte is not the answer," Tabia said gazing into the distance.

"How would you know?" Aissa questioned. "You are no different than us. You have never set foot on our home planet."

"Aissa, please. You have heard the prophecies just as I have. Nowhere in Shadow Realm is life the way it was meant to be."

My ears perked up and I leaned forward in my seat. "What prophecy?"

Jayde's eyes rolled and she twisted her body around to an upright position. "There is a prophecy of the supposed *one* ... the Goldenborn. I am sure you must have been taught it as a child in your own village. Well, so were we except when it was told to us she was the chosen daughter of the Amirites. She would soon come and save us all from a life of unrest and servitude."

I sank back and deeper into the chair. Of course I had heard of the prophecy, I had practically been accused of its realization but when Mira mentioned it and when Galê Sarai attempted to convince me of its validity, the daughter was always Marinite. What could it mean that Amirontians had a belief of their own in this daughter coming to free their people?

Suddenly my skin, eyes, and every other genetic flaw were

placed in perspective. There was no truth in it. It was simply a myth that got spread across the planet and manipulated to serve the needs of whoever was telling the story. A bedtime tale of sorts likely told to help little children sleep at night.

"It is true, Jayde," Tabia cried out with passion.

"It is a myth. It is a tale our elders created in order to give themselves hope ... to make life bearable for *them*."

"No. No!"

"Tabia, listen to yourself," began Aissa. "You have been brainwashed."

"Ye of little faith."

"Foolish girl," Jayde uttered.

Tabia stood from the sofa and addressed me. "It most certainly is true. In our villages the Goldenborn is Amirite, in yours she is Marinite. She changes to make her familiar to the children the divination is being told to but it makes her no less real."

Jayde groaned loudly, becoming more fed up with the topic. "How is it possible, Tabi? Huh? She is Amirite? She is Marinite? Which is it?"

"She is both," Tabia ended, facing Jayde.

Jayde shook her head. "You are a loon." Refusing to further entertain the topic, she climbed over the back of the sofa and departed to the kitchen.

I, again, involuntarily touched the area where the crescent was. "What do you mean, Tabi ... both?" I asked.

Tabia seemed pleased to have a captive audience, even if it

was only me. "She is a combination of multiple cultures. Her fate extends beyond the saving of Marieux alone. She is destined to save all of Zephyrnox Theta from those cruel forces that oppress us. Not only will she overthrow the Allegiance but she will also take control away from the Kedt clan of Arethoxx and restore power on the individual planets to the west of the Starr of Tayle to whom it rightfully belongs."

Her eyes lit with excitement. It was clear that she had invested a lot of time into studying this subject and she knew more than I had ever heard with regards to the prophecy of *the one*. But I was not certain that I was buying it.

Jayde re-appeared in the doorway of the sitting room. "Tabi, if this all mighty daughter of whoever's planet does indeed exist, what the hell is taking her so long to do her job?"

I looked to Tabi for an answer. My faith in this myth and its truth lied in her hands. She fumbled, struggling to find a plausible answer. Aissa laughed and stood, retiring to the room the two shared. Jayde signaled for me to join her in the kitchen. Tabia had lost me. It seemed she did not know as much as she let on. I stood and walked across the room to the kitchen, leaving her behind fuming and stewing.

I took a seat at the breakfast table. Jayde opened the cooling box and pulled forth the remainder of the freshly made bottle of carraplum juice and poured me a refill.

"Tabi is not right," Jayde said, pointing at her temple. She stood leaning against the cooling box, drinking the remaining juice from the bottle. "She saw her mother hanging there in the shanty. She was the one that found her. I think she may have lost it that day. She was so young. We were all taught of the prophecy, so were our parents. But by the time the story reached us most of us were wise enough to understand what its true purpose was. We think Tabia latched on to it as a way to deal with losing her parents the way she did. We have all suffered hardship and choosing to believe in some make believe super hero is not going to change a thing."

I looked at Jayde. I almost wanted to tell her about my skin, hair, and eyes ... the unexplained partial crescent and get her take on it. But I did not believe the story either. It was a great tale but it simply was not true. Were it true, Mira would have prepared me for it. If it were true, if this supposed daughter was me, how was one little girl barely in her seventeenth day to, not only to take down Henry Kelsard, Taaman Dupec, and the entire Shadow Realm Allegiance, but also overthrow a clan that had been in power for centuries *and* save planets on a side of the Starr of Tayle that she had never even seen?

I opened my mouth to speak. "Diana is shooting blackberries."

"Unbelievable."

My eyes locked onto the wall. I could not bear to see the hurt and disappointment in Jayde's eyes. I finished off my juice, waiting for what I knew was coming next.

"Are you ... stealing?"

I glanced at her, then looked away. Blackberries was a much more expensive habit than caniron sticks or obi red. She was a little shy of the tax payment. I could only earn so much doing odd jobs for Wally; I had to make up the difference somehow.

Jayde pulled a chair from the table and sat beside me. She danced the empty bottle between the tips of her phalanges.

"Jayde—"

"No. No excuses. You have to get a job. Period. You are doing this to help Diana, is that what you wish to say to me? If you are locked away indefinitely how then will you help Diana? You do not want me to go to Amironte, I do not wish for you to be remanded to the Facilities."

"I understand that but Jayde, we have already been through this. I am not willing —"

"I will not hear it, Liv. No. I have a friend. He knows a guy who owns a shop downtown, near the markets. You need to work, he needs another assistant." She looked away from me, her energy suddenly shifting. She appeared discomforted. "It is also time you ... it is time you took leave of the SOTA building."

"No. no, I cannot do that."

"Olivia—"

"I will not do that."

"You have seen seventeen days. You do not need Diana's guardianship any longer. Technically you have not for a year."

I sat my hand forcefully against the table. "No, Jayde. No. Fine, I will try things your way. If you can work the job out, I will give it a try but I will not leave Diana. She has no one but me and she is all that remains of my family." I looked at Jayde directly, saw the wheels of her mind spinning but she would not sway me on this. "It is final."

She sighed and nodded. She took my hand in hers and squeezed. "I will get you the job."

I squeezed back. "Sure."

†

THERE WERE NOT VERY MANY OPTIONS FOR EMPLOYMENT on Marieux. You were either working for Kelsard directly or indirectly. Anything else was against SRA law and would be certain to have the perpetrator remanded to the Facilities indefinitely for the crime of taking out of SRA's economy.

Villager's harvested crops and the creations their special gifts and talents enabled them to make they bartered with fellow farmers or sold at market. In The City the options were limited to soldier, SOTA, pusher, clerk, factory administrator or factory worker. Every job available benefited or financed SRA. I was never interested in contributing to Kelsard's twisted cause. But I had made a deal with Jayde that I would not steal and the only way to assure that I held up my end was to accept the job that she set up for me.

Undoubtedly Jayde kept her word. Barely a week passed by before she sought me on the streets around SOTA to tell me when and where to report for duty. A friend of hers from the factory she performed admin duties with had a relative who ran a small shop downtown near the markets. He needed an additional clerk to cover the shop, assist customers, and help keep thieves from being successful (what irony). His last one was placed in custody during the tail end of enforcement. He had not been seen or heard from in over a week and was presumed to have been remanded.

According to the friend, the owner did not get into The City much. He ran a farm on a village over 60 tms away. He entrusted the handling of the shop, which specialized in Marinite delights, to a young head clerk who had been successfully employed with him for several weeks. I would report to him and he would familiarize me with the ways of the gainfully employed.

The market was lively when I approached. Merchants were calling on passing patrons, displaying fresh fruits picked from their fields just that morning, fish pulled from the streams of the Apigara, the Lux, or Lake Ittas, and flowers the women hand selected from their gardens. Sweet treats, handmade garments, and beaded jewelry were all showcased and ready to be bargained.

I eyed the various shops that lined the lane looking for the one that Jayde had described. Finally recognizing it, I paused just outside its door contemplating going inside. Technically in accepting the job I would not be directly betraying my own beliefs and standards by working for SRA, but nonetheless every dime I would assist this shop in earning, an unhealthy percentage would make its way to pad Kelsard and Dupec's pockets.

I was nothing if not a woman of my word. I inhaled deeply and stepped inside. A bell rang over the door announcing my arrival and a voice cried out asking me to be patient; I would be assisted in a moment. The voice momentarily stilled me but I shook it off. I glanced around the shop as I waited. There were large cases in front filled with powdered babali and jellied mashoroot, amongst other sweet breaded delights.

Racks displayed packages of dried green obi berries and cured batuchee. My mouth watered and I was nearly tempted to take a pack or two for myself. But I remembered that I was here to halt crime, not indulge in it. I returned to the counter to wait. I glanced over the drink menu and was thrilled to see that the shop made shakes of all flavors including, my favorite, the red kakali nut milkshake which was sweetened with three different red berries.

"Sorry for keeping you waiting. May I help..." The voice trailed off and I glanced up to see the clerk that was speaking to me. He stopped short, then smiled and continued forward using a rag to wipe his phalanges clean. "...you."

I swore beneath my breath. The voice, the silky bass-filled voice that I was so certain that I recognized when he first called to me, was indeed connected to the clerk from Kel's. I should have known then and I should have left. I glanced back and out the shops window and into the lanes. Soldiers, in their black uniforms and stoic faces, walked the aisles of the marketplace.

I turned back to face the clerk. His smile revealed teeth the whitest I had ever seen. He continued to wipe the sweetness from his hand as he approached the counter. He leaned against it, his eyes upon me. I watched his moves.

"Hello? Anyone there?" he asked, chuckling and waving a large hand in front of my face.

"It is you."

"You found me."

"I was not looking for you."

He nodded his head and stood upright. "So what brings you to this side of town?"

"A job."

"You must be Olivia."

I swallowed hard. The clerk who recognized my face now had my name. I shifted, uncomfortable beneath his gaze and trying like hell to remember his name.

He sat the towel on the counter. "Okay, somehow I think that I have discomforted you. Whatever I have done, I apologize. How about we begin again?"

The bell ringing above the door interrupted us. He excused himself and tended to the customers as I fell into the background. A group of elder Marinite women who could not seem to decide on what and how much they wanted, haggled over the price.

I glanced at the door during their transactions, pondering whether to depart, and finally settled on that decision. I turned to leave but was stopped when my eyes fell upon a woman in the group. My heart weakened. "Mira?" I whispered, unable to move. I could only watch as the group collected their packages and exited the shop.

"So," he began, jarring me back to reality, "you are my newest assistant."

I nodded. "I suppose so."

"Then how about we get you started. You can come on around to this side and get comfortable. You will take the orders, I will ring them up until you learn the system, then you will do both," he spoke as I slowly made my way to where he stood. "I will soon introduce you to Obsidian. He is in the back and prepares everything you see here. Oh, you can hang your jacket and hat there."

I paused. I had not considered the possibility of being in public without the benefit of my jacket and especially my hat. "Why? Do I have to?"

"Well, no but you might get hot wearing this jacket over that one. Besides the oven is always going, we make the pastries fresh throughout the day. It gets warm in here."

I laughed spontaneously. I was being foolish and paranoid. For the first time ever in a public place, I removed my jacket and hung it on a notch on the wall near me. I took the uniform smock from the hook beside it and slipped my arms inside.

"The hat stays," I said pointing to it.

"Oh, okay."

"Now what?"

"Now you are one of us," he said to which I smiled. "Your smile is beautiful. You should do it more often."

"Thank you." I felt a heat crawl up the back of my neck as he watched me. "Okay, so what do I do?"

He thrust his hand toward me. I took it in mine. "I think we should maybe, finally, formally meet. Do you not? Hello. I am Charleston Kelsard."

Involuntarily I pulled away and stepped back, my paranoia returning and in full bloom. "What is this?"

"Apologies. I assumed you were told who you were to meet."

He tossed his hands in the air defensively. "I am not the bad one. I do not even know Henry Kelsard. You have my word. He is a distant cousin, three generations removed. My father knew him as a boy, my mother, my brothers and I never met him. My family has never stepped foot on that compound nor do we respect what he stands for and what he has done to our family name."

I looked at him skeptically but decided he was being truthful. If he were attempting to set me up he could have done me in by this point. I looked into his eyes and felt a feeling unlike any ever before. But more importantly my instincts told me that I was safe.

I released my wariness and stepped forward, placing my hand in his once again. "I am Olivia Aleyk."

"Very nice to officially meet you, Olivia."

I blushed. I had never blushed before. I had a new job and if I were not careful, maybe just a little more.

Love Hurts

Six

A UNIQUE BENEFIT TO HAVING A JOB, THAT I HAD NOT counted on, was the feeling that my new life provided. Besides having the ability to save a respectable amount of money toward Diana's and my future (that I now stashed beneath a floor board whenever Diana was not around) and aside from finally being able to enjoy certain delicacies, not to mention eating well on a regular basis, was the rare feeling of being ... normal. For once since leaving my life on Ashtwor behind, I felt normal.

I awoke early, departing at first light to make the trip to the marketplace where I assisted my new boss and friend, Charleston Kelsard and our baker, Obsidian Omris, in opening and preparing the shop for the day's business. I did not focus on my genetic flaws during this time, nor did I concentrate on Diana's occupation and preoccupation. And though I continued to avoid trouble by sticking near the shadows, especially when returning home in the evening hours, I no longer stressed the presence of SRA.

I enjoyed working side-by-Charleston's-side more than anything else and this fact was the greatest surprise of all. Though I had only been working at the shop for a short period of time I already knew, barring circumstances beyond my control, I would stay on at the shop for as long as Diana was obligated to SOTA.

†

IT HAD BEEN A RELATIVELY QUIET DAY AT THE SHOP. IT WAS the start of another endweek, my third one there. I had learned during my experience that business was light on those days. We were cleaning for an early close. Obsidian had already gone.

I swept up the last of the crumbs and dumped them into the receptacle in the back while Charleston locked the drawers. I took the broom and placed it inside the dust closet and turned off the lights. I removed my smock as I returned to the front of the shop. When I glanced up, Charleston was standing, waiting, leaning against the display glass watching every move that I made.

I smiled.

He pushed off the glass and walked across the space toward me, taking my jacket from the notch. I rushed toward him, reaching to take it away.

"I will get it," I cried out.

"Olivia, Olivia, I got it. I am only going to help you into it, not take it away from you. It is called chivalry. I am certain you have not been exposed to much of that living in the heart of The City."

I twisted my lips, a bit embarrassed but I allowed him to help me into the jacket. I was taking pleasure in having a normal sort of life; being a normal sort of person ... maybe this was part of it. Charleston grabbed the sleeve of my jacket and edged me forward. With my free hand I tugged my hat down further on my head and followed his lead, giggling for no real reason along the way.

I stood off to the side of the shop while he locked up. My eyes roamed his frame. Much taller than he should have been with muscles protruding from every visible inch, his body was like art. I wanted to ask if he was sure that he was full blood Marinite. But then again, I hated when assumptions of Amirontian ancestry was placed upon me simply because evolution worked in my favor.

When he was done he turned toward me. He grinned. I blushed.

"So. I guess I will see you in a couple days," I said, privately dreading our departure and feeling very much like what it must have meant to be an average girl.

"Are you in a hurry?"

"Well, no, not actually."

"Good."

I was confused. "Okay, what does that mean?"

"Come on." He flashed those white teeth at me and I could

not resist doing as told. I followed him, walking alongside quietly, in our own world. It was as though we were anywhere but the world in which we lived. Soldiers were ever present but they did not matter.

We walked together. Silent, but offering one another the occasional smile that said those things which we were not yet prepared to say. We walked, me carrying my bag of private goodies on my back and he carrying his. We headed into an area I was not very familiar with though I had passed by a few times. SRA presence dropped off more and more as we continued.

"This way," he said nodding to the right.

I followed his lead until we reached a large clearing where ahead the sheath grass was tall, nearly as tall as me. He took my hand in his before we entered. If we were not careful we could be separated in its fullness. My stomach flopped at his touch. He slowed his steps and looked back to me, checking to see if I were okay. I lifted my chin to the sky and pretended that his touch did not affect me. He smiled and continued to guide me.

We continued forward another tanometer or so until we reached a large panati tree. He released me and I found that I was disappointed. He removed his bag and sat it on the ground. I stood looking around. I gazed up at the huge tree that cast a wide shadow across the field. Large kakali nuts dangled low. I reached up and grabbed one. I twisted the shell until it popped. I nibbled on the seed inside, sucking the sweet milk from it as I slowly walked around the tree, brushing my phalanges against the feathery softness of the sheath grass.

"Come here," Charleston commanded.

I crept around to the other side of the tree and peered at him. He had spread a blanket across the space around the tree that was free of the thick grass. He sat and pulled two containers from his bag.

"You brought shakes?" I asked astonished.

"Of course. Come on, have a seat. This is the best place to be this time of day."

I eased toward the blanket and took a seat beside him. "This is great Charleston, but we cannot really see much from here beyond sheath grass."

"Just trust me, okay. Enjoy your drink."

I grinned and took the container he handed to me. I took a sip and my eyes widened. "Red."

"Your favorite."

"It certainly is."

We sat with our backs against the beautiful panati tree listening to the rustle of the wind as it grazed the top of the grass. I glanced at Charleston. He was indeed very handsome and I greatly enjoyed his companionship. This nearly normal life was kind of working for me.

"So," he began, "how long have you lived in The City?"

I wiped the sweet milk from my mouth. "Four years."

"Really. I have seen you there ... noticed you only, maybe a few months ago."

"How? I mean, where?"

"I saw you occasionally by that big SOTA building. Do you

live there?"

I nodded and took another sip of my shake. "With my cousin. I was an illegal when I arrived here so she became my guardian. I cannot leave her there alone."

"I thought, how beautiful you are. It was clear you had managed to avoid being recruited. I thought it amazing that someone as angelic as you could have the nerve to flaunt that beauty directly in the face of SRA soldiers and yet manage to not be taken away."

My cheeks warmed. "That does not seem possible. You do not reside near here, so how could you have seen me?"

"Work. Before I came to work for Golê Turit I was head clerk at Kel's Diner. You are familiar with Kel's Diner."

I swallowed hard and nodded. "Kel's, yes. I may have been there once or twice before."

"It was a decent job. That is until a beautiful stranger slipped in somehow and lifted seventy dashii's from the safe." He faced me.

My heart stopped beating. My blood was no longer being pumped and I was choking on a partial piece of fruit that had not been ground fully. I glanced about discreetly. If I had to escape I needed to remember from which way we had come. The trouble with being normal was that I lacked focus while it was happening.

"What?" I asked, clearing my throat. He patted my back until the fruit broke free.

He chuckled. "Tiakalu is a fool but he did not blame me for the loss. He actually passed the blame to our cook. I did not care to work for him any longer, not after you told me that the kakali nut shakes were less expensive at the Amirontian locations. I went to the other shops and checked. Did you know that manteles come with the sandwiches there?"

I laughed awkwardly. "I know."

"It felt too much like being SRA. Just do me a favor, okay? Do not take from Golê Turit. He is a fair man and one of us. He is already being robbed blind by SRA as it is."

I concealed my embarrassment. "It had not crossed my mind."

Our eyes met. "It is time." He took my shake and his and set them aside. He took my hand in his and guided me down. We stretched out on the blanket, lying on our backs. The sight was breathtaking. It was the exact perfect location at the exact perfect moment in time. We were looking at the divide line. There was darkness and stars where the western sun had set, blending into the beautiful array of colors being cast by the setting of the eastern sun.

I whispered Charleston's name. "It is ... amazing."

He squeezed my hand tight. His voice was low, abyssal. "I am thrilled that you like it."

I did not see him move, only felt his heat as he hovered above me. His lips met mine, soft and gentle ... as though testing the boundaries. I had never before been kissed. And as his body pressed deeper into mine, I could only think how happy I was that my first one was with Charleston Kelsard.

†

WORKING AND SPENDING TIME WITH CHARLESTON RESULTED in my missing too many endweek celebrations with my best friend. I was very much missing Jayde. With the new law imposed, she had not bothered me much about meeting up at Mole's but as enforcement faded further and further into the recesses of our minds, she became less accepting of my leaving her with little buffer between she and Tabi.

I was enjoying the time that Charleston and I found to be around one another outside of the shop. I had never had a relationship with a man before and though there was no declaration set forth between the two of us, I nevertheless looked forward to his companionship.

Jayde had yet to meet my new friend, the one who stole kisses in alleyways just out of sight of the greedy eyes monitoring all local activity. He often expressed a desire for a deeper, more personal connection ... a claim on my emotions, but I was not sure that was something I was ready to give.

When I lay on my back on the tattered mattress at night and looked up at my darkened hands in the shadow of eve, I wondered how someone like me could ever have a true involvement with the opposite sex. Would I ever really know that sort of love? A kiss, a touch, to be held but beyond that, things became too risky.

He would eventually press for an explanation about my attachment to my hat. How might I explain that the phantom feeling of golden roots and unruly curls, even after I had shaved my hair close to the scalp, was the reason I always wore it? I was not comfortable without the accompaniment of the jacket I cherished or the long sleeves I wore regularly. I could never confess my dependence upon concealant for what if he wished to see me without it. The risk involved was much too great. For these reasons, every day I worked beside him I vowed to negate any intimate involvement, but the moment I saw him my heart said something different.

I invited him to join me ... was curious whether he had the courage to brave the territory at night and venture into a land forbidden to us past the setting of the eastern sun. Wondered if he was prepared to escape the Amirontian neighborhood in the middle of night. A challenge he accepted without question.

I had more experience with keeping below the radar than most but Charleston was able to hold his own with me without a problem. Together we slipped past guards in transport cars and made our way to the heavy gate. He followed my lead to the cement steps leading to the hold where Mole's was located. I was introducing him to my world, its fun and its thrills and equally its dangers. He proceeded uninhibited.

"Liv," Jayde called out over the bass laden music Silhouette was mixing. She stood at our usual table shared with Aissa, Faraji, and Tabi. Charleston and I made our way past the sea of faces. No law would squelch the temerarious spirit and endweek alcoholic living inside the Marinite (or any other culture on the planet to be quite honest).

"So this is the handsome gentleman who has kept one of our dearest friends out of our company for so long," Faraji stated as he stood, extending his hand to Charleston.

"I do not suppose you can blame me, now can you?" he answered, shaking Faraji's hand.

"Not at all. Maybe you should sit near me. I can share all

the dirty little secrets Liv will conveniently forget to tell," Faraji laughed.

I stepped forward. "You steer clear. He is a good guy, not used to such disreputable behavior as what is typically displayed at this table." I laughed and made introductions, acquainting Charleston with those that I called my friends (and Tabia). Faraji ordered a round for the table despite the lack of companionship by a cute little giji boy to pay (undoubtedly out of a mixture of guilt for the capture of Madan and the fear of expressing his taboo love in front of a male stranger).

Jayde leaned closer to Charleston. "Half-blood?"

"Excuse me?" he replied.

"You are an unusual Marinite. Are you half-blood?"

"Jayde," I scolded.

"Do not Jayde, me. I am so sure you have wondered the same. He is very tall and though he has the smooth head of a Marinite he is not quite the color."

"He is not the color of an Amirite either."

"Touché. So, what are you?"

I glanced at Charleston who only smiled and assured me it was fine. "Sorry to disappoint but I am full blood Marinite."

The strength in his answer caused a chill to pass through me.

Faraji edged in closer, lowering his voice just enough that we could hear him without nosey ears absorbing too much of our information. "So, word around the panati tree has it that you are not only a full blood Marinite but you are also a full blood Kelsard. Any benefits to that?"

I felt Charleston's eyes land on me as mine shot daggers at Faraji. I turned back to face him. He smiled as though forgiving me for having shared so much without warning him.

"I do not condone the things he has done in our family name." His answer received only faint enthusiasm. His honor was appreciated but the group quickly grew bored with what was formerly the excitement of his heritage. "But, do not think I do not find occasions to have it work in my favor and keep unsuspecting soldiers on their toes. You should see them falling all over themselves trying to please me. *Oh, young Kelsard, we did not know. Please forgive us the disruption. Is there anything we can do for you?*"

The table exploded into appreciative laughter.

"So coming tonight should have been the first relaxing trip Liv has taken to this part of The City," Aissa said.

Charleston chuckled. "Actually no. She was determined that I do things her way. But, perhaps we can have a little fun en route back."

I jumped in to defend myself. "You did not mention these advantages you now speak of."

"You, my dear, did not ask."

I blushed. Uproars of laughter swept across the table as Charleston shared stories of his antics while taking advantage of the Kelsard name as a means of taking advantage of the soldiers of SRA.

Jayde leaned across the table toward me as he spoke, and mouthed the words, *I like him.*

I liked him, too.

†

JAYDE WRAPPED HER ARM AROUND ME, PROTECTIVELY embracing me as we stood outside of Mole's at the close of business. She said her good-byes to those passing while I rested my head against her.

"Charleston," began Aissa, "I hope that our antics have not scared you off. We are actually pretty decent people ... I think. Do you not think so, Raj?"

"Oh, most certainly," Faraji replied.

Charleston laughed. "I am not simply the sweet farm boy you may think of me, nor am I so easily put off."

"Very, very good information to have," Faraji said. "Liv, I think your little worker boy has a few deep, dark secrets of his own. Maybe even a few tricks up his sleeve. Feel free to use them on her; she does not realize how much she needs it."

I waved my fist at Faraji.

"Charleston," Jayde began, using her matriarchal tone, the one I dreaded and loved at once. "Please, feel free to join us again ... anytime."

"Thank you, Jayde."

"And Charleston, take good care of my little one. She is precious to me and I can be a very pernicious Amirite when I am angered."

Their eyes were locked passing an order and receiving understanding. Jayde released me slowly into Charleston's care. The mood in the hold became slightly strained.

Jayde broke the gaze and cleared her throat, disintegrating any lingering tension. "We should leave now. Soldiers are a bit friskier these days. Olivia, Charleston, thank you for coming and please ... be careful."

"I always am," I said.

Her hands landed on my shoulders as she looked into my face. Suddenly and unexpectedly she pulled me in for a tight embrace.

"Jayde, please, the girl is not running off to get married," Faraji said. "Laid maybe ... hopefully, but certainly not married."

I glared at him but smiled as we ascended the stairwell to make our departure.

†

We did it his way. For the first time since I had lived in The City I walked from one district to the next without hovering in shadows and becoming one with inanimate objects. We strolled side-by-side, with Charleston leading the way and covering us with the Kelsard name.

We stood on the walk at the bottom of the steps leading to the SOTA building that I called home. The benefit of being with a Kelsard being displayed the moment the first bored soldier approached, his aggression diminishing once he recognized Charleston's face.

"My apologies, Young Kelsard," the soldier spoke before scurrying away. "Carry on."

Desperate Sisters who had not yet secured a date for the

evening hovered close, circling like vealadar birds. Those Sisters who had passed me by without noticing that I existed were certainly aware of my presence now.

Charleston stepped close to me. "Someday you are going to let me take you away from this place."

I smiled up at him. "Not a chance."

"Certainly you do not like coming home to this, Olivia," he said, sounding astonished.

"I hate it but it is home. Until my cousin's presence here is no longer required, this is where I will lay my head at night."

He appeared disappointed in my answer but leaned forward, pressing his lips to mine. He kissed me slowly and with great passion. In that moment I forgot about the soldiers and the SOTA whores and their blazing glares ... forgot all about the turks creeping about after their work hours ended at the factory to spend their earnings on what they could have gotten at home for free.

"Good night," he whispered, while looking over and gazing into my eyes but not moving away. I was very certain my knees would give way right then and there. I pushed him playfully, ordering him to go home. I ascended the steps, trying hard not to look back at him but I knew he was at the bottom looking up at me.

As I entered the building I wondered if he would be that one for me. Would I find the strength to tell him the truth? I was cursed but I was still me, was I not? Could Charleston see beyond skin, hair, and my natural eyes?

I went inside, smiling all the way to the flat. Diana was alone, the room dark save for the candle that was now little more than a ball of wax. My beautiful fantasy world with its pastures filled with panati trees and five-foot high sheath grass began to fade into obscurity. I swallowed the lump forming as I watched Diana sit still on the bed gazing into nothingness. My eyes moved to the clump of flickering wax and the syringe emptied out and resting beside it.

I could not leave Charleston's essence behind 100%, not yet. In the middle of night, when the Sisters were busy either entertaining or looking to entertain, was a great opportunity for me to refresh my concealant. I peeled off my garment and hat and tossed them into my space, grabbing what I would need to freshen myself.

"I will be in the communal if you need me." I was not sure why I bothered to tell her. I did not know if she had even heard me or, for that matter, cared.

I stepped inside the little room the entire floor shared, locking the door behind me. Immersed in complete blackness, I felt around for the string and shed dull illumination across the space. I looked at my darkened face in the permanently stained mirror. For a moment, I thought I could see my skins natural glow shining through but I realized it was merely a reflection of my joy. I smiled at myself, thinking of how silly I was.

I pulled the long sleeve shirt over my head and tossed it across the edge of the tub. I removed everything down to my undergarments and set them aside. I stooped low, opening my bag and removing a clean rag and jar of concealor.

I worked from the bottom up in small spaces at a time, never, ever removing all the concealor at once, as Mira would do to me as a child. These days it was much too dangerous to do so. One never knew when they would have to flee on short notice.

I finished an undercoat on my arms and paused to allow it to settle into my pores. A loud bang on the door jarred me. I jumped but quickly stilled myself. It happened occasionally; not often but sometimes a desperate Sister would stake her claim to the communal in the middle of night.

"One minute," I barked to the Sister on the other side.

"Olivia," the strong voice sang my name.

I was winded. I had to pull myself together and fast. I glanced down to my arms and the subtle glow emitting from beneath. "I-I will be out in a minute," I stammered.

"Open the door, Olivia. You have nothing that I will not soon see."

I cursed, looking across to my clothes then down to my arms. My garments were only a few steps away but something ... instinct maybe, told me there was no time. A heavy thud landed against the door. It vibrated beneath the force. My eyes moved to the open jar of concealor moving toward the edge of the sink caused by vibrations from the door being rammed.

I would not keep him out; I could not. The wood of the door frame splinting seemed to happen in slow motion. I had to react. My arm swung backwards firmly, smashing the bulb, and subsequently the mirror. The thin glass crashed into the sink as the door burst open wide revealing the outline of Legatus Ja'ali Dupec.

"What happened in here?" he asked.

"Had a little accident."

Dupec stepped from the dimness of the hall and into the blackness of the communal, revealing the presence of Diana. Her face was drenched in tears. I stood still, my back pressed firmly to the edge of the sink. My eyes went to hers, she looked away avoiding contact.

"Diana," Dupec barked.

She looked back to me, discomfort and fear on her face. Her eyes were pleading. "Olivia, you have ... I need for you to..." Her voice trailed but her point was beginning to register. The day had come. Ja'ali Dupec did not want her anymore. Her enhanced drug use likely accelerated the inevitable.

Dupec licked his lips slowly, his eyes roving my near nude frame. "Your cousin and I made a deal. I will not retire her and will even continue to finance her. In exchange, you will be taking her place."

The floor dropped from beneath me and the wind left my sails. Diana had sold me or, rather, exchanged me for an ability to continue a habit of blackberries. My eyes were deadlocked on the side of her head that she showed me because she was too ashamed to show me her eyes.

My hurt emotions escaped in a pool of wetness.

Dupec stepped forward, his hand moved up to softly caress away the tears trailing my cheek. "She had better be as good as you used to be, Diana. How old did you say she is again?"

Diana sniffled and spoke just above a whisper. "She is young, just barely seen seventeen days."

I bit down hard on my lip, swallowed the feeling of pure disgust welling up inside of me. Dupec moved in tighter, digging his weight into me and burying his nose in my neck. I reached back slowly; carefully felt around the inside of the sink as his large hands moved to fondle the nudeness beneath my top.

"She smells fresh. She smells young. This will be a great pleasure, for this one has never before been touched."

I steadied my breathing, felt the shards of glass carefully until my phalanges grazed one that seemed sufficient. I grasped it slowly, cautiously. I had made up my mind. I would not allow him to follow through. I would kill him first.

My arm rose steadily as he smelled me while fondling my breasts and mumbling words of pleasure against my flesh. Diana gasped my name and redirected my attention to her. Until that moment, I had not realized that I had moved the glass to only inches from the side of his neck. She shook her head vehemently, begging and pleading non-verbally.

"Yes, I am going to enjoy you," Dupec said, straightening his back as I lowered my arm.

The feel of my own blood trailed my hand before dripping into the sink. My eyes met with Dupec's. He again licked his lips slowly as his phalanges grazed the space between the top of my undergarment and flesh.

"I am sure you will."

He paused and chuckled. "Oh yes, I do like you. Feistiness runs in your bloodline, does it not, Diana?"

His hand moved from my waistline to his own. He moved a few steps back to get a better view of me in the dimness, his phalanges slowly unbuttoning his pants. I thoughtlessly squeezed the glass tighter, its sharp edge digging deeper into my flesh. I would slice. If he revealed himself to me he would know regret.

He edged nearer to me, tugging at his zipper, the sound filling up the small, stuffy place. I eased my arm forward and placed it at my side, bracing myself for what was to come.

"Legatus Dupec. Come in, Lega Dupec." The scratchy voice came through loudly from the *Com Device on his waist.

Dupec groaned and took a step further. He snatched the device from his uniform pants and pressed the button on the side. "What?" he growled.

"Orders have come down from headquarters. Your immediate presence is required."

Dupec scratched the side of his neck. Even in the dark I could see the anguish on his face. "I am busy right now," he stated, lustfully looking me up and down.

"My apologies but *Commander* Dupec has specifically requested your immediate presence."

We stood breathless and silent. He growled angrily and turned his back for several moments before turning to face me again. He stepped close to me and grazed the tips of his phalanges across my flesh as he licked his lips. He leaned in, his breath humid against my cheek. I cringed at the feeling of his tongue slowly trailing backwards across the path that my tears had created. Satisfied, he stepped away. "Ready the transport. Over."

I remained poised, ready to attack ... ready to defend my honor no matter the consequence. Dupec began to adjust his uniform but halted. He stepped toward me again, firmly grasping my neck, lifting me slightly and forcing me to look into his face. I fidgeted with the glass, my mind reeling, trying hard to make the right choice while my toes strained to touch ground and I struggled to hold onto what remained of my oxygen supply.

"Do not worry. I will back for you, little one."

His lips pressed to mine and my arm swung forward, the shard aimed directly at his most vital internal organs. I tried hard to make contact but could not. I had not noticed her move but she had. Diana stepped forward right on time, catching my arm and holding me back with all that was in her.

Dupec dropped me. He moved away, looking suspiciously from me to Diana. My arm relaxed and her hand discreetly moved to mine, taking the shard away and gently placing it into the sink as I gasped for air. Dupec smirked. He charged by, bumping her violently into the hallway. His hurried steps faded in the distance.

"I am sorry," she managed to utter once we were certain he was gone. She caressed the back of her head as she rose to standing, and rushed to my side.

Angrily, I pushed away from the sink and walked to my clothes. I stepped into my pants as she begged for my forgiveness.

"Do not," I said.

"Olivia, please. You have to understand—"

"Do not," I cried out.

She opened her mouth to speak but paused as the sound of doors opening reached us. We listened to the stampede of soldiers from various floors, exiting rooms at once throughout the building. We were quiet, watching as two rushed past. My curiosity piqued. When it seemed as though our floor was clear, I gathered what remained of my belongings and charged past Diana.

"Olivia, listen to me," she pleaded, tears thick in her throat. "I could not stop him. Even if I said no, you think it would have stopped him?"

I turned to face her. "I can deal with him coming for me if that was his will but you *gave* me to him, Diana. You delivered me into his arms."

I continued forward into the flat with Diana close on my trail.

"You were already recruited; you just did not know it."

"What is your point?"

"I was doing you a favor."

"Do not dare. You do not dare!" I walked to the window, looking down into the lanes as I wrapped my bodyrag tightly around my sliced open hand to cease the bleeding. I carefully pulled my sweater over my head. I wondered what was happening. Soldiers were loading into transport cars and departing their posts.

"Olivia, listen. He was going to take you away. It was either SOTA compound or stay here with me ... take my place."

I turned. "This was not done for me. Maybe I could forgive you if it were. You did not want to lose the money. You did it so that you would not lose money. No dashii's, no obi red, no blackberries!"

She opened her mouth to speak but no words formed. I dressed quickly, gathering what meager belongings I could stuff into my bag. I tossed it on my shoulder and rushed across the room. I knelt forward, prying the floorboard free with my good hand and removed the dashii's hidden beneath.

"Olivia, 'lil'eail." Her voice was soft ... innocent, but I was beyond making amends.

I counted out two months of my portion of the tax fee and extended it to her. She shook her head no.

"Take it."

"I cannot. I do not want it."

"You do, that is the problem." I passed her and tossed it onto her bed. "I will suggest you find someplace safe to hide before Dupec returns."

I pulled my hat down firm on my head and adjusted the bag on my shoulder as I headed to the door. The sound of Diana's sorrow filled the room. I paused, my hand on the knob. I swallowed my emotions and moved ahead, exiting the door and leaving her selfish despair behind.

Seven
Goodbye to Love

I STOOD ALONE BENEATH THE LARGE PANATI TREE. IT perfectly mimicked my emotions. The majestic tree with its twisted limbs and sprawling branches whose leaves grew large enough that one alone could mask an entire face. There was nothing for tanometers wide, nothing but sheath grass as far as the eye could see.

It was alone in a field, accompanied occasionally by the beautiful creatures that circled about taking occasional refuge on its limbs and leaves, suckling sweet nectar from the exotic flowers that were miraculously born at its base.

I stood in solitude, a recruited Marinite girl on the run. I had made a tremendous mistake. I had thought I could be normal, could settle into a conventional existence. I thought I had found love, could keep love. I had visions of lying in the arms of a beautiful Marinite with sweet kakali nut skin and weary eyes. I imagined my natural skin pressed against his richly dark flesh. In my dreams his phalanges danced across my golden tone because he loved it ... because he loved me.

There were nights where I saw us as we would be when we grew old. Together since seventeen and his age twenty-one, until the days when my golden hair turned silver and our skin became defenseless against gravity.

I had been foolish, a silly girl hoping for what could not be in the world in which we lived. A world firmly planted in corruption and degradation. I had been a fool and that foolishness had nearly cost me my freedom and my virtue ... and would have very quickly cost my life.

Had my thoughts not been pre-occupied with Charleston maybe I could have altered fate or at least prolonged things enough that I could figure a way out for Diana and me.

When Dupec reached our floor I was in labor birthing anointed babies that I would protect but refuse to conceal. When he passed me by in the communal, I was barefoot and frying pendi while the little ones helped mix a fresh bowl of rutarb sauce as their father checked on the veggies in the field.

Had I been where I should have been, a dirty little communal with a low wattage bulb assisting me in protecting myself from the grip of villains, rather than wasting time with pointless visions, maybe ... just maybe I would have sensed that something was wrong. Possibly could have avoided the entire scene altogether.

I stood beneath the panati tree ... alone, gazing at the setting western sun and plotting my next move. A soft breeze rustled the tops of the sheath grass.

Nevermore.

Love was not for people like me. Happiness was not penned upon my fate.

Nevermore would I let down my guard and get my hopes high. I would have to continue to fight for my survival ... harder than ever before.

†

THE LANES NEAR THE MARKET PLACE WERE SURPRISINGLY vacant given the day of the week and extremely limited SRA presence. I had been in seclusion for three days trying my very best to clear my head and find forgiveness in my heart for Diana. I was also working to rid myself of the frustrating feelings I had for Charleston Kelsard.

I stood across from the shop, shielded by no more than the limited girth of the red rubrum tree. From there I could see him working, wiping down the countertop. Frequently he looked up and out the window in both directions, as though he were looking for something – or someone.

I watched as he dropped the rag and rounded the counter, walking out the door and into the lane. I sank deeper into the shade of the tree and further out of his line of sight. I observed as he peered down the lane in both directions. An approaching customer sent him retreating to his post.

I stayed my ground though it was a challenge. I convinced myself that this was indeed the right choice for both parties involved. The solemn look upon his face nearly weakened me and for a moment I almost caved. I stepped from the cover of nature. Had he looked up at that moment he would have surely spotted me.

Obsidian, the old Marinite baker, appeared suddenly from the back of the shop. Whatever he was speaking to Charleston about halted and his bony phalanx aimed directly at me.

I was out of sight before Charleston could look my way. I was gone with no intention of encountering him again. I almost thought I heard my name echoing off buildings above but convinced myself that it was merely a hallucination as I retreated down the nearest alleyway.

It was the easiest journey I had ever taken alone as there was practically no SRA presence on the lanes and the few who did not have enough rank to get out of policing the proud citizens of Marieux, were too preoccupied to do much of a job. Jayde worked at an SRA plant, I wondered if she had heard anything about what was happening and what it would mean for citizens.

I glanced toward the eastern sun. The position and shadow cast let me know that I was right on time, Jayde would arrive. I thought to slip into the crack beneath the stairwell where I normally awaited her. But with the soldier's attention diverted toward whatever was happening at headquarters, I thought it as opportune a time as any to wait for her on the steps.

Patiently I waited, trying to decide where I would go. Maybe a trip to Ashtwor was in order. But what would I tell Sarai and Pete of my whereabouts over the past four years, if they were even still alive. There was Kalaath and Aleyk but neither village knew of my existence and I was not so sure how I would be received. I had enough dashii's to sustain me for awhile. I could afford to rent the vacant shanty I saw on the Marinite boards. It was on a small patch of land located just outside The City limits, but I would have to find work before my funds ran low.

I looked up at the sound of heels landing hard against the gravel. I stood slowly. Jayde stopped abruptly. Her face displayed a mixture of relief and anger.

I began to speak but she held up a hand to silence me. My eyes dropped to the pavement. I was not certain how much she knew but it was clear that she knew something. She continued forward and up the steps signaling for me to follow. She was tight-lipped until we entered the flat and closed the door.

"Where have you been?" she asked, continuing forward.

I followed her hurried steps to the kitchen where Aissa sat at a table in front of some sort of dish I did not recognize, but nevertheless made my stomach growl. She jumped from her seat when she saw me, wrapping her arms around me tightly.

"Liv," she sighed.

I allowed the embrace but did not return it. My worried eyes were on Jayde.

"I had to get away," I said.

"Away from what?"

"Everything. I just had to go."

Jayde turned up a bottle of carraplum juice. She wiped the violet wetness from her mouth with the back of her hand. "You could not tell someone this?"

"There was no opportunity."

"Charleston is worried sick."

"Charleston," I sighed.

"He came to the plant looking for me, looking for you. You had not shown up for work for two days."

"Three ... now, I mean ... three days."

The look in her eyes caused me to look away. "Do not be cute." Jayde sat the half emptied bottle on the table forcefully and walked from the kitchen. I followed with Aissa trailing me. "You know I called in a favor to get that job for you and this is the thank you I receive? I thought that I knew you better."

"Jayde."

"What?"

"Exactly. You do know me better and you know that if I did not honor my commitment to you there must be a very good reason. It is not about the job. I *had* to leave."

"Why, Olivia? Why did you have to leave?"

I swallowed hard and took a deep breath. "I have been recruited."

Jayde collapsed into the chair she was nearest to. A pained expression was painted on her face, and fluid sprang into her eyes.

Aissa grabbed my arm and turned me to face her. "This is not true. This cannot be true."

"Legatus Ja'ali Dupec. He wants me to take Diana's place. He will not officially retire her nor will he send me to SOTA compound. He wants me to himself."

"But ... and forgive me, but you are Marinite and of prime Elite age. How can he barter in such a manner?"

"I do not know. This is something ... I do not know, he is creating his own rules. I suppose I would not rank if I remain at SOTA house and so there would be no rule to stop him. Officially he would be there for Diana and she is Level 1 so race does not matter. Who would know? Who would tell if they did? Matters not, as I would never allow him to hand me over. I would sooner see the Facilities."

Jayde rubbed her forehead in frustration. "So what happened?"

"He spared me once. During the last enforcement I was captured."

"You never told me that."

"It did not matter. But whatever is happening here, whatever pulled the soldiers away, took him away from me. It saved me though I am certain it is only for the time being. When he returns he will look for me and if he finds me, I will kill him before he has an opportunity to destroy what little soul lives in me."

The room fell silent. Aissa eased onto the sofa, completely caught off guard by this news. I scratched my scalp through my hat and walked to the window, looking down into the lanes. Amirontian workers were returning home from the plants. Children were playing with much less apprehension. Two soldiers idled in the distance near a transport car focused more on what was going on inside than out.

"Where have you been sleeping?"

"Here and there."

"Good. Now you are staying *here*."

Jayde's words came to me but I paid them no mind.

"Jayde, no," Aissa spoke up. "And what of my brother?"

"Forgive me, Aissa, but this is not Razi's home alone. He does not make the choices here."

I asked, "What of the new regulation? Razi has SRA on his side."

"In case you have not noticed, something much bigger than a minor district regulation is going on. I am confident that Razi will not get much support. It will be temporary ... until we can find suitable accommodations listed on the Marinite boards."

"Jayde."

"We will have to find you new employment. You will be unable to return to the shop."

"Jayde!"

"Olivia, it is settled. You will share my bed until we figure the rest." Jayde stood from her chair and walked to her room, ending the discussion.

I wanted very much to fight her but I was exhausted and had few options as it was. I sat on the floor, resting my head against my knees. I had not slept in days.

"I think she is right," Aissa spoke up softly, reluctantly.

"And what of Razi?"

"I would not worry much about Razi. You have not had the privilege of seeing Jayde when she has her mind set on something. She can be a rather vicious Ami."

I looked up, my eyes locking on Jayde's closed bedroom door, asking myself whether or not I could do this.

†

THE ARGUMENT WAS AGGRESSIVE, THE MOST VICIOUS WORDS were spoken in the language native to the planet the two had descended from. A language I could not easily translate and given the brutality present in their tones, I was completely comfortable in my ignorance. More than once I contemplated disappearing out the window. If only Jayde did not live so high up.

I paced around the room, but stopped at a stack of hand drawn images. Jayde's creations. Most were of Aissa and Faraji; others were of people I did not recognize. At the bottom of the stack there was an especially beautifully crafted one. I pulled it forth to get a better look. The heavy papyrus was dated. It was creased at the edges and slightly discolored. The image was of two women without smiles. One appeared to be Jayde at a much younger age. I did not know who the other was but ventured a guess that it was either her mother or an elder sibling.

The door swung open forcefully, jarring me. I nearly knocked the stack to the floor.

"What are you doing?" She barked, her face contorted in a way I had never before seen.

"I, um ... I was just... " My mind drew a complete blank.

"It is my mother."

"What?"

"The picture you are pretending not to hold. That is what

you wonder, correct? That is – *was* my mother. She is dead."

"Oh ... I..." I carefully replaced the picture at the bottom of the stack.

Jayde landed heavily on the bed, exasperated. Her phalanges moved to her temples and massaged. Her eyes moved up to meet mine, the tension beginning to fade.

"Try to maintain a distance from him. One can only try to contain Razi for so long."

I nodded. "Jayde, you know–"

Her hand went up, silencing me. "I am tired."

She moved fully onto the bed, crawling beneath the thin blanket. I cautiously removed my jacket, carrying it with me to the bed. I reached up and pulled the string to turn the light off. I tugged at my hat, pulling it down as far as it would go. I kicked my boots away and climbed in bed beside her.

†

I SAT UP WITH A START. I LOOKED AROUND AND FOR THE moment completely forgot where I was. Light from a street post outside streamed through lighting the space enough for me to achieve some recognition. I rubbed my eyes and twisted my body, swinging my legs around and feet to the floor.

I tried to make sense of what had just happened. Was it a dream? It seemed to be real but I could not exactly recall what it was. I leaned forward, placing my head in my palms, putting my weight on my elbows that rested against my thighs. I tried hard to recall ... to remember something important.

The vision was disappearing. I focused, tried hard to take myself to those last moments before I awakened. Whatever it was, it was real. It was as though I were right there witnessing it. I gasped.

"Diana."

I jumped from the bed, feeling around for my boots. I found one but the other seemed to have vanished. I swore louder than I had intended while sliding beneath Jayde's bed. My phalanges brushed the edge and I pulled it forward. The bed dipped beneath Jayde's weight as she adjusted.

I grabbed my jacket from the floor and threw it around my shoulders.

"Olivia?" Jayde mumbled.

"Go back to sleep, Jayde."

She yawned and blinked her way into consciousness, the process seeming to accelerate. "What are you doing? Where are you going?"

"I have to go. Something is wrong with Diana."

Jayde flung the blanket from her body and jumped from the bed, rushing around, cutting me off before I made it to the door.

"Oh no, you will not leave this house to return to that place. After what I just went through with Razi for you?"

"I appreciate your fighting for me but this is not debatable. I have to go to Diana. I cannot explain ... nothing like this has ever happened. It was as though ... as though I saw something that was happening. It was like I was there."

Jayde calmed, her demeanor changing. "What is it? What did

you see?"

I shook my head, defeated. "I do not know. I cannot recall but I have to know that she is okay."

Jayde stepped away. "Then I am coming with you."

I wanted to tell her no, this was my battle but I knew without a doubt that I would be wasting my breath and I had no time to waste. She dressed quickly and the two of us slipped out into the night unnoticed.

We were surprised to see soldiers on the lanes. Not many however and they still seemed to be in their own world. I did not wish to take any chances. I guided Jayde through the shadows to the district of SOTA.

When we emerged, our attention was drawn to the small cluster of visibly shaken Sisters huddled in front of the building. I debated exposing myself versus slipping in through the back way. Jayde parted from me before I could stop her. She approached the group as I watched from a safe distance. I observed her face drop. I bit my lip, waiting impatiently for her to return. Instead, she signaled for me to come to her.

"Dupec," she said as I approached.

I turned and ran as fast as my feet would carry me up the steps and into the building. I thought my heart would explode from anticipation as I traveled through the building and to the flat. The door was open wide; several Sisters were inside looking on in awe. I shoved past. I stopped, gasped. Diana sat in a heap on the floor. She was being tended to by an elder resident Sister.

"Diana," I croaked her name.

Her head lifted slowly and my blood boiled. Her face was hardly recognizable. One eye was closed tight and swollen to at least twice its normal size, maybe greater. She was covered in her own blood. A terrified look swept over her face when she recognized me. She was speaking, but it was difficult to comprehend what she was saying.

The attending Sister addressed me harshly. "She wants you to leave."

I ignored her and continued forward. I knelt beside her. "I will kill him, I promise. I will kill him."

She shook her head slowly, like it hurt to do so. Her voice was hardly a whisper. "Give me a minute."

The elder Sister eyed me suspiciously before rising. I returned her glare until she stepped away. Diana whispered. "Olivia, you must not be here."

"I am not leaving you again. I should never have left you in the first place."

"He will return for you—"

"And this time he will find me."

"Olivia, listen to me ... please. I was wrong for bartering you. You were right, I am more addicted than I had recognized but that is no excuse." She coughed harshly, spitting blood onto the floor. "You must not be recruited. You are the only hope that our people have."

"What are you talking about?"

Her voiced dropped an octave lower than it already was. I leaned in closer to hear. "You are *the one*, Olivia. You are the

Anointed Child of the Marinite. You are the one the elders tell prophecies of."

I was confounded. Never before had Diana implied such. We had never even spoken of the possibility. "No, Diana, I am not—"

"You have heard the stories, you have seen the signs."

"Mira would have told me."

"Your mira wanted to protect you. She had already lost everyone dear to her. Your mira was being selfish, she knew that she only had you for a short time. She knew that she would not see seventeen days with you ... when your gifts would begin to manifest she would not be around."

I shook my head. "Diana—"

"Quiet. You are all that matters. I will be fine, I always am but you must leave now before he returns."

"But Diana..." My voice trailed as my eyes watered.

A shaky hand came to my face, touching it gently. "I love you, Olivia and I am honored to have been chosen by all that is good and sacred to have given birth to you. I need you to obey me. I want you to leave here, now."

I touched my hand to hers, carefully so not to hurt her. I placed her palm to my lips and kissed. "I cannot..."

"You must."

I sighed, defeated. "Be careful. I love you ... Mother."

I whispered the words. Tears flooded Diana's eyes. It was the first time she had heard that word from my lips. I helped her to ease her arm back to her side. She mouthed the word *go*. I stood and rushed out without looking back. I moved quickly from the building but stopped abruptly at the exit. I looked down to where Jayde stood looking guilty. I did not need this now.

I descended the steps slowly as Charleston left Jayde's side and approached me.

"You should not be here," I said without stopping.

"Olivia, talk to me." When I did not stop he caught up to me, catching my arm in his hand. "Olivia."

I turned. "Forget about me, Charleston. This cannot work. I am not the one for you."

"Forgive me, but I am man enough to make those choices myself. I get it; your life is hard ... complicated. Let me be there for you."

I shook my head vehemently. "You should not even be here."

"I saw the commotion and then I saw Jayde, so it is a sign. I happened in the area and ... I needed to see you. Needed to know that you are okay. Are you okay?"

I looked into his eyes. A mistake. I was weakened momentarily. I could not involve myself with him, not for his sake but my own. I was weakened by him and for me to be weak, particularly in the situation I was in, could be deadly.

I pulled my arm away. "I have to leave here now."

"Olivia." There was hurt and anguish in his tone. I had not wanted to wound him, only protect myself. "I love you, Olivia."

I stopped. It felt as though all of my breath had been knocked from me. I pulled myself together, piece-by-piece. *I love you, too*, I thought. That was the problem.

I continued forward down the steps and to where Jayde stood

waiting for me. A million questions were upon her tongue. The look on my face silenced them.

I darted into the shadows with Jayde close on my heels.

High Alert *Eight*

As a young girl growing up in Ashtwor, by midday each day, my mira would pull me from the fields or the river and drag me, anxiously, back to the old shanty. I never wanted to go. Perfectly content with the activities that I earned the right to engage in by being obedient and helping out in the gardens at the rising of the western sun, I could have stayed there all day.

But, as always, I was lured home where I sat under the idle threat of a lashing if I did not obey. It did not take long for me to be content as Mira shared the stories of our heritage as she knew it, and answered, with pleasure, the many questions that formed in my young mind.

I took immense pride in the knowledge that our people were descendants of the great human race from the former planet Earth. I had heard mostly good about the people and place where intelligence and innovation influenced a galaxy. But we had advanced as a race beyond even their capabilities. Though technologically we nowhere matched the Earthlings, our peaceful disposition and appreciation of nature made us a better and more advanced race than theirs, whose greed and environmental disrespect led to their self-destruction centuries before.

While there was no definitive answer to the question of the origin of The Anointed, Mira explained the belief that it began with the falling of grace of *Hezkiah, the sibling of Deus the Good. This brother, Hezkiah the Balance, expressed a jealousy so great that it ripped a hole in the galaxy, creating the Veloxx Continuum and eternally destroying their union. Finally free, Hezkiah struck a foothold in humanity, steering them toward mischief. In response, Deus used his own light to pass along his anointing (which would explain the fated golden tinge to the skin, hair, and eyes) as a means to restore order.

It was spoken of an unexplained favor over the lives of those touched — in a sense, things naturally went their way. It was as though an invisible force followed them throughout life, offering protection. Some rose to great heights and overcame incredible feats. There were even whispers that perhaps the Arethonian leader, Katashi Kedt, was of an anointed bloodline, one blessed by Hezkiah in his quest for power and autonomy.

And while it was arguable whether the power that came with a distinctive skin tone could be used for a purpose of good or evil, or if there was any actual truth to any of the tales to begin with, there was a unanimous belief that wasted gifts (or misused ones) died from the bloodline with the last breath of the carrier.

There was reason to support and dispel the theories of my being a carrier of this legacy. I certainly seemed to slither from tight spots in most incredible ways, but I had yet to see any great benefit bestowed upon me for this so-called "gift". And there was a colossal difference between being what was known as a *chosen one* and *the one*. I was living on borrowed time, sleeping as a neighbor to a man who was biding his time waiting for an opportunity to see me to my demise, while quietly mourning the loss of the first and only man I had ever loved. If this was the life of any form of an anointed, then I felt truly sorry for an ordinary being.

†

I BALANCED MY WEIGHT ON TOP OF A WOODEN STOOL staring down onto the lanes below from a window in Jayde's bedroom. I had spent the better part of the past three days in the same position lamenting the pain that I had inadvertently caused Diana.

I wanted to seek out Ja'ali Dupec, do unto him as he had done to Diana in his quest to find me. Because I was nowhere to be found when he came calling, she had endured a great suffering. She had already been through so much, already had the permanent physical and internal scars to prove it. And now I was forced to sit by while she endured further pain and humiliation at the hands of the Allegiance.

She had been retired, certainly, and I knew not where she would live. This was not how it was to be. I had saved diligently for the day that she would be free to be her own woman, make her own choices. I had done all of this in vain.

I had not eaten for days, my appetite dissipated. I sat by

hopelessly waiting for something. What, I did not know. Tapping on Jayde's bedroom door interrupted my mournful thoughts.

"Yes?"

"May I enter?" I could not distinguish which female roommate the voice belonged to.

"I suppose so. This space is not mine."

The door opened cautiously and Aissa poked her head through. "How is it going?"

"Fine." I turned away, my eyes retreating to the action on the lanes below.

"I am preparing lunch. Shall I fix you something?"

"No."

"Oh ... well, I just mixed up a fresh bottle of carraplum. I know how much you enjoy that."

"No. Thank you."

Aissa sighed. I heard the sound on the floorboards as her weight shifted from one foot to the next. She turned away but immediately turned back.

"Olivia, meli, please eat. You are going to shrivel up and die in here. I know that you are upset—"

"You do not know the half."

"I suppose not. If you change your mind—"

"I will not. But thank you."

Aissa unwillingly conceded and backed away slowly, easing the door closed behind her.

Commotion in the lanes distracted me before I could think too much about Aissa's discouragement. I tried to piece together what was happening. A transport car that I had not before noticed, idled below. An officer at the helm, another struggling with a citizen ... a female. She cried out, the piercing screech carrying on the wind to enter every open window.

I stood involuntarily, straining to get a better look ... trying to recall if I had seen her doing something even remotely illegal. I had only barely noticed her at all before now, walking along in her SRA administrative uniform, same as what Jayde wore daily to serve her duties at the plant. She was heading home from work. The transport car, I was certain had not been there before. It came out of nowhere and took her away for seemingly no reason at all. Had she been recruited? It happened all the time, though I had not ever bore witness. It was possible except, she was already Allegiance. Even SOTA recruits were forewarned before being hauled to Kelsard's seedy lair.

I walked from the window, a nagging sensation running through me. I was suddenly very anxious for Jayde to walk through the door. She was due soon and she was never late. Not ever.

I paced, glancing out and gauging the time of day. I tried to settle on a reason why a citizen would have been taken. Especially one who clearly worked for the regime and who was in her own neighborhood in the middle of day. Certainly soldiers had harassed citizens, words exchanged and a pleasurable, though utterly ridiculous, recitation of the crime committed given before one was forcefully hauled away. But never before had I seen a citizen swept off their feet in this way. No words. No grand display of power and presence.

I paced and found myself inside Jayde's private communal drinking cool water from the faucet. I jumped slightly at the sound of the bedroom door opening. Immediately I turned off the stream and walked back into the interior of the room. Jayde stood by her bed, leaning forward, removing her heels.

I opened my mouth to speak but she beat me to it. "I know where Diana is."

And like that, all that I had witnessed from above was gone from my mind. "She is okay?"

"Somewhat, I suppose. That is my understanding, at least. We can visit her today if you want to check on her and her living arrangements."

I smiled for the first time in days. "I do, I do."

"I am starved. We will eat something first. I will not have you withering away under my care."

I agreed. Suddenly I, too, was starving and actually feeling as though I had not eaten for days.

†

SOMETHING WAS WRONG. I COULD NOT JUSTIFY THE EMOTION but there was certainly an air of discontent and I felt strongly that it was related to the female Amirontian citizen being snatched from the street and taken away.

The lanes were quiet as Jayde led the way to an associate of hers who waited patiently for us in a transport car. They would carry us safely to the place where Diana was being temporarily holed up.

It was not very far outside The City, on the border where the dust and gravel became grass and the orange sky began to clear. I leaned my forehead against the glass, forlornly mourning the days of peace and relaxation that I had planned to share with Diana. It was difficult to imagine that soldiers roamed these lanes and pathways but I knew with certainty that they did.

The grass grew taller, soon replaced by the feathery, honey colored sheath grass that complemented the natural decorum of most villages. It amazed me that one could find the way in its denseness. There was nothing but sheath grass for as far as the eye could see.

The transport car turned left, taking us deeper into a heavy patch of the beautiful grass, its tops wafting lazily in the late day breeze. I squinted at the sight of a shanty in the distance.

"It is just up ahead," the driver said to us.

"Where are we?" I asked.

"Ayercroft."

My anxiety level increased though not from instinct, but heightened emotions. I sat upright and stilled as we came closer, before coming to a halt. I knew not what to expect. I feared Dupec had beaten her more after I disappeared because I had not returned, as I am sure he ordered for her to make happen. Curious as to whether she had been further disfigured by the incident, but fearful of finding out.

A sizeable woman with an extraordinarily attractive face and hair displaying the distinguished marks of elder age met us at the door. A deep scowl was our greeting. She did not appear pleased to see us.

"Beltan," she called out to the driver of our transport car, her powerful voice sending a chill through me. "You brought two of them here? I thought that I told you to bring the one girl."

"They were together, a package deal. This one knew where the girl's cousin was. She would not get her if I did not allow her to come along."

I glanced up at Jayde, taking in the look of satisfaction on her face. Her eyes dared the woman to question her motives. The woman placed her hands firmly into her hips, her eyes roving both Jayde's and my frame. She visibly relented, though only slightly.

"You should have waited until after dark." She pursed her lips and shook her head in disappointment. She turned away toward the door. "Come on inside. You three had better not have led any soldiers to me. I have lived here all of this time, in peace, far from their watchful eye and I will take down anyone who ruins that for me, you know I will."

"Yes, Galê," Beltan responded.

The woman turned and headed inside the shanty. The driver nodded for Jayde and me to follow. The inside was much larger than it appeared from the outside, larger than the shanty Mira and I had lived in once upon a life. It was a place like I had never seen, colors that I did not know existed. A huge black shelf filled with books covered an entire wall. I had seen a few, learned to read from the ones that my mira salvaged over the years, but books were illegal without a permit and somehow I doubted this plump little Marinite woman, had obtained a book permit from

SRA.

"She is back here."

We, Jayde and I, followed along the long walkway leading to the back of the shanty, nearly as big as a normal house. I fought the urge to reach out and touch the colorful pieces hanging on the wall. We were led inside a room that smelled faintly of mangalee and my stomach began to speak. I swallowed hard at the sight of my birth mother lying there in the huge bed beneath a brightly colored blanket pulled to her chin. She looked nothing like I expected. She was peaceful ... rested.

I sighed, relieved.

"I will leave you to her."

Her eyes fluttered open, one wider than the other. She gasped. "Olivia."

Jayde touched my shoulder and turned away, leaving me alone with her. I walked across the room and took a seat in a wooden chair beside the bed.

"How are you feeling?" I asked, touching her hand lightly.

"What are you doing here?"

"I was worried. I had to know that you were okay."

"How did you find me?"

"Jayde found you."

"Oh."

We sat together in silence. I did not know what I should say or if I should say anything at all. I caressed the back of her hand.

"Olivia." My name was a whisper from her lips. I looked up.

"Do not feel bad about what happened to me. It is worth it to protect you. I had not believed in the prophecy–"

"Diana–"

"Just listen to me. When my musha, Elizabeth, would tell me stories of my mother when I was a child, I did not believe. Even with your birth I was unsure. Things were so bad ... so many had lost so much, how could anyone possibly believe in change? Some glorious infant would come along and make the world better for us all? My meager belief faded the longer I was gone."

I reclaimed my hand and stood. "Diana, please do not do this."

"Hush. Just listen to me. I am very sane and know that what I am telling you is what I believe to be truth." She took a deep breath. "I saw – I saw my mother. I saw Carolyn. She came to me."

I sat heavily in the chair. "What? What are you talking about?"

"I know it sounds ... unlikely–"

"Impossible. Diana, Carolyn is dead."

"I know."

"She has been dead for more than fifteen years."

"Am I fool? Am I not aware of this fact? She was *my* mother." Diana adjusted herself on the pillows, turning slowly, painfully to face me. Her eyes locked onto mine. "It was the night ... the night Ja'ali came back to retrieve you. Before he arrived ... I thought it was the – I thought it was the blackberries. Thought they caused me to hallucinate. They do that at times, y'know. There was a bright golden glow, reminded me of the night you were born. I called her by your name for I was sure she was you.

"She warned me that Dupec would come, told me that I must protect you at all cost. You are the savior of our people but more than that, the savior of all the Shadow Realm."

"Diana," I groaned. I shook my head vigorously. It was impossible. How could a dead woman possibly give advice? How could a young girl who had only barely seen seventeen days be responsible for an entire galaxy of people? "What is it that you expect me to do with this information? This makes no sense. What would you have me do, show up at Kelsard's door and request control of Marieux? This is foolish."

"This is your responsibility. If you refuse I do not know what the fate of our people, our planet, let alone our realm will be. The anointing has passed for generations and finally it has found you. It has matured in you. Something is happening here, I do not know what it is but it is major and citizens are fearful. Your destiny is calling. You need not know how to proceed. The answers will come. You only need be willing."

"So, what does that mean?"

"It means our fate is in your hands and you must answer the call."

It was heavy ... what she was sharing was much too heavy to process. I wanted to believe her but I did not know that I could. It made absolutely no sense. I was only happy knowing that she was alive. I stood again, leaning forward and pressing my lips softly to her forehead. I loved her dearly but believed her encounter with Ja'ali Dupec, paired with her fondness for blackberries, had shaken something loose inside her head.

I made my way absentmindedly to the sitting room where Jayde, our driver, and Diana's caregiver were sitting at a small round table. The trio surrounded a clear pitcher, drinking from glasses chilled with cubes of ice. The caregiver stood abruptly when she saw me emerge.

"Have a seat, girl," she ordered, offering the chair she had vacated.

I obliged respectfully. She poured me a tall glass of the juice and I drank its sweetness.

"Look, I do not mean to be rude but I have been off SRA's radar and balance sheet for a long time. Taaman Dupec would love to get a hold of me for reasons I am not at liberty to say." She exhaled heavily. "You cannot come back here. She is protected and again, for reasons that I am not at liberty to say or rather am uncomfortable confessing, I will care for her. But I cannot afford for you to risk either of our lives ... nor your own."

She looked to me and for a fleeting moment I saw vulnerability in her eyes. What had Diana told her? She looked away and was her previous stern self.

She continued. "You can sit on the veranda, I have a beautiful garden that you may pick from. I will prepare a meal for you to enjoy before you depart. You may leave after dark."

†

IT WAS WELL PAST THE TIME THAT BOTH THE EASTERN AND western sun had dipped below Marieux when Jayde, Beltan, and

I departed from the hidden shanty where Diana lay protected and healing.

Her caregiver, known only to us as Galê Tas out of a fear of us having knowledge of her full name, stopped me before I could enter the awaiting transport. Her eyes locked onto mine, holding for a moment longer than natural. I had not known if I should say something or if she would.

She hemmed and hawed a bit before opening her mouth to speak. "Bless you child. If it is true, bless you and Deus keep you. I will care for your mother so you do not need to worry."

I gasped ... began to speak, forming a defense in my mind but she silenced me, instructing me to go about my way and to be careful, very careful.

I walked to the transport in a daze.

Jayde said my name as we left the location behind. "Is everything okay? What was that old hag speaking about?"

"Nothing," I whispered. "Nothing ... important. Hey, how did you find out Diana was out here?"

Jayde shrugged. "By chance really. I went by to check in on my cousin and while I was there, asked if she had heard an update on the status of yours. She had not but another Sister happened by at that very moment who told me that this Marinite elder had come by and taken Diana in the night but she did not know where to."

I was even further confounded by it all. "So how did you know where to take me?"

The driver, Beltan, raised his hand. "That would be me. I

had been in the area for two days waiting for you to show, waiting to inform you that this Diana was being cared for, as I had been instructed to do. Your friend here was doing all the asking and through probing of my own determined that the best way to reach you was through her. She was not to accompany but ... well."

"I insisted."

I half-smiled, half-relieved that Jayde was with me in this. "So this woman we have just left, this Galê Tas told you to find me. How did she know about me? Who is she to Diana?"

"You have many great questions, little one. Unfortunately I cannot answer. My instructions were clear in bringing you here. There was one ... minor hiccup but my instructions are just as clear in returning you. I am sorry but I can say nothing more."

I leaned back into my seat. I had no choice but to respect his position.

†

THERE WERE DIFFERENT STORIES REGARDING THE ORIGIN OF the prophecy. Most connect it to the legend of Nosgrz, a Marinite elder that was the head of Marieux's oldest family. Deep in the mountainous ranges was where they resided, near where SOTA Compound A sits today. They say she was a powerful woman who managed to keep her entire village family safe from capture during the Shadow Wars.

It is rumored that she had lived well over a century and showed no sign of letting up. She predicted numerous high profile events on the planet, including the Ustek invasion and overthrowing of Ittas, and subsequent leadership of Henry Kelsard and Taaman Dupec. It was during these days of bloodshed and civil unrest that she apparently emerged and spread hope among the residents, reminding them that a brighter day would come with the birth of a child, an anointed daughter.

She had claimed knowledge of this child's lineage, however it was entirely too dangerous to reveal. That secret died with her when soldiers, under the orders of Savitri the See-er (who was known for working exclusively for Henry Kelsard), torched the entire mountainside in order to keep secrets from escaping its borders.

Others insist that it was not Nosgrz who spread this news but an ageless Citoberian See-er. A woman called Kharish, the elder sister of the See-er, Savitri.

Some believe that it was Kharish herself who, during the latter days of captivity, appeared amongst those confined behind the walls of the university school assuring them that a champion of the people would come along and set them eternally free. And with nothing in life other than pain and suffering, they believed. It gave them hope and motivated them to survive.

Whether believing in the Marinite elder or the Citoberian, neither would reveal the anointed lineage or timeline for the birth. It could have been anyone born at any time. Anyone at all – including me.

But, even if I chose to believe that the appointment was mine, that did not answer the question of what to do with such information? I had never been guided in that direction, never trained for such a magnanimous battle. What did they really expect for me to do? Simply knock on Kelsard's door and inform him that I was there to take him down? And then what? Would he shiver in his netil skin boots and hand me the keys to the compound? How silly. When mobs of SRA soldiers stormed the compound gates in response to my foolish announcement, what then?

These thoughts occupied space in my mind as I crept from SOTA district, where I had sort of hoped to find Dupec, and back to the Amirontian district that I laid my head down at night. My senses were on high alert.

Though there had been no sign of the reinstituting of the most recent enforcement that prohibited me from being in the area after eastern sunset, I had not gotten over the sight of the Amirontian citizen being dragged away and was nearly positive it had happened again. I had heard the scream but witnessed nothing but the departure of the SRA transport.

I would seek Jayde's assistance. If this responsibility was truly mine to bear I could not proceed alone. I would need someone to help guide me ... someone I could trust with my life and my secrets. And if Diana had trusted this mystery woman, then maybe that was my cue to have a confidante of my own.

The lanes were eerily quiet when I emerged and darted up the back steps above the crack where my friends and I occasionally hung out. I used the spare key that Jayde loaned me to gain access to the premises, moving hurriedly, as I was anxious to speak with her one-on-one and reveal my truth before I lost my courage.

"Who is there?" Faraji's voice called as he entered from the kitchen. He answered before I could. "It is just Olivia."

Tabi and Aissa emerged in haste.

"Liv," Aissa began, "tell me that you have seen Jayde."

My heart raced. "I have not. Is she not here?"

"No she is not and I am terribly concerned for her well being. Citizens have been disappearing – women. Jayde is never late. She has never before been late."

Aissa was frantic; Tabi's eyes were glassy.

"You do not think–"

"We do not know what to think."

My stomach dropped. I was suddenly ill.

Faraji walked across the room and stopped near me. "What are we to do?"

"Find her," I replied, as though the answer were obvious. To me, it was.

"How?" Tabia asked. "We do not even know that she is truly missing."

"And what would you suggest? Should we all make our way to SRA headquarters and file a missing citizen's report? Wait the requisite hours to see if she turns up?" My voice rose in anger. "She is not home and it is well past her daily curfew. Whether or not she is truly missing, I am not waiting here to find out."

"I am coming with you," Aissa said following behind me.

I paused, putting a hand up defensively. "I do not think so. I work better alone."

"But she is my friend! I want to help find her."

"Then form your own search and rescue team."

"Olivia. Olivia!"

I was out the door and gone from the building before she could make things more difficult.

Nine

Missing Person

TABIA HAD BEEN CONCERNED ABOUT SEEKING OUT JAYDE considering we had no real reason to believe that she had actually gone missing. As far as we knew and could prove she was only late coming home from work.

Maybe her superior had ordered her to stay late and complete some mundane task that she was responsible for or maybe one that he himself was responsible to fulfill but was too lazy to complete. Possibly she had met someone who intrigued her and stayed behind to flirt. I understood what that was like. For a brief moment in time I had found love and happiness in Charleston Kelsard and would often lose track of time.

There were a number of possibilities to explain Jayde's absence and each and every one was logical. But none were true. Jayde was gone and against her will. The question was how to find her and bring her home.

The answer lied with the Marinite Wally.

I cautiously made my way from the Amirontian district and returned to SOTA territory. I took to the alleyways behind the buildings quietly and carefully, and I crawled into the hold where Wally's flat was located. The light from inside illuminated the area. Were there anyone nearby I would surely have been noticed. But all was silent, not a soldier around.

I tapped the window lightly at first, then harder when there was no response. I hoped there was no one there that would give Wally trouble for my shady presence in the middle of night. There was most certainly no wife to complain, so I pressed my luck. Wally, at this point, was my only hope.

The curtain pushed back and his angry eyes met with mine, softening when he recognized me. He moved quickly, he and I meeting up at his entrance at the same time. I waited as patiently as possible, listening to the sounds of the locks being undone.

The door swung open and Wally instinctively looked both ways and took immediate inventory of our surroundings before addressing me.

"Liv, what are you doing here?" he asked, pulling me inside the doorway.

"I need your help."

"Why do I get the feeling this is not about a quick job?"

"What do you know about what is going on around here?" I asked directly.

"Please, be more specific."

"Why are women disappearing and where are they being taken?"

"And exactly why would I know the answer to that?"

I contained my sudden bloodlust incited by his decision to play coy. He had close relationships with many soldiers and that made him privy to all that happened before the average citizen was made aware. Everyone had his or her survival tactics and this was his. To violate or threaten violation would not help my cause. I was angered, fearful, and in a great hurry, but I had to maintain composure.

"I do not exactly know how you obtain the information that you do. All that matters to me is that you do and I am certain you have the information I want."

Wally paused reflectively. A decent man, Wally had been there plenty when I needed an opportunity to earn extra dashii's to survive but he was far from sainthood. The wages I earned from the small jobs I did for him paid less than half their worth. He knew that people like me were desperate for survival and he capitalized on it.

Getting this information out of him would not come without a price.

"It is possible. I may know something."

My jaw clenched as the games began. "What do you want in exchange? You know I have nothing monetary."

He smirked and his eyes scanned the length of me. "I am sure that we can arrange something."

"Wally." My temperature began to rise.

"Do not flatter yourself, little girl. You are much too tall for my liking. But you do look strong. I sense that you can handle the job."

I listened as Wally submitted his request. A woman that he was involved with had confessed that a close relative had been taken away in, what he referred to as, The Sweep. She was much too distraught to fulfill the terms of their illicit involvement and, as her own husband seemed disinterested in doing anything about her predicament, he wished for me to attempt to find the girl and bring her back.

I agreed. "Where, Wally? Where can I find her?"

"Why did you come to me for this information? Who is it that you are seeking? I could not help but notice that Diana has gone missing."

"Do not concern yourself with Diana's whereabouts. I am not looking for Diana." I paused to compose myself so that I would not reveal my own weaknesses and vulnerabilities. "Jayde."

The wind left Wally. I thought I would have to catch him to keep him from landing with a thud. I jumped, moving swiftly toward him but he raised an arm, palm open, stopping me from proceeding.

"You could have opened with that."

"I saw no need for another to worry and potentially get in my way."

"You are just a kid, Liv. This is bigger than you."

"I do not have a father. I need one now less than ever before."

Wally took a deep contemplative breath. "Dorolard."

"What?" My eyes widened and my heart nearly stopped. "On the other side of Tayle? That makes no sense. Why there?"

Wally pulled an old bent chair from the table and sat his hefty frame inside. A stubby phalanx pressed into the center of his forehead as if trying to ease a mounting pain.

"That part is unclear. Kelsard is up to something and I am certain it involves the expansion of SRA to that sector. I have tried to find out more but…"

"Expanding to the *west* of Tayle?" I asked. "But how is that even possible? What of Kedt? He will never allow this."

"My assertion is that Kelsard and Dupec are aimed to somehow overthrow Kedt Clan and institute SRA rule system wide. It is the only thing that makes any sense."

I took a step away and walked toward the window, gazing at the level of the lanes. All was quiet. A set of shoes moved quickly past, clearly a mother, wife, daughter, or sister, trying to get home without being swept away.

"Why Jayde, though? Why Dorolard?" I mumbled my thoughts aloud.

"Word around is whatever SRA's scheme is starts with Dorolard. I know little about the planet other than it is very industrial. It makes economic sense to begin there. It is a dangerous mission; lives are guaranteed to be lost. My assumption is they are recruiting for the soldiers to be stationed there. They would not wish to jeopardize selected SOTA and Level 1's are not worthy of ranking officers."

"Recruiting," I repeated the word, confused.

Wally did not immediately reply. I turned at the sound of the chair scraping across the floor. Wally stood and walked to the cooling box. He offered a poppy beer. I declined.

"What do I do?" I asked, feeling hopeless.

"I can lead you to the base but getting aboard a ship and to the planet is a feat that I fear I cannot guide you in."

"I am going to get Jayde and bring her home."

"Are you certain that you wish to do this? It is crazy and if you are caught, and you likely will be caught, it is certain death."

"I do not fear death. I am going, with or without your guidance and if you want this adulteresses relative returned, may I suggest you tell me everything that I need to know now so that I may be on my way."

"Fine. Have a seat."

†

THE IDEA OF SHUTTLES, OVERSIZED TRANSPORT CARS that were capable of taking citizens from one planet in the realm to another light years away seemed impossible. I remember as a child, Mira sharing tales of ships that could travel to such places as near as Amironte or to as far away as Ntozaint or Arethoxx. The thought was farfetched…utterly impossible.

Sitting there, crouched between shuttles in the middle of a space station had me both on edge and in awe. Hidden by a massive vehicle, I peered at a much larger one in the distance. The wails of captured women echoed off the walls and bounced back to me. They were every size, every variety. They were mothers, workers, Amirontian, Citoberian, Marinite. There was a pregnant one and I was made sick.

Wally arranged for late night transportation to an area near the base but once the driver dropped me off I was on my own. He believed that two ships left daily, shuttling soldiers and new recruits. There was a possibility that Jayde remained on the planet. The only way to be certain was to stow away on the ship.

SRA presence was not as tight as one would suspect it would be, but surely that did not make my task any easier.

"Sir. Commander Dupec, sir."

I shrank against the massive metal at the sound of the voice not very far away. I cringed and heat spread throughout my frame. My breathing intensified. I tipped carefully toward the voice, being very mindful to stay flat.

"What is it soldier?"

"The transport is prepared, the recruits are boarded and contained. Conditions are good for departure."

"Where is the General?"

"En route to the compound."

"Very well. Carry on, soldier."

I swallowed the heavy lump in my throat. I had not counted on seeing him again and anytime soon. I crept carefully to the edge and beneath the tail of the craft. I could see Dupec's frame though I did not completely recognize it. He stepped forward, moving in my direction.

I gasped involuntarily as light cast upon his face. He was much larger than I anticipated. This was not Ja'ali Dupec receiving information and giving orders. I was looking at one of the founding fathers of evil – Taaman Dupec.

"Amen Deus," I whispered reflexively.

I watched, in awe, as this giant of a man strutted in what seemed to be slow motion across the base and toward the ship that I had watched women being boarded onto. His dark uniform seemed to caress every muscle that bulged from his massive frame.

I shook away my fascination and anger. I had to keep focus. I had to be aware of what my instincts instructed so that I could follow through. I had to save Jayde.

Taaman Dupec disappeared into the shuttle. I sat, crouched low in the shadows, watching and waiting for the moment to make my move. I stilled myself, body and mind, tuning out all distracting thoughts. I crept, edging closer to the imposing figure that was the transport. I wondered if Jayde had already gone over or if she was still on board. I knelt low beneath the large wing, managing my breathing.

The sound of footsteps landing hard against the steel steps echoed throughout the vicinity. I crouched lower, inching back slowly.

"Everything appears to be in order, soldier," Taaman Dupec's voice came to me.

I listened as the leader and his cronies wrapped up their final details, their voices and steps fading into the distance. I moved swiftly and immediately, gracefully ascending the platform and ducking inside the machine. I paused thoughtlessly, taking in my surroundings and marveled at all I saw. Foreign voices jarred me to reality and I darted off to the side, concealing my presence behind a beam near a door.

Cool tingles crept up my spine and slowly radiated out as the beings came closer. I glanced about. Though I was out of their sight, I was virtually in the open. I held my breath and opened the door, disappearing behind it and quietly closing it behind me.

Darkness engulfed me. A blue light was all that illuminated the place. I stepped carefully, keeping close to the walls and trying to determine where I was. I eased my arm up inside my sleeve, my phalanges feeling for the manipulation in the lining. I stuck my phalanx inside and flipped my blade from holding. I moved my arm back down the sleeve, my hand appearing palm up and open right on time to catch it. I had not a clue what I would encounter here and I needed to be prepared for the worst.

I maneuvered through the space with great caution. As my eyes adjusted to the absence of light, I took in the sterility of the place. The air was void of scent, which in and of itself was incredibly odd.

I knew not what to do, how being here would lead me to Jayde's rescue. It was the first time I felt truly helpless. My phalanx grazed a cold steel tray top as I paused. I looked up and took notice of a row of slim doors spanning the entire room. A couple were ajar but the others were firmly closed.

I crept across the space to one of the open doors, pulling it wider. I looked inside. The space was tight and empty with the exception of two sets of restraints, one at the top and the other embedded into the floor. I turned slowly to face the door. Small holes had been drilled inside.

Oxygen holes.

I jumped out of the cell and walked to the end of the row and stood at the side of it investigating. It was not attached to the wall. Across from where I stood was a large cage. I shook my head. The smaller cells would not fit inside; they were too tall.

I returned to an open cell and looked closer at the brackets hanging from the top. It was on a track. I eased it forward, careful not to make too much noise. I moved it back and stepped out, walking across to the big box that I was sure was a cell. The door unlatched with ease and I entered. The space was stuffy and though breathing was possible, it was a challenge.

In the blackness of the space I could see nothing. I stood on my toes and reached toward the top but the ceiling was too high. I glanced to the door and an idea popped into my mind. I straddled the door and used all the strength in my core to push my body up until the tips of my phalanges turned cold from the feel of metal track.

"Jayde," I whispered into the loneliness.

Suddenly there was movement. Caught off guard, I was thrown from the door and sent crashing into the heavy steel wall.

†

I DID NOT KNOW HOW LONG I WAS IN AND OUT OF consciousness. I awoke surrounded by a starless night, groggy with pain shooting from the knot that had formed on my head. My movements were in slow motion.

I was relieved to see a dull light illuminate the edges of

the big door as muffled voices came to me through my fog. I peered around though it was unnecessary; I could see nothing. I wondered what was happening, wondered where in the galaxy we were and for how long I had been out cold.

I struggled to my feet. I would need to pull myself together much faster lest I meet a fate matching the one destined for the women stolen from their lives and family. I steadied myself against the wall listening as the voices became louder. Fear attempted to rain down upon me but there was no time for that. I could not possibly be of any use to Jayde were I murdered or taken captive.

The ring of light provided just enough of an advantage. I glanced about. There was nothing to shield me from prying eyes. I glanced up; there were no other options. I turned my back to the wall and planted my feet and hands firmly. I moved quickly up the wall to the corner, tucking myself away inside. The door creaked open and I convinced myself that I was invisible as I concentrated to keep from slipping down.

"This one is lovely," a voice traveled to my ears from somewhere below. "I do not know how she managed to avoid capture for so long."

"Well, she is captured now. And I think when we get a leave, she is going to be my first feast away from home."

"Not if I get to her first."

"You are no bother to me. It would be nothing to overtake you."

"Oh really? I would like to see you try."

"Soldiers," a stern voice called from the doorway. "We have landed, this means that there is work to be done. Enough of your bickering over a whore who you are not likely to have before I have drowned her in my seed anyhow. Now hurry!"

"Yes sir, Lega," the two said in unison.

My palms and feet pressed firmly into the metal walls, supporting my weight as I watched in emotional and physical anguish from above. Semi-unconscious women were led inside and handed off to be secured for transport from the ship. These were not SOTA of any breed; these were women—workers, mothers, and wives. Then I remembered that, though nowadays it was not uncommon for a woman to enlist, this was how SOTA had actually begun, and I felt ill.

In many homes across the planet children were waiting at empty tables and husbands would cry themselves to sleep in the darkness, angry for being unable to protect whom they loved. I breathed in and out, carefully and quietly. I worked to calm my emotions; they were draining me of my strength. I closed my eyes momentarily and took in a deep breath, channeling the energy to keep my muscles steady, while beads of sweat pooled together on my face and body.

The last woman was secured. The two soldiers departed the chamber, closing the door tightly behind them, a follow up clang signaled that the door had been locked. I wanted to try to call out for Jayde, find out if she was in my presence but the air thickened quickly making breathing difficult.

I slid much too quickly and landed in a heap in the corner, the little breath I had being knocked from my lungs. Using the back of my hand, I smeared sweat from my forehead. I would need to keep my mind alert and my body poised. I would soon be forced to retreat to the ceiling once again.

†

THE CELL WAS EMPTIED. THE VOICES OF SOLDIERS FADED into the distance. I slipped from hiding and peered from behind the large and heavy door. An armed soldier was several feet away. I checked the opposite direction. It was empty. I took in my surroundings. We were inside some sort of structure that had the appearance of a hollowed out cave. There was an unfamiliar chill in the air and I tugged at my hat.

We were far from home, that much was clear. The look and texture of the place that the lot of us had been taken made it obvious that this was not home.

An alien language that I did not understand tugged at my ear. I shrank behind the door, looking out into the unwelcoming environment. Two beings, dressed like soldiers but looking like nothing that I was used to, discussed indecipherable business in their tongue. Both were half my height. Dorolardian. I had seen one or two in my time at Mole's but never had I fathomed seeing one up close and personal on their own land. I waited patiently until the soldiers disappeared before quickly moving in the direction the women had been taken.

I was clueless, I did not know precisely where the women wound up. I tugged at the first door I came across but it did not budge. I swore softly. I had not figured how I would get to Jayde, not to mention how to get out of this place once I got to her.

The sound of keys jingling caught my ear and I looked down the dark hall in that direction. A soldier from my own planet was exiting a room a short ways away. I moved toward him without considering my actions. I was on him before he could place the key inside the lock.

"What are –?" He was unable to complete his question. I ran at him, using the wall to propel me forward so that I could wrap my arm around his throat. Locking his head between my forearm and bicep, I held with force until his body slumped into a pile of flesh and bone near the door.

I froze, alarmed for a millisecond while staring at his stilled body. I had not killed before. I did not want to nor was I certain that I could. I hoped more than anything that I still had not. I removed the trepidation I had been feeling before opening the door and discovering, thankfully, what I had been looking for. Partly unconscious women were spread about the huge warm and surprisingly luxurious space. I grabbed the fallen soldier and dragged him inside, closing the door behind me.

I collapsed forward, breathless, pressing my hands to my thighs. I wondered if I had killed him but was not yet prepared to find out. After stripping him of his uniform and weapons, I stood above, staring down at him trying to determine my next move.

"Liv?"

I looked up. My heart moved from my chest and exploded into my throat. "Jayde."

She looked weary. She held herself up with the support of an archway but barely. I rushed to her side, taking her into my arms. I had found her, or she had found me, I could not tell which.

"Are you really here?" she asked. "Am I ... hallucinating?"

"No. Praise Deus, you are not. I am here."

"Where are we?" her voice was coarse and low.

"Dorolard."

"Impossible."

"Apparently not."

"Amen Deus."

I led her, carefully, to a plush red seat and eased our bodies down. Once she was stable, I grabbed her and pulled her into my arms. Jayde's head landed heavily upon my shoulder. Her breathing was rough and labored.

"You are going to be okay. I am getting us out of here."

"How did I get here?"

"I was hoping that was something you could answer for me."

She shook her head and then moved her hand to press against it as she leaned away. It was clear she had been drugged. I wanted her to get her bearings but there was a near nude soldier on the floor only a couple feet away and I was not certain that he was actually deceased. I was sure I had seen his chest move.

"We have to go," I said. "I know you are tired but–"

"I know. I understand."

"Do you think you can walk?" I asked.

"I will have to manage."

I helped Jayde to her feet and attempted to guide her to the door.

"I got it," she mumbled. I ignored her insistence and continued trying to lead her. "Liv. I said I got it."

I stopped. "I told Wally I would try to return his friend's relative. I gave my word in exchange for information on finding you."

"Do you know this relative?"

I paused. "I have a description but...I am not certain."

"You know I like Wally and I know your word is your bond but do we really have time to find out?"

I glanced toward the room she had come from. My eyes darted to the soldier who shifted on the floor, hinting a return to consciousness. I sighed and groaned but turned my attention to the exit, moving in its direction with Jayde holding her own behind me.

I stopped short of pushing the heavy door open. Jayde opened her mouth to question me, irritated from having awakened from a drug-induced stupor to find herself on another planet, but I silenced her.

I always followed my instincts.

Ten
The Hunter

ALTHOUGH I HAD RESCUED JAYDE, WE WERE FAR FROM SAFE because we were far from home. Stranded on a distant planet, surrounded by darkness, granite, and unfamiliarity. Left to fend for ourselves, to the west of Tayle with no plausible means or plan for escape.

We managed, though barely, to break free of the structure which held Marinite and Amirite united in captivity but instinct would get us only so far.

Jayde was mostly free of her fog, able to think clear and offer some suggestions and wisdom for what it was worth. But knowing no more about this foreign territory than I, meant her offerings had little constructive basis. As for me, I had been knocked unconscious by invisible forces, holed up in darkness when the transport was made and had no idea from which direction we had traveled.

We paused, trying to fight fatigue, confusion, and the urge to fight one another for the advice we were each giving. What worked in our favor was the quiet in the lanes, if you could call them that. There was little activity in the distance allowing us precious time. We had to try our best to hold to the shadows, as we would stick out like sore thumbs.

"What do we do now?" Jayde's voice was low and deliberate.

"I do not know."

"We cannot just stand here, Liv. We will be spotted."

"I am aware."

"I am not going back there."

"Just give me a moment to think … please."

She exhaled heavily in frustration. "We do not have a moment. So now what? What is your instinct telling you?"

"I do not – I do not know."

"Liv, think. How did you get to me?"

"I arrived the same way that you did, in a transport box. It was black. Had I not been knocked unconscious, I would not have seen anything anyhow."

A noise to our rear re-directed our focus. Our eyes locked briefly, mine darting to the left milliseconds before I moved with Jayde by my side. We crouched low, hiding behind a heavy, unidentifiable structure. SRA soldiers. I paid particular attention to the direction from which they were coming.

I eased back, deeper into our hiding place.

"I have an idea," I whispered.

We waited impatiently, not breathing and longing for the cool orange skies of home. We waited until the lane was again silenced before emerging. I gazed into the direction the soldiers had come from. If that was indeed where escape lied we would need to be extraordinarily cautious heading that way. There would be soldiers with weapons who were not intimidated to use them.

"Now what?" Jayde whispered.

"That way. Stick to the—"

I stopped speaking. My heart raced. Something was wrong. I stretched my arm wide before Jayde's body, easing her back.

"What is it?" she asked softly.

"I do not know."

We waited for something to happen. I waited for something that would justify the horrid feeling that had washed over me. I looked in all directions but saw nothing or no one. Yet, I still felt heaviness as though something was terribly wrong.

"Liv, I know that you are loyal to your instincts but we have to get out of here now."

"Jayde, wait."

"We cannot wait. There is no one. We have to go."

She stepped away from me before I could stop her. I tried to tell her again to wait but her body was dropping before the command could finish escaping my lips.

My eyes widened. I squealed her name quietly as I dropped to her side. I reached to check her out; to see what happened but my body reacted ahead of my mind. My arm rose above my head and reached back, gripping the wrist of someone … or something. My heartbeat accelerated. A blade was centimeters from my throat. My widened eyes moved down to the gray arm connected to the weapon that, had I reacted a moment later, was prepared to slice my throat wide open. I gulped in slow motion, fearful that the inside of the lump created in my throat would be exposed.

I discovered physical strength that I had not known existed. I pulled the arm with the blade away, ducking low and spinning out, coming eye to beady eye with what, I was not certain. The creature was larger than I, much taller and lean, visibly strong. The physical makeup of a human male with gray flesh and a bald head tattooed with unrecognizable symbols.

His hands were abnormally large with long phalanges and nails like talons. In his eyes was as much surprise as I was certain that was in my own. A surprise that did not last long before turning to vengeance, his eyes pressed into lines and the muscles in his jaw clenched.

He growled, pulling forcefully from my grip and sending me reeling from the sheer force of his strength. I recovered and found my footing. He sneered and then was gone. I did not see him move, only saw a blur that could have easily been mistaken for my imagination until I instinctively ducked again, turning and catching both wrists, again, both hands clenching what happened to be swords that glistened in the darkness.

Whoever it was, whatever it was, wherever it had come from, it was certainly aimed to murder me on this dark, foreign planet, far from home. He was closer to his goal this time, eerily close.

One blade was mere centimeters from my abdomen with the tip of the other drawing blood from the side of my neck. I could feel his heat enveloping me as his own anger accelerated.

The warmth of my life fluid leaked from the surface wound. I listened to it as it traced a path to my clavicle. Fear filled me first – then rage.

"Grrragh," I cried out, using his strength to support my weight as I catapulted from the ground while leaning away from the blade. My feet planted firmly against his chest. With force I pushed him away as I tried to backflip to momentary safety. But the weight was gone suddenly and I nearly slammed to the ground below. I somehow managed to right myself landing hard on my feet and hands. I looked around, dismayed. The creature was again gone.

I turned about, looking to and fro trying to find where it could have gotten to so quickly. I abruptly paused.

"Jayde," I exhaled.

Her face lay in a pool of blood. My knees buckled as I ran to her. A chill ran through my entire frame. I was certain I was in a dream; it had to be a dream. My breath shortened as anxiety filled me. I pushed my body from the ground and ran faster, landing harshly by her side, my palms splashing her still warm blood.

"Get up, Jayde," I cried foolishly. "Jayde, please. Get up, please."

My vision blurred and my heart ached. Why was this happening, I wondered. I could not understand what had gone wrong. My sadness fell from my eyes and landed with a thud into her blood.

I leaned away swiftly and just in time to avoid the cold steel that passed by my sweaty flesh. I filled with hate and rage. I moved without thinking, led by an intense emotion. I twisted my body, landed with feet planted firmly, poised and ready for a fight to the death.

But it was gone…

And so was she.

Jayde's body vanished along with the large, gray being. I charged back to the puddle of her cooling blood. I fought the onset of hysteria.

"Jayde. Jayde." I swore and looked about, praying that she would appear but knowing that it would not happen. "Jay—"

My heart beat faster; so much so that I thought my chest would explode. She was gone. She was gone. Nothing remained of her but blood.

I stopped, my eyes to the dark sky while attempting to steady my breathing so that I would not pass out. I had traveled, oh so far, to save my best friend, I would not quit now. This was indeed a setback, a minor one. I would find her. I did not know how but I knew that I would, that I must.

Soldiers were approaching. I could hear the commotion grow nearer. I stepped forward, ready for war, prepared for a rampage but swiftly halted. I found myself kicking and fighting against an unseen force that had somehow managed to cut through my defenses and work around my instincts. I was pulled back from the open lanes on a foreign planet in sight of my very best friend's blood, all that remained of her, into the cover of darkness feeling much too angry to be afraid.

A force covered my mouth, despite there being no threat of me screaming. I no longer had a friend there. Danger loomed for me at every turn. I could feel the presence of my captor against my damp flesh. She whispered a request for my compliance, warned that I was in grave danger, and that upon my release, I should not scuffle or create a scene. I reached to pry her hand away – but there was none.

The force dissipated, and I turned quickly to come face to face with this person whom I would surely soon kill. But no sooner was I released than the lane from which I had been snatched came alive. She had rescued me. My eyes met hers, and I read the order to retreat beside her.

The two of us, my savior and I, stooped low, quiet in the dark, hardly breathing. Hearing the activity in the lane nearby, the voices of soldiers calling out orders and strange accented responses demanding answers, encouraged me to keep still.

Jayde. All I could think … all I could see was Jayde. Her last words, the sound of her voice rested upon my ears. And now all that remained was her blood on my clothing and flesh. I fought the emotion that was trying to sweep over me with as much vigor as when I had fought her killer mere moments earlier.

Time ticked by. My questions going unanswered. They would have to wait. The presence of soldiers grew and their questions and concerns would take precedence over my own. I relaxed slightly, relieved that the presence at my side remained and there was an opportunity to resolve those burning queries that were haunting me.

†

I DIED THAT NIGHT. SITTING IN THE HOLLOW, FEELING the presence of foreign and domestic soldiers edging dangerously close then retreating. Toying with me. I tried to remove myself mentally. Foreign and domestic soldiers everywhere.

I felt my spirit escaping my being, leaving but an empty shell of a person that only remained alert because of the unnerving continuance of a requisite heartbeat.

I had not noticed when the lanes emptied … when the voices died and there was no one left but myself and my savior who I was coming to resent with each passing moment. Why had I been rescued? Why was I spared when I not only allowed my friend to be murdered, but her body taken.

Who was foreign on this planet? The only thought that kept me sane was that question. Who was the foreigner? Me? Or the ones that spoke in an accented tongue?

There was movement beside me. I was reluctant to follow. I was not even certain if I had the ability to do so.

"Olivia, come."

I froze. My heartbeat stopped. Only my eyes moved from the spot on the ground that they were transfixed to, into the direction the feminine voice came from.

"How do you know my name?"

"I know who you are, Olivia. I have been watching you–"

"Watching me?" I asked incredulously.

"–waiting for you to come of age. Waiting for your watershed moment. And it is here ... it is now."

My nostrils flared and I moved quickly toward her, more than prepared to strike a deadly blow if need be. "Who are you?"

"My name is Kharish. I am a Seer* from the planet Citober though I have never been far from you."

"How is that? I have never before seen you."

"From the day your mira brought you into this world, in a shanty in your home village of Kalaath, when you were being raised and trained to conceal your truth in Ashtwor, I was never far away."

I swallowed hard and took a deep breath, steadying myself. I looked hard into her face as she informed me of the many occasions in which she had been nearby. She was beautiful, a typical Citoberian, with dark and glossy hair that cascaded in soft waves to her waistline. She was not golden as I was without the help of my treasured concealor, but her olive-tone skin, kissed by the suns, glowed ethereally.

I was suddenly overwhelmed with fresh anger. My hand aimed to wrap firmly around her small neck but I was blocked. It was as though an unseen force kept me from her. I tried, repeatedly and with everything in my being, but I could not connect. Weary, I gave up.

I collapsed, hands upon knees ... more winded from the act of attempting to exact revenge upon her than the creature who had stolen Jayde's life and corpse. "Then why ... why did you not stop it?" I muttered fiercely.

"Stop it. Stop what?" she replied plainly, as though the answer were obvious, the question ridiculous.

I whisper shouted, "*Any of it! All of it!* Mira's death, Diana's capture … *Jayde's murder!* Is my tortured life your entertainment? Do my travesties find with you amusement? Pleasure?"

"You suggest that I should somehow stop fate? As though that were my role?" The Seer asked the question in the voice of an educator. She spoke to me as an elder speaks to a child who only knows foolishness.

I was stunned. I became a ball of fire. "Explain this to me, all of it! What just happened? How do you know who I am? *Where is Jayde?*"

She watched me from a place that, despite being level with me, felt as though she were floating above. "I am sorry, Olivia, but your friend is gone. And unless you wish to meet a similar fate, we must use this time to help you escape."

"You are sorry? Well, that just makes this all okay because you are so—" I groaned and bent at the waist, clutching my chest with both hands and struggled to breathe. I clawed at my neck, trying to create an opening in my airway. I felt certain that I would soon lose the meager contents of my belly. Ignoring her voice my weary voice asked, "Gone? Gone where?"

She continued as though nothing out of the ordinary had happened. As though I were not experiencing the worst pain of my life. "You did battle with a Miltvarian Hunter and lived to talk about it—"

"I do not care about that. All I care about is finding my friend."

"Do you understand why that is?" she continued as though I had not spoken. As though I should somehow be patting myself upon the back for my valiant effort.

"Did you not hear me? I do not care."

"You have a responsibility, Olivia. It is time."

My face was drenched in sorrow and my breath shallow puffs. I did not want to speak any longer. Fruitless conversation would get me no closer to rescuing Jayde. I gulped oxygen and squeezed my wet eyes tight.

"Time? For what? An imaginary creature, something born in the nightmares of little boys and girls just murdered my best friend and took her body away. I do not have *time* for this. I need to know where she is. I need to take her body home. She has friends. She is my family…" I turned to depart but paused, trying to figure out which way I should go.

"Olivia. You are *the one*."

I stopped. My body, my breath, my heartbeat ceased. "What did you say?"

"Our time is short so I will be direct. You wish to find your friend's body—but you do not find a Hunter. A Hunter finds you. Now that he has picked up your scent … is aware of your existence, he will find you again. Your next meeting however, you *will* be ready and you *will* have your vengeance. But for now … for now my dear Olivia, you have a responsibility to your people, to Jayde's people … and to—"

Her eyes became cloudy as they rolled to the back of her head. She seemed to fade, if that were possible, and for the briefest moment, I forgot that I was in mourning. I reached for her, but while this time I could connect, it was like swatting the wind—intangible. I wanted to call to her, to get her attention, but

I had already forgotten her name.

"Hey. Hey! What is wrong with you? Are you ... are you okay?"

"Olivia?" she said, her tone tinged with uncertainty. She glanced around, seeming to assess her surroundings. Though she still appeared before me in her strange, floating, and unreachable way, something about her had changed. It was as though during the time it took for me to blink she had become somehow younger.

"Yes, Olivia, we established that. What is going on? Why do you look ... different?"

"I did it," she said to herself.

"Did what?" I asked, agitated beyond measure.

"Listen, I do not have much time. I am Mala and I am your Seer."

"I thought you said–"

"I know what you have been taught your entire life and how you have been raised. I have waited patiently, what feels like an eternity for the time to come."

"Yes, I get it. My watershed moment."

"Your what?"

My eyes locked onto hers. Somehow imperceptibly different from the pair looking upon me not long ago. Slow and methodically I began to form my posture into one suited for fighting. In my heart, I realized something was off ... something had indeed changed with my so-called seer. But my mind...

Suddenly my mind no longer cared.

My thoughts went to Diana. I deflated, became small. "I care not who you are or why you have come. I just want to go home. Can you see your way to do right by me for once and help me off this forsaken planet?"

"Yes, home you shall go, my child. Home you shall go."

Eleven

Discovery

MY FACE WAS DAMP. SWEAT? MAYBE. PERHAPS IT WAS FROM tears. I could see nothing around me. I was alone. My Seer had gone, to where I did not know. My throat began to constrict making breathing a challenge.

My hands went to my scarred neck and massaged, trying to open the passageway. I wanted to survey my surroundings but could not move. I felt trapped ... claustrophobic. Surrounded by darkness. I was empty inside. I felt as though I had been gutted but I could not recall anything. Had it all simply been a bad dream?

Jayde...

Jayde...

History returned in unchallenged flashes. How had I lost her when I had saved her? But she was gone. I knew that she was because of the cold and empty sensation of death that bound itself to me.

But what exactly had killed her, that was the question. I remembered the gray flesh, hard and rigid to the touch. The razor sharp claws that looked like swords threatening to see me meet a fate equivalent to that of my best friend. Her blood covered the lane ... covered me. Seemingly more than one body could contain, should contain. Warm. Wasted.

I twisted, trying to pull myself from this world between the living and the comatose. The undead. Neither of which would guide me back to Jayde's side. Neither of which would have any power to impact the course of events that had already taken place.

†

I SAT UPRIGHT IN SEMI DARKNESS. WHETHER IT WAS THE start of transition from nighttime to day or from day into eve, I could not determine. My breathing was harsh. My racing heart pounded loud in my ears.

As my eyes focused, I racked my brain trying my hardest to recall or recognize where I was, not to mention how I had gotten there. My mind was in a dense fog. There was cushion beneath me, the harsh cold was gone—a bed.

I glanced about the space. A string dangled low, one that solely controlled the single light source above. My eyes roamed, pausing at a dresser. I jerked my body up and around and looked behind me to the set of windows.

"Amen Deus," I mumbled as I quickly jumped from the bed and to the floor. I was poised. It was as though I anticipated that some unseen entity would jump from the shadows and attack. I stood for what felt like an eternity, stooped low, arms wide, waiting and surveying my surroundings.

Nothing appeared. There was no movement other than my own, no heartbeat except mine. My arms slowly descended. I reached up and involuntarily grabbed my hat and pulled it from my head, allowing my cursed curls to breathe and my scalp to cool. Water streamed from my eyes as I forced myself to walk back to Jayde's bed.

Scattered remnants of a tumultuous journey began to return to me: the odd, seemingly shape-shifting woman who was constantly just out of reach, guiding my steps and acting as the backup I needed to avert danger. The signal to my ever-reliable instincts had gone dead. Were it not for this curious woman, apparently called Mala (though I was almost positive that she had introduced herself by a different name initially), I might have been left as dinner scraps for displaced Hunters from the planet Miltaver but taking sabbatical on Dorolard.

For my inability to save Jayde, or at the very least her corpse, that was likely the fate I deserved. I had made it home, a truth that was too impossible to believe. Unable to face my friends, I snuck inside after all was still and had taken refuge in Jayde's bed.

I leaned over, pressing my hands against the cooling spot that I had moments earlier occupied. Cautiously, I reached across to "her side", the side she should have been on. The side she occupied the last time that she and I shared this bed. As expected it was cold. Untouched.

I swore and spun away. Walked across her space with hat in hand, trying to recount the events that led to her untimely demise and determined at what point I had failed. The only images playing on repeat in my brain was Jayde's shredded chest and the eyes of Mala. I caressed the wound on my neck, confirming that all of this was not simply a realistic dream.

She claimed that I was indeed *the one*. But really, who was she? And if she knew so much, why could she not have warned me? Warned Jayde? Why did she not protect Jayde?

The one?

Could it be true? No. No, it was not possible. There was no *one* and indeed I was not it. If I were, would I not have been a better protector of Diana and had the ability to encourage Mira's heart to beat longer?

And what of Jayde...?

I entered her communal. I swallowed hard. Her essence was present. Less than a day ago she had bathed and prepared herself for her daily responsibilities in this very space. I gently fondled her ritualistic tools, hoping to regain some piece of her in doing so.

I walked in slow motion across the small space, stopping at my reflection. I looked into my eyes, staring deeply. If anyone ever bothered to look hard enough ... if they even knew what to look for, they would recognize the faint glimmer of light that haloed my irises. I continued to look, to soul search. To attempt to see beyond the foil of color used to deceive soldiers and civilians seeking favor from SRA.

If I am *the one* ... what does that even mean?

I do not know why I did it, did not know why I bothered to remove the color. Maybe hoping for some sudden sense of clarity. My natural eye sparkled. Literally, like gold in sunshine. Even beneath the dim lighting, they shone brilliantly. I hated my eyes, hated their dangerous radiance.

I hated what they may symbolize to others.

I looked away in shame. I focused on the tattered green hat in my hand. And despite shielding my eyes reflection, I was certain that I could somehow still see clearly their glow.

I am the one. Could it be true?

I, again, raised my eyes to meet their reflection. Without looking away, I grabbed a cloth from a bar embedded in the wall. I turned the handle and heard the sound of the waters fall breaking and placed the cloth beneath, soaked it through. I moved my hand to my forehead but hesitated. I had not seen my true self with my own eyes in so long. Not since childhood.

I swallowed hard and moved the cloth across my flesh. Wetness poured over my eyelids and I blinked it away. I did not want to see but I knew that I must. I did not have a choice.

I inhaled deeply, then pressed the cloth to my face again and began to scrub with vigor. I moved my arm back and forth, applying sufficient force until finally … a patch of golden flesh shown through. Tears welled and I did not know whether the wetness that trailed my cheeks was from the cloth or my dying spirit. I continued to scrub with wide, untamed strokes.

I wet the cloth again, wiping away excess concealor. I continued to separate what I had adhered for my mother's and my own protection. A concoction that had existed on my skin for so long that it had nearly replaced it. If only it could have.

Slowly my face began to show through. I scolded myself, commanding myself to stop the madness yet finding that I was unable to oblige the demand. The water poured and I worked the cloth in ways that, at times, made my flesh feel as though I was peeling the skin clear off.

I stopped. Abruptly ceased, allowing the towel to drop from my hand. I stared at myself. A few brown streaks remained. Red, patchy abrasions formed. I sighed heavily as I rinsed the cloth and squeezed the excess liquid, then wiped the last bits clear.

The cloth slipped forward from my phalanges. I scanned my skin and curly locs, typically cut as close to my scalp as I could manage, and dark save for the fresh roots shimmering through. I stared at my reflection and hated with passion what I saw staring back.

"Amen Deus." The wispy voice was not mine.

My heartbeat postponed and my eyes widened in fear. I turned without thinking and regretted it immediately. I looked away, reaching for the door and slammed it shut.

"*You!*" Tabia gasped.

"Go away, Tabi!"

"It all makes so much sense. I ... I knew something ... something was different. You are the Goldenborn. It makes so much sense." She spoke to herself more than me.

"You know nothing! You are just a foolish girl that thinks she has all the answers!"

I shielded my eyes from my reflection, angry that I had nearly allowed myself to truly believe the things that Mala had tried to convince me of.

Tabia's muffled and excited voice carried through the door. "The Anointed Daughter—here all this time! You are the Goldenborn. Deus be praised!"

My palms balled tightly. I pounded, gently against the edge of the hard, cold porcelain trying my best to figure a way out of my dilemma. I was trapped, confined to a tight place feeling as though all the oxygen was being sucked away by my tension.

I was completely vulnerable. Golden and glowing. My hair and eyes exposed. I had not brought my concealor with me, had not anticipated needing it immediately. Had not even considered the possibility of being caught.

Where were these instincts now? How had I not recognized her presence before she recognized mine? I was so absorbed in my own thoughts that I had left myself vulnerable. A deadly mistake. My reality was, again, the prelude to my potential demise.

"Go away!"

"Praise Deus. Praise Deus for your existence!"

I breathed steadily, my eyes locked upon the back of my hands, appreciating their darkness. Emotions are a weakness. Emotions equated to death and destruction. I would get out of this situation and vowed to never again allow my despondency to impact my awareness.

"Tabia, please." I had to act. Think. Quick. "Aissa. Get Aissa for me."

"Oh, Liv. This is such an incredible honor—"

"Get Aissa. Now please."

I moved closer to the door, my hand hovering the knob. I detached myself from all emotion. Sadness. Fear. Anxiety. One deep breath in and I exhaled it all away. I remembered who I was and the feats that I had overcome. I was, am, and will always be Olivia Vala Eso Kalaath.

I waited. Tabia's praises obediently faded into the distance and I moved quickly. I turned the handle and re-entered Jayde's vacated space, hurrying across to seal and bolt the entry.

I turned and dropped hard to my knees and thrust forward, pushing my body partway beneath the bed. I stretched my arm until the tips of my phalanges found the edge of my bag, and then guided it to me. I took it into my arms and rushed back inside the small communal, digging out my half-filled jar of concealor. I swallowed hard. I would need to replenish and soon.

I had made perfect the art of concealing under pressure. The task took little time and results were flawless. I pushed my head deep into my hat and turned to face this new bane of my existence. I caught the glimmer of gold and swore. Frantically, I grabbed at the colored foil and pushed one in. I reached for the other and fumbled to place it properly. The small foil slipped from my phalanges. I caught it before it was lost forever, and managed to place it over my left eye.

I blinked a few times to be sure they were secure in their position. I could hear Tabia in the distance calling my name and the mumbles of incoherent explanation to her companion. Her fist landed hard against the door and I knew I had only moments before she gave up and forced her way inside.

I stuffed my belongings back inside my bag and returned it to a new, temporary home inside the communal. I took a breath and steadied myself before moving forward. I told myself that, with the exception of my loss of Jayde, nothing else had changed and Tabia was as twisted as ever.

Tabia was hard at work, attempting to convince Aissa of my existence as *the one* as Aissa remained steadfast in denial. Good girl. I unbolted the door as I shook off the last remaining fears of retribution for having been exposed, and walked into the main living space as though oblivious to Tabia's claim to have witnessed what she had indeed seen.

Noticing me, Tabia stumbled back and appeared startled by my presence. Aissa shrugged off her aggravation, walking away.

"What have you done?" Tabia asked mystified. "Why have you done this? Why are you doing this?"

"I have not done anything. I know not of what you are speaking about." I attempted to proceed forward but Tabia blocked my path.

"Take it off," she screamed reaching for me.

I reacted, catching her wrist in my hand. My eyes locked on hers. I refused intimidation. "What are you trying to have done to me? We all know that you do not like me but must you set out to destroy me?"

"I only want you to do what is right by my people." As if thinking better of her response she added, "For our people."

I glared at Tabia, loosening my grasp though not letting go. She was unfazed. I looked in the direction of Aissa's footsteps. Her attention was on the glass of carraplum juice she was drinking.

I released Tabia and stepped back. Aissa appeared livelier, more alert. Her expression was bright as she approached me.

"So, where is Jayde? Is she awake? She must be with Tabia's morning insanity," she said accusingly. "What happened? How did you find her?"

Recognition finally hit Tabia. "Liv, where is Jayde?"

My chest became so heavy that I feared it would cave in and crush my heart. I could feel the stress and tension caused by those explosive questions gripping my throat firmly and suffocating me.

I was instantly transported back into that world. One with strange, jagged surroundings, many soldiers, and gray creatures with horrendous talons. I had not realized that I had not uttered a response until Aissa called my attention to her again in a voice that was now filled with terror.

This time she did not wait for my reply. A decision that was best for I did not know how to respond. She moved past me with Tabia, who had clearly not noticed Jayde's absence in her determination to make me her savior, close on her heels. I walked slowly to the glass and looked down to the lanes below. Jayde's blood stained the foundation. Warm heat permeated my frame and I began to hyperventilate.

The voices in the distance came to me louder. I blinked and the lane was once again clear. There was no blood. The sun shone brighter than it had in some time. I chuckled at the irony.

"Where is she?" Aissa stepped aggressively in my direction.

I shrugged. "I do not know."

"You did not find her," she sighed.

"I did, but–"

"Then where is she?"

"I do not know! She is dead. She is … she is gone. The thing … something … it killed her. Too fast. It was … I cannot even say what it was. It nearly killed me but … my reflexes … better." I swallowed the knot and turned back to face the lane. "Her blood was … I fought hard, I tried to destroy it. An eye for an eye, his life for hers but it was much too powerful."

All of the air left the room.

"Her body…" I did not know which the tiny voice had come from. It did not matter.

"Gone. I-I-I do not know what … I do not know how." I turned to face them. "We battled but he had phalanges like swords." Thoughtlessly I caressed the wound already healing at an accelerated rate. Faraji stood in the background, a horrified look upon his face. I glanced away from the guilt. "I could not stop him. Never encountered anything so fast. I dodged a blade. Looked up, he was gone. And so was she."

"A Miltvarian Hunter." Faraji spoke.

I returned my gaze to him, interested to know what he knew.

"You are aware of this creature?"

"I have heard of them. How they smell the blood of any Marinite or Amirite within range and seek to kill them. The bodies they take back as a trophy. Liv, where exactly *did* you find Jayde?"

"Dorolard," I said as casually as if the answer was Mole's.

I ignored their confused expressions and clarifying questions. My blood boiled again. This creature that murders senselessly, does not for survival but for recreation, took my friends body simply as proof of its triumph? My mind whirled and my face felt damp. I panicked, briefly wondering if my concealor was failing me. But Faraji, Aissa, and Tabia remained firm in their concern for Jayde's soul and I relaxed.

"What is done with the body?" I asked.

"I do not truly know. I have only heard there is a celebratory feasting on the … the blood," Faraji's voice dropped out a moment, then returned. "Marinite and Amirontian blood is a delicacy. They crave it but because they cannot survive on our planets, it is rare. They drink it like it is sweet carraplum or green obi. When the tribe has had their fill and their fun, the body is tossed away to decompose."

"Why have I never heard of this before?"

"Opidin legend on Amironte. Because no one had ever seen one – or maybe never lived to tell its tale, no one believed it was true."

Tabia's voice was small when she spoke. "Sort of like the Anointed." Her eyes were fixed on me. I felt it but ignored her.

Tabia's soft sniffles combined with Aissa's and filled my ears. My body tensed. I, too, had shed tears of my own but how could I have not? I had witnessed this evil, an evil that had taken a life dear to me and I would not forgive nor ever forget about it. I would only seek to destroy and weakness and tears would not make a difference. A symphony of tears would not bring her back.

Rage filled me to the brim. I turned sharply to face Aissa and Tabia who were holding one another up.

"What value hold your tears? What sort of Amirites are you?" I screamed. "You have been softened by this planet, indeed. And though that is not a bad thing entirely, where is your pride? Where is your outrage?"

The pair was rocked by my forcefulness. I had no time for weakness, only action. I turned back to Faraji. His strength was impressive. There was no heartbreak in his eyes, no slump in his stance. His spine remained erect. His eyes fixed on mine. Hate filled him and I, somehow, knew that he was awaiting my order. An order that was hesitant to come.

"How do I find it?" I asked.

"It finds you. No one ever escapes death where a Hunter is concerned. Never. Somehow you managed. I guarantee it is already seeking your scent."

"And I will make his job easier. Since he cannot come to me, I will go to him."

"How?"

"He was on Dorolard. He can survive there. That is where he detected my scent, so that is where I will return. This time one of us will die."

"No … no, you cannot." Tabia cried.

Shamed, Aissa stepped toward me. She pulled herself together quickly; recalled her Amirontian heritage. Stood taller. Eyes dried and focused down upon me. Muscles taught.

"I am going."

I looked past her, continuing my silent debate with Faraji. I could hold my own; this had been proven. I did not need more bloodshed on my hands. Faraji was certainly powerful, definitely much larger than me but so had been Jayde and she fell instantly.

I broke my gaze, signifying my answer and faced Aissa. "No."

Her brow furrowed. "I am going." Her reply was aggressive and meant to challenge me.

"No. Neither of you will go. This is my battle. I allowed her to die. This is my battle. Mine alone."

"How is that?" Aissa questioned. "She is our family. Been our family for years before your existence was even known. I know you loved her, I know she adopted you as family as we had done her but she was ours from day one. We gave our life to one another and we will give our life *for* one another. It is a matter of Amirontian loyalty, Amirite pride and no Marinite – not even you, can ever interfere in that!"

I inhaled deeply. Mentally matched her height, a feat I would never in reality achieve. I considered being defiant, adamant about avenging Jayde solo. But it was, as she said, Amirontian pride that drove them. A pride that I had reminded her of. It was a cultural requirement and I would have to kill all three of them if I wanted to get by them alone. Certain death by my hands, or potential death at the hands of an abominable creature on a foreign planet with soldiers that would seek to imprison us if not murder us in cold blood if we were detected by them first.

My shoulders softened and subsequently theirs did as well. I had absolutely no plan. Follow the shadows to the base. Crouch in the hold nearest until the final sun set before using the cover of darkness to blanket our mission.

"She is *The Anointed*," Tabia screamed as she charged toward us. "You cannot go! She cannot go, she is The Anointed!"

My jaw clenched tight and murder filled my eyes. "You know not of what you speak, now move before I move you!"

She challenged me. "Then you will do what you must. You are right, Liv. I have never truly liked you and I *never* will. But this is not about you. Unfortunately, Deus presented *you* with the gift of savior. I have no right to question what She does and can only accept and respect this reality. I love Jayde and I fully understand the rights, responsibilities, and rituals that my heritage dictates but no Amirite is greater than this. Not even Jayde is worth this sacrifice."

"What has gotten into you, Tabia?"

"You do not understand, Raj. You need to trust me. You have to understand. Liv could die and that would seal a fate that you do not even wish to imagine."

"Then she will die at our side defending the honor of one of ours."

"She is *the one*!"

"Are you mad?"

"This is greater than honor! You believe in the myth of the Hunter but not of The Anointed Daughter?"

Aissa stepped forward. "Honor is everything. You have no proof of this allegation but I know for a fact that Jayde is dead else she would be here. Let us go and find this creature."

"I will not."

"What?" Faraji's face contorted. "Coward. I should kill you where you stand."

"These threats coming from a disgrace who prefers the company of giji boys. Do as you must but Liv is The Anointed Daughter. Foolish Ami. Because you choose not to believe you will seal our fate forever. I would rather die!"

Faraji moved forward with Tabia anticipating his move and following his lead. I hardly blinked before each held a grip on the neck of the other. Eyes were red and spittle edged their lips. They would die by their own hands.

I used the opportunity to dart past. I would not be able to bargain with either as both were beyond reason. I cared not what they did to one another. My focus was in one place and I was determined to achieve my goal. They were Aissa's responsibility, not mine.

I exited before they noticed I was gone, leaving their disagreement behind. Leaving Aissa confused but ultimately choosing Jayde as her priority. I heard her footsteps traveling quickly at my rear.

I had no idea how the battle would end, no clue if Tabia would lose her life to Faraji. I did not care. For me, in the moment, the only thing that mattered was avenging Jayde's death and, with any luck, I would even retrieve her body and allow her a proper, traditionally Amirontian burial. I kept forward, fixated on my goal with the trail of one, then suddenly two sets of footsteps following me.

Twelve
Recon Mission

GREEN PASTURES SURROUNDING ME. I STAND IN ITS midst, gazing out. My heart swells and its beat skips. My eyelids lower and my head falls away as the familiar scent of braised kindali balls waft toward me and tickles my nose. I look around frantically then stop. My eyes fall upon that hypnotic rocking of the Apigari's delicate waves.

For a moment I frown and doubt what I am witnessing with my very eyes. I am unsure if this is even a possibility. I walk forward, slowly at first but progress quicker until, before I realize what is happening, I am running.

I hear a scream or more like a squeal, a shrill noise that deafens my ears. It takes a moment before I realize the noise has escaped from my own lungs. I run in circles, kicking my legs and sending the rivers spray up to water the land near its edge.

I am a child again. It is an impossibility but I do not care, not at all. The warmth of the sparkling waters embrace my legs up to my knees before I halt. I turn sharply, facing the vast spans of land. And there it is.

I gasp, exhale awkwardly then manage to catch my breath.

"Mira," I gasp. "Mira?"

I repeat her title as I fight against the force of the powerful fluid and stumble onto dry ground. The shanty is in the distance, in the same serene location as when I was just a child running wild on Ashtwor. It is the same place that I was raised. It has not changed, not a bit.

And I reason against the unreasonable. If the Apigara continued its magnificent flow and the home of my youth remained in tact eleven tanometers from the water's edge...if the greenery that lined the distance of my path home continued to grow the sweetest green Obi berries one would ever have the privilege to taste, then my Mira must certainly still be inside the little shanty alive and well.

So I run while simultaneously working hard to calm my nerves and uncontainable exuberance, lest I collapse from the strain on my heart. Thoughts and curiosity regarding Pete and Sarai cross my mind as I land hard on the stoop before the front door.

I jump back from it, afraid to touch it ... afraid of what I may encounter beyond it. The door is ajar and that scent is much stronger and even more alluring. I swallow the lump in my throat and try with all within to steady my nerves.

Slowly, I raise my arm and reach for the door, pushing it

lightly, my phalanges shaking terribly. I push a second time with greater force and wait as the door creaks open wider.

It is dark on the inside. The only light streaming through the small openings is from outdoors. I step in and look around, straining to see. As my eyes adjust I realize that nothing has changed, nothing is out of place. It is as though time has stood still and rather than being comforted by this familiarity, I am bothered by it though I cannot understand why.

Panic rips through me. Suddenly I am terrified of what discoveries may lie beyond this room. I open my mouth to speak but there are no words. I clear my throat and try again. A hoarse sound leaves my diaphragm and I walk across the shanty, careful not to make too much noise and stir an unseen force.

A soft noise, like the sound of a floorboard being disturbed, rattles me and I turn toward the cooking room. My pace quickens with my heart, motivated by an intense curiosity.

I stop abruptly at the entrance and stare at the back of a woman sitting before the huge table in one of the large chairs. My eyes trail the length of dark hair that conceal the entire backside of the chair. My eyes water and my hands tremble incessantly.

"Mira?" I ask uneasy.

She adjusts then turns in her seat to face me. Her eyes are wet with tears of her own when they meet mine. Her eyes belong to my mira – but that is not who I am looking at.

"My child," she whispers.

I instinctively take a step back. "You are not–"

She stands, this woman with my mira's eyes, and seems to

float in my direction. I force myself to stand my ground. Little in life has ever roused fear within me but in this moment a chill runs down my spine.

"Olivia." She speaks my name clear. She speaks it as though she knows who I am.

My head shakes non-stop. "You are not Mira."

She smiles gently. "No, I am not. I am Carolyn, Elizabeth's second-born child. I am your musha."

"No. That is not possible. My musha — Carolyn, she is dead. Dead before I was ever born."

She stretches her hand toward me and though at first I flinch and move out of reach, as though by some magical force my arms move forward and allow her to take my hands into hers.

"I have already visited with my daughter, Diana. She is prepared for what is to come. Prepared for her sacrifice. You must allow her the opportunity to fulfill her obligation to destiny, my child. You must fulfill your own."

I shake my head in a state of confusion. The thoughts running through my mind are chaotic but the only words I can find the strength to release are, "I do not know…" an incomplete thought.

"You are tied to a much greater destiny, Olivia. I know you fight against believing the things that you have been told, and you are right to do so. But that does not mean others are wrong about you."

I snatch my hands away and return them to my possession. "Who are you? What do you want from me?"

"You are so beautiful, just like your mother. You look very much like me as well but … Deus' light shines brighter than anyone who has ever carried it. The aura is extraordinarily powerful in you. It is clear that Deus has chosen you."

My being reflects in her eyes. Trepidation consumes me. I look down to my hands. No concealor is present, only the golden glow of my natural flesh. I push the sleeves of my green jacket up and am horrified by my discovery.

My jaw drops open and my eyes go to hers. The glow of my eyes reflect in the glow of hers, the intensity nearly blinding me.

"For now, Olivia. For this generation, *you* are the one. My blessing was passed on to you but with much greater strength. Your aura is at its peak. Now is your time."

I cannot find words to properly express the emotions consuming me. "What is the meaning of this?" I command, referring to my own skin. "No. No! Who are you?"

"There is no time for foolish questions and there is no time to waste. I know that my very own mother pretended to not believe and in teaching you not to believe she did you – did us all – a grave disservice but now, my lil'eail, you must find a way to part with the fallacies you were bred upon and step into your rightful place as mother of a new and just nation."

"This is preposterous. You are not here. You are not alive!"

"Olivia, you must listen to me. You have a responsibility. The aura was passed from my mother to me but it was not strong enough that I was able to survive and fulfill prophecy. It was not written for me. Do you really not see what is right before you? Are you so blind, naïve, or so stupid that you truly cannot see what is right before you?

"Or maybe you are afraid of your reality. It was written into *your* destiny and you must not allow your own foolish pride to doom another generation of people. If you fail, Deus only knows when the aura will return and even worse, how many more generations will have to suffer."

I stand beneath the archway listening to what she is saying, questioning how any of this is even possible.

"I do not even know how I came to be here—"

"I summoned you."

"And you expect I should listen to someone I do not even know? A ghost? Someone who claims to be my musha? My musha is dead. Gone before I was even born. Gone when Diana was barely even living!"

Rage shadows her face. "Yet you were prepared to believe that I was your mira who, too, is dead! It is now *your* responsibility. And if you fail to accept, the collapse of an entire generation of Marinites will weigh upon *your* head and yours alone!"

Her eye color shifts, becomes clear. Reminds me of the Seer Mala.

"My only responsibility is to myself, Jayde, and Diana."

I turn and head to the door. Unaware of how I came to be at Ashtwor, I would gather mud at the bank of the Apigara and find my way back to The City no different than I had once before.

"And by giving your life to fulfill a responsibility to Jayde, how will you meet your responsibility to Diana?"

I freeze. Diana. I wonder if she is still where Jayde and I left her to heal, wonder if she is safe.

I shake off the effects of the warning—or threat. I know it is a trick. It is none other than Mala trying to meet some agenda—what, I do not know—but I will not fall victim. I must save Jayde's soul. I cannot allow her to stop me.

The ghost is gone and I am outside facing a closed door. I jump from the stoop and run from the shanty, run into the field. But I stop so abruptly that I nearly lose my footing and topple forward. I look to the waters and know that something is, in fact, different. The flow is reversed. How did I not notice before? I close my eyes and shake my head, open them and look again.

"Olivia," her voice calls after me. "Olivia!"

A figure is standing in the distance between the river and me. I gasp. "Charleston."

But when I blink, he is gone.

✝

"LIV, IT IS TIME."

I jumped to my feet quickly, poised for attack. I was vulnerable. Disoriented. I did not know where I was. In the dim light I focused on the face of the person before me speaking, but was unable to comprehend what was being said.

I glanced about. The luscious greenery was replaced by granite and gravel. The crystal waters evaporated into darkness, its dank humidity the only evidence of its previous existence. Panic shot through me and I looked down to my hands that I had thrust before me. I pushed the sleeves of my jacket up.

I needed more light and rushed forward to the mouth of the hold, looking over my arms, brown and rich, and sighed my relief. I shook away my dreams and beautiful fantasies and welcomed my reality as best as I could. I turned around and looked into the face of Faraji, as masculine as I had ever seen him, awaiting my directive on how to proceed with our seek-and-destroy mission. His face held a concerned expression. His lips moved but I heard nothing.

A feeling nagged at me, an annoying awareness that told me that what we were about to do was not right. My fantasy faded in the face of a harsh reality and I found it difficult to recall just what the message had been.

Aissa stepped closer. "Liv, are you alright?"

I shook away my fear and discontent. "I am fine. Let us do this."

Faraji and Aissa stood poised and ready for a war but were unable to proceed without my leadership. I still had not made a move and the two were unfamiliar with the territory and had no idea what to do next. There would be an obscene amount of soldiers inside the base. Were we confronted with battle we would never make it to Dorolard and our anticipated confrontation with the Hunter who was now the hunted.

"Olivia—" Faraji began.

"Follow my steps. Stick to the shadows. You must become invisible. You must not so much as breathe. If either of you are even suspected we are as good as dead."

The pair nodded. I inhaled deeply and crept quietly to the very edge of the hold and peered out from its darkness and into the darkness of night that we had patiently awaited the arrival of. Distant sound created an acute awareness of the danger that loomed.

The three of us eased into the stygian night. The dark, our protector ... our sentry. A weight pressed down upon my shoulders. The responsibility of another's fate, let alone two, slowed me. I focused and refocused as we braved the ways leading to the base.

I stopped abruptly, reaching my arm back, palm up. My entire being stilled. I listened and waited. My brow furrowed and I snapped my head back and looked between Aissa and Faraji. I tuned into the two for a moment before my angry glare fixated on Aissa. I narrowed my eyes and gently placed a phalanx to my lips. The sound of her breaths died into a mere inaudible whisper.

I returned my focus to our surroundings and we proceeded forward onto base – the lion's den. We moved deeper inside, surrounded on nearly all sides by impending danger, heart held in a vice grip to muffle the threatening sound of its beat. Adrenaline coursed through me as we dodged the eye of a camera with a mission of its own – to capture rogue citizens and escapees.

But we were not after them, not here on a rescue mission. I was no longer interested in SRA's purpose. They need not pursue us. Our enemy was their enemy, which, in essence, made us an ally of the Allegiance. If captured maybe we could plead our way to freedom and free access aboard a ship aimed for Dorolard, as the very nature of the beast we sought out put their soldiers directly in harms way.

We would be an asset.

"Halt! Who is there?" I froze. I knew that I was clear but turned to see which of my companions had been detected. "Identify yourself."

Confusion swept through me as I assessed Raj and Aissa's confounded gaze at me. It appeared that Faraji had been seen, but how so without the lot of us being noticed. He looked from me to the soldier who was looking and aiming his weapon in his general direction.

The soldier commanded, "Show yourself, now, or I will shoot!"

I assessed the scenario quickly. For a brief moment my line of vision went beyond Faraji and I understood what was happening. Fury and angst exploded inside of me. Just as I fixed my lips to whisper a command for Faraji to stay put, he defied every law of covert ops and stepped from our protective shadows, revealing himself in the light.

"Wh-what is the meaning of this?" the soldier asked, cocking his weapon for release.

I cursed myself for ignoring better judgement and leaving Faraji as a sacrifice, but rather let my presence be known by jumping in front of him, hands in the air.

"What is going on here? What is this?" His eyes raised and, confused, he asked dumbly, "Who are you?"

Faraji, realizing that he had unnecessarily blown our cover, swore.

I moved my head cautiously, just enough to see the original focus of the soldier's attention, but not so much so to get myself killed. The true target, dressed convincingly in the fashion of

SRA leadership, casually stepped to where we were being held hostage. "Who am I? *Who am I?*" he asked in a raised voice and incredulous tone.

"Should I recognize you, sir?"

"Who I am is Charleston Kelsard, soldier. Now release your lever and lower your weapon before you do something that you will surely regret."

"Kelsard, sir?"

"That would be correct."

"And ... forgive me sir, but how will you prove this?"

Charleston exhaled, intentionally displaying his annoyance at being questioned as he retrieved his forged citizenship card and shared it with the low level worker.

"Is this sufficient?"

The guard lowered his weapon but did not holster it. "My apologies, sir. I am very sorry."

"Your pathetic apology will not restore the dignity that you have stripped me of, you imbecile."

"I apo–... I am sor–... with such a delicate mission, sir ... you must understand my hesitation. But sir, what I cannot understand is why – and please forgive me for questioning your authority ... sir."

"Well, perhaps you should not deem to question me," Charleston snorted arrogantly. "I appreciate your thoroughness soldier but while you were focused upon me," Charleston reached into the dark, grabbing Aissa firmly by her neck and snatched her forward, "you were going to simply allow these three rogues to slip by."

I cut my eyes to meet Aissa's, sending an unspoken message that I could only hope she would understand and heed. Her eyes connected to mine and the flickering flames died slightly.

"Sir, I did not–"

"Of course not. Soldier, check the perimeter for more rogues. I will deal with these three myself."

"Yes, sir. I will radio for backup."

Charleston stepped closer to the Marinite soldier. "That will not be necessary. Two females and a giji boy? I think I can handle them."

Charleston eased a weapon from his side and aimed it at Faraji's head.

"But sir, this is not your responsibility. Maybe it is best for me to summon back up."

Charleston seemed to, for a moment, ponder this option. "I will tell you what. Maybe it is best not to take soldiers from their post and risk other criminals getting by them. I will hold them here while you secure the perimeter. When you are done, you can be the one to take them in."

The soldier hesitated, as though he thought better of it. Though clearly not convinced he turned away, lifting his weapon defensively and did as he was instructed.

"Hurry soldier. I will be waiting."

"Yes, sir."

We were still and silent as we waited for the soldier to disappear around the bend. Raj's and my hands remained in the sky, Aissa still held firm. Once the soldier was completely out of sight, Charleston released his grasp. Aissa gasped for air as her hand went up to massage her throat.

"You had better damn well have a reasonable explanation for this," Aissa hissed.

My arms dropped to my side and my facial muscles drew together as I charged him. "What is the meaning of this? What are you doing here?" I asked, my voice a raspy whisper. "Are you trying to have us taken captive or killed?"

"Now is not the time to discuss this, Olivia –"

"You have ruined everything. Now they know we are here –"

"Which is why we must leave. Right now."

"What do you hope to achieve –"

Charleston aimed his weapon at me. "Walk. Fast."

"I should kill you," I snarled.

"If you do not move right now, we will *all* be killed. If you have ever trusted me before, I need for you to summon that faith now. All of you. Now again, walk. And be quick about it."

Charleston grabbed Aissa once again, with great force, pulling her to him and placing his large loaded weapon at her temple. I looked from her murderous eyes and into Charleston's serious expression before nodding my approval to Faraji and doing as told.

As we moved further away from our goal, I cringed and boiled inside my fury. Further into the open we were led, making our presence fully known. I seethed. With each step that led me from my self-prescribed healing, Charleston made himself more of an enemy to me.

We were mere steps from the exit of the base. Mission involuntarily aborted, for now at least. I would accept his will. Deal with him in my way when the time was right and return to fulfill this duty on my own. Had it been that way to begin with, none of this would have happened. No soldier would have spotted me let alone the likes of Charleston Kelsard.

The sound of laughter rang out. Charleston hesitated but decided to move confidently forward.

"Hey. You there."

The four of us turned slowly to find ourselves face to face with a small cluster of soldiers.

"Carry on, soldiers. I have control of this situation here," Charleston attempted.

The group halted and looked to one another to answer the unspoken question of proper protocol. Charleston gave instruction for us to proceed as though he truly had ultimate authority. We continued forward as a soldier, previously unseen, stepped from the back of the group.

He strolled casually toward us as he took a drag off a caniron stick he held to his lips. He turned and handed it off before speaking.

"Identify yourself, sir," the soldier commanded.

Charleston's voice was strong and assured when he replied, "Does my dress not exhibit my authority, soldier?"

"I beg your forgiveness, sir. Your dress may speak authority, however your face is unrecognized. This mission, as you well know, sir, is extremely restrictive with very limited superior officers involved."

"Of course."

"Well, it seems that we have a slight problem here."

"It would seem that way."

"We have been personally notified of each superior that we are to report to ... sir."

"I do not know what to say to you. Apparently someone failed to do their job this time."

"Indeed."

My eyes were locked upon the soldier's hand. I picked up the rhythm of his phalanges as they drummed the weapon at his side. My line of vision shifted cautiously as I surveyed my surroundings and the demeanor the soldier's colleagues wore. I watched as courage returned to their hearts and they stood at the ready of the one taking lead.

"And what of these citizens?"

"Infiltrating rogues that I have personally captured. Clearly someone else is not properly doing their job."

"What the hell is going on here, Liv?" Faraji asked me through gritted teeth.

I whispered my response. "No idea but ... trust him."

The soldier stepped closer. "Allow us the honor of doing so now, Lega—"

"Kelsard."

The soldier reflexively stepped back. His confidence fleeting, but making swift recovery. He mumbled the name. "Forgive my rudeness, sir, but you do not quite have the traditional appearance of Marinite."

"I am unclear what that means but I will be certain to pass the message along to my parents. Now, carry on so that I can deal with these prisoners."

The soldier, clearly unconvinced, frowned. "Why not allow us to take care of that little inconvenience. Quath, radio the tower—"

I watched as the soldier's hand moved slowly away from his weapon as his arms rose into the air. I glanced back to see Charleston's extended arm, ready to discharge death from his blaster rod into the center of the soldiers head.

His tone was even when he spoke. "Go. Now."

I asked no questions. Did not need to be told twice. I fled with Faraji and Aissa on my heels before his command even had time to catch up to my ears.

I had no idea where I was going or whether or not more soldiers awaited me. Death whizzed by and I ducked low. I could not understand what Charleston's purpose was in putting us in this position. All I knew is that he was clearly on our side.

My options had run out, I had to trust in him and whatever his mission was. I turned back to see if he was even still with us. A beam shot past me.

"Get down," I screamed to Aissa and Faraji.

Faraji dropped just in time to not have his head split in half.

"Come on!"

I heard the voice and looked up to find Charleston nestled anxiously inside a transport. I shoved Raj and grabbed Aissa firmly and pulled her inside as Charleston used his weapon to stave the soldier's off.

"Can you drive?" he asked. I hesitated. "Olivia, can you drive?"

"I can." Faraji jumped into the seat as Charleston climbed out.

"Follow," he instructed as he passed his weapon to Aissa.

I climbed into the back of the transport with Charleston. He reached further back and pulled forth a large, glistening object and tossed it into my hands.

"Deus knows, I hope your instincts are as good as legend claims them to be," he said as he grabbed a much larger version of what he had given to me.

I looked to him, trying to figure out what I was to do when he opened the top hatch and stood, pulling the object through and placing it on his shoulders. His phalanges reeled back a trigger followed immediately by an explosion.

A weapon!

I shot through the opening as Faraji peeled through the night with soldiers hot on our trail. I reeled back and released, letting the ammo explode taking a soldier down, hopefully permanently. Adrenaline sent a rush to my head. The soldier's weapons were incomparable to what we were using. Weapons I had not ever before known existed.

Another shot caused one of the official transports to swing

out and cut off a second. I used the opportunity to aim dead center, reel back and release. A flash blinded me momentarily, followed by the sound of contact being made with my target, destroying both vehicles and likely eliminating everyone inside.

Charleston followed up my round. The transport he aimed to wreck swerved, then pulled back and was soon lost beyond the yellow ball of heat and flame that I had created.

We stayed our position, poised and waiting for more brave soldiers to reveal themselves. The night quieted and the flames died to a flicker in the distance.

"Where do I go?" Faraji called out, anxiously.

Charleston re-entered the transport first, then me. He advised Faraji that he would take charge and the two switched places. I nudged Aissa and she followed Raj to the rear of the transport. I aimed the weapon, my newfound plaything, at the side of Charleston's face.

He did not flinch nor look my way. My expression and voice were controlled when I spoke. "I am going to ask you this question once again, now that I do not have SRA soldiers itching to kill me or take me into custody. What is the meaning of your presence tonight?"

"Olivia, you may want to put that away before you accidentally do something that you will regret."

"Who says it will be an accident?"

He heaved a heavy sigh and grunted. "You were about to make a terrible mistake. I just saved you from yourself."

"You have no idea what I was about to do. I did not need

saving. I was about to right a grievous wrong!"

"You were about to die!"

"Then that would have been my choice! I can take care of myself."

"Oh, I do not doubt that."

I pondered, then lowered the weapon. I turned away and looked into the darkness ahead of us.

"What is this thing?" I asked referring to the heavy piece of artillery that I caressed as though it were an innocent marineal.

"An X15 Lanier – junior." He turned to me and winked.

"Never heard of it."

"My father is a weapons maker. These are his creations."

I nodded. Silence settled between us for a few moments.

"Is this it?" Aissa asked, enraged. "You show up out of nowhere, take us hostage. And like that, the dialogue is done? Turns to weaponry and family business?"

I turned to face Aissa, my expression giving up nothing of my inner turmoil. As difficult as it would be to admit, there was a small part of me that was relieved. I was no coward but I was not ready to leave Diana childless again.

"What more would you like for me to say, Aissa?" Charleston queried. "I did what was right."

"How did you know *where* to find us? *Why* did you find us? What exactly do you *want* from us? Start there."

Charleston's eyes remained fixed on the path ahead. "All very good questions."

I returned my gaze to the road.

"Have you any equally good responses?"

"In due time."

Aissa was flustered. She had every right to feel so. I settled into myself, content that, for the moment, I knew exactly all I needed to know. Something in his voice, his expression … his eyes, something had betrayed him and given me what I needed to know.

I was not exactly aware how he came to know my plans but, more importantly, I knew – and was beginning to accept – why.

Thirteen
Revelations

I ALLOWED MYSELF TO DRIFT AWAY INTO A LIGHT slumber, grateful that no dreams of fate and fallacies filled my mind, disrupting my opportunity for rest.

For the moment I was at peace. For the first time in quite a while I felt at ease and I knew the reason for it was behind the controls of the transport. Charleston's presence somehow made everything okay. I did not feel a need to be a warrior when he was around, though my defenses never dropped fully.

Simultaneously I felt toward him a way that caused me discomfort. A paradox I was in whenever Charleston was around. His scent possessed me. A mix of crushed dragena and another, unfamiliar fragrance. I tried my very best to pretend as though I was not disturbed.

The path beneath us smoothed out and I relaxed, occasionally being jarred to life by the negative emission of emotions coming from Aissa who sat behind me. She was desperate for answers that I wondered if she would prove strong enough to handle.

I thought of Diana and wondered whether she was comfortable. I hoped she was healthy ... safe. I had not thought of her on my mission to Dorolard. In a sense my going could only be beneficial to her. I was the reason she was in her present state of despair. I was who Dupec wanted and in my absence she was mishandled. She was beat down but not destroyed.

If I were gone for good ... murdered on a foreign planet, I saw no reason for her to be any worse off than she already was. I had done all that I could to care for her, all that I could to protect her. Now she was done with SOTA and living in a home in a secret village far away from The City. For all intents and purposes, safe.

Better off without me.

The transport slowed, turned and slowed more. I was jarred back to consciousness as we stopped. I looked about at our surroundings beneath the reddish haze of an early morning. My eyes took in the breathtaking view. The sun revealed a selection of colors that even the finest artist could not articulate.

Rolling greens created a path for miles and exotic flowers jutted from rich soil. Trees flanked each side of a massive cabin home. Charleston gave energy once again as he turned the wheel and aimed at the most kept shanty I had ever seen.

The transport rolled to a stop on the gravel road. Dust spiraled up and about us. Charleston sat in silence, enraptured by his intimate thoughts. His eyes fixed to the side of the wooden structure. It was as though he could see through it from where he sat.

"Well? Do we now get to know what is going on?" Aissa asked.

Charleston unlatched the door and climbed out. He appeared even taller in the early morning sunlight. I exited with Aissa and Faraji following.

"Charleston, where are we?" I asked placidly.

He gazed into the distance. "My father's compound."

I took it all in. An awe-inspiring visual that stimulated the senses. Huge royal poincianas provided shade to much of the land. Their orange leaves blazed beneath the rays of the rising sun. Glorious unrecognizable plants edged out the soft green blades of grass.

I placed a hand broadside against my forehead and gazed into the distance at what appeared to be a massive pool of glistening jewels.

"Is that—" I began.

"Ittas Lake."

My arm fell to my side. "You live here."

"I was raised here. My father raised us here … on this land."

Aissa and Faraji seemed to have momentarily forgotten that they had come to be here strictly by force. So had I.

"Ittas Lake," I repeated. "Why?"

"What?"

"Why would someone that had the ability to live here…to

live surrounded by such beauty, why come to The City to live and work?"

Charleston exhaled heavily and chewed at his lower lip before nodding his head in the direction of the shanty.

"I need to share something with you, Olivia."

"Okay. What is it?"

He signaled for me to come toward him. I looked over to Aissa and Faraji and signaled for them to follow. We trailed along a small paved lane adorned by flowers that ran alongside the shanty and led to a shed in back, nearly as large.

"My father, Akelo Kelsard," Charleston began as we approached the large green shed, "comes from a long line of hard working blacksmiths. They have crafted and perfected some of the finest tools in our history. During the Shadow Wars my great-grandfather, Oüske, was recruited by Claude Ustek who knew that he would need weapons if he hoped to stand any chance of eventually defeating Kedt.

"Although we were not a family of armorers, but merely blacksmiths, Great Grandpa was especially talented and he soon began creating weaponry of exceptional quality. When Henry Kelsard and Taaman Dupec took charge, he and my grandfather were forced into servitude. My father was committed to continue in their place and so on. It became our legacy of sorts, albeit one forced upon us."

Charleston grabbed both handles of the shed and, with a bit of force, pulled the heavy doors open wide. My gasp attached itself to Faraji and Aissa's giving the sound of one heavy wind gust.

Charleston stepped aside allowing us entrance. Weapons of every form were everywhere my eyes landed. I stepped inside and stopped. My eyes roamed from one end of the shed to the other. I eased forward in slow motion. My jaw dropped in my amazement.

He continued to tell his tale. "My father created arms for SRA for many long years, until one day he decided our family had fulfilled their duty."

My phalanges grazed the edge of a large, awkward shaped object that was unfamiliar, though I was sure was packed with the power to destroy.

"Can one simply decide that? To be done?" Faraji questioned.

Charleston chuckled cynically. "No. No, one cannot."

I turned on my heel to face him. "Wait a second. You told me that you did not know Henry Kelsard. Said you never set foot on his compound."

He looked ashamed. "Partially true. I never met him."

"Why did you lie?"

"I did not want to scare you away. *Henry Kelsard is my relative* is not always the best pick up line."

"Sooo, what? He just left SRA? Put in a 2-week resignation notice?" Faraji asked this question while carefully lifting a magnificent sword.

Charleston chuckled. "Nooo ... if only it were that simple." His mind seemed to drift away once again. Was as though he were recalling something distant, far away.

"Charleston," I spoke.

He snapped back into reality and turned to face me. "If you are going to do battle like a soldier, you must have a weapon to match."

I approached a table in the center of the shed where swords of a variety of shapes, sizes, and styles lay in wait. I touched one delicately, as though I were afraid that disturbing it would cause it to jump up and slice me.

Charleston stepped behind me, closing in and violating my personal space. I could feel his breath against me, and a chill and tingle simultaneously shot through my body.

"How can I know which weapon to choose? Will you recommend one for me?"

His hand landed on mine as I stroked the casing of another sword.

"Olivia, you do not choose a weapon. The weapon chooses you." He stood close enough that his lips nearly touched my ear.

I swallowed hard my affinity for him and nodded while trying to figure just how to solicit the desire of the perfect tool.

"Liv," Aissa called to me. "You should leave those silly knives along and come over here. Choose something with fire power."

I nodded while stepping away from the table and sidestepping Charleston. "Aissa is probably correct." I glanced back just long enough for his eyes to lock onto mine, causing my cheeks to warm. Swiftly, I broke our gaze and walked toward Aissa to review the options that adorned the wall.

"What sort of ridiculous weapon is this?" Faraji asked. We turned to see the small wooden block that he held under examination in his hand.

Charleston grinned. "*That* is the most powerful, most effective piece of equipment on this table. The best in this room. In the right hands, that is."

My head cocked and my eyes narrowed, focusing onto what Raj held.

"It is a piece of wood," he said, turning it over and over in his hand before bouncing it up and down.

"To you," Charleston responded.

Faraji looked from the wood between his phalanges to Charleston and back. He shrugged and sat it down, moving on. Bored with the less than impressive accoutrement, Aissa turned back to evaluate the arms, mentally comparing and contrasting to be prepared in the event she was offered the opportunity to take one.

I looked away to examine a weapon with the letters DI100 etched on the side but my mind returned to the innocuous block of wood.

"Liv, how about this one here?" Aissa asked, her eyes on a massive piece of metal. "It looks to be very powerful."

"Uh hunh." I turned away. Still fascinated by the wood and curious as to how it could possibly be deemed 'most deadly', I walked to where it sat amongst large and lavish swords. I took it into my hand. It was a smooth, polished solid wood, petite enough to hold between my thumb and initial phalanx. I turned it over and over looking for something, some sign that made it special. Some justification for the feeling that was washing over me.

"Charleston," I began, "how do you know?"

"How do you know what?"

"When an inanimate object is calling you, how do you know?"

His eyes widened as he pushed himself off the wall that he was leaning against. His gaze connected firmly to mine.

"You know. I cannot explain how, you just know."

Aissa turned to me. "Amen Deus, child. What will you do with that thing? Give someone a nasty knot?"

"Raj, I highly recommend you step as far away as you can. Quickly," Charleston ordered.

Faraji said no words. He hesitated but soon his footsteps took him out of my range as I continued to fumble with the object.

Aissa laughed and rolled her eyes in frustration as she began to approach me. "It is merely a block of wood. What is the big deal?"

"Aissa, no!" Charleston yelled.

It all happened so fast; before I realized I had made a move. I stood holding my breath with the wood block firmly inside my hand, my eyes wide with amazement. I surveyed the room slowly.

Faraji stood near the open door, drained of color with his heart in his throat and eyes filled with stupefaction. Aissa lay partway on the ground with Charleston on top of her where the pair landed after he had saved her life. She looked up at me; mouth agape, reeling from her brush with death.

My eyes landed on the tip of a blade. It glistened in the light and curved, three small teeth protruding. A hook jutted from the other side and curved in the opposite direction.

My eyes roved slowly, trailing the incredible length until I reached the small wooden block, continued beyond my palm and followed the second blade that was a perfect opposing replication of the first one.

"How did you do that?" Faraji whispered.

"I-I-I do not know."

"It is true." Charleston spoke more to himself than anyone around him.

I looked up, startled by his voice. "What? What is true?"

"I cannot … I cannot believe … I know that I must but…"

I swallowed hard and looked from him to the incredible and impressive piece of steel in my control. I hesitated, then pressed my thumb and flicked my wrist left then right and within a millisecond, both blades returned to their rightful home, tucked safely inside a small, innocuous block of wood.

I opened my palm. The block rested peacefully. Aissa and Charleston pushed themselves back to their feet. Faraji approached with reserve. My eyes went to Charleston's.

"This is it. This is the one."

Charleston took a deep breath and smiled, revealing all teeth. "As are you."

"What are you talking about?"

"My father did not just have the sudden presence of mind to leave SRA. My family had served as Armory Makers for three generations. I would be groomed to take over. My father left with me when I was small. He was instructed to leave. My fate, he was told, was directly connected with that of the Anointed Daughter."

My smile dropped. My joy fled. I sat the block firmly upon the table and walked to the open shed doors. "I do not want to hear anymore."

I listened to the sound of him hurrying to follow behind me. "My pregnant mother made him go. An Arethonian half-blood, she was mighty and strong-willed and she and my grandfather and great-grandfather so believed, that they sacrificed their lives so that my father could escape with me. So he could create your perfect weapon. So that he could bring you and me together to fulfill our mutual destiny."

I stopped and faced him. "Oh, so now there is not a one but the two?"

He stepped as close as he could and looked down into my eyes. "There is only one. Just you. There is only you."

"No. No, not you too with this nonsense."

"My father had a vision on the night of the third lunar moon, seventeen years before when the eastern sun had settled."

I covered my mouth with my hand and looked away from him. "When I was born."

I stood silently, searching for a defense or some sort of explanation. There was none. Charleston reached toward me slowly. My eyes returned to his, watched as he reached for my beloved hat. I did not stop him. I allowed him to ease it away, revealing the short curly locs with the golden roots.

He took my chin between his thumb and phalanx, his eyes

never leaving mine. With firm, gentle strokes he scraped at the concealor on my cheek. Its freshness gave way with ease and in moments a golden streak had been revealed.

I heard the sound of a sharp intake of breath. I faced Aissa.

"It is ... true?" Her voice trailed away first, then raised aggressively. "It is true?!"

I let go a ragged breath. Leaning my head forward, I took my phalanges to my eyes and removed the dark film and, for the first time, revealed my true self in front of my friends.

"You *are* the one," Faraji spoke with certainty. "Tabia was *right*? Well, I will be a graydurs second tail, Tabia was right ... you really are Goldenborn."

Aissa turned away, shaking her head in disappointment – or disbelief. I called after her but, with a raised palm, she continued forward.

"Issa, please."

She ceased abruptly. Turned angrily toward me. "We are friends, Liv. We are *supposed* to be friends. You kept this from us. How could you do that? Why? Why would you?"

"Because I did not believe! I figured I was simply a Concealor, like every other. A Concealor that got lucky on occasion. What would you have had me to do?"

"Tell us the truth. Give us that much respect. Did you think we would turn you in? Are we so untrustworthy?"

"It is not that. What if Razi had found out? He would have turned me in to SRA without thought, and no intervention by Jayde or by you would have stopped him. I would have been the ritualistic sacrifice for the furthering of his political career and you know that I am correct, Aissa. "

"Razi would not have found out."

"You cannot be so sure, nor could I. I wanted to, I really did but it was not worth the risk."

Faraji spoke again. "Tab was right. She was actually right about something."

I shrugged my shoulders and shook my head. "I am sorry, what more do you want from me. I had to protect myself."

"I do not know, this is all so much. We were going to Dorolard."

"To find Jayde's body."

Aissa moved in close, pointed a phalanx. "You could have died!" Her eyes reddened, the brims filling with fluid.

Reality hit me. The reality that I had tried to escape for all the days of my life, finally hit me. "I am sorry."

"I am not sure what to say to you right now. The fate of ... Amen Deus. Did Jayde know?"

I shook my head. "She only suspected that I was concealing."

"This is so hard to believe. All of this time."

"Then can you imagine how I have felt all of my life?" I turned to face Charleston. "So now what do I do?"

Charleston took my hand in his, then turned it palm side up. Carefully, he placed the wooden block inside.

"You step into place."

I nodded in agreement.

†

THE RETURN TRIP TO JAYDE'S FLAT WAS SHROUDED IN danger and heightened emotion. Anticipating trouble, we were heavily armed. My specialized weapon, I was told, was called a bêti. An ancient word that, roughly translated, meant *mercenary*. The word originated from Charleston's mother's native tongue, Thonti.

"So that nonsense about being full-blood?" I questioned. His response was merely a look of remorse. I paused then asked, "Do you recall anything about your mother?" I held hope that a lighter conversation would ease our tensions.

Charleston smiled brief and uncomfortable. I nodded and looked away, watching the lanes for any sign of trouble.

"It is probably not wise to travel all the way," Faraji warned.

"I agree," Charleston replied. "We will stop about 12 tms short and journey the rest."

Silence fell upon us once again and fear infected our space. We worked individually to steady ourselves, suppress the shakiness of our nerves. Engaging in combat with SRA soldiers on their territory was not unprecedented but rarely heard of. It would not be taken in stride.

"She was beautiful. Tall. Taller than my father." His voice was small and child-like when he spoke. I listened quietly. "She was ... she was the wisest, most intelligent person I have ever known. Very intelligent. Very. She knew all sorts of things. Even spoke ancient Gelish, two dialects."

"The ancient language of Marieux?" I asked in awe. He

nodded. "Is that even useful?"

"In the hills it certainly is. Some elders still speak strains. She spoke Thonti, the language of her father ... a direct descendent of Kedt."

I turned sharply at this revelation. Aissa spoke up before I could manage my thoughts. "Let me get this straight. You are a descendant of both Kelsard and Kedt."

Charleston nodded slowly. "Seems that way."

"Are you sure that *you* are not the one?" I inquired, only half serious.

He chuckled. "Quite positive. Katashi Kedt himself was her grandfather. She never knew him. She knew none but her father who secretly stowed her and her Marinite mother away somewhere on Arethoxx."

"How does a Marinite woman wind up on the planet of Arethoxx with a mixed blood for a child?"

"Good question that I have no answer for. She died long before I was self-aware enough to question it. And my father did not like to speak about her. Too painful. So the story is compiled of bits and pieces of information I have acquired from relatives over the years. But what I do know is that although Katashi Kedt does not like outsiders, he holds greater contempt for mixed blood."

"He found out."

"That he did. I cannot imagine one can get away with hiding anything for too long from a powerful person like Kedt. Imprisoned her mother and murdered her father for treason.

But in a weird and somewhat sadistic twist, it seems he holds a very high regard for blood*line*, even bloodlines contaminated by another.

"His own beliefs, albeit contradictory, would not allow him to murder one who shared the same blood as he without just cause. She was only a child. She was not at fault."

Faraji asked with intrigue, "What did he do?"

"Put her aboard a transport and dropped her here, on her mother's planet. If she would die, it would not be by his hands or order. She had only seen her 7th day at this point but she somehow managed to survive. She met my father only a few years later."

I smiled knowingly for I understood what it meant for a child to survive in foreign territory. I returned to observing the lanes ahead. I nodded as I held firmly onto the bêti that had been gifted to me, and stroked one of two Blazer R9's that were nestled in my pockets. My mind drifted to Diana and her plight. We all had our demons, all our own sad tales of pain and despair.

Fight or flight.

Some of us would fall to our knees and die in the face of despair. The others would live to fight another day.

"So she was pretty." I stated without looking up.

For a moment Charleston was silent. Was as though he were going back in time to see her again. "She was stunning. When my father was persuaded to talk, it was generally of her great beauty both inside and out. He told me that he lived in constant fear of her being taken to Kelsard or Dupec's bed and claimed as theirs. The innate Arethonian warrior in her made her extraordinarily headstrong and difficult to manage–"

"Amirontian women are taken all the time," Faraji interjected in defense of his people.

"With all due respect, Amirite women are meek when compared to an Arethonian. An *Amirontian* woman may be quite strong and aggressive but an *Arethonian* woman is vicious and deadly when trifled with."

"If you say so." The air of having been insulted rested in Aissa's response.

Charleston turned briefly toward me and smiled. "Yes, Olivia. My mother was beautiful. From what I can recall of her, she was phenomenal." Our transport pulled into a dark alleyway and slowed to a stop. "Okay kiddies. This is where we get off. I assume we all know our way from here."

Aissa and Faraji affirmed.

"We are separating?" I asked.

Charleston sighed. "I think we stand a better chance that way."

I agreed. "But you have never been here before. And you cannot creep about the darkness seeking out identifiers."

He nodded. "I will follow you."

The four of us exited the transport and slipped into the night. Activity could be heard in the distance, the lanes seemed busy. My heart raced and a euphoric sense swept over me. I had not before recognized it but this was what I lived for. The rush. The thrill. The danger. I loved it. It empowered me.

I steadied my grip on the heavy metal inside my pockets. I

looked to each member of my group who awaited my leadership in this, the area of my greatest strength.

I nodded my affirmation. And we departed.

Fourteen
Nemesis

As a child I loved to run. Running was freedom. My legs moved gracefully. The wind gathered beneath my heels and carried me forward with enviable speed. Mira would attempt but she could never keep up with me. She gave up every time. Out of breath and struggling to laugh, she would collapse into a heap upon the grass. When I realized that she had, yet again, conceded, I would stop and turn back to her, laughing and smiling and collapse into her open arms.

There we would lie upon the soft bed of grass, side-by-side, staring up into the clear sky swapping tales that we would invent, inspired by the shapes that the fluffy white clouds created.

I ran from Ashtwor. Ran most of the way into The City and I had yet to stop. Now I was running to Jayde for help. How would I know what to do ... how to proceed?

My mira was gone and Diana had no answers she cared to share with me. And Mala … I was unsure of her intentions. My best option was to return to the flat where Jayde's presence resided and hope that perhaps clarity would come. Or, maybe Tabia, who apparently dedicated much of her time to the study of this anointed phenom, would have a few ideas to spare.

†

"Pssst…"

I peered cautiously from our little hideaway below the flat my Amirontian friends called home. Several minutes had gone by and Charleston and I were becoming concerned.

"Liv?" A female voice responded.

I stepped beyond the sanctity of the crack to come face to face with Aissa. I looked both ways for a sign of Faraji but the alleyway was otherwise empty.

"Where is Raj?" I whispered.

"Amen Deus. I hoped he were here already. Where is Charleston?"

"Here," he answered emerging.

"What do we do?"

I looked into the distance again, biting down on my lip in contemplation.

"Shall we wait longer?" Charleston asked.

"There is no time to waste. He is likely to go directly inside when he arrives and does not see us. We will have to meet him there."

"But what if—"

"He is not, now lead the way."

Aissa nodded and looked both ways before guiding us up the steps and to the door of the building. She hesitated, concern peppering her face. Concern for her friend's safety. I gave her a moment before I nudged her forward. She sighed and pressed her weight into the door.

The heavy sound of footsteps jarred us, causing the three of us to jerk around, my counterparts with weapons drawn. Faraji bound the bottom steps, and then paused abruptly with hands in the air. A relieved smile lit Aissa's face.

"Did you miss me?" he asked nervously.

"Took long enough," Aissa complained as she continued forward.

"You wanted me here quickly or you wanted me here at all?"

"Touché."

We climbed the slim, steep stairwell in a tense single file. Aissa entered her key, working it until the lock popped and door creaked open.

I frowned. Something did not feel right. The aura was different. I whispered for Aissa to wait as I pushed past her and stepped inside of the flat ahead of the group. I looked around, stepping lightly. Nothing appeared out of place.

Charleston followed me inside. "What is it?"

I did not reply, just continued to move about quiet as possible, looking for something – anything to be wrong. I turned to face the others standing just inside the doorway. I shook my head. Something was wrong; I knew it but could not place it.

"I do not … I do not know," I mumbled. "I do not trust it."

"Everything appears normal, Liv," Faraji spoke.

I nodded. "I am going to gather a few things. I will … umm, be right back. Charleston, can you please come with me."

I led the way to Jayde's space, closing the door behind us. I did not know what to say. I did not know what to do or how to proceed but I could not look helpless in front of Aissa and Faraji. They were depending on me. They had gone from adamantly doubting the existence of this myth referred to as the *Anointed Daughter* to putting all of their faith and trust into the power that my newly acquired title beheld.

They were not on the mission that they had not more than a day ago signed up for; the mission to rescue and properly put to rest the corpse of our sister Jayde Nestyton. They were now at my side on a journey to save the world and I did not even know what my first step should be.

I wanted to say all of this to Charleston, pour all of this out and hope he had something for me. I trusted him and even maybe … I hoped that he could give me some guidance but I could not say a word to him. As I gathered my thoughts we were interrupted by Aissa's frantic cries. I turned and ran from the room with Charleston hot on my heels.

"What is it?" I called as I ran into her space. She did not answer me. She did not have to. I gasped, stopping abruptly steps away from Tabia's body which sat on the floor slumped over with her back to the wall, the handle of a blade protruding from her right side.

Charleston eased closer leaning into her. "She is breathing. She is still alive."

I dropped hard to my knees beside her. "Who did this to you?"

She gasped for oxygen several times, gathering up the strength to answer.

"My brother," Aissa replied before Tabia could gurgle out a response.

I looked up to her. My expression must have been sufficient to voice my inquiry for she began to answer before I could actually make an utterance.

"It is his signature. He is sending a message." Aissa swallowed hard and stepped away. Her arm swung back, tight fist landing hard against the wall causing a small crater to form. "He … he did not want her to die immediately. He counted on someone returning and … and finding her this way. Alive, but barely."

"What? Why? What kind of message and why would he need to kill Tabia to deliver a message to…" My mind trailed for a moment. I thought hard, trying my very best to make some sense of this. "The message is for me."

"No. No way. Why?" Aissa asked.

I turned to face Tabia once again. "You told him what you saw, did you not? You told him I was Goldenborn."

She struggled to nod.

I growled furiously and jumped to my feet.

"What did she see?" Charleston asked.

"Me. She saw ... *me*."

Aissa's eyes lit. "When you returned, she kept yelling at you ... rambling on about you needing to *take it off*. She *knew* what you were ... what you are."

"And you told *Razi?* Tab, why? Why would you do that?" Faraji asked. Both distressed and upset, he dropped beside her.

"But wait," I began, "he does not believe in this. Right?"

Aissa nodded. "Razi does. Always has."

Charleston joined the conversation. "Clearly I do not know anything about this brother of Aissa's, but this is not making a lot of sense. What sort of message is killing her sending to you?"

I did not understand it either. Tabia's death would not have a great impact on me. I liked her about as much as she did me, which did not speak well of our affection for one another. Torture of her that would eventually equate to murder was not a way to hurt me. Then what was it?

I lowered myself again. "Tabia, listen to me. Did Razi say anything ... before this?"

She swallowed painfully as she struggled to nod. I noticed, for the first time, the phalanx prints branded into her neck. I closed my eyes and took a deep breath. I did not like Tabia but she did not deserve this.

Her voice was a hoarse whisper. "He said ... you will ... be taken care ... of (*cough, cough*) and ... she. So will ... she."

"So he wants me to know he plans to kill me?"

She shook her head lightly and I frowned. If the message was not a threat on my life, then what?

Tabia's next words were hardly audible. I leaned in closer. "You will … you (*cough, cough*) to … him. Come to (*cough*)…"

"…him." I completed her sentence. "He wants me to come to him. But why would I … what makes him think I will just come to – Diana!"

I jumped back to my feet and pushed past the group. Rage inflamed my being. My breath came in spurts and my hand squeezed so tightly into itself that I felt the pop of skin breaking. In my pocket rested two lightweight yet very powerful weapons waiting for an enemy to be used on. And I had found an enemy in Razi Las, or rather he had found an enemy in me.

Aissa rushed after me. "You do not know that."

"Am I to be made a fool? Why would I possibly go looking for trouble in Razi? For what better reason?"

"You two do not like one another. You are Marinite and he—"

"Are you really so naïve? Or is it loyalty that compels you? What better way to make rank in SRA? Your brother is very ambitious. Hurdle over foot soldier, base, and compound guard and land directly beside his idol Taaman Dupec. A feat Dupec's own brother could not manage."

"By taking a SOTA whore like Diana?"

I cringed. "You fool. By using her he gets to me. By handing me over to Henry Kelsard and making up for a mistake that allowed my birth in the very first place."

"Diana is not who you claim, is she?"

I turned to face Charleston, leaving Aissa's question to linger in the air.

"I am going to Ayrecroft."

"What is all the way out there?"

"Diana better be. If not, I will track down Razi Las as he predicted. Unfortunately for him, and this I promise, the outcome will not be what he anticipates."

I pulled the wooden block forth and looked it over. I grazed my phalanx across it delicately and my eyes shot up to Aissa's before I continued to speak. "You are with me or against me. If you cannot go in against your own blood, against your brother, I understand but in that case you should stay. But, knowing what I intend to do, if you feel the need to fight for his honor speak up and we can settle this right now. You are armed − and so am I."

"Olivia," Charleston attempted to intercede, taking my forearm in his hand. I snatched away keeping my sights on my friend. I watched her carefully, reading her expression as her emotions and loyalties switched forward and back and around again. Ultimately her arms rose in sweet surrender and I relaxed.

I turned to face Charleston. "I am driving."

"Do you even know how?" he asked in horror. I glared. "Okay, fine. You drive."

I moved to the door feeling Aissa's eyes on me. I turned to face her. I understood her favor toward me to be conditional. That was fair. She had not believed in my existence, not since childhood. I had never believed in it myself and now she was to decide between protecting me for a greater good or standing against me on the side of a brother she had escaped to this forsaken place with.

I was fairly certain she understood that I would kill her if necessary. I would not want to but I would sacrifice her before I allowed Razi to take me down and hurt Diana. Faraji, who recognized that Razi would do the same to him as he had done to Tabia without hesitation, found no moral dilemma in choosing to side with me.

†

I WAS HAPPY THAT I HAD RELENTED ONCE THE LOT OF US regrouped at the transport. I had only experience on foot, not with technology. I focused on recalling the path we had been taken the day that Jayde and I visited Diana.

That had to be what Razi's message was. Nothing else made any sense. It was me that he wanted. Capturing Diana and delivering her to SRA's headquarters could do very little for him. It meant nothing, proved nothing. The return of a demoted whore to the home she once knew would benefit no one. The child of said whore would, however, fare quite differently.

I recognized the surroundings. The house where Diana had been left behind was very near. Charleston kept on the path that I had guided him but there was no sign of life in the distance. The sheath grass was quite tall but I recalled that there was a frame of no greater than 10 minutes beyond the place where the honey colored grass became dense before seeing the top of the home.

But I did not see it. I saw no home – but I did see smoke.

"There! Ahead!"

My breathing came crashing down hard upon me in waves as we rode nearer to the once beautiful little shanty that I had left Diana behind to call home. I had not realized that I was mumbling my angry thoughts aloud until Aissa asked what I was saying. I had no response.

We neared the home. I pushed the door open and jumped from the moving transport. Scrambling to steady my feet, I rushed toward the smoldering remains of the shanty.

"Diana," I cried out. "Diana!"

I felt myself being grabbed from behind. I did not look back nor care who was there. My eyes were focused on charred beams of wood. I could not tell if the difficulty I was experiencing breathing stemmed from my twisted emotions or the smoke that was saturating the air.

"Liv!"

I turned at the sound of my name, snatching from the grasp of Charleston. I looked across the pathway. A feeling of electricity shot through my skull. I stepped away slowly ... walked across the gravel path still lined with beautiful beds of flowers.

I took a deep breath and tilted my head, taking in the sight. The body of Galê Tas sat slumped against a tree nearest the place that she had called home. A blade protruded from between the right fourth and fifth ribs, same as Tabia.

I walked closer to her, slowly ... cautiously. Unfortunately, unlike with Tabia, we were too late. Galê Tas was already dead. Whatever message she had for me was gone to wherever her spirit had departed to.

"What do we do now?" Faraji asked from his position beside me. "Do you believe that he killed Diana in the fire?"

My eyes burned. Galê Tas' eyes were wide open – like Tabia's. I stepped closer though I had not intended to do so. I could not move my eyes from her cold, dead stare. There seemed to be life beyond the surface. I was reacting through some subconscious force that I was only vaguely aware of.

I reached out into the darkness that overcame the world around me. I could hear a voice, a voice that faded and got lost in the confusion of sounds that took over. Curses. Yelling. A strong voice commanding silence.

"Who are you? What do you want?"

The sound of physical violence, precious items being broken. A scream. Diana. The smell of wood burning coming to me stronger and louder. Screams fading into the distance. I turned my shaky palms up and looked down. Blood. Bright red blood dripped through my phalanges.

I heard my name yelled. I wanted to respond but could not find my voice. I felt paralyzed.

"Liv!"

I could see the fear in Diana's eyes. Wide open like Galê Tas' were when she was stabbed. She tried to scream for help but she could not. Something was obstructing her … or someone. I found the strength to shake my head side to side as light returned to the world. A figure faded into recognition before me.

"Olivia, answer me!"

My body was being shaken. My eyes focused on Charleston's face.

"She is not dead. He did not kill her. Not yet."

"What?"

"Diana is not dead."

"Then where is she? And how do we find her?"

I looked across the lane curiously at the sheath grass. A nerve in my temple jumped as I stepped around Charleston. There was something odd about the grass pattern. Something that did not seem to match the rest.

I nodded across the way. "I do not yet know. But he does."

I approached the edge of the lane but stopped. My jaw clenched and my eyes locked on the image of Razi Las emerging. My arm moved slowly toward my pocket.

Razi stepped closer. "You would not be reaching for something to hurt me with, now would you?" He raised his hands into the air to show me that he was unarmed.

"Are you here to return my cousin to me, or to make my killing you that much easier?"

He returned an expression that looked as though he had been startled. "Your *cousin?* Interesting. I forget, that *is* the tale you like to tell."

"Are you here to return her?"

"Now why would I go through all this trouble just to do something foolish like that? No, I do not think so. If you want her, you will have to come get her."

My ears perked up at the sound of weapons being readied behind me but I did not react to my group.

Razi continued. "Sister. Why am I not surprised to see you here."

"You killed Tab! How could you do something so cruel? She was our family."

"You are my family. And now you hand your loyalty over to this Marinite? Tabia was weak. Where is your honor?"

"Where is yours?"

Razi laughed and shook his head. "That is right, you never had any. You are weak as well, always were. That is why you spend so much of your time with this little giji boy. Jayde was the only one with any true Amirontian honor. So sad that she did not know her place. Oh dear sister, how I will enjoy killing you."

"Not if I kill you first, brother."

"Anointed Daughter, I highly recommend you order your pathetic little army to stand down before one of them gets hurt– or killed."

"I think I sort of like my little army and how they think," I replied.

"Well, do not say you were not warned, for if you come at me for a battle I will give you a war and you will never see Diana again. And as for this sorry little troupe of yours, if you value them at all, you will think long and hard about your next steps."

The sheath grass rustled behind Razi. No one emerged, merely made their presence known. I could feel their artillery aimed at us in return beyond its beautiful honey glow. I reluctantly signaled for my three to lower their weapons.

"That is more like it. You have until the next setting of the western sun to turn yourself in. If I do not return in good health and you do not show, soldiers will scour every inch of this planet looking for you. And Diana, your mother, cousin, whatever she is … she *will* die."

Razi smiled at me. I watched him carefully, every move. His eyes darted beyond mine and back so quickly that I barely knew that it happened. I moved without thinking. Moved to my left reflexively. A chill went through my body. I was in front of Aissa, the death end of a blade pointed at my face from its position in my hand. A trail of blood instantly dripped down my arm and to the dirt below. My heart raced. Razi's laugh rang in my ears as he disappeared into the sheath grass.

Aissa's voice was a hiss when she spoke. "He was going to kill me? My own brother! Had you not … he was really going to kill me."

"How did you know–?" Faraji asked astounded.

"We must go," I ordered, thrusting the blade into the ground. "Get to the transport now before Razi changes his mind and picks a fight here."

"Olivia, you are bleeding."

"It does not matter–"

"Olivia."

I exhaled heavily as I pulled the knife from the ground and used it to tear away part of the bottom of my shirt. I wound the material tightly around my open wound. "May we go now?"

"To Kelsard's Compound?" Charleston inquired knowingly. "How do we do this? It will be tricky. Very heavily armed, particularly since they know you are coming."

"We are not going to Kelsard's."

"Excuse me."

"She is not at Kelsard's Compound."

"Of course she is. Where else would he possibly take her?"

I turned to face Charleston. "Razi Las is no fool. You do not know him, but I do. He is Amirontian in every sense and stereotype. He is cunning and he is clever and he would not make things too easy for me. This is a game for him. It is all a game. Were it not, dare I say it, you would all likely be dead right now."

"So what are you trying to say?"

"How did he know Diana was here? Think about it. How could he have possibly found her so quickly?"

"The same way that you and Jayde found her," Aissa volunteered.

I laughed. "It took days to find her and we had help because someone was sent to look for me. Razi went right to her. He knew. I may not have believed it myself but ... I believe Jayde knew something – about me – and so did Razi. He arranged for Diana to be brought here and he is responsible for Jayde's capture."

Aissa took a step back. "No. No, Razi would never do that to Jayde."

"Really? He nearly murdered you, how quickly we forget. And he all but confessed it moments ago."

"If she is not at Kelsard's, then where?" Faraji asked.

I shook my head, gazing into the direction from which we had come. It was Razi Las who was attempting to do battle and instead would have war. I pulled my jacket from my body. The blade that I had kept booby trapped there for years I replaced with the bêti.

I took my old, trusty weapon and snapped it open. I looked up and squinted toward the sun, then looked out into the distance. With a flick of my wrist, I whipped the blade forward. It landed point down, firmly into the ground casting a shadow that pointed south.

I nodded. "She is at the Facilities."

The three passed about a shared look of extreme discomfort.

"And you are sure about this?" Charleston asked, nervously.

"I would bet my anointing on it."

Where Souls Are Lost

Fifteen

I WAS FILLED WITH APPREHENSION MUCH GREATER THAN I could have ever anticipated as we crossed The City's limits. The lanes were bustling and though there seemed to be nothing out of order, I knew that suddenly, for us, everything had changed. We were headed into the dragon's alternative lair, a place where souls were lost – or stolen – for the purpose of trying to play savior to one before it was too late.

Razi, and whomever he had convinced of my existence, would only wait so long for my arrival. The expectation would be that I would come to the compound, seeking out Diana with vengeance. It would only be a matter of time before he realized that his plan had failed and a search party sent to capture us.

Were I correct in my assertion, there would not be much

time. We would have to get in, find Diana, free her and get out as quickly as possible.

Night settled around us, the Western and Eastern sun tucked well away for the evening. Death loomed eerily at every turn but that was not what bothered me. The task ahead, though daunting and terribly dangerous, incited no fear. As far as rescuing Diana ... finding her alive, that was the weight that I carried with me.

The transport slowed to a stop several tanometers from the Facilities. The air tightened. A large rubrum tree cast a threatening shadow over the place where we sat communing. I took several deep breaths, tuning everything about me out and preparing for my mission. I could not fail.

I turned to meet the surprisingly excited expression marked on Charleston's face. "You three wait here," I said.

He guffawed. "I am going with you, Olivia."

"No. No way. Diana is my ... she is my responsibility."

"And you are mine."

For a moment words escaped me. I stared into his coal colored eyes, lost and trying hard to find my way back.

"I am going as well," Aissa spoke softly. "Raj can man the transport and drive us away when we come out with Diana."

And just that fast I was back. I shook my head vehemently. "No one is going. You will all wait here as instructed."

"Listen to me," Aissa began, "I am ... coming to terms with the reality of your prophecy. Okay? That it may be true ... that you are ... *the one*. But that does not make you special or somehow suddenly different. You are still Liv that wears that awful green hat and dumb jacket even in the warmest weather. You are still the same Liv that drinks up all the carraplum juice with little regard for others. I have lost my sisters and I have lost my last blood connection. If you are to die tonight, I will be at your side. You saved my life today. I owe you my bravery."

Her tirade, though endearing, frustrated me. I did not have patience for nobility or sympathy. I opened my mouth to speak but Charleston spoke first.

"Part of being powerful is allowing yourself to be vulnerable. You stand a much greater chance of walking out with Diana alive if you have help. My fate is tied into yours as well and you have acknowledged your gift for less than a day. Do not get ahead of yourself."

"Fine," I growled. "Do as you must. Just be quick about it."

"Faraji, be alert. Stay here where you have a better view. When you see us, do not hesitate."

"No worries," Faraji stated.

"Let us go." I opened the door and stepped from the vehicle followed by Charleston and Aissa.

I had never seen the inside of the Facilities nor had I before felt any desire to. From a distance, the building appeared to be quite magnificent. Its high towers looming above The City could be seen from nearly every location throughout. A constant reminder of the destiny that lied ahead for those that refused to obey what SRA commanded.

I did not know what type of security was in place inside. The only thing I was certain of was that there must be more artillery on the inside than out. I could not imagine many trying to force their way in but those remanded must certainly attempt at every opportunity possible to free themselves.

High-branched rubrums outlined the structure helping to conceal us from prying eyes. I stopped and looked up. Each level was lined with windows that were boarded up blocking out the world beyond.

"Follow me," Charleston ordered.

My brow furrowed and I eyed him curiously. "Are you certain you know where you are going?"

He turned to face me and sighed. "Trust me, Olivia. I know where I am going. I have done this before."

"What?" I asked in confusion. "You have been inside the Facilities? For what?"

"I had," he paused and gathered his thoughts, "...I had to rescue someone important to me."

"Who could be so important that you would risk your freedom to enter this place?"

He appeared suddenly flustered. "Do we really have time to discuss this right now? What matters is I have done what you aim to do. Security is generally lax here. Most people are afraid to enter and those inside are either too drugged or halfway to insane and are not thinking clear enough to attempt anything as daring as making a break for it."

I stepped back. "Your story just keeps getting better and more interesting, does it not. How do I know that I can trust you?"

"Look, I understand your hesitation but if there were any

reason that I could not be trusted I am positive you would have sensed it by now." I hesitated to proceed with him. It was all beginning to be too much. Razi. Mala. Jayde. Tabia. Diana. Charleston's continuous revelations. "There is a door below that should be simple enough to pry open. Women are held on the second floor in individual locked cells."

"So how do we retrieve her?" I questioned.

Charleston glanced up and around as though assessing our surroundings.

"The key. We have to get the key."

I groaned out something unrecognizable even to me.

"And just how do we manage that?" Aissa asked on my behalf.

"There is a master key. It unlocks all cell doors. However, there is a chamber guard in each wing that mans the cameras and has the ability to open cells remotely."

I regained my ability to verbalize my thoughts. "Surely he is not the only person responsible for a level."

"No. No, of course not. There are patrol guards who monitor the aisles in sync. They would have master keys but in order to obtain one it would require taking one out. Doable, however if another guard comes along and spots him or even notices that he is missing it will alert the others. Easy in. Not so easy out in a pursuit."

"So we go for the chamber guard," I deduced.

"Best bet. It would take much longer for anyone to notice a problem there. We would need one of us to stay behind to guide us to Diana and avoid bumping into a patrol guard."

"Let me guess," Aissa spoke, raising her hand partway.

"Do you think you can handle it?"

"I am an Amirite, true blood regardless of what my brother thinks of me. I can handle anything."

Charleston nodded his appreciation of her pride and confidence. "That is what I am counting on."

He signaled for us to proceed. We cut across a patch of field toward the towering building, crouching low, avoiding being spotted by one of three tower guards above. Up close the buildings age was apparent. Huge peeling gray boulders made up its structure. We crept alongside the building until we came upon a steep stairwell that led into a crack beside the building and outside of a weather-beaten door, all that appeared to stand between us and our rescue mission on the other side.

Charleston reached inside a pocket and pulled forth an object that I could not make out in the darkness. He inhaled deep and shot us a worried glance before prying the door open and cautiously stepping indoors. Aissa and I followed him into near complete darkness. A low wattage bulb dangled somewhere in the distance emitting a faint glow.

Having been in darkness already, the transition was nearly seamless. A pungent odor assaulted our senses. My stomach churned and I swallowed nothing repeatedly, suppressing the urge to dry heave. The sounds of creatures scurrying about rang in my ears making me aware of their presence though I was unable to see them. We crept forward toward the light and found ourselves at the entrance of a tunnel heavily guarded by spiders.

Charleston sliced through a thick web. A chill ran though me less from foreboding, but from the cold breeze that engulfed the air. It took a moment to recognize that we were standing ankle deep in water. I looked down. Try as I might, I could not see through the sludge to the bottom. A greasy film shown on the surface.

The heavy chill gave the feel of being surrounded by death and I knew with certainty, in that instance, that the rumors were true. We sloshed forth through the tunnel, beyond the bulb that illuminated the space and allowed me to see a glimpse of what dodged my steps.

Tension wrapped itself around every bone in my body. We would find Diana and leave with her, defeating Razi Las at his own little twisted game. And once she was safely tucked away, I would go after him once and for all.

We approached a door but Charleston veered suddenly right, plunging us, once again, into absolute darkness. I felt Aissa's anxious hand against my back trying to make sure that she did not lose me.

"Step up," Charleston whispered.

I stumbled slightly but found the stairwell. Almost as suddenly as we were placed in darkness, were we greeted with a halo of light. Charleston, very carefully, pulled a door open partway. The light flooded my eyes and momentarily blinded me. I blinked rapidly, bringing him into focus. He stood stock still, silent and alert. His body was taut and ready to flee or fight, whatever the situation may call for. I took his non-verbal cue and several deep breaths, steadying myself. I only hoped that Aissa could handle herself under pressure.

Charleston signaled with a nod, then pushed the door open just far enough for Aissa and myself to slip inside. He was careful to push the door up behind us, giving it the appearance of being closed. There was no handle on this side of the door. If it closed I hoped that he would know how to get us out.

"There is about a six minute delay in patrol shifts," he whispered. "The chamber is just around the bend and directly ahead. Though there is no camera here, once we exit we are completely vulnerable."

"So how do we get there without being caught?" Aissa whispered.

Charleston fidgeted. "It is unlikely the guard is watching the monitor."

"That is it? That is the best we can do? And if he is watching?"

"We are taking a chance even being in here. Yes, it is the best we can do. I will go. You two wait here. Do *not* turn this bend until I say so," He commanded. I rolled my eyes away. I had successfully completed a great many covert ops. I did not now see the need for anyone to begin fighting my battles for me. "Olivia, please. Do not allow pride to ruin this. Wait here."

"Do not attempt to handle me. I am as strong and swift as anyone – even you."

Charleston gripped my forearms. I did not flinch. "You will have many opportunities to prove yourself. If you want to save Diana, I suggest you swallow your pride this instant."

My jaw clenched and eyes became slits as I stared, unblinking, into his eyes. I conceded. He nodded and released me, then edged nearer the bend. He waited a moment, listening carefully before taking in a deep breath and darting from the illusion of safety.

I stood waiting impatiently. I fidgeted, anxious to proceed while finding it hard to believe that I could not have succeeded in this mission solo. I glanced to Aissa and observed the concern etched across her face.

My success or failure was to lie in her hands. What had she done lately to prove her worth? She was a good friend but I was certain her survival in The City had been more courtesy of Jayde and her twin Razi. And now Razi had become her greatest nemesis and Jayde was deceased. She would possibly be dead herself were it not for me. Or maybe, she will die because of me.

"Would you stop it?" Aissa whispered angrily.

"Stop what?"

"All of that. Fidgeting and pacing, you are making me nervous."

"Sorry." I closed my eyes and attempted to steady my nerves.

"Is it … is it true?"

I gave her a look of annoyance. "What? Is what true?"

"Diana? Is she really your mother? Razi implied … well, that she is your mother and not your cousin."

My greatest secret had been revealed. What difference would it make to openly confess to Diana Kalaath having birthed me? I looked at her. She did not look away. The sound of footsteps clicking across the floor and casual whistling silenced us.

We were beyond view from the aisle but that did not mean whoever was out there would not check. I steadied my breathing so carefully that I was hardly breathing at all. My hand pressed against Aissa's abdomen signaling for her to control all bodily functions.

I wondered if Charleston had been successful, wondered how long we should wait to find out. Aissa moved and stumbled slightly, her foot banging the edge of the wall creating a small sound that seemed much bigger in silence.

The whistling ceased, as did the heels clicking on the floor. I turned sharply to face Aissa, my eyes narrowing. We eased further into the darkness, closer to the door we had come through and waited. The quiet was stifling. I closed my eyes and swallowed in slow motion. The footsteps echoed closer and closer as though the someone out there were drawn to our fear.

My hand slipped into my pocket, seeking out a defense. There was the sound of a shoe scrapping the linoleum then the resuming of whistling and footsteps leading off into the distance. I waited until the sound was no more before I allowed myself a decent breath.

I decided I would wait no longer. I waved Aissa forward. If she protested I would just leave her behind. The way I figured, according to Charleston's calculations I had six minutes to make the most of. But no sooner did we reach the mouth of the bend that had protected us than I heard my name whispered upon the stale air. I nodded toward the aisle and Aissa and I fled to the chamber.

It was a small, claustrophobic space with numerous camera monitors and a seemingly endless supply of buttons and levers. The chair that the guard used to do his job was toppled over and across the room. I looked to Charleston and for the first time noticed the bruise on his cheek not far from his eye. A small trail of blood escaped a superficial wound on his lower lip. He looked around intently as he flexed his hand repeatedly.

"Where is the guard?" I asked hesitantly. He responded by pointing beneath the station. Aissa and I walked around and peered beneath. He looked to be sleeping peacefully rather than knocked unconscious. A ridiculously large man who appeared quite odd curled beneath his workstation. I looked from him to Aissa and back. It would be her duty to monitor the activities in this wing of the Facilities, guiding us safely to Diana. What would she do if the brute awoke?

"What happens if he awakens before we return for Aissa?"

"He will not." His tone was laced with remnants of anger.

"How can you be so sure?"

He looked from where the guard lay quietly and to my face, his brow furrowed and expression intense. Aissa stooped lower to get a closer look.

"Because he is dead," she replied, startled.

My head jerked back involuntarily. He looked away from me and walked to a wall where rows of hand-held intercoms were housed as I mulled the revelation over. Murder. I had not considered that Charleston had the gall to do what was necessary. He grabbed one and adjusted some knobs on it before tossing it to me.

"Have you ever used one of these before?"

I shook my head, ceding dominance to him for the moment. He took another for himself and walked to my side and gave me an impromptu tutorial on how it was to be operated. Aissa took the chamber guard's from the counter top. She waved Charleston away as he approached her.

"I was once assigned an assistant position in a security booth at an SRA factory. Worked it steadily for nearly a year. Used a Com Device and this board is nearly identical. I am good."

Charleston nodded and exhaled, clearly relieved. "She is in sector 4. Either cell 3 or 5, the writing is difficult. Aissa, you only need to tell us when to hold back or take cover. Once we have her we will meet you back here."

"Where is the master key?"

"We do not need it. Aissa can–"

"I want it."

He opened his mouth to speak but tightened his lips as though thinking better of it. Instead he did as requested, walking around the station and stooping low. When he returned upright he held the key in hand, which he dropped into my open palm.

"Can we go now?" he asked, exasperated.

Aissa studied the monitors before giving us the all clear.

†

OUR PACE WAS STEADY AND OUR SURROUNDINGS, SILENT. Tension was all that was between us. I could not imagine what could have been bothering him. It had been his idea to join me on this mission, not my own. I fixed my mouth to question but thought better of it. I had greater concerns.

"Are you upset with me?" The words came of their own

volition. Like regurgitation. This is what being normal got you.

"Now is not the time." He kept his eyes focused ahead of us.

He was right. It was much too dangerous to allow personal issues to interfere. So I was amazed at myself when I spit more pointless words out. "So you are."

He stopped and I nearly bumped into him. His jaw clenched. "You do not trust me. I never turned you in, never told your secret. Even when you stole from me. Still, you do not trust that I am a man of honor. You do not trust that I am capable of doing those things that I say I can do."

"I do not trust anyone. Trust is a luxury I cannot afford. Besides, what am I to think when your story keeps adjusting?"

He chuckled cynically and continued forward. "I am not the bad guy you are determined to make me out to be. You are just going to have to learn to break those old habits. Let us just get this job done and get out before – "

"Guys," Aissa's voice came through as a whisper across the private channel of Charleston's Com Device, hijacking our attention. "Guard less than a minute before reveal from bend ahead."

I looked around for a place to take cover but Charleston grabbed me and pulled me in the direction we had just conquered. A small aisle connected one sector to another. It was dark but if the guard were to look longer than 20 seconds he would likely be able to make us out.

Charleston dropped to the floor, pulling me down with him. "Lie flat," he ordered. I obeyed.

Our ears perked at the sound of the guard approaching in the distance. His steps halted suddenly, not far from us. I did not look up but I imagined him looking in our direction and hoped he would only look ahead and not down. More specifically I hoped he would not check. A dead soldier would invite trouble.

His steps resumed.

"Clear," Aissa informed.

Immediately, we jumped to our feet and rushed from hiding, leaving whatever problems that existed between us behind where it belonged. At least for the time being.

Sixteen
Deja'vu

BEFORE CAROLYN DIED SHE USED THE BRIEF TIME SHE HAD
left to spend quality time with her mother, while Mira worked
fervently to save the infant Diana. The two had lost so much time
when SRA had taken her away.

Mira attempted to talk to her daughter about the things she
had experienced while in captivity during the days leading up
to labor and delivery but Carolyn refused. Her time was limited
and she wanted to remain as far away from Kelsard's compound
as possible and that meant physically, mentally, and emotionally.
She knew that she was going to soon die and there was some
power in this knowledge in determining, for her, how she would
spend her last days.

But something changed as she began experiencing labor.
Suddenly, for the purpose of either deciding her mother had a

right to know how her child had lived and husband had died or simply as a way to distract herself from the pain, she opened up. And Mira would absorb and hold onto every word spoken, each of which she would eventually pass along to me.

She described a romanticized version of slavery. Naked in her captivity, her young body having been violated repeatedly, she would wrap herself in a thick, soft cotton sheet she had fashioned to resemble a dress so that she would not feel vulnerable.

She described a chamber lavishly decorated with the finest quality furnishings and accent pieces that she had ever seen in life. The bed she slept in was round and could fit at least four full-grown bodies at once. Her coverings were trimmed in gold. There was one window that did not open, and was too small to fit through even if it had.

She had been supplied every trinket and beauty supply a girl could ever desire. There was a wardrobe but its presence was redundant as a SOTA girl had little use for clothing.

Books were generally discouraged but she was one of the lucky few with a shelf lined with several editions worn from constant reading and re-reading.

Carolyn spoke of loving the morning time. Business was conducted in the mornings. Orders were given and carried out and deals made in the morning. The solitude granted her the opportunity to read or imagine. She would climb upon her bureau beside the bed and gaze out the small window into the field and pretend it was her village. She would see her mother tending her vegetable patch and her father chopping wood for cooking and to heat the home come sunset.

She would see her brother running in the fields and avoiding labor. She would even see herself with her favorite girl relatives picking green obi berries or playing with the dolls their mothers had carved out for their pleasure.

Some afternoons, if business took precedence over her service rendering, she may be allowed to keep company with another Sister for a short time.

But one day the door was flung open much earlier and much harsher than on any other occasion. She had been daydreaming and when she saw her father, Franklin, standing in the doorway beckoning her, she was so certain it was an illusion that at first she did not move.

It was not until he rushed to her side and grabbed her by her wrists that she realized this was not an illusion after all, and reacted. The pair ran wordlessly from the chamber through halls and down stairwells.

He was her hero. She knew not how he came to be there, all that mattered was that he was there and she would soon be free and back in the secure embrace of her mother, Elizabeth. Her farmer father yielded a sickle, slaughtering, without hesitation, anyone that crossed his path. The two survived the journey to the lower level and in sight of the main door. Her heart raced and her eyes watered with tears of joy.

She would be free at last.

But just as the pair approached the door, a feeling of overwhelming anxiety consumed her to the point that she could hardly breathe. Her knees buckled and she fell hard to the floor beneath her, reaching out and begging her Papa to not open the door.

But it was too late. The knob was already in his hand and he pulled it toward himself before Carolyn's warning could be heard. When he turned to face her for his final breath (a sword shoved deep into his abdomen and breaching his spine) his eyes were wide open and blood poured over his lips.

She thought to go to him, hold him one last time and tell him that she loved him but a powerful instinct kicked in and she turned away and fled in the opposite direction. The story ended there and any other details of her escape was a mystery that died with her.

†

DIANA HAD NO CHAMBER, MERELY A 4x4 DRAB, GREY CEMENT cell. Her small window was covered with a wood plank making it unusable for such things as inspiration and imagination. No sun, east nor west, could gain access. Only a small rectangle opening in the heavy metal door with a non-exclusive view to the wide solemn passage gave any sort of escape from the captivity she was in.

The air was chilled. Not quite able to be described as cold, but something else. Something much more disturbing. On Aissa's command, we entered the aisle where Diana was being held.

"You have 6-minutes before the next guard comes through so be swift. There is no place to hide outside of the stairwell."

I glanced at Charleston who looked down at me as if to ask if I was ready. My eyes told him that I was. We observed the first cell number and rushed forward to the one containing Diana.

"Here," I said, snatching the rectangle open and peering inside. It appeared empty. Blood rushed to my cheeks and my nerves tingled. "Diana? Diana."

I heard movement but still saw no one. I called to her again. "Diana, if that is you, please answer me."

A moment passed before her voice came to me, weak and groggy, "Olivia." She gasped like it was her final breath.

"Yes, yes it is me." I exhaled my relief, only then realizing that I had been holding my breath.

"What are … why…"

"To get you out of here. Why else?" I answered, knowingly.

I heard a soft click and pulled the door. Aissa had done her job. I stepped inside and at first saw no one. I turned to my right and looked down and was aghast at what I saw. Diana sat crumpled in the corner nearest the door, curled into a fetal position. Black bruises filled her legs and her tattered hair was matted. Her jaw was swollen and discolored.

The taste of hate permeated my palette.

I dropped down beside her and caressed her hair, spying the dried blood. I tried to help her to her feet but with each movement she flinched in pain.

"Charleston, you are going to have to carry her."

Her eyes were fixed upon the wall and she did not acknowledge my presence. It was as though she was no longer aware that I was even there. I said her name again and she suddenly became cognizant.

"It has to happen … it must be this way," she spoke.

Charleston stepped deeper into the cell and crouched low, attempting to take her into his arms but she recoiled, not allowing him to touch her.

"Diana, please," I pleaded.

"It has to happen. She said … she told me that it must … be this way. If I want to save you…"

"She who? Diana, Razi Las put you here. Who do you speak of?"

She shook her head carefully.

"Olivia, I do not mean to rush but we have very little time."

I shook my head vehemently and remained focused on Diana. "Listen, Charleston is going to lift you. He will not hurt you."

"No. I cannot… He knows now. He cannot harm what belongs to him. He cannot. If I go…"

"Diana." I said her name firmly and through gritted teeth. Reluctantly, I grabbed her cheeks and forced her to look my way. She flinched and I felt guilty. "I do not know who these people are but we have to go now or else we will be caught and all killed or worse, locked here forever. Can you hear me? Mo … mother, we have to go now. Charleston will carry you."

Recognition lit her eyes and she turned to face me. "Olivia."

"Yes. Yes, it is me. We need to leave. Right now."

I nodded to Charleston who reached beneath her and easily took her into his arms and carried her through the heavy door, dirty and covered only by a thin tattered layer of clothing. The sound of static that preceded Aissa's voice over the Com Device caught our ear.

"Guys, we have a major problem."

I grabbed the device from my waist and held it up to my mouth and questioned whether a patrol guard was coming our way. We had who we had come for and I was set to do whatever it took to get out.

"Worse. We have company."

"What does that mean? What sort of company?"

"The kind that would love to see you captured and the rest of us dead."

"Razi."

Charleston slowed and faced me. I waved for him to continue.

"Yes."

"How could he have known…"

"Mala." The voice was faint. It was neither Aissa's nor mine. It was not Charleston's. My eyes cut to Diana and my feet simply stopped moving. I tried to press forward, was aware how crucial time was but I could not will my legs to move.

"What did you say?" But she fainted in his arms. I rushed to her side and shook her arm. "Diana, wake up. Please. How do you know about Mala? Diana."

Charleston turned to face me, pausing and encouraging me forward with a head nod. "Olivia, we have to go."

"Why did she say that?"

Charleston shrugged slightly. "I do not…"

"Mala," I repeated.

"Who is Mala?"

I swallowed hard. "My see-er."

Aissa's voice cut through my thoughts and encouraged my legs to work. "You have to hurry. The guards on the inside are going to know we are here. The soldiers on the outside are trying to get in and someone else is bound to grant them access."

We turned a bend and rushed down a corridor, oblivious to any danger that may lie ahead yet not caring about it.

"What of the other chamber guard?" I asked breathlessly.

"What about him?"

"You said there were two. Can the other guard grant access?"

"I do not know. I imagine it is entirely possible but I would rather not find out."

"And what about the warden Chrekal?"

For the first time, Charleston looked lost. "I … I do not know. I do not know if he is here at this time of night but if he is —"

"It will not be good."

We approached the stairwell that we had accessed to get to Diana and pushed through the door. We ran down the level and Charleston reached to open the door. I hurried ahead of him and stopped him. Diana looked to be asleep in his arms though she was mumbling incoherently. I stood holding the handle firmly, listening to the sound of footsteps approaching, getting louder, then ultimately passing.

I pressed the side of the Com Device and whispered Aissa's name. "What is going on there? We nearly ran right into the arms of a guard," I questioned, once she responded.

"My apologies but you had better move quickly. The others are inside."

I cursed fiercely and glanced to Charleston, meeting his eyes.

Aissa continued. "It was not me. Must be another chamber guard. They rang twice already commanding to be allowed entry. They are on the other side but are headed this way."

I jerked the door open and held it so that Charleston could get through. I relaxed slightly when I recognized that we were nearly to the chamber guard tower that Aissa was waiting for us in.

"We are approaching," I warned. "Be ready."

We slowed at the bend, hesitant to continue forward without careful consideration as we could very well have run directly into dangers cold embrace. All was still. I did not sense anything out of the ordinary. Charleston looked to me for guidance. I nodded my approval and he, with Diana still in his arms, stepped into the open.

"All clear," he whispered.

We moved as fast as we could through the aisle. We were mere steps from the chamber door when a powerful sensation overwhelmed me. I held up an arm to stall Charleston as I surveyed the area but could see nothing of concern.

I shook it off assuming my paranoia was creating confusion within me. Previously, my instincts always kicked in on their own. This was the first time that I had ever attempted to channel the energy in the air myself and supposed, maybe, my feed was incorrect. Maybe I was creating concern where there was none.

Charleston arrived at the chamber door a couple steps ahead, as I was preoccupied with verifying that all was sound. I whispered into the Com for Aissa to join us in the aisle. There was no response from her but suddenly a soundly sleeping Diana was wide-awake. He eyes rounded and filled with fear.

"Let me down," she hissed, squirming. "Release me. Please."

"Diana," I spoke in a hushed tone. "It is fine. He is with us."

"No. No. Release me."

"Olivia," Charleston began, "you have to calm her down before we are captured."

"Diana, you have to be quiet."

"I said, release me."

Charleston reluctantly allowed her to fall from his arms though he managed to continue to hold her in a way that she would not harm herself nor escape.

"I will not hurt you," he tried to assure her. "I am going to get you out of here."

"No. You cannot. She will not let you. They will not…" She was shaken. She looked confused. It was as though she could not determine what to believe. Then just as suddenly she was calm. It was as though she was in this place as an invited guest rather than a drugged and subdued prisoner. Her eyes came to mine but … they were not the eyes of Diana. Something was off, something unclear. I recognized the eyes but could not figure how this made sense.

Diana smirked at me and I gasped. "Mala." I looked to Charleston just as his hand reached for the handle. "Charleston!

Do not—!"

My order came too late; the door had already swung open. He looked to me, unsure of what to make of my present state. I peered into the chamber. Aissa stood in the pit looking directly at us but not budging. I scanned the room quickly but saw no one.

"Aissa, hurry," Charleston instructed.

I moved without thought, pushing Charleston with all of my weight away from the doorway just in time for the harbinger ray to miss taking his life or a limb. Diana fell hard and slammed into a corner.

"Grab Diana!"

Charleston scooped Diana up and charged toward our exit. I followed, reaching into my pocket, fumbling slightly before pulling forth the arms created by Charleston's father. I turned and stopped, aiming the weapon and waiting for Razi to emerge.

I blasted on sight but he ducked into the room, scarcely escaping with his life. A ray shot in our direction but anticipating retaliation, I dodged, throwing my body into the small corridor. Charleston's expletive outburst refocused me.

"What? What is it?" I asked breathlessly.

"It is closed."

"What?"

"He closed it!"

"No, no, no!"

My name rang out in a singsong manner. "Where are you going? The party was just getting exciting. I underestimated you."

I stood in the darkness while Charleston considered how to free us. "I have Diana, I have what I have come here for! It is over!"

"Over?" Razi questioned. "I do not think so. If it is, why not leave? Ah, that is right. You cannot. Your little secret passageway sealed off, huh?"

I looked to Charleston, hoping for an answer. I glanced down to the weapon in my hand. "I can shoot it."

He shook his head. "You cannot. Against this metal, the blow back could kill us. "

I peered cautiously into the aisle. Razi had crept closer, a strong forearm wound tightly around Aissa's throat, his Harbinger pointed in the air. He looked at me and paused but did not point his weapon.

"So you have your mother, but you are not so cold that you would leave here without your traitorous friend."

I tried hard to not look into Aissa's eyes. I had gotten who I had come for. Aissa was not my responsibility. She was *his* sister and that made her *his* problem. Whatever sibling quarrel they had did not concern me. But I lost my battle and our eyes met. I had expected to see fear but she lacked emotion.

I relayed a mental message to her that I hoped she would somehow receive. Razi would not kill her, not today. I knew that now. What he had done back at Galê Tas' shanty had strictly been a test. Maybe this was all a test. He needed some assurance that I was indeed who he thought I was. He knew I would save her. She was not my responsibility but if I did not face him, he would never relent. That much was clear. But I could not do it now. Not with Diana in harm's way.

"Face me, Olivia. Right here, right now and I will let your mother and boyfriend go free."

"That will not happen."

"Come on, Anointed Daughter. If I wanted all of you dead I could have easily arranged that. It is just me. Surrender yourself and your people will go free. I will tell you what, I will even spare the life of my twin. I am not heartless. This is a fair deal, Liv. You have nowhere to go."

"Is that so, Razi? Is that what you believe?"

"Until you prove me wrong." I stepped into the open and faced him. "That is my girl."

I turned away, rushing past Charleston and Diana with armory drawn. I leapt into the air and without thought or hesitation, aimed my taut legs and kicked the door open. I landed poised and prepared to tear a whole through the chest of anyone who happened to be waiting on the other side. There was no one. I signaled that it was safe to flee.

"How, in the name of Deus, did you do that?" he asked as we ran as hard and fast as we possibly could.

"I have no idea."

Razi screamed my name. Venom laced his voice. The sound rounded the bend and followed the three of us through the damaged door and continued down the dreary tunnel. We ran, murky waters splashing and soaking our legs.

"Be cautious, Olivia. He certainly has support."

I was not concerned though maybe I should have been. I

continued without slowing, weapons drawn. I charged through the door, blasting without hesitation. A Harbinger ray took a chunk out of the wall just as Charleston passed through.

"Get down," I cried, as I ran up the steps taking aim at every soldier that I caught in my sight. Fear fueled my adrenaline. Never before had I been in face-to-face combat. I was not a soldier. All I knew to be true was that I would fiercely protect what I loved.

Charleston, with a freshly battered and disoriented Diana in his clutches, followed close behind me. My arms were extended, muscles taut but though the soldier's weapons remained drawn and aimed, they seemed to retreat. Their actions, though favorable, baffled me. I did not know what to do. If I shot, they would surely retaliate. But was this part of their plan for my capture? Make us believe we were safe, causing us to drop our guard … become vulnerable and then take us down one by one?

We moved as fast as we could toward the transport, my back to the sudden rush of footsteps coming upon us. I turned sharply, ready to fire but halted when I recognized it as Faraji.

"What is this? What is happening? Where is Aissa?"

I answered all questions with one breathless response, "Razi."

"You have to go back. We have to rescue her."

"Look around you," I cried out.

"We cannot just leave her!"

"We will get her back, I promise," I answered as I grabbed his arm, attempting to force him back in the direction of the transport.

Charleston's voice was strong when he spoke. "We have to

get out of here. I do not know why they were ordered to stand down but we should go before Razi changes his mind."

"But he will kill her!"

"No, Faraji. He will not," I attempted to assure him.

"You do not know that." Faraji jerked, freeing himself from my loose grasp. He took two steps before a soldier cocked his weapon and prepared to fire, causing him to hesitate and rethink his previous position.

"If he is going to kill her, she is already dead. Let us go."

I left Faraji to make his own decision while Charleston placed Diana hastily inside the transport. I slipped in beside him as he took over the wheel.

"Are you coming?" I asked as Charleston brought the vehicle to life.

Faraji glanced toward the Facilities but seemed to think better of it and instead, took us up on the ride to safety.

Secrets of the Panati

Seventeen

SILENCE.

The quiet was so loud that my ears began to hurt. The darkness gave me peace. It gave space to think and plan. I looked ahead although I had no idea what our destination was. I did not care.

I needed to sort things out but more specifically, I needed to separate my enemies from my friends. I needed to gain a clear visual of who was out there and who wanted me handed over to SRA to be murdered or enslaved and forced to do their bidding.

I tugged gently at the inside of my right sleeve and felt the hard, smooth wooden surface roll down my forearm and land in my open palm. I focused on the seemingly harmless piece of weaponry. Based on appearances alone, the most damage it could inflict was as Aissa had said, giving someone a serious knot

291

if you chucked it at them. It was discreet and powerful, deadly and destructive. It was like me. It was made especially *for* me, likely, especially for this purpose.

There was more ... so much more to it. Created by Charleston Kelsard's father. A man who had never met me nor my family and yet was convinced of my existence and what it represented and that someday this piece of meticulousness would get me out of whatever corner I would be backed into. So far I had been too intimidated to use it. What it represented was apparently more than I could handle and thus settled on blasting heat like every other planetary citizen in trouble.

According to Charleston, in a sense his mother had sacrificed her life for my protection. She was convinced of my value at a moment where I had barely entered the world. But what of Mala? She, too, claimed to have this vested interest in me. According to her, she had been charged with the duty to look after me since the moment of my birth. She knew everything about me for she claimed it her responsibility to protect me.

But somehow I did not feel protected by her. Anything but.

†

"WHERE ARE YOU TAKING ME?" DIANA'S GRUFF VOICE recalled my attention to her presence. I looked toward her. She was seated with her knees pulled tight to her chest and her legs crossed at the ankles. Her long, dark hair covering her eyes, and dark skin made her barely visible in the night. Her forehead was pressed to the glass. She raised her head slightly and with effort to return my gaze and then turned away.

I returned my attention to the road. "Where *are* we going?"

Charleston opened his mouth slightly to speak but hesitated. He glanced at me, then looked quickly away. "My home."

I turned partially in my seat so that I was facing him. "No. No, we cannot go there. That is much too far away. We still need to find a way to get Aissa and–"

"That is my father's home. We are going to m– ...to *my* home…" his voice trailed.

I eyed him curiously. He turned his face toward me and locked his eyes on mine momentarily before turning back. I took my cue and readjusted myself in the seat.

During my period of confusion, the time that I had mistakenly assumed that I could have a normal life with Charleston Kelsard, I had questioned him about his home. I had, on occasion, inquired about where he retreated to when he left the shop in the evening. I wanted to know where he rested his head at night. Every time, he ducked my inquisition telling me no more than that he resided on his father's land.

I reached up and tugged at my hat with the tips of my phalanges, pulling it slowly forward and from my head. I exhaled as the heat contained did the same from my scalp.

I snuggled deep into my seat, running my phalanges through my mangled locs resolving not to put much thought into it. I assumed he had his reasons and that they were valid.

"Olivia," Diana whispered. I sensed the paranoia in her voice. "Olivia."

"It is okay, Diana. They know … they already know."

I looked back to her. She looked uneasy about the revelation but said nothing.

The transport slowed, turned and then slowed more until we came to a complete halt. Charleston faced me. I looked into his eyes. Tried to show him that there was no love lost and we would be okay.

He exhaled. "We are here. This is it."

I sat for a moment after he exited the transport and took a deep cleansing breath as Faraji climbed out from the back. I followed, then paused, looking into the darkness and trying to make out our surroundings. I blinked, trying to adjust my eyes to the darkness. Sheath grass, there was a field of it across from us.

I turned away and began to walk around to assist with Diana but turned back suddenly. I looked into the dense grass, leaning forward and straining my eyes. I began raising them slowly, sizing up the lone panati tree in the distance. I swore under my breath but exhaled my anger. He had his reasons.

"Liv," Faraji spoke. I turned quickly to face him. "We are going inside."

I nodded and looked back at the tree, the very tree that Charleston and I would lay beneath watching the eastern and western sunsets. The one place with a clearing so perfect it allowed us a glimpse of the Starr of Tayle in the great distance. A gorgeous tree and one like I had never before nor since seen, no more than half a tanometer from where I stood.

I turned away and followed my party to the home. Smaller than a cabin home but certainly larger than a shanty. Quite fitting for a distant Kelsard youth out on his own.

The door swung open. A dim light haloed the entry illuminating the frame of a petite woman who donned two braids that hung to her waistline. Likely of Marinite descent but who could tell these days? I swallowed hard the emotion that was battling with me for a right to surface.

"Oh, Charleston," she cried out, stepping forward and falling into his arms. "You are safe. Deus be praised. I was beginning to become so concerned … I *was* concerned. You should have allowed me to come with you. I could have been of use, you know this. What happened to your face?"

He eased uncomfortably from her grasp, instead holding her delicately by her wrists. "I am fine. No need to worry for me. I can handle myself just fine out there."

Her eyes moved reluctantly from his face and her arms slipped slowly to her sides. She appeared vaguely startled when she looked past him, as though noticing us for the first time. She stood straight, hands clasped before her, giving us a swift assessment. Faraji, who held a helpless Diana in his arms, glanced at me. I refused to meet his gaze and instead kept my eyes ahead of me, passing just by the woman's head. I understood his question but had no answer. I did not know who she was.

"Well," she began, moving her arm in a sweeping motion. "Come on inside where it is warm."

Charleston led the way, following the unknown woman. She motioned and Faraji carried Diana to a sofa and placed her carefully upon it while the mystery woman walked about lighting candles. I recognized the heavy scent of dragena in the air and suddenly felt ill. Faraji stepped away and rejoined me near the door. We stood shoulder to upper arm waiting for some instruction, introduction … explanation. Maybe permission to make ourselves comfortable in the couple's space. I glanced away as Charleston walked to us.

"James," he said softly and the beautiful hostess turned. He cleared his throat and continued, "I would like for you to meet my friends."

My palms curled into tight fists. I had not meant for them to. There was just something about the sound in his voice and the reference to me as a *friend* that disturbed me. She walked our way with seeming reluctance, an arm extended. My hands relaxed.

Charleston continued with his introductions. "This is Faraji and this … is Olivia."

"Of course," she said and my head jerked.

"Of course. Faraji and Olivia, this is James."

"You are Charleston's sister?" Faraji asked hopefully.

James looked quickly to Charleston, then shook her head gently. Her braids wafted with her movement. "I am Chas' *wife*."

I stumbled slightly but Faraji caught my elbow and I regained my balance. My eyes went to Charleston's. I channeled my negative energy in his direction and I was certain that everyone in the room could detect it. He refused to acknowledge it.

My eyes went back to James … his wife. Movement broke some of the tension and I looked beyond her to the two bodies rounding the corner. A female and a much younger male.

James turned in their direction and beckoned them to her. I looked back at Charleston as the child and girl approached us cautious and suspiciously. Charleston stepped back slightly. It was as though he did not wish to be affiliated with the group.

"Faraji. Olivia. This is my younger sister, Jiliane."

I looked sharply at Charleston and then back to Jiliane who did not speak and did not seem very interested in meeting new people. I looked her over as she looked me over. Though small in stature, she was quite a bit taller than James.

"And this...," She continued while offering up a tiny smile while caressing the arm of a thin and adorable young boy who was just as tall as she was, "...is Silver, my son. Jiliane. Silver. Olivia is ... well, she is the Anointed Daughter."

Silver, looking pleased, stepped forward and shook our hands. "It is a pleasure and an honor to meet you."

Jiliane turned away. "Who, in the name of Deus, is this?" She cried out in disgust, redirecting our attention.

Charleston raised a hand to me that begged permission to allow him to handle it. My jaw clenched tight. Nothing graceful would escape my lips and so, being in the presence of a child, I kept quiet.

Charleston walked toward the sofa. "That is Diana."

"And was this Diana recently rescued from the streets?"

"Jiliane," James hissed.

I swallowed my own anger at the girls disrespect. Deciding to make myself at home before anyone had invited me to do so, I walked across the room to where Diana lay half-dazed and half-dead.

I looked at Jiliane. "The Facilities, actually."

Horror streaked across the girl's face. Aside from height, she was a replica of her sister. "No, James, no! Who are these people that we should risk *everything* for them?"

"You know who they are and you know why we must help."

Jiliane approached me quickly and looked me over again. "She is only a child. Anointed? We are probably the same age. We have done well here. We cannot have SRA knocking on our door for harboring some escape con and Charleston's little girlfriend!"

"Watch your mouth."

"You hardly believe this yourself. I know you well enough, Sister."

I stepped forward before James could answer. "You are right. Who are we that you should risk your lives and freedom? I am not The One. I am not anyone. We will leave."

"No!" James turned to me, pleading. "No. I apologize for my sister's ignorance. You are welcome to stay. We will do our duty and assist in any way we can. You must ... please, understand. We just expected ... more."

I chuckled cynically. "I cannot believe this, insulted by strangers. Faraji, get Diana. Let us go."

Faraji fidgeted. "Liv, please. They are offering to help. Why do we not just leave her here and let her get some rest. We can come back for her."

"You know me *very* well, Raj and you know that I do not stay where I am not wanted and I certainly will not leave Diana behind."

"Where will we go with her?"

Charleston finally found his voice and approached me.

"Olivia, leave Diana be. You will stay here while we figure out our next move."

I glared at him. "*My* next move."

"What does that mean?"

"I will figure out *my* next move, *Chas*." My chest heaved heavily.

"Olivia, do not do this."

"Okay, stop." James put a small hand in the air and walked between us. "You three will stay here. She is weak. You cannot travel with her. She may not make it."

"No offense, *Charleston's wife*, but I do not know you and clearly we have no reason to trust one another. And besides, I have … greater things to tend to. There is no time to play one big happy family in the forest."

"No offense taken but she has clearly been through a lot and needs an opportunity to recover. It is obvious to me that she has been drugged … starved. Beaten and medically neglected. Now unless you are prepared for her to die or have a better plan readily available, I strongly suggest you swallow your pride and stay here for the night. My sister is just an ignorant child. Ignore her."

I looked down at Diana lying there, oblivious to what was going on around her. Bruised. Battered. Dirty. Doped. And shivering.

James continued to instruct. "Silver, please go and run a warm bath for our guest. And use a capful and a half of my special minerals. Jiliane—"

"No."

"Jiliane Aëru–"

"No, James. What if–"

"What if Uncle had not stuck his neck out for us? I know that you find it hard to believe that she is … what if Chas had not stuck his neck out? For Deus sake, my sister, were it not for those who defied logic and took a chance, we may have been captured or killed by now."

Jiliane huffed a bit and her eyes rolled in the low light. "What would you like for me to do, *Sister*?"

"The malta stew, warm it and prepare a bowl. Add a gram of honeycram herb. Chas, please show our guests to the shanty–"

"I am not leaving her alone with you," I said.

"I will not harm her."

"No. You will not."

James conceded. "Show Faraji where he can rest. I will show Olivia when she is ready."

Charleston accepted the orders and signaled for Faraji to follow. He did not move immediately. He looked to me and I nodded. Charleston looked back to me before leading him away but I averted my eyes.

I walked over to the mantle and stood with my back turned as James adjusted a half-dead Diana with little assistance from her. I turned to watch her with my mother. James was a striking beauty with strong yet feminine features. Her round brown eyes were brighter than her skin. Her own beauty was likely comparable to Diana's in her youth. She called my name and I snapped back to reality and to attention.

"There." She pointed. "Please hand me that coverlet."

I grabbed it, taking my eyes off of her as short a time as possible. I wondered how she had managed to avoid being recruited. She stretched the blanket over Diana's body. Jiliane returned with a small bowl and handed it over to James.

"Thank you. Please make sure all is secure. Then take Silver and return to bed."

Jiliane glanced at me curtly with disapproving eyes before wordlessly disappearing. James carefully propped Diana and gently moved her hair away from her face. She spoke softly, words only the two of them could understand. Diana nodded weakly and James scooped up a spoonful of stew and fed it to her.

"We have been married for nearly two years. That is what you are wondering, is it not?"

I did not respond. I walked to a chair and took a seat.

"It is an arrangement. I love Chas. Love him for who he is … for what he has done for my family, but our marriage is merely an arrangement. It is not that kind of love."

"This is not my business."

"I know who you are."

"I gathered. I just wish I could have said the same."

"No. Beyond being the Anointed Daughter. I know who you are to him." She paused and looked my way while Diana digested what was given to her. "Do not be angry with Chas, Olivia."

"Charleston is … he is like a helper. He is nothing to me. He helped me rescue my mo – Diana. So I do not care about his personal life."

James nodded and fed Diana more stew. "I reached my 16th day without being promised to anyone. In my village that was the greatest shame a girl could face."

"It is none of my business."

She looked my way, her eyes piercing and glittering in the dim light. "I was a fighter ... trained by my father in the physical arts. It was an odd choice for him. Not only was I a girl child but a very small one. But he had no boys and I was good. Boy was I good. Strong. Agile. Swift. Being small has its advantages. But who wants a woman that behaves like a man?"

I leaned back deeper into my seat. My lids became heavy and I fought hard to keep them open.

"Juliane. I was given the name Juliane Eësa I'kimi Aëru."

"Eësa?"

"Roughly translated means champion. It was as a result of all the time I spent training with my father, Jameson Aëru, that the elder men in my village began to refer to me as Pica Jameson and eventually, simply James."

"Why are you telling me this?"

James dabbed at Diana's mouth. "Half past my 16th day I finally met someone. He was wonderful and we were immediately married and I became pregnant with Silver within a matter of weeks. The first couple years were great. Just wonderful. But Rothdene wanted more children and my womb was cursed. I lost every seed planted. He blamed me, of course. Said it was all the training. Told me that my constant behaving like a man caused me to lose my ability to be a real woman. I cannot say that he was incorrect. And then one day he came home after a long day in the field and informed me he was becoming a soldier for SRA."

I looked her way. She had my attention.

"I had seen how SRA changed the men in my village and Rothdene was no different. I had to get away and as you may know cultural law requires a 6-month separation period before a woman can claim a default release. He would not formerly release me. Instead he wanted to hand me over to SOTA. Collect a profit on me."

"What about Silver?"

"Rothdene's mother would raise him in my absence. She was okay with it."

"So you disappeared."

"Yes."

Diana finished her meal and James set the bowl aside. "Your mother has been through a lot."

I sat upright. "She is not my—"

"Like I said, I know who you are. Chas did not tell me, only confirmed it. I was once captured during an enforcement. I thought I would never see Silver and Jiliane again. But while in captivity at the Facilities I had a dream. It warned me that I would one day, very soon, be responsible to assist the Anointed Daughter."

"You are who he rescued," I said knowingly. It was now clear how he knew so much about the inner workings of the jailhouse.

James nodded. "That was part of my purpose in life.

Charleston's marriage to me was merely so that should Rothdene discover me, he could not lay claim to me. And it was the only way that my uncle could lawfully provide me a dowry that allowed Chas to purchase this land from his father so my family could have a home."

I leaned forward, resting my elbows on my knees. "So you do love him."

"I believe I have already addressed that."

"You know what I mean."

She tilted her head slightly. Light from a nearby candle danced in her eyes.

"I believe that I do. For what he has done for us, for Jiliane, Silver, and me. How could I not? But his heart as of late is uh ... shall I say, preoccupied." James placed her palms on her thighs and pushed herself to standing. "Help me. Your mother is in terrible need of a bathing. She is fully influenced but the stew and a warm bath with excalibur crystals will soon bring her down."

I nodded and stood. Together, James and I led a disoriented Diana to the communal.

†

"We have to leave here, Liv."

Those were the first words that Faraji spoke when I stepped into our little guest shanty. I did not respond. My head was pounding. I walked directly to the bed that was prepared for me and sat, my body arching forward and my face landing in my open palms. I could hear a commotion nearby but I did not budge. I could feel Faraji's presence as he hovered above me. Still, I did not move.

"What are we waiting on? We must go to Kelsard's compound as soon as possible. We have to rescue Aissa. We cannot just leave her there to be killed or prostituted."

I attempted to tune his voice out. I did not need a reminder of my responsibilities. What I needed was an opportunity to process my emotions.

"Olivia." A much deeper voice, one that would not be ignored, invaded my thoughts.

I raised my head slowly and looked into the direction that my name had been called. Charleston's strong frame blocked the doorway. Seeing no support would come from me, Faraji turned to plead his case in the opposite direction.

"Charleston … Chas, whatever you prefer to be called, we must go and now. We cannot just leave Aissa there."

"What we need, Faraji, is rest. We have been through a lot in a very short frame. We stand no chance against Kelsard and Dupec's army if we do not at least re-energize."

"Listen to me. Razi could kill her. I know that means little to you but she is everything to me."

"And if we enter that compound blind, exhausted, and unprepared, she will be as good as dead and so will we."

"But please, just listen—"

"End of discussion. We leave at first light. Olivia, may I speak with you for a moment?"

"This is not your call. Who are you anyway? You may be a Kedt and a Kelsard but you are not *the one* and I do not answer to you! It is your fault we are in this mess to begin."

"It is no one's fault. Olivia."

"Indeed it is. *You* had barely known Jayde but she was *our* family and we had a responsibility to her, a responsibility we were prepared to honor until *you* came along. Some glory hound itching to earn some recognition off the back of the Anointed. How did you know we were there anyhow? How do *we* know that this is not all part of some plan on your part to turn her in ... get the prize yourself. Live up to your family name?"

"Faraji, you know not what you are speaking about and I will *not* discuss this with you. Olivia, please."

Finally, I looked up from the darkness of my palms and turned my face toward Charleston.

"Yes, *Chas*. How *did* you know where we were?"

"You do not believe in these accusations, Liv."

"I do not know what I should believe."

Charleston sighed and deflated. He moved closer, past Faraji who offered a firm shoulder shove in passing, and took a seat beside me. "There is not some shady tale as it seems the two of you believe. Fine. A woman, she appeared at my father's doorstep and I happened to be there. It is as though she knew I would be there. She was ... some sort of see-er. Clear eyes that seemed to be able to see through to my soul."

"Mala?" I whispered to myself.

"I do not know. Aged ... bent. She told me where you were ...

what you were up to. Said it was my duty to stop you and bring you back. She confirmed what I already knew, that you were *The Anointed*. She had come to my father once before which is how I wound up working in The City near you to begin with. She reconfirmed what my father had told me, that part of my destiny was being in servitude to you."

I shook my head and stood. I believed his account, but for reasons I could not explain, believing in a Seer was a great feat. Mala was neither aged nor bent. She was youthful and beautiful. What was her true purpose? What did it all mean?

"Aissa–" Faraji began, looking pleadingly to me.

"We will save Aissa." I yawned as I rubbed my eye with my right index phalanx. "You have my word. Now rest, please. I need you at full strength if I will be able to pull it off."

Faraji stood in the dimness longer, worried and fearful. His world had come crashing down around him, all in a matter of days. Jayde and Tabia dead, and now Aissa had been taken. And Razi Las, I believed, was solely responsible for it all. Faraji shook his head but heeded my promise and reluctantly returned to his bed.

"I am very sorry that I did not tell you about James before," Charleston interrupted. "It is a difficult and very complicated situation and I did not know how or if you could handle it."

"Like I could not handle your relationship to Kelsard and to Kedt … your connection to me." Charleston looked away, ashamed. "It is of no consequence."

Charleston approached me as I turned to lie down. He cut me off, gripping my arm firmly and looking down into my eyes intently.

"Do not say that, Olivia. I love you. I never meant to hurt you. I only did not want to push you away."

I was speechless. I felt winded hearing those words come from him – again. He turned me slowly to face him and his eyes bore into my own, making me weak.

…making me weak.

I pulled away. "I cannot deal with this. I already told you, this relationship you have going here is of absolutely no consequence to me. That you love me, I am sorry indeed, for I do not love you. Now, please. Go. Rest. We have a difficult task ahead."

I pulled my body away, using little force to free myself. I pulled the thin, worn, green blanket back, exposing a measly pillow.

"I am not going back. I am staying here with you."

"Go, Charleston. I do not want you here. Go back to your wife … to your family."

"Stop it, Olivia."

"To your marital bed."

"Stop it. You are just using this as an excuse!"

"An excuse for what? That is why you never brought me home, is it not? I was a fool. I thought I wanted a normal life, for once. Just once. To know what it was to love and to be loved. To make love. But you could not bring me home. Always a reason, always an excuse. And now I know why.

"She is beautiful, Charleston. She is a woman. A real woman, and I am merely a foolish girl. Like her sister said, just a child. A child who hides herself behind concealor and denies her fate out of fear. Go to your wife whether she is that by choice, chance, or circumstance. We are in danger. Diana may very well be dying for all I know and Aissa? I *have* to save her. It is the only way that I can possibly begin to redeem myself before the memory of Jayde. So your supposed love for me is rather insignificant under the weight of it all. So go. Please ... just go."

I stood, holding onto the edge of the coverlet with my heart crumbling inside of my chest. Charleston did not walk away immediately. His eyes remained on me though I could no longer bear to look at him. I knew that his heart was crumbling as well.

But it was best for all concerned.

I had a dangerous task awaiting me. The greatest challenge I would experience yet and a true test of my calling. Charleston made me weak and that was an unfortunate consequence of his love that I could not afford.

Compounding Issues

Eighteen

IN MY FANTASIES ALL I EVER WANTED TO BE WAS NORMAL. Whatever that meant on a planet ruled by dictatorship, it was what I wanted: a mother and father in a village with family and friends. Betrothed to some fair young gent from a nearby village who would make me his wife and mother to his children. To feed my family healthy meals with ingredients and spices handpicked from a garden. Even paying my tithes into SRA because, despite the iniquity of it all, that was an element that a normal life entailed.

An ordinary existence is what I believed that I wanted. It is what I had strived so hard to achieve, to be normal with Charleston Kelsard. That was a dream that I had dared to bring to reality. But what I learned is that being so-called "normal" enervated a person, and when that happened you became vulnerable.

What I seemed to want so much was the one thing that I was not and would never be. I had been foolish to have even tried. If that was what Charleston wanted he could have it with James, Silver, and Jiliane. Normalcy was not within my realm of possibilities.

I was born to be different. I was conceived with a purpose, as part of a prophecy. It was time to forgo the perception of normalcy. The time had come to stop asking questions and seeking answers to those things that did not matter in the greater scheme of things. I needed to lay claim to what was to be mine.

Charleston had stirred within me emotions that I grappled with as I stood on the edge of potential personal destruction. They clouded my judgment and slowed my reaction time. Were I not careful, they would be the death of me and I was not yet ready to die.

I could have none of that.

I stood in the field, partway between the home that Charleston shared with James and the magnificent panati he had once shared with me. The eastern sun would soon awaken and with it, the sleepy eyes of Faraji and Charleston, luring them into a preparation to sojourn with me on this mission for Aissa's freedom and Razi's downfall.

I walked through the grass to the clearing behind the home where there was a substantial trench where fresh water flowed. I pulled a torn piece of coverlet from inside my pocket and dipped it into the clean waters and proceeded to scrub my face.

I worked hard, my flesh becoming raw. I dipped the cloth again, rinsing it clean and returning to the chore of freeing myself of my mask and facing my vicissitude. Once I began, I refused to cease. I cleansed face, neck, hands, and arms, continuing until I could see myself for what I really was. Scrubbed until my glow created a haze in the darkness that could have just as easily been caused by the rising of the sun.

But it was the Anointed Daughter that was rising. Rising to take her position and instigate the destruction of a regime that had destroyed the lives of her very own for far too long. Rising up against anyone that had any ideas of grandeur that would encourage the belief that they would take up where the Shadow Realm Allegiance would leave off.

When I was confident my task was complete, I stood upright and removed the hat that had contributed to my concealment for so long that it had become a living part of me. I held it between my phalanges before managing to summon the courage to toss it into the river to be carried away. I walked toward the shed as the sun began its ascent. I passed by the transport car as slumber slowly lifted its veil from Charleston's eyes. I preferred the transport bike that was stored there, one I had discovered earlier during my secret tour of the grounds.

I had already palmed the key. I had driven one similar to this in the past under Jayde's instruction. I climbed aboard as Faraji turned and blinked burning eyes that would soon discover my absence and as Charleston whispered adieu to a restless James who shared his bed. In the moment that Faraji would call my name and rise to find me, I prayed to Deus that he should watch over Diana but, more pointedly, a woman named Juliane (but regarded by the name of her father) as I was leaving my mother in her care.

And just as Faraji readied himself to run to the main house to alert Charleston of my absence and his concern that I may have been taken in the night, I revved the ignition and rode off into the sunrise hell bent on destruction.

Razi Las first. SRA to follow.

†

THE COMPOUND WAS FAR BEYOND ANYTHING I COULD HAVE imagined. I had always heard tales from this ex-SOTA Elite or that AWOL soldier. People who had never had any business requiring they set foot on Kelsard's compound swore they knew it inside and out. My expectations had been high but nothing could have prepared me for what I saw.

I sat in the distance, perched high on a hill beneath a panati tree, the transport bike asleep by my side. I sucked the juice from a kakali that I held in one hand while looking through a pair of binoculars I had stolen from Charleston's shed in the other.

The residence was massive … simply magnificent with sprawling hills of green cascading all around. From where I sat in the distance I could see clearly that security was at least as tight as I had anticipated. Armed guards roamed the premises and armored trucks came and went seemingly on a scheduled rotation.

Getting inside, though a terribly difficult feat, would not be impossible. But finding Aissa would be something of a task in and of itself. I did not even know whether she was still alive though something inside convinced me that she was.

My eyes roamed the picturesque scene ahead, seeking out a

weakness that I could exploit. I jerked forward, dropping the near drained kakali from my hand, which I now used to balance the other end of the binoculars. I focused. Zoomed in and focused again. I rose slowly and stepped forward, keeping my eyes glued to the spot I had located. The weakness in the chain-link. A portion of unguarded wall nearly buried in vegetation flowing off a large tree of a breed I had never before seen. Try as I might, I could not see very well beyond it but it was my best chance for entry and thus would have to do.

I zoomed out slowly and found the path that would lead me to its exact location before dropping the binoculars at my side, turning the compound into nothing more than a grand dollhouse. I rushed to the stolen bike while adjusting my jacket and pulling the oversized hood down as far as it would go over my head. I turned the machine on and the engine purred softly like a sleeping kitty, then took off in the opposite direction of the compounds location.

I dipped up and down through the hills and valley until I was positioned directly opposite the trail to the woods that flanked the compound. I drove to the edge of uncertainty and pondered whether to proceed. The engine of a transport bike was practically silent. Practically being the operative word. There was surely some security measures in place protecting this edge of land and a disturbance of this sort, even the crackling of a twig breaking in half, could attract undesired attention.

I eased the bike into a heavily wooded area and quietly concealed it. I checked that my bêti was in place and easily accessible before taking off across the fallen leaves and between trees where night owls bedded after dark. I stepped lightly into wilderness, being keenly aware of my surroundings.

A small shack sat ambiguously in the distance. I was sure it was occupied by armed guards anxious for some action that would justify their presence out here in seclusion. I slowed my steps considerably, taking every precaution not to rouse suspicion. I was overcome with relief when I spotted my little piece of wall in the distance and made my way toward it.

It was much taller than I had realized. I ran my hand across its nearly smooth surface and contemplated my strategy. It was no wonder Kelsard and Dupec had not bothered to use much manpower at this location. The likelihood of the average person scaling the massive obstruction was none. I was not the average person.

I glanced around taking in every detail. My eyes locked onto the tree that grew beyond the wall. My solution was clear. Whoever was responsible for the landscaping had neglected to care for this particular area. This would certainly be to my advantage. I latched onto its body and pulled myself up its rugged surface, using all of my strength to hoist myself until I reached a branch high up.

The branch, though thick, was suspicious and I wondered how long it could support my weight. I decided I would have to scale across quickly to avoid the possibility of plummeting to the greenery below and having a slew of soldiers running to my side with weapons drawn.

I extended my leg and stepped across gingerly, planting myself amongst the leaves and branches at the top of the wall. I looked to the other side, fully expecting to see at least one guard waiting for someone with as much bravado as I. The space was empty. Noises came to me but from a distance.

It was now or give up, leaving Aissa to the will of her brother and the Allegiance. I climbed over, supporting my weight with the tips of my phalanges. I dangled above a neglected flower bed momentarily before allowing myself to free-fall. I paused, poised and readied for action but no one appeared. I looked both ways but saw nothing and no one, however ahead was a door also surrounded by thick vegetation.

I fidgeted with the lock to assess the difficulty in picking it. To my surprise it opened with relative ease. A security breach, how wonderful. I entered into dimness, walking inside as if I belonged. After several steps I found myself beneath a wide stairwell. I felt overcome with emotion. I imagined Carolyn and her father rushing down these very steps, my great-grandfather yielding a sickle that made him difficult to take down.

I questioned how I would make it up and if I did, how would I find what chamber Aissa was being held. But when I took another step a rush of energy consumed me. It was the same sensation I had felt when Diana was in danger. But it was Aissa and her spirit that was calling to me.

I peered deeper beneath the stairwell, making out the frame of a door. I approached but reconsidered the stairs. That is where Carolyn had been held, on the upper level. But a force tugged at me, leading me to the door. I eased it open and stared into the unknown, dark – save for the faint light in the distance. I waited at the top of a stairwell that led beneath the compound. I took a deep breath and quickly stepped inside, pausing until I was confident that all was clear.

I crept softly down the steps easing up as the light became

brighter. I pressed my back against the wall as I descended. At the bottom, I took a breath and peered around the corner, immediately pulling myself back. A soldier stood guard, Harbinger in hand. I swore mentally. I knew not what else awaited me but I had to proceed. I reached deep inside my jacket pocket feeling the kakali nuts that I had stored there, and pulled two forth. I took one and tossed it forward, its hard shell echoing when it made contact with the concrete.

I pressed my back so close to the wall I thought that I would fuse with it, and eased up a couple steps. I listened as the soldier reacted. I waited, listening as he crept closer to investigate the sound. When I felt him upon me, I threw the other. He reflexively turned toward the noise, allowing me the opportunity to leap upon him wrapping an arm around his neck and using my other arm to lock my hold.

He scrambled to free himself as I constricted his air passage while lowering his body to the floor. His weapon slipped from his grasp and sat itself gently on the ground while his hands went up to his throat and attempted to peel me away. I held on with all within me as though my life depended on it, which it undoubtedly did, until he weakened and his body became limp.

I released him and he dropped like a lump of clay. I wiped away sweat beads as I checked his pulse to make certain that I had not murdered him. He was alive but unconscious. I claimed his weapon and wrapped it around my body, then grabbed him beneath his armpits and dragged him deeper into the den. A guard station sat abandoned in the middle of the space surrounded by cells. Some sat open and empty but most were sealed shut.

Screams of defiance and dispute rang out, mixed with

the sound of male voices and sinister laughter. A cell door sat propped open at the end of the row. From where I stood there was no way that I would be able to see inside. I swallowed the bile that made its way up to my throat and glanced at the other cells as I cautiously approached the sounds. The energy was strong and I knew at once that I had found Aissa. Knees bent, I walked slowly, dragging the unconscious soldier along.

I stopped. The cells were similar to the ones in the Facilities with the exception of the rectangular opening for one to look in or out of. I dropped down beside the soldier and patted him down, searching his uniform. Then I found it – a master key. I jumped up, placing the key into the lock and turning until it clicked.

In this space the sound was loud and exaggerated and I fully expected unwelcome and unwanted company. But I presumed what the other soldiers were engaging in made it difficult to be aware of any unexplainable noises as there was no response.

I pushed the door partway open. It creaked terribly as though it needed to be oiled, and I stopped abruptly. I poked my head inside where I found a terrified Aissa backed into a corner, fully expecting to see the business end of a Harbinger aimed at her from the hands of an SRA soldier.

She exhaled heavily when she recognized my face. "Olivia. Amen Deus," she cried out as she rushed toward me.

My mouth became a thin line and I held up a phalanx to quiet her. I jerked my head toward the exit. "Hurry. The other soldiers are … busy," I whispered harshly.

Her eyes dropped to the body of the soldier at my feet. "Is he dead?"

"No, now help me. Careful." I sat the Harbinger aside and the two of us grabbed the passed-out soldier and dragged him inside of Aissa's former cell. I closed the door as gently as possible and locked it.

"This way," I whispered, reclaiming the large weapon and heading toward the stairs. I stopped and turned to see Aissa standing still outside of the cell. I beckoned to her but she did not budge. "Come on. What are you waiting for?"

She jerked her head. "We cannot just leave her like this."

I groaned and stepped close, my mouth to her ear. "I did not come here to save all these women. I came for you, now let us go."

"Liv, they are *raping* her."

We were in a standoff. She was free. I should have left her, I had done what I set out to do. But I could not. I swore and turned back planting the Harbinger comfortably in my hands and cocked it.

I walked directly to the open cell door. So appalled at the sight was I that it caused me to stumble backward. I watched another wasted minute, a soldier forcing himself upon a young girl, likely younger than me, while his partner joyfully waited his turn with his pants down around his ankles. I recovered and continued inside placing the barrel of the weapon firmly against the standing soldier's temple. His sick laughter stopped and his body became stiff.

"Off the girl. Now," I ordered.

The molested girl turned toward me. Pleading and hopeful eyes bore into the shadow that covered my face.

"What the hell – " the violator opened while reaching around for his weapon, yet not pausing to remove himself from the girls body.

"C'mon, you heard me. Off the girl."

"Who do you think you are speaking to? How did you even get in here?" he asked stretching his body to reach his weapon.

"Ah, ah, ah. I would not do that if I were you," I said as I pulled one of the R9's from my pocket and took aim at his face. "Now, please. I have more important business to attend. Behave, Soldier."

Aissa approached unnoticed, claiming possession of the guard's weapon that I held in dispose. She aimed it and I knew she would gladly follow through.

"Off the girl," she repeated with great force.

His tone was less forceful when he responded. "I do not know how you managed to get in here but you must know that you will not make it out."

He twisted his neck; trying to get a good look at me. Maybe figuring where I had been picked up or what cell I had broken free from. But it was a challenge. The oversized hood on my green jacket shadowed my face as was its duty.

I decided to help him out. With one hand, I eased the hood back until it fell free. The soldier gasped, disconnecting himself from the young girl.

"You are ... the..."

"I am."

"You are real."

I agreed, encouraging the girl, who was in awe as well, to hurry and join us.

"Grab their Com Devices," I ordered the girl as she quickly dressed.

I stepped back as Aissa claimed the final weapon. My soldier turned cautiously to face me, fearful he may die but needing to get a look at my face nonetheless.

"You *are* real," he pronounced, repeating the sentiments of his partner.

I smiled as Aissa rushed out past me. "I am. *Very* real. Tell your friends," I answered as I backed out closing and locking the cell door before they could utter another word or regain some bravado.

When I turned, the girl was bent forward, bowing to me. I looked to Aissa who merely shrugged and raised an eyebrow. Gently, afraid I would frighten the poor child, I touched her shoulder and encouraged her to rise.

"What are you doing?" I asked.

"Honoring you," she replied as though it should have been obvious.

"Why?"

Her shoulders hunched and she turned to face Aissa, apparently seeking support. Finding none she turned to me again.

"My mother told me stories of you when I was just a small

child."

"I am not a deity. I am a girl, just like you."

She chuckled shyly. "You are not like me."

I placed my hand firmly upon her shoulder, locking my eyes to hers. "Just. Like. You."

A moment later she nodded in agreement, albeit reluctantly. I shook it off and turned my attention to Aissa. "Take your weapons – and take her – " I turned and glanced again at the girl momentarily, "– and get out of here. Follow the stairwell and go left and you will find an exit. There is a wall ... a tall one but–"

Aissa shook her head aggressively. "No."

"What do you mean, no?"

"No. I am not leaving without you."

I paused; slack jawed with eyes fixed to hers. "Aissa, I need you to go and take – what is your name?"

"Ramona," the young girl responded, bowing again.

I rolled my eyes to the back of my head and returned my gaze to my friend. "Take Ramona and get out of here while you can. Someone is going to figure out what has happened down here and that someone –"

"I am not leaving."

"You are."

"You are not in charge of me."

"I beg to differ. I am *the one*, remember. I would like to think that little fact puts me in charge."

"Since when? Yesterday?"

"That is not the – fine. Whatever. Ramona–"

"I will not leave either."

"Amen Deus." I scratched my head aggressively for lack of anything else productive to do. "I did not just save you – both of you – so you can die for your stubbornness and stupidity."

"I would be honored to die in servitude to you," Ramona said, again bowing.

Frustration bubbled over. I grabbed Ramona firmly by her forearm, pulling her body upright. She winced from the pain.

"Will you just please stop bowing? Why am I having this conversation with the two of you? I have done my duty and freed you. Should you be killed, your blood will not fall upon my head."

I pushed past the two who appeared completely content with their decision. The choice was most certainly theirs to make, whatever they wanted to do was fine by me, so long as they did not get in the way of my going after Razi Las.

Nineteen

The Commander

I MADE PEACE. THAT WAS THE ONLY WAY THAT I COULD move forward and face absolute uncertainty. Making peace with myself was the only way that I could make peace with my mira for having been less than honest with me all of our life together. It was the only way to make peace with Diana for her not being a better mother to me when given a second chance, and equally for my not being a better protector of her given I had the ability.

And with Jayde.

In making peace with myself and rescuing Aissa from the Hunters of our world, I made peace with Jayde. And although we had lost any opportunity we may have had to rescue what remained of her being and lay her to rest as her culture dictated, I prayed that Deus would not forsake her soul, and grant her the blessing to rest in peace.

Razi would be something different altogether. It was my prayer that when I slay him, the demons I was most certain he worshipped would rise to his heels before me and drag him kicking and screaming directly into infernum.

I had a job to do and, if I hoped to be successful at it, I would have to fend for self. It seemed that I could not convince Aissa and Ramona to save themselves. If faced directly with danger, self-preservation would be their only lifeline.

I entered the guard's station, the place where the now detained soldiers were supposed to have been rather than raping young girls. The security panel was elaborate, much more complex than the one at the Facilities. Before me were three rows that contained three monitors each, all displaying the inside of the cells. There were scores of buttons and levers on either side. With the exception of the two that I had in use, all were empty. The first soldier that I knocked unconscious remained so and I wondered if I had done more damage than intended.

To the left were more monitors. Activity on one of them caught my eye causing me to double take. I moved closer, trying to get a better look but it seemed that in whichever room it was located, the camera was too far away. Aissa approached slowly, then halted only steps from where I stood concentrating.

"That is my brother," her voice was low and I was unsure if I had in fact heard her at all. A moment later her words firmly grabbed my attention. "Who is he talking to?"

Her question was thoughtless and I was certain she had not expected me to have a response. But I did have one. "That, meli, is Taaman Dupec."

"Taaman Dupec? *The* Taaman Dupec?"

I nodded. His frame was burned into my brain. I would recognize him anywhere. The two seemed to be deeply engaged in conversation. I watched, pondering how I would find them in this massive structure. The camera angle adjusted suddenly, startling me back to my reality. I turned to see that Aissa was fidgeting with knobs, giving us a look around. Ramona had crept beside us and was watching over her shoulder. I returned my attention to the monitor.

"Stop," I cried. "Go back."

Aissa did as instructed; shifting the camera angle back over the area she had just covered. She stopped on her own, noticing what I had already, a woman standing and facing the men. She wore a long flowing gown that covered her feet, and appeared to be holding a set of beads between her phalanges. I leaned in closer, trying to make out the frame or face but could only see one side of her.

"Can you get closer?" I asked, planting my hands on the counter and leaning forward.

Aissa thought for a moment, evaluating the various buttons before choosing the one that made the woman fill the screen. My forehead scrunched and I eased into the guard chair, not believing what I thought I was seeing.

"Who *is* that?" Aissa inquired, looking at me.

I watched the screen, being cautious not to blink for fear I would miss something vital. The woman shifted, she was now speaking. Whatever was going on, she seemed to be angered by it. She took a step forward, then pointed. She stepped back and turned away, facing the camera.

"Mala," I exhaled. My body trembled as rage consumed me. Slow and searing. My fist landed hard against the station. I growled out her name again. "Mala."

"Who … who is Mala?" Ramona asked timidly.

I turned sharply to face her. I had forgotten she was even there. I was seething. "Where is this room?"

Ramona, appearing horrified under my surprise interrogation and mood change, shrugged and struggled to give me useless information. I focused on Aissa instead who, though jarred, remained relatively calm.

"Let us see if we can find it," she said in an attempt to appease me.

"I must get to this room."

"But Taaman Dupec – " Ramona began, but the hatred in my eyes when I looked her way silenced her.

Aissa went to work trying to get me the answer I sought. I had no time to waste. I knew not the routine on these premises. At any moment a soldier, or soldiers, could enter this space and discover us and discover the crime we had committed.

No, I had not time for that. I jumped from the seat and grabbed Ramona by the arm. I shoved my stolen Harbinger into her hand and snatched one from beside Aissa. I proceeded to drag the frightened girl with me to the cell containing the two guards. I unlocked the door and pointed.

"You. Come with me."

The soldier, confused and nervous, looked to his colleague for assistance. He only scowled. I stepped inside confidently; Harbinger cocked, and grabbed the soldier I wanted. He did not resist. I backed out of the cell and signaled for Ramona to close and lock it as I jerked the unusually slender male out into the main area.

Resentment toward the soldier and an upper hand gave Ramona a confidence she had not earlier possessed. I knew any false move and she would blow his man parts free. I held his arm tight and led him to the monitors.

I pointed at the one where Dupec, Razi, and Mala were. "What room is this?"

He attempted to make himself upright and defiant, trying hard to summon a fleeting courage. He, instead of responding, averted his eyes and tightened his lips.

I jerked him closer, grabbing his face and forcing him to look at the screen.

"Where is that?" I inquired again, relatively calm.

His answer was mumbled. "I do not know."

My jaw clenched and I swallowed my anger. "You do not know," I stated more than asked.

"I do not know."

I nodded and released him. I turned away and fidgeted with my hands. If I hurt him too badly, or worse, killed him, I would get no answers. I glanced at the screen. Mala was now sitting and fondling her beads and my blood pressure rose. I turned swiftly, my tight fist landing hard against the soldiers jaw. He went reeling backward, his feet lifting slightly from the ground. Before he could get his bearings, I snatched one of the Harbingers from Ramona. I held the weapon mere centimeters from his nose.

"Would you like to look again?" I asked. He gulped and nodded.

I stepped aside, moving my arm in a sweeping motion, inviting him back to the monitors for a chance to redeem himself.

"This is Commander Dupec's council room."

"Is that far from here?"

He appeared to contemplate ignoring my question but one glance at Ramona and her itchy phalanx and he thought better of it. He shook his head sullenly. "Up the level and down the left bank. You will see the grand doors to your right. You cannot miss it."

"Oh, I will not because you are going to be my guide."

A pained look crossed his face and he resigned to helplessness. I wondered what the penalty for helping us would be.

"Liv." Aissa interrupted my thoughts. "Someone is entering the room."

I stepped away from the soldier and watched as a large, dark, bald male entered. He first saluted Dupec and then Razi Las. I looked back to the soldier.

"Who is this?"

He exhaled heavily. "That is Keluc, head of security."

I nodded, taking one last look at the scene, secretly imagining a variety of scenarios that explained what was really going on in there. I pulled my hood down over my eyes.

"Let us go," I said and led the soldier forward.

†

THE FOUR OF US STOOD STILL AND SILENT BENEATH THE stairwell that led to a life of servitude. Faint sounds of activity traveled to us from the foyer. I recalled the sight of trucks making regular rounds outside the front gate. From my position beneath the panati I could not determine the frequency at which the soldiers entered and exited the premises but it was clear that it was a busy place.

"We are not going that way," I said.

I stood, positioned beside the soldier. He stood casually, as though I were not holding a powerful weapon aimed at his side. Ramona took up the lead. If anything unexpected occurred we would be given notice through her sacrifice. Aissa took up the rear.

Our soldier could no longer bear to look at us. Instead, his eyes stayed directly ahead.

"It is the only way to get to the left bank," he responded with much attitude.

"We are not going that way."

"What do you want from me? You broke into an SRA compound. Soldiers are everywhere. You *will* be caught."

"Not if you do as you are told." I sighed. "Lead us. If we are confronted and have to fight I am making you this promise – I will not kill you. But I will shoot off your testes, then leave you at the mercy of your leaders and their disciplinary tactics. I may die as well, but you will wish that I had killed you first."

I waited as he considered my threat.

"This way." He jerked his head in the opposite direction. I nodded my approval and followed.

The activity faded into the distance as we walked. It became challenging to not outwardly express awe at the beauty we were witnessing, beauty that none of us had ever in life been exposed to. I battled inside the desire to stare at the golden statues and glorious paintings that adorned the compound's walls.

The soldier instructed us to turn into, what I assumed to be, the left bank that he had previously spoken of. It was an aisle that appeared endless. Chandeliers hung from high ceilings in measured distances, illuminating our path. An exquisite rug replete with the requisite tiny gold and green embroidering padded it.

Silence enveloped us. Too much silence, an unnerving amount. I glanced up, scanning the outer edges of the aisle. There was a camera perched high and I fixed my gaze upon it. It was possible that someone would, by now, know of our presence. Or, possibly the feed led only to the lower level which we had left unsupervised.

As though sensed, my question was soon answered when the sound of footsteps entered from the rear and armed soldiers greeted us ahead.

"Drop your weapons and release the soldier."

There was no response from our end. Not even Ramona flinched. We stopped walking but stood our ground as I assessed the situation. I looked to our hostage. His eyes held their forward stare. Nothing of his emotions betrayed him. Not relief. Not fear.

Not shame for having been captured by a small fleet of females. Just a disciplined soldier awaiting his orders.

We had no upper hand in the matter but I did not accept that. They could kill me; kill us. Murder us in cold blood. I could guarantee, however, at least one, if not more, would accompany me on my travels to the infernum or wherever my soul would find its final resting place.

"You are making a big mistake," said the same voice which ordered our obedience. "I do not wish to kill the three of you. That would indeed be a waste of good product. But if you do not drop your weapons and release my soldier, I will be forced to take more aggressive action."

I looked closer, focused more on the source. Recognition set in. It was the head of security as pointed out by our soldier. My jaw clenched. Certainly he had enough authority in this matter to do as promised but I was not yet ready to surrender.

"I believe you are looking for me."

The familiar voice commanded my attention far more than Kelsard's security Lega had. I inched about, trying to see the person that I expected to see. The crowd parted and Razi Las stepped through appearing much more authoritative than the last time I had seen him. Once he reached the front of the small gathering he stopped, a shadow of a smile on his lips.

"Hello again, sister," he offered.

Aissa, filling up with a hatred so strong it formed an essence of its very own, raised her weapon higher. Every soldier present responded in kind. "I should kill you."

"Tsk, tsk. Now that is no way to treat family. You were raised much better than that, I am certain of it."

"You turned me over to SOTA. How could you?"

I reached back and gently eased her weapon down, issuing a non-verbal warning.

"Olivia, Aissa, and ... you, whoever you are, put your weapons down and release the soldier."

As there was no longer any reason to resist, I did as instructed without hesitation. My eyes never broke from Razi's as I acted. Aissa and Ramona reluctantly followed my example. When they were again upright, I released my grasp on the soldier.

The head of security spoke up as he charged my way. "Take those two to lock up. I will take care of this one. Jefferson, gather the weapons and head to debriefing."

"Sir, there are two soldiers locked in the SOTA holding cells below."

Keluc rolled his eyes and shook his head in disappointment. "Release the soldiers and order them to debriefing."

"Yes sir." Jefferson saluted his commanding officer and retreated.

"Bring her to me." I looked away and saw Taaman Dupec walking toward me.

Legatus Keluc responded. "Sir, with all due respect, General Kelsard has commanded that–"

"You, a Legatus in second nature, dare question me? I suppose you know what is best."

"No, sir."

"Now, please bring her to me."

"What of the others, sir?"

"Carry on as you see fit."

Keluc nodded and led me, with much more force than was necessary, to Dupec. My eyes, however, remained deadlocked on Razi as I was drawn nearer to him. He smiled. Everything in my being wanted to break away and be killed whilst slashing his throat with the bêti that I held in concealment. Instead, I contained my rage. I believed firmly that this would not be my last opportunity.

I was led into a large room that was decorated as immaculately as the aisle outside of it. The very room we had not long ago observed Dupec, Razi, and Mala convene in. I instinctively looked around for her, prepared to threaten answers out of her. Other than Dupec, Keluc, and myself, the room was empty. I glanced up to the camera as Dupec dismissed his head of security.

I paced slowly, taking in all that I saw. The bronze statues. The velvet drapes. The marble inlay. A framed painting of a life-size Taaman Dupec hung from the wall. I cringed and swallowed a small amount of bile.

"So," he began once we were alone, "the prophecy is indeed true."

"And what prophecy would that be?" I inquired, feigning ignorance.

Dupec chuckled. "Oh, this is the game we are to play. Fine, I will go along. The prophecy of the Anointed Daughter of the Marinites."

I raised an eyebrow behind the shadow. "Have I heard that one? I am not so sure. You hear many tall tales when you live in The City. My friends tell me that the Anointed Daughter is of Amirontian decent."

"Do they now? Pray tell."

"They do. But well, it only matters if you believe in such fantasies."

He nodded thoughtfully. "Why not remove your jacket? Get comfortable. You are going to be here for awhile."

My eyes rose beneath the shadow of my hood. I looked to him for a moment before walking away. "Thank you for the offer but I would rather not."

"At least remove your hood so that I may have the pleasure of seeing who it is that I am speaking."

"I am fine as I am."

"Suit yourself."

I approached a small station with a couple monitors, accompanied by levers and buttons same as in the room below. My eyes locked on the one containing the image of my arch nemesis.

"This is how you knew that we were coming," I mumbled.

"Push the red button and you can zoom in for a closer look."

I had been so engaged in my bloodlust that I had not realized that Dupec had moved closer. I did as advised and got a closer look at Razi's face. He appeared relaxed … at ease.

"Is there something between the two of you that I should know about?"

I looked to Dupec and frowned. I walked away. "What is it you plan to do with me?"

"Well, you are the revelation of prophecy. A very significant one, I might add. I should be asking you that very question."

I stared into his face. Surprisingly, it was not a bad face. Did not look like the face of evil. Had I not known with whom I was dealing I would not have fathomed that this man before me had such propensity for hate.

"Despite what you may choose to believe, I am not here for you or General Kelsard."

"You have come for him, then. This Razi Las."

I nodded.

"Why, if I may be so bold as to inquire."

"He has become the bane of my existence and the world will not be set right until he is destroyed."

This time Dupec nodded. "I see. I knew your mother. Were you aware of that?"

My head jerked so quickly that I was nearly afraid I had snapped a bone in my neck. "My wh ... who...?"

"Oh, come now, let us not play silly games. I believe we are beyond that."

"I do not know who it is you speak of."

"Diana. You know precisely who it is that I speak of."

"Diana is my ... my cousin."

"Cousin."

I swallowed hard and nodded. "Yes."

"You are aware that she was once an elite on these premises."

"You have had many women on these premises. Why would you recall *her*? Besides, my cousin Diana is Marinite and I find it hard to believe that a soldier of your caliber would have even been friendly with such a Sister."

Taaman Dupec sat upon a red sofa with the grace of a debutante, the sofa that Mala had sat upon earlier fondling beads. His face took on a subtle softness, a dream-like quality as he reflected.

"Diana Kalaath was absolutely beautiful. And feisty," he said as almost an afterthought. "Feistiness not dealt with since SOTA's inception."

My lids lowered as I stepped in his direction. Taaman Dupec knew something. He knew more than he was now saying and for the briefest of moments, Razi Las was meaningless to me.

"Do you know … do you know whose woman she was? Can you tell me what soldier she belonged to?"

"Indeed I do and can."

My heart pounded in my chest. For the first time in my life there was a possibility of my getting closer to the identity of my father.

"Then who—"

The door to the room burst open with force, interrupting our bonding. Reflexively, I jumped back, separating myself from Dupec. Keluc rushed inside.

"Sir, we have another security breach."

Dupec jumped immediately to his feet. "How is this possible?

You are in charge of security and yet citizens are running rogue on this compound under *your* watch!"

I eased unnoticed toward the monitors, nearly choking on disbelief from what I saw. My eyes lit and my heart skipped. My hands reached inside each of my pockets, very slowly. Very cautiously.

"I have to get you to safety."

"How is it possible to have soldiers occupy nearly every inch of this compound and we be breached twice in one day?" The rage that filled Dupec made him unrecognizable. He was nothing of the calm leader that sat poised and respectful of my boundaries only moments earlier.

Feeling surprising relief, I turned my focus toward the two men. "No worries, sir. They are here for me."

Keluc aimed his Harbinger in my direction just as I drew both of my weapons.

"I do not have time for games, little girl. Drop your weapons. Sorry to disappoint your friends but you are coming with us."

"I do not think so. You can point me in the direction of Razi Las or I can kill you and your Commander and find him myself."

"And why would I do that?"

I moved my eyes to meet with Commander Dupec's. He smiled and nodded. I recognized something in the gesture, something I had no time to explore.

Dupec touched Keluc's Harbinger ever so gently. His weapon lowered and he ushered Dupec toward the back of the hall. "It matters not. You will not escape. Go on, have your fun with Las and when you are done, you will get to watch your friend's die. I will take my pleasure in crushing your soul with my bare hands later. You should realize, you work for *us* now"

The security head Keluc, hatred and disappointment in his eyes, disappeared with Dupec behind a door that looked to be nothing more than a wall panel. I assumed that was where Mala had disappeared. Temporarily, I returned my weapons to holding and attempted to follow to no avail. The door would not open for me.

I cursed and turned away. I would get her in due time. I vowed that after I dealt with Razi Las ... Mala Belroth and Taaman Dupec would be next. My list of enemies was growing steadily.

Serve and Protect

Twenty

RAZI LAS MURDERED JAYDE.

For what purpose he had her life taken was as much a mystery as Mala's involvement. Whether he meant for her to actually die was yet another question that I had no answer for, not that his intentions mattered. She was dead, that was what mattered. What I knew without a doubt was that their mutual presence at the Kelsard compound and in Taaman Dupec's company was not a mere coincidence.

But the why still nagged at me. Razi had spent many years with Jayde; she was like family. What purpose had her death served? How did it benefit Razi? He would not have done it were it not of benefit to him. And furthermore, if Mala had indeed spent a lifetime watching over me ... if she was duty-bound to protect me, why was she involved with the likes of someone hell-bent on my destruction?

I shook myself free of distractions. Answers would come in time. I stepped away from the panel that had allowed Taaman Dupec to disappear before my own soldiers arrived, still curious as to how he and Keluc had gotten through and where the escape route led.

I backed away, my phalanges outstretched to the wall until I was no longer able to touch it. I had to find Razi, had to deal with this conflict for both the sake of vengeance as well as resolution. If I did not stop him he would continue to come for me and he would destroy anyone close to me. Saving Aissa and stowing away Diana would not be enough. He had one, if not both heads of SRA aware and interested in me and my purpose and goals. The planet was not that big. Unless I traveled deep into the mountains it would only be a matter of time before my whereabouts were discovered.

Besides, I was no coward. I would not run. The idea of hiding out … laying low, it did not appeal to me. I was about action. I was about facing my demons head on and dealing with the matter until it was dealt with. I returned to the monitoring station and investigated each image, hopeful that my enemy's face would re-appear.

"Charleston," I gasped. I ran across the room to the large double doors and pulled one open, poking my head into the surprisingly empty hall. "Charleston," I cried out softly.

He ran in my direction, weapons still drawn just in case. I stepped back allowing him entry. He tucked the artillery away once he saw we were alone, then firmly closed the door. He turned to face me, relief drained color back into his cheeks.

He stepped forward and grabbed me, pulling me into his arms and held me tight. His power enveloping me felt good, felt safe. He pried away though not far, his deep brown eyes connecting to mine.

For a moment, I forgot it all. I forgot where I was or why I was there but remembered only what it was like to be in his world. He leaned in but before our lips could meet I recalled those little all too important details. I remembered James. I remembered Silver. I remembered the place he called home with the hostile sister-in-law. And I recalled his lies. And then, and more important, I recalled the danger on the other side of the door.

I leaned back, giving a loose attempt at freeing myself but he would not let go.

"You frightened me, leaving like that."

"I had no time to waste. You want to play Home, I had a friend to save."

He glared at me, then dropped his arms, allowing me the freedom to walk away. "That is unfair."

"I do not care about equality right now. There is more at stake."

"Indeed and you could have been killed coming here with no one to back you."

"But I was not killed, Charleston." I pulled one of the Blazer R9's from my pocket, held it away from my body and aimed just past him and at the door. I tilted its heaviness to the side and my eyes went back to Charleston. "I could say the same to you, you know."

"I have back up." He pulled a Com Device from his waist. "Package received. Over."

To my dismay a female voice came through soft but crystal clear. "Reconvene at Borg."

My head jerked. I understood that they meant to rescue me, except I was not in need of saving. I rushed forward and snatched the device before Charleston could respond.

"Negative."

"What?" Charleston asked dumbfounded.

James gave a similar response but I ignored it. "What is your wife doing here?"

"James is a trained mercenary, Olivia. Her father prepared her for this sort of battle since she was a child. She and Faraji are my back up."

"What about Diana?"

"With Jiliane. Do not worry, she is fine."

"I have to save Aissa – again."

"Aissa does not need saving, she is with James but if we do not leave here quickly it may not stay that way much longer."

"Then go."

"Not without you."

"You do not seem to understand. I came here for Razi Las and now it seems I have unsettled business with Taaman Dupec. I am not leaving until I get what I came for."

"Taaman Dupec? *Commander* Dupec. You cannot be serious." I did not respond, only stared at him. "You are going to risk your life to settle a score? We have Diana and Aissa, they are safe. You will have your day with the Commander – the entire organization, but today is not that day."

"This is bigger than you can imagine."

"It is, which is why we need you alive."

"I am not leaving with you."

Charleston nodded and seemed to ponder for a moment. "And I will not leave without you."

"That is *not* a good idea."

"You have not offered one good idea yet."

I exhaled heavily. "If this does not end well, it is your funeral."

Charleston reclaimed the Com Device from my hand and activated it once again. "Go on without me. Liv is staying so I am staying."

The static voice came through. "Chas, no. You *must* make her leave."

"Soon you will learn that no one can make Olivia do anything. If she will not leave, I will stay and fight."

"I will track you," James responded without hesitation.

Love. She down-played her emotion for him. Only love would make her do something so foolish. She was not sacrificing her life for me alone. I walked to the monitors and observed the chaos. It would not be much longer before someone realized that I was no longer captive but free to create havoc. I watched as James, Aissa, Ramona, and Faraji rushed down the aisle. Moments later the double doors opened.

James was breathless. "We must hurry. Whatever it is we are doing, we *must* hurry!"

The sound of an alarm rang out before anyone could utter a response. James cursed and yelled for us to follow. I glanced back to the monitors and watched as armed soldiers charged ahead. My expression must have betrayed me because Aissa soon asked what was wrong.

"The soldiers. I have never seen so many at once. We have to get out of here."

Without further hesitation, Faraji turned back toward the heavy doors and we exited the room just as the soldiers that I had witnessed on the monitor entered the aisle where we were located.

"Go," James cried. But how could I leave her to do battle with a brigade, a mere civilian? I would not leave her the task of covering for me. I stood my ground, prepared to assist. "Olivia, go. *Now!* I can handle this; trust me. I have spent my life readying for this. The prospect of bringing SRA to their knees, it is what I live for. It is how I have survived all these years!"

For the first time I noticed the long, thin, red and gold, curved pouch that she carried on her back. She reached back, grabbing the handle of a sword and delicately pulled it forth. In her other hand an R9 was at the ready. I stood stunned but only for a moment before I led a way with all but James following.

I had no idea where I was going or what I could expect to find when I got there. I tuned entirely into what signals the energy around me sent and kept on course. We ran until we could go no further. We stopped abruptly. There were two options presented to us, left or right. I bent forward at the waist and listened intently despite Charleston's nudging for a quick decision. I held up a hand and mentally separated myself from his impatience.

I nodded to the right. "This way."

I led us forward into uncertainty. We came upon another grand set of double doors similar to the ones that closed off Dupec's meeting quarters. They were made of a thick metal with intricate and detailed carvings likely created by the indentured servitude of captured mountainside Marinites.

I eased the doors open with caution. More than prepared for a battle, I was surprised to discover the enormous hall vacant. I took a couple steps then paused and scanned our surroundings. Large columns flanked us on either side and huge paintings of fallen SRA leaders hung on the wall. I looked up the length of the walls to the high ceiling, ironically painted to pay homage to Deus, the greatest leader of all.

Slowly, my fixation moved down and forward. Across from us was a platform. Heavy blood red curtains created the backdrop, the irony was not lost on me. Before it, a large wood carved table sat horizontally with eight regal chairs posted behind it. I could only assume this to be where *The Board convened, where the most important decisions were made. This was likely the place where unfair and unreasonable laws were crafted.

Taaman Dupec stepped from behind the dark curtains, Keluc in tow. I had not excused my score with Razi Las, but for now Dupec and I had some unfinished business and he was the most accessible of the two. He had piqued my interest and I would get answers before I left this place.

"Dupec," I called loudly so that my voice would reach him. "We have not yet concluded our conversation!"

A smirk crossed his lips and if I were not mistaken, a look of pride lit his face – or disdain. He adjusted his stance, locking his eyes to mine, though not verbally responding. Keluc stepped forward in an attempt to establish his authority.

"Who knew that the Anointed Daughter would prove to be so foolish," he said. "*You* are who we have been concerned about all of this time?"

"Lega," I addressed Keluc, "I respect that you have a job to do but I will ask only once that you not interfere in that which is of no concern to you. I have come here to harm neither your Commander Dupec nor General Kelsard. I only wish to conclude our conversation."

"Unless it is the will of my leader, you know that I cannot allow that. Besides, what is your hurry? General Kelsard will be expecting you when he returns to the planet. So long as you do not force my hand, you will not die immediately. I cannot say the same for your friends."

I had no time for useless banter with a low life security soldier. I grew bored with him and quickly.

"Catch me if you can, sir. *After* I conclude my business." I redirected my attention to Dupec. "Allow me to proceed. Talk to me Commander. This can be quite simple or unnecessarily difficult."

The room fell completely silent as Dupec observed me and Keluc awaited his orders. I could feel Charleston, Aissa, Ramona, and Faraji behind me. There was a sudden shift in their aura.

They would be forever changed on this day and I trusted that I could count on them. Even Ramona.

Dupec raised a hand and gestured ever so slightly that if I were not paying such close attention I may have missed it. But I had missed something significant. Keluc stepped forward and shifted his weight before turning. It was in that moment, mere seconds before he commanded *Get them,* that I sensed the imminent danger about to overtake us.

I took strong, swift strides toward the sound of footsteps in the shadows and reached into both pockets, pulling my weapons forth as an army of soldiers charged. Heavy metal in each hand, I dropped to one knee and fell forward, swinging my arms back and sliding the weapons. One for Aissa. The other for Ramona – I only hoped she would know how to use it.

We were indeed changed. We were now one. I had no doubt that they would follow my lead. Charleston's father, seventeen moons prior had created a weapon designed specifically for the Anointed Daughter of the Marinites. That daughter was me, Olivia Vala Eso Kalaath, granddaughter of the clan Aleyk. And as the small block of wood made its way, of its own volition, to my open palm, I felt myself being transformed. I had not reached for it or initiated it in anyway. Instead it was as though our relationship was suddenly symbiotic and all I need do is summon it with a mere thought. As I accepted the fate that Deus had chosen to bestow upon me, I felt myself swelling with a power like never before.

With the bêti in my hand, I was re-born.

I closed my eyes and tuned into the sounds of the footsteps of the soldiers coming toward me and those of my team at my rear dispersing. The sound of ammunition discharging filled my ears. I eliminated all thought, becoming one with my power and instinct ... with my faith. As I rose from the ground and back up to my full potential, I used my free hand to push away the hood that shadowed my identity. I wanted each and every soldier I encountered to know the face of righteousness being represented.

"Aaaargh," I cried as I charged into the onslaught of soldiers, releasing the bêti's knives into the crowd. I would set the tone of this battle. I swung around and ducked, destroying one soldier's Harbinger and another's limbs. I ran through with force, dropping low as a ray passed over my head.

"I want her alive," Dupec bellowed from his post. "*Alive!*"

A collective feeling of disappointment very obviously swelled inside the chests of those surrounding soldiers. Weapons holstered would level the battlefield for me. But weapons holstered would put the soldiers on the frontline at a disadvantage as they faced me. I was not a threat to Dupec, not at this moment in time. If only I could reason my way through the onslaught. I did not wish to kill these men. They had, at one point, been husbands and sons and fathers. These same men had once been lover and protector of those they now helped to enslave. Perhaps for this reason I should have sought to have all of their heads. Though maybe allowing them to live was in Deus' will, as all deserved an opportunity to see the error of their ways – even if they had wasted years of their lives furthering SRA's cause.

I restored the bêti's knives. No longer was anyone trying to take my life, though they were seeking to destroy it. My instinct alone was enough to secure it, so long as I maintained focus and ventured quickly. Dupec wanted me alive and only me. The others were merely collateral damage. But they were my responsibility, their blood would be on my hands and I would, therefore, need to end things swiftly in order to keep them alive.

I sought them out, my small army, but they were lost in the scuffle. I had done my best to keep an eye turned in their direction but had no choice but to trust that they could handle themselves and look out for one another. Soldiers surrounded me, closing in confidently. They no longer sought to kill me, but each wanted more than the other to turn me over. Whosoever did would be elevated another level. The ultimate prize. My conscious did battle with the savage within me. This, my first true battle, would define who I was at my core.

Destroy or show mercy, who was I to become?

Preserve and protect, that was the credo for myself and for my team. Needing to create space and opportunity, I again released the bêti's knives causing the allegiant dogs to fall away.

My eyes scanned my surroundings as I sought a solution, while holding my attackers temporarily at bay. I locked on Dupec who watched with a smug and self-assured look etched across his face. The same calm and callous expression that he had worn when we spoke previously.

"Liv!"

At the sound of my name being called I returned to the present. I ducked and swept the legs from beneath the soldier that had miraculously closed in from the rear, prepared to take me out with the R9 that he aimed at my head. So much for the order to keep me alive. He fell forward and dropped the weapon as I quickly returned to my feet with the closed bêti pressed firmly against the back of his neck; whilst my eyes remained trained on the brazen soldiers who warily moved forward.

"This could have been the end of your life. Is *he* worth it? Is *any* of this worth it?" I hissed.

His answer was a hoarse whisper, "Yes."

Heartbroken, though not surprised, I smashed the wooden block into the back of his head, rendering him unconscious. I concealed my weapon as I propelled my body forward and collected the soldier's abandoned one, using it immediately to assist in clearing a path. There was no longer room for grace – my brains were very nearly in my own hands. I now knew who I was – who I must be. For this life that was chosen, there must be consequences.

I raised my arm, moving and shooting continuously, and aimed to maim any soldier that stood in my way. And should, in the chaos, my attempt to injure result in finality, that blood burden was not mine to bear. I closed the gap between Dupec and I, although not fast enough. I could not risk his growing bored and deciding to leave. Adrenaline fueled me and my aggression. A round ripped into a soldiers chest, my last one. With no ammo remaining, I slammed the hard, cold metal against the face of the nearest soldier, before throwing it forcefully at the forehead of another on the approach.

I retrieved my bêti and released just in time to take an arm with a Harbinger attached to the hand. I turned quickly, catching it, and blasted myself a path. I picked up speed, ducking, dodging, and diving over the bodies of the fallen. My heart raced with the realization that Dupec was well within reach.

I did not look anywhere beyond my target. To break concentration could prove deadly. I could only trust that the four that had sacrificed themselves to back me would be successful in their own individual goals. After what seemed like an unreasonable length of time, I finally approached the platform. Taaman Dupec was nearly mine. I dropped the arm with the spent Harbinger. A soldier stood before me, foolishly attempting to keep me from my destination. He appeared to still be a child, barely beyond my own days. He looked afraid, though he attempted to mask that fear with feigned bravado.

"Stop her!" Yelled Dupec, angrily.

"Graaah!" I ran at full speed. Against orders but out of options, the young soldier timidly raised his weapon and pressed the trigger. I swerved just as certain death blasted from its mouth. My arm wrapped around his neck. I used the force of my momentum to counter his body weight that attempted to push us forward, using it as leverage to propel me onto the platform. I felt his spinal cord snap in the space between my elbow before I released him, and landed beside Dupec. I swallowed hard. He was just a boy, and I had killed him. I took solace in that his sacrifice put Dupec in my grasp, with the closed bêti pressed firmly against his throat, before he even realized what happened. Keluc, appearing startled, fumbled to aim his Harbinger at me.

"Call off your soldiers," I ordered. Keluc, dumbfounded, continued to unwisely hold his ground. "Call off your soldiers or his blood will be on your head. Explain *that* to your General when he returns."

Keluc's mouth tightened in anguish but he still would not comply. Slowly, I moved the wood slightly right so that if I released the steel it would cut into Taaman Dupec's flesh, ending him immediately.

"Do as she commands," Dupec gasped, addressing his soldier.

Reluctant to give in to me, Keluc finally turned toward the battle. He whistled, signaling for his soldier's attention.

"Stand down," he cried out. "Hold your positions."

The commotion began its gradual decline. My eyes went to Keluc's weapon, which was still aimed at me.

"Sit the Harbinger down, slowly. Now step back. Further. Good."

Once compliance was achieved I glanced quickly over the hall. The dead and the wounded littered the floor. The prospect of murder had once bothered me. But now I knew better. Bloodshed is how we came to this place in history. Bloodshed was inevitable. I scanned for my friends. Miraculously all were accounted for. Aissa helped Ramona to her feet, battered but surprisingly alive. Weapons were aimed but no ammo discharged.

I looked to Keluc to be sure he did not try anything foolish, then to Charleston, nodding for him to join me. He ran past eager soldiers who would give anything for the chance to take his life. My eyes went to Keluc's weapon and Charleston seized it and stepped away. Once I felt secure, with one weapon aimed at Keluc and another on Dupec, I eased my grip and took a step back. Dupec stumbled slightly while massaging his throat.

He faced me, that calm reserve once again washing over him. His voice was even when he spoke. "You do know that you will be made to regret this."

"Maybe. But not today."

"What is it that you want from me? You think you will threaten me and poof – SOTA is no more." He laughed, deep and guttural as he paced slowly. "You *believe* that a fear of your reality will change what is. Are you really so naive?"

I swallowed hard, feeling every bit of a small, immature child. Needing an answer to a question that I was terrified to ask. "What I want ... is to know if you are my father."

I felt Charleston's eyes on me but I did not acknowledge his reaction. Taaman Dupec was a respected and high-ranking Amirontian SRA official, and I was no more than a peasant Marinite girl who had been born of a Marinite whore. I knew how what I said sounded. Confusion lit Keluc's face as he looked from me to his leader. But Dupec bore no reaction. He did not appear to be the least bit surprised by my assertion.

He chuckled. "You know who I am, do you not?"

"Of course I know. But my mother was an elite here. You knew her, you admitted as much."

"A *Marinite* elite. There are laws prohibiting–"

"Laws which you help to create and can therefore break."

After a thoughtful pause, he spoke, "I am not your father."

"I do not believe you. If not you, to whom did she belong?"

He shrugged. "A Marinite ... by the name of Warren, I believe."

"That is a lie," I cried out. I gripped the edge of my top and raised it halfway, exposing the partial crescent birthmark. "*Every* Amirite has a crescent birthmark somewhere on their body.

Where is yours?"

Dupec again chuckled, but this time it was not so self-assured. "And what should this mean to me?"

"That my father is not Marinite. That whosoever he is, he is of … he is of Amirontian descent."

"And you know this because of a birthmark."

"Yes."

"That is not even a crescent."

"Half crescent for … half-blood." I felt sick even suggesting such a notion. But it was the only thing that made any sense to me. I could not completely explain it but somehow I knew it was true. I was the daughter of Taaman Dupec. The answer had been clear the first time he smiled at me. I knew that smile, had known it all of my life. It was my smile.

Dupec's face suddenly became serious as he stepped closer to me. Charleston raised his weapon but I signaled for him to lower it. I stepped closer in response, near enough that our words would be left between only us and those in close proximity.

He tilted his head as he eyed me carefully. "Do you understand the penalty for such an act?"

"I do not. But I am certain if you participated, or even orchestrated the inception of the law, you would feel superior to it. After all, you are second-in-command of an entire planet."

"I am not above the law – laws which are in place for a reason. Should my actions have led to the impregnation of a Marinite whore, that act would be treasonous. I am not above the law if my actions led to your creation." His face had become pure evil. His eyes darkened with the hate that filled them.

I swallowed hard, returned his malevolence. "You would not have presumed that such a thing would happen. How could you have known that she was even able to bear a child? After all, she was fixed, was she not? How could you have known that Diana carried the anointing? That she was the daughter of Carolyn Kalaath?"

"She what?" An incredulous look covered his face.

"You said yourself, she was beautiful and feisty."

"Many are. That is how they come to be elites to begin, silly little girl. Why even take the chance? Why create the law, only to defy it?"

I watched him. Read his eyes. My voice became softer. "My guess is it was because you loved her. You did not mean to, you were not supposed to. After all, she was Marinite and whether Henry Kelsard accepts it or not, you despise the Marinite people. But her ... you loved her. In your own sick and twisted way, you loved Diana Kalaath."

His silence said so much more than I could have imagined it would. I had indeed found my father and for as much as it hurt, I was glad that I had.

"Olivia!"

My name being screeched out nearly knocked me from my feet. I stepped aside and turned sharply toward its sound. All of the wind escaped my body and for a moment I thought I would fall from lack of oxygen. Razi Las stood taunting while holding firmly one of Diana's forearms.

"Is this...? No it cannot be. This is not some sort of family reunion we have here, is it?" Razi asked with pleasure as his gaze went from me and to Dupec. "Not quite where I had expected this day to lead, though I am thrilled that I am fortunate enough to be part of it. Thank you for having me."

"Tread lightly, Mr. Las," Dupec responded in kind.

"Why is Diana here? How did you find her?" I dumbly questioned, looking to Charleston for an answer.

"You may want to ask her those questions. Were I to venture a guess, I would say that she was trying to help you out in her own drug induced way."

"If you hurt her—"

"If I hurt her, what? Huh? What will you do, Olivia?" Razi jerked Diana away and stepped forward. Anger shadowed his face. "Avenge her death like you seem to think you are going to do for Jayde? Is that what you are going to say? *You* killed Jayde, not me. If it were not for you I would not have had to have her taken into custody and she would not have been slaughtered by a Hunter on that forsaken planet.

"And your mother? She came here. Should I kill her on this day you cannot be mad at me. Were it not for *you* she would not be here. Therefore, as I see it, *her* death will be on you as well."

I stared at Diana through watering eyes. She should not have come. She knocked me off balance. If I was concerned for her, how could I know that at my side Charleston, too, had been shaken out of focus? How could I know that Dupec picked up on the opportunity and managed to communicate it to Keluc? She should have known better.

The distraction of Diana and my consideration of what needed to be done to protect her blocked all instinct. This is how Keluc managed to knock the Harbinger from Charleston's grasp and toss it to Dupec. This is how power shifted and how I came to be the one held hostage with death at my temple while Diana looked on helpless and apologetic.

"Taaman, no," she pleaded as she tried her best to free herself from Razi's grasp. "Please, please do not hurt her. You cannot do that; you know it to be so."

"Silence her," Dupec ordered.

Razi laughed. "So soon? She has quite the infectious personality. Besides, I am rather interested in what it is she has to say."

Tears drenched Diana's brown cheeks. My heart crumbled inside my chest cavity as I watched her try to save my life. My pain was not for me. If I died, the greatest regrets I would have would be not killing Razi Las and Mala Belroth. Not avenging Jayde. Not protecting Diana.

"Please, Taaman. Take me, do what you will. Just do not harm our – do not hurt her. You cannot do that!"

"Silence her!"

"If you insist." Razi reached around and into a sheath at his side. My eyes widened and I struggled against Taaman Dupec.

"Razi," I cried. "Razi, no!"

The sound of Diana gasping for air echoed throughout the hall and met my ears as Razi plunged the knife deep into her abdomen. I felt helpless. Where were my instincts now? That which had protected me for all of my life was failing me when I needed it most.

Razi released Diana and allowed her traumatized body to crumple to the ground. I had lost Jayde. I knew there was no possibility of my being any good to anyone, including myself, if I lost Diana as well. The room went red. My ears blocked and I could hear nothing but my own heartbeat. I did not know if I had been injured but a pain shot through my entire being. My strength left me and I would have fallen to my knees had Dupec not held such a firm grip on me.

A scream welled up deep inside. I opened my mouth but there was hesitation before it escaped. "Nooooo!" My hand reached into my pocket and pulled forth my blade, the one that had previously been solely responsible for my protection. Old school war tactics. With a flick of the wrist I opened it and flung it at once, aiming at Razi's head. He moved my target but still caught the tip of the blade deep in the flesh of his upper arm.

He cried out in pain, his wail combining with the noise of the small commotion behind me. A hard sound caught my and Taaman Dupec's attention. I took advantage of the distraction, jerking back, causing him to lose his footing long enough for me to break free. I cried out as I immediately released the knives from the bêti and swung it around, hoping to take my father's head off but he ducked in time to survive. When I rose I saw James standing in a pool of Keluc's blood.

"Go," she yelled. "Get Diana!"

With Keluc dead and Dupec, though no longer held hostage, in clear and present danger, the battle resumed. I slayed my way across the space but when I reached Diana, Razi was gone. I looked up and back toward the platform and saw that Taaman Dupec had made his escape as well. I grabbed Diana. Blood spilled over her lips as she tried to speak. I pulled her out of harm's way while granting early termination rights to every representation of the evil of SRA that came our way.

I had come to this place not just to save Aissa, but also settle things with Razi and in the process found which way my blood flowed. Taaman Dupec and Razi Las had not seen the last of me, but for the moment the only promise I had any hope of keeping was the one that I made to keep my mother alive.

Twenty-one
The Beginning

AT THEIR END, THE ONLY THING I REALLY WANTED FOR Mira and Jayde was an opportunity to have a proper burial. One that would show respect to them by honoring their respective cultural traditions. I wanted for them a homegoing that would pay homage to their spirits and those of their ancestors.

For my mira, Elizabeth Aleyk, I was hopeful that she had been honored by Pete and Sarai Ashtwor. However, for Jayde, there was the unfortunate reality to face up to. She would never be sent over properly, a daunting reality that I would have to carry with me for the rest of my days. A disappointment that would haunt Aissa and Faraji for just as long.

If I could help it, no one else in my world would fall victim to such a fate, and I was hopeful that the same promise would be kept for me.

I, and those that remained of my makeshift family, stood huddled beneath a rubrum on the outskirts of a service designed to send a fallen daughter into the arms of those before her. Grieving relatives comforted themselves with the knowledge that she had at least been returned home. A great relief as it had been their belief that she would never be seen nor heard from again.

It was warm on this side of the planet but I kept my jacket closed and my hood drawn. I had no opportunity to properly reapply a coat of concealor and did not want my presence and appearance to distract from what was most important ... from why we were all gathered. To bury her body and usher her spirit toward the light. To go unnoticed was best.

My heart ached for having been unable to save her life. She had given hers for mine. There had been so many tragic deaths in such a short span of time and they all deserved vengeance. My own father was out there somewhere, waiting for the opportunity to send my spirit to the light as well.

Being with my ancestors did not sound so bad, but I was not ready to go. Not yet. Not without sending Razi Las to the darkness. Not without finding out the truth about Mala, and though my friends deemed it foolish and impossible, not without tracking and destroying the Miltvarian Hunter that took Jayde. And in the midst of it all, I would dismantle SOTA and eradicate SRA and all that it represented. Rule would return to Ittas clan, wherever they were. Some must have survived and I would find them. That was what the original people wanted and it was the justice the planet needed.

But that would take time. And after all of the work was done, when Deus called to me, I would go in peace.

Aissa sidled beside me. Her wispy voice came to my ear. "I hardly knew her. So why does it hurt?"

I wrapped an arm firmly around her shoulder and leaned my head against hers. I directed my attention to the Grand Priestess who called order to begin the Light Service, a Marinite death ritual that required an appointed village elder to assist in guiding the soul of the fallen into the light, where the ancestral spirits would take over.

I thought of Diana and our time together in The City. It had not been all hardship and abuse. There were a great many fond memories to recall should the need ever arise.

"Thank you to those who have gathered here to usher our fallen daughter, Ramona Inatai Borana Sulari, into the arms of her musha and her father who traveled before her…"

A soft breeze passed over us, drying the stray tear that trailed my face. Though we had not known Ramona Sulari, she fought hard with us and gave her life for a greater good. She was a credit to our planet and my people and I would carry a piece of her in my soul every time I entered into battle.

Charleston stood behind me, much closer than I was comfortable with being that James was standing at my side, but I tried not to think about it. I respected James for what she had done for me and it was important not to violate that in any way. She saved my mothers life and I owed her more than I cared for him. Charleston would have to respect my decision.

"…go forth into the light. Be brave little butterfly, and use this vision as your guide."

The Grand Priestess raised her arms high and opened her

clasped hands allowing a large black swallowtail to float into the sky. I watched, from where we stood, as Ramona's mother reached out for the butterfly while tears washed over her cheeks.

I could no longer partake in the ritual. It brought too many emotions to the surface. I turned, leading Aissa away. James, Faraji, and Charleston, who carried an injured Diana, followed. A flutter in my peripheral caught my attention but when I glanced back there was nothing there.

We continued across the grass, a new family with a new perspective and mission. Quietly, we headed toward the road. I would get Diana settled in safely, not leave her behind again. Were it not for James's great ability as a trained medicine woman, I might have lost her for good.

And there it was again. The fluttering wings of the Black Swallowtail. Ramona. She had not gone forth into the light but rather selected to stay behind in our world, in darkness. Maybe through a deemed obligation to help us destroy that which had nearly destroyed her, and subsequently taken her life.

An unusual rustling of the sheath grass across the lane redirected my focus. Without thinking first, the bêti had been released and found its way to my opened palm.

The energy around me shifted and I knew that something was wrong. I stopped, slowly raising the wood block high as my team respectively reached for their very own weapons of choice. The Swallowtail floated by, landing softly upon the woods edge.

Another warm breeze wafted past, bending the grass in the general direction of The City. And then it was gone. Razi Las had made his presence known to me, wanted to be sure I realized our business had not concluded. I had not seen him, but knew it to be true. Since accepting my fate and becoming one with my bêti, my instincts had become stronger than I ever deemed possible.

I smiled a bit, as I lowered my arm, signifying to those with me that the danger had passed – for now. I stepped forward, heading in the direction the grass had pointed.

Led by Ramona.

Led by Jayde.

Covered by my mira with Deus by my side.

Turn the page to read a preview of:

Olivia

RISE

of the Anointed

One

Disappearance

3 MONTHS IN FUTURE

THE SOUND OF THE DROPLETS OF WATER FALLING FROM between the warped wooden slats above to the insecure floor below reverberated throughout the small, stuffy space. It rarely rained on Marieux. Years had passed since residents and transplants had experienced the release of fluid from the chemically tinted sky.

Rain was not a sign of prosperity on a planet such as this. The naturally moist ground could not withstand much of the solution before the threat of ruined crops and flooded shanties sent residents running to dust off emergency contingency plans, hoarding food, and fleeing to higher ground.

The young Marinite swallowed his fear slowly, cautiously. The blade pressed firmly against his abdomen, threatening to tear through his flesh with any sudden movement, potentially ripping vital organs necessary for sustaining a proper quality of life. He quickly and discreetly scanned the faces of the men surrounding him, their presence thickening the air. They were undoubtedly soldiers, representing the Shadow Realm Allegiance, known colloquially as the SRA. He didn't recognize any of their faces, and the reason for his abduction eluded him, although he suspected his younger sibling's dangerous discovery had everything to do with it.

A large Amirontian with a deep complexion and broad shoulders paced before him. He hadn't laid a hand on him yet, though he had allowed one of his subordinates the pleasure of delivering a couple of blows to the young man's jaw. It was clear that whatever they wanted, they were deadly serious about obtaining it.

"You wonder who I am," the Amirontian began, his voice deep and cavernous. "You do. I see the question marks in your eyes."

The young boy searched for the courage to respond, then cursed himself for being stumped by such a simple question. "Yes," he replied, his voice a hoarse whisper, fearing it might not have been heard. He debated whether to repeat himself, tensing and fully expecting to earn another blow.

The man began to nod slowly, signifying that the answer he expected had indeed reached him. He wore a black uniform with a tan patch over the left breast, adorned with the SRA emblem. His position of leadership was clear. Initially, the boy had pegged him as a *Legatus and was thus puzzled by the reference to him as

*Auctoritas. His sheltered life had kept him away from SRA ranks, but his mandatory survival training had taught him to distinguish between the dangerous and the deadly. But Auctoritas? This title would put him on par with Commanders Henry Kelsard and Taaman Dupec. Only members of The Board were referred to as such. The term literally translated to "Of Authority." However, Auctors were known not for fieldwork but for delegating tasks to lower-ranked individuals. Politics worked that way. Nevertheless, this Auctor had delegated this boy's ordeal. Despite this, his presence seemed unusual.

"You know what it is that I seek from you," the Auctor stated.

The boy quickly shook his head and whispered fearfully, "No … I …"

A hint of a smile brushed across the man's lips as he leaned in, studying his prey. "Are you certain?"

Whatever courage the young boy possessed waned as the man's dark eyes bore into him. No matter how hard he willed himself to respond, he found no breath to complete his reply. He could confess, give up the information he believed was desired, and spare himself. But what consequences might that unleash upon his sister? He swallowed the swell of tears building in his chest at the sight of a subtle nod to the soldier by his side, the one eager to deliver another blow. The boy tensed, mentally preparing himself, yet no preparation could shield him from the force of the next punch. His breath was knocked out of him, and his already tender eye swelled rapidly.

He silently pleaded for the torment to cease. He wasn't a

warrior, hadn't been trained for battle. He was a simple farm boy who'd managed to avoid such terror for all his sixteen years of life, fortunate to belong to a clan that had settled far enough away from SRA's radar. Until now, his contact with SRA had been minimal. He prayed to Deus for relief, and as if answering, the man signaled for his henchman to stop. A breathy "thank you" escaped his lips.

"Would you like another chance to answer my question? I would take it if I were you. Second chances are rare in my world."

The boy gently rubbed his tongue against his tender, swollen bottom lip. "I ... I do n—"

He flinched as the large fist drew back again, but to his surprise, the Auctor moved swiftly, catching the fist before it landed. Everything happened so quickly that the boy questioned his perception. The Auctor seized a blade from a nearby guard's hand and plunged it into the renegade soldier's side.

"Did I instruct you to lay a hand on the boy?" he growled.

The soldier, clearly pained and bewildered, shook his head while enduring the injury.

The man scanned the room, assessing reactions, as though preparing to face them all. Blank stares met his violent act against one of their own. The Auctoritas looked satisfied, nodding at a companion.

"Take him outside to die in the rain. And clean my blade while you are at it."

A compliant soldier sprang into action. "Yes, Auctor."

Satisfied, the Auctor returned his focus to the frightened boy. "Apologies for the interruption. Now, you have wasted enough of my time. Let's get to the point. You have met the Anointed Daughter, haven't you?"

The boy's stiffened posture betrayed his attempt at loyalty.

The man leaned closer, allowing himself to be seen clearly by the boy's good eye. He revealed a new blade, identical to the one previously used. Long, broad, serrated. The boy pondered the Auctor's actions, realizing that if he could be so ruthless with his own soldiers, the consequences of withholding information could be dire.

His sole experience with SRA was when his sister was taken. It was his fault; his idea to join their elder cousin on a secret journey to The City. For one day, they gained a lifetime of experience, feeling rebellious and courageous. It had been worth it until his sister was spotted and abducted. He couldn't save her, so he didn't try. He betrayed her, and now he was asked to repeat his mistake with another sibling.

The boy felt the cold blade graze slowly across the flesh near his good eye. "Be cautious how you answer from this point on."

A small drop of liquid trailed from the corner of the boy's eye onto the blade. He wasn't sure if it was his tears, blood, or the fluid leaking from above. He whispered a breathy affirmation.

"Tell me, what is your name?"

"Eda ... Edan."

"Edan. Good. Edan, the Anointed Daughter. You know who she is, do you not?"

He swallowed hard. "No—yes! I mean ... I have never seen her, but I know ... I know ..."

The Auctoritas nodded, smiling. He stood upright, retracting the knife. "Excellent. You know where I can find her?"

He sighed, defeated. "Yes ... no. Not ... not exactly."

"But you have an idea."

His response was barely audible.

The man's patience waned. His face darkened, contorting as he moved forward, aiming the blade's tip millimeters from the boy's eye.

"Do not play games with me. Enough of these games; my patience wears thin. Where is the Anointed Daughter? Where is Olivia?" His voice, grave and furious, resonated throughout the room, anger manifesting as threatening fangs.

The boy found his voice. "I do not ... I do not know, but I can find out. I will find out."

"How?"

"My sister," he answered with a flinch. Mentioning her pained him, but he was a poor liar, struggling to buy time.

"There is a sister I should threaten instead, it seems."

The Auctor stood, smiling—almost genuine—a sight more terrifying than his scowl. "There is always a sister entangled in unrighteousness. So, where is she, your sister?"

"I do not know, but I will find her. She snoops ... she knows their location but will not lead me to their camp. I can uncover it, though!" His final thought slipped out as the blade crept closer to his pupil. "I will find out!"

The man paused, seeming to consider the response. He raised an eyebrow and nodded as he leaned back. What use would the boy be dead or blinded? If he betrayed him, his fate would be far worse than his current ordeal.

"Yes. Discover where The Anointed and her band of miscreants are camped. Will you do me that favor? We are allies now. Are you a loyal friend, Edan?"

"Yes, yes I am ... I will be. And when I do, how do I locate you to report back? What's my next step?"

"Report back?" The man chuckled. "That will not be necessary. Simply locate her. And when you do, relay a message for me. Tell Olivia that Razi Las sends his regards."

†

PRESENT DAY

Where I come from, it is said that little girls are born into their destinies. And as a child raised in secret, it seemed my fate was to be on a small plot of land at the edge of the modest village of Ashtwor. There, I was kept safe and out of sight, away from danger. It was there that I heard prophetic tales of a girl child burdened with the destiny of freeing the people of my planet, Marieux. This prophecy, passed down through generations, did not bypass me in my secluded corner of our world. The elders called her the Anointed, consecrated in the womb.

This traditional folk tale offered hope for a better future to the citizens. A future free from the harsh dictatorship that shattered our planet's peace and community. For years, our home had been oppressed by a ruling force.

Marieux, the smallest in the Zephyrnox Theta system, was once a peaceful agricultural planet. It thrived under the leadership of Vincent Ittas, a descendant of respected leaders from the Ittas clan. During his reign, we felt the unity and pride that came from being part of a family

But, as all good things eventually end, ours did with the Shadow Wars. The ruler of our neighboring planet, Amironte, used his silver tongue to convince our leader into a treaty that he promptly violated. Claude Ustek, the greedy leader of Amironte, aimed to join forces with Katashi Kedt of Arethoxx, the most powerful planet in the system. Their allegiance led to the massacre of Ittas and his Council—a brutal betrayal.

Life as we knew it crumbled. Ustek flooded our streets with transplants from his planet, disregarding our ways and traditions. But his plans were thwarted when karma or his own greed led to his downfall at the hands of Kedt, the ruler he sought to align with. With no government, chaos reigned. Aggressive transplants disrupted our culture, pushing Marieux into chaos.

Amidst this confusion and destruction, the cry for leadership grew louder. The descendants of Ittas had vanished, assumed murdered. This left a void for a young Marinite, without rightful claim, to seize power. Henry Kelsard, under Amironte's guidance, gained the trust of the desperate collective. They missed or ignored the warning signs of another form of destruction, long-term and without a clear solution.

This union held our planet hostage for years, until now. Though I do not know the tale's origin, I have accepted its truth and the realness of the prophecy. A girl child was born, destined to bring order and justice to Marieux, the smallest planet in Zephyrnox Theta—a modest agricultural planet.

That girl is me. I am Olivia Vala Eso Kalaath, and I will not stop until our oppressors lose their dominion and all power returns to its rightful place—with the people.

The End.

Giving Credit Where Due

OF ALL THE BOOKS THAT I HAVE WRITTEN TO DATE, THIS one is a dream come true.

No, really. It literally is a dream come true. Once upon a midsummer's night, during an especially vivid session of REM sleep, I dreamt that I was an observer of a particularly horrific incident that occurred on a planet far, far away. A dark and ominous place made mostly of granite. Scantily clad women were out and about, posted up against fences and walls and attempting to sale their "goodies" to whatever john that showed an interest.

This occupation, however, was not theirs by choice. They were not even from this planet, but were brought by force in order to assuage the needs of the soldiers whose jobs it was to keep order. When a creature, one made up of thick gray skin and lean muscle, standing at least 7' in height with phalanges like talons, stepped from obscurity and proceeded to terrorize the already tortured group of women.

They ran, but one unlucky woman's lifeless body dropped to the ground in a bloody heap when a sharp nail sliced her neck from ear to ear. Her best friend, Olivia, did battle with this creature of the night and sent him fleeing deep into the foreign territory.

Who knows what I ate before I went to bed the night before, that would cause my imagination to run so free. But after describing this to my spouse, it was his idea that I further explore.

According to him, I had dreamed the makings of a really good book. It was now my responsibility to bring it to life – and make it great.

And so, after thanking the almighty Deus bka GOD for dreams, talents, and gifts, I wish to say thank you to my hubby, Shay Glorius L. Martin for encouraging me to step out of my literary box and explore new and unchartered territory. Hope I did you proud and showed that I have range.

To my sunn Storm Ariane, thank you for listening to my ideas and contributing some of your own (Velox Continuum, that is all him!). Shonell Bacon, Layne Bellamy II, LC, Janika, and Karrye: Thanks to those "fans" who pushed me to write so that they could read. Thank you Grammy, Auntie Shellene & Uncle C, and the entire Martin family for embracing me as one of their own. To my own family (The Johnsons with love) because they are so incredible and I adore them all so very much.

Special love to my baby sis Trina Wash and The Juice Crew members, Jennifer Richard, Alichia Johnson-Noble and Michele Adams. You guys are my world and a part of you will always be part of me.

I dedicate this one to the babies: Kyla Simone, Ameena Simone, Angel, Gabby & Bella, and my very first nephew who is on the way!

Love Always, *"Bunky"*

READER'S GUIDE

Olivia: Rebirth of the Anointed by Miki Starr

Discussion Questions:

1. What does it mean to be "the Anointed Daughter," and how does Olivia's early life complicate or affirm this role? Consider how prophecy, identity, and concealment shape her self-perception and survival strategies.

2. Olivia's relationships—with Mira, Jayde, and Diana—drive many of her decisions. What does each relationship teach her, and how do these bonds prepare (or hinder) her for what's to come?

3. Much of the story unfolds in spaces controlled by oppressive systems (SRA, SOTA, The Facilities, etc.). How does Olivia navigate these structures, and what tools—literal or spiritual—help her resist or subvert them?

4. Exile, hiding, and performance are recurring themes. What roles does Olivia play throughout the novel, and how do these layers of disguise protect or endanger her?

5. Many characters carry both personal pain and public purpose. How does Olivia's pain differ from others'? What does she do with it—and what does it awaken?

A Note from the Author

Rebirth came from a different life, a different rhythm. It began with a dream I couldn't explain and ended with a girl who refused to stay quiet. I didn't know it would become a trilogy. I just knew Olivia had something to say. And all these years later ... I'm still listening.

With gratitude,

REBIRTH IN SOUND

CHAPTER	SONG TITLE	ARTIST
Intro Track	Ibeyi (Outro)	Ibeyi
Prologue	Courage	Lianne La Havas
1	Orange Colored Day	Arima Ederra
2	I Am	Jorja Smith
3	Borderline (An Ode to Self-Care)	Solange
Interlude	Woo Woo	ALA.NI
4	Mother	Kacey Musgraves
5	Collide	Tiana Major9 & EarthGang
6	Hope is a Dangerous Thing…	Lane Del Rey
7	This Woman's Work	Maxwell
8	Wayfaring Stranger (Acoustic)	Eva Cassidy
9	Breathe Me	Sia
10	Into Dust	Mazzy Star
11	Blackbiird	Beyoncé
12	Cherry Blossom (Moors Remix)	ALA.NI feat. LaKeith Stanfield
13	Don't Let Me Be Misunderstood	Nina Simone
14	Control	Halsey
15	Fyrsta	Ólafur Arnalds
16	Angel	Massive Attack
17	My Mind	Yebba
18	Weary	Solange
19	Gallows	CocoRosie
Interlude	Rise	Solange
20	Bottom of the River	UGA Noteworthy
21	I Carried This for Years	Ibeyi
Closing Track	No Room for Doubt	Lianne La Havas

Created June 2025

Miki Starr is the author of

ZELLA DORA, THE SKINNY GIRL'S GUIDE, DISORDERED,
and the meta-fiction extended short PSYCHO.

She is a loving wife and mother of one biological child and two cat-babies.

Originally from Chicago, Illinois, she now lives in the Twin Cities MN
area where she does freelance graphic and web design.

www.mikistarr.com